A Casa de Familia

a novel

Joe Marvici

Trafford rev. 09/08/2021

 www.trafford.com
North America & international
toll-free: 844-688-6899 (USA & Canada)
fax: 812 355 4082

About the Author

I was born and raised in Springfield, Massachusetts and was named after my grandfather in the Italian tradition that named the first son after his grandfather. My father Pasquale was also named after his grandfather. Though my mother was not Italian we were raised in the Italian tradition and live in close proximity to the family. Springfield had a large population of Italians back in the 1950's. I was always proud of being Italian and was always curious about my family history though the past was seldom talked about and always mysterious.

I left home and got an apartment with a friend at the age of 17 which was frowned upon by the family as the tradition at that time was to live at home until you got married. My Father found out where I was and caused a terrible scene where I ended up having to live with my sister and was not going to be allowed to live on my own. I moved to New York City within 2 days of that event and afterwards moved Boston and then Washington, D.C. and then back to Boston. It was from Boston that I left with friends in1969 heading for San Francisco and eventually settling in Denver, Colorado. I worked for several years in Denver in the concrete business as a foreman until I was able to buy land in British Columbia, Canada.

Moving to British Columbia in 1973 I worked in the concrete business for several years before changing occupations, becoming a faller in the logging industry and in the 1990's operated my own logging business.

Having played guitar and wrote songs for many years I recorded a Cd of original music in 1993 and since then produced five more Cd's, publishing more than 50 original songs.. The last two being solo recordings under the name of Mudcat Joe. I currently live in Prince Rupert, B.C. and operate a home repair and renovations business called Add-A-Man Handyman Service.

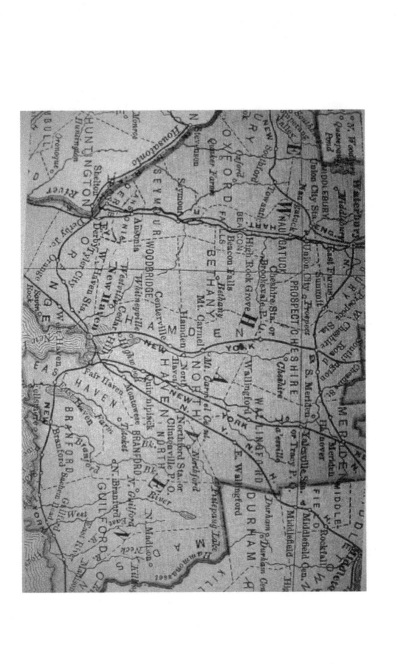

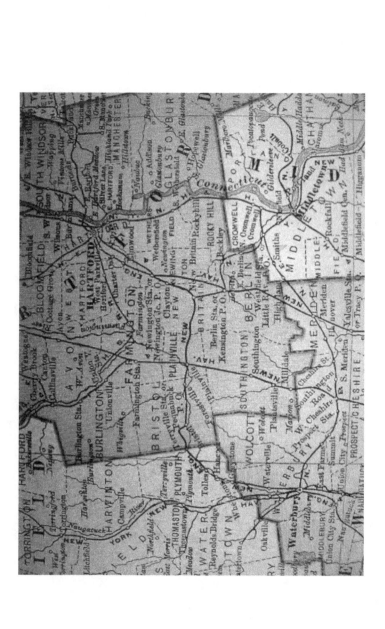

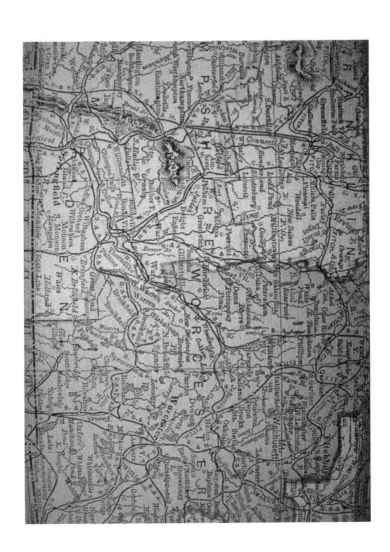

Chapter 1

We pulled up to the departure area at the Vancouver airport. MC was in the van with me. He was going to look after my van in Eugene, Oregon while I was gone. I was catching a plane to Melbourne, Australia to meet a bunch of family members that I never even knew existed a couple of years ago. Only their name was different from our family name in North America. We were the Marvicis and they were the Mauricis. There are a lot of Mauricis in the world but only a few Marvici's so I suspect that Marvici is the newer version of the name.

It was only a couple of years ago that Joe and Angela Maurici and Dominic and Francesca Foca came to New York from Australia and began the search for the other side of the family. It all started when they talked to Tony Bartolo in Sydney. He knew my uncle, John Marvici. Tony had met John at a wedding during the summer of 1993. Tony met a few people that day and forgot all about it until he was talking with Joe Maurici in the Italian club in Sydney about 6 months later. Because Tony was living in America the conversation turned to the U.S. Joe was telling him that he knew he had relatives in the eastern U.S. but did not know where they lived. The family had come from a small town on the Mediterranean coast called Samo and nearby Caraffa in Reggio Calabria.

As they talked, Tony started to recall the conversation with Uncle John and the remarkable similarities in their last names.

"Whena you go to the States again?"

"I gotta no plans righta now but ifa you know somebody thena we go."

"You know, thisa guy John Marvici might be one of your relatives" Tony said to Joe. "When I getta back to the America I'ma gonna looka him up and I'll calla you."

Tony got back to the U.S. a couple of weeks later and looked up John's telephone number in the phone book. He dialed the number and John answered the phone.

"Hello John Marvici."

"Yes this is John"

"John, comosta, This isa Tony Bartolo. We met at the Augustino girl's wedding last summer"

"Oh yea, I think I remember."

"The reason I ama phone you is about your Australian relatives."

"Australian relatives? What do you know about Australian relatives?"

"You have relatives in Australia?"

"I don't know. I think I have relatives in Italy, but I don't know about Australia."

"Wella I thinka that you might. I met a man, a Joe Maurici in Sydney and we thinka you might be related."

"What makes you think that?"

"What town your father from in Italy?"

"Caraffa, in Calabria."

"That'sa the same town. That'sa what he tola me."

"You sure?"

"I think I'ma sure. I don't know, but it soundsa like you are related."

Tony phoned Joe Maurici in Sydney and told him about his conversation with John Marvici. Joe made plans to come to New York and he would call Tony from there and then Tony would get hold of John and they would go to Massachusetts and meet him.

About a month later Joe, Angela, Dominic and Francesca land-
ed in New York. They got a hotel in midtown and phoned Tony.
Apparently Tony had already talked to John again and he gave Joe
John's phone number.

John picked up the phone on the second ring, "hello."

"Is this John Marvici?"

"Yes it is and who am I talking to?"

"This isa Joe Maurici from Syndey, Australia."

"Oh, are you the guy Tony Bartolo talked to me about?"

"Yes, I have talked to Tony. He must have tola you that we think
you might be our cousins."

"I never heard of having any cousins in Australia. And even
if you are why are you calling me? Are you looking for some
money?"

"No we're not looking for money. We are your cousins and there
are lots of us and we just want to know our cousins."

"Where are you now?"

"We are in New York, at a hotel."

"You know where we are?"

"You're in Springfield, Massachusetts."

"That's right."

"We gonna hire a car to come to Springfield tomorrow."

"Alright then, you call me when you get to Springfield."

The next day they hired a car to go from New York to Springfield,
Massachusetts and met up with Uncle John and Aunt Carmela. They
were the only two of the Marvici kids of their generation that were
still alive. My father Pasquale and my uncle Frank had both passed
away.

After meeting and talking for a couple of days everyone was
satisfied that we were all from the same family and that side of the
family had gone to Australia in the 1950's but our side of the family
resided in the northern east coast of the U.S.

We were all astounded that we had family in Australia and an
open invitation was extended to us all to come there.

So here I was at the Vancouver airport getting ready to get on
the plane bound for down under. I tried to get someone to come with

me but nobody seemed to be able to make it. I even tried to coax my aunt Carmela to come. Even though she had both the time and money she said that she was too old to travel that far. No matter what I said I couldn't change her mind.

I checked my bags and by the time I was done MC had parked the van and found me at the Air Canada counter. I had about an hour and a half before my flight left so MC and I went out on the top level of the parking garage and smoked a joint I had rolled up and ready. It would probably be a while before I smoked any B.C. bud again. I gave a second joint I had to MC and then headed to the gate to get my flight.

It was a long flight and made longer with all the stops and changes. We landed in Hawaii and then in Raratonga and then in New Zealand where the dogs must have picked up the smell of the joints I'd had in my pocket in Vancouver. I was asked to the back room where they searched all of my belongings. That took a couple of hours to get through and then I got a hotel room for the night where I washed out my pockets good so that I wouldn't get searched again when I landed in Australia.

By the time I got there I was bug eyed and jet lagged from the flight. I had sent a photo ahead so that they would know who to look for when I got off the plane.

"Joe is that you?" an attractive blonde woman was yelling over at me.

I put my hand up in the air to let her know that I heard her. As the crowd thinned out I got closer to her and she greeted me. "Hello, I'm Marie and this is Michael. We came to pick you up."

"Hi Marie" I said extending my hand. "And hi Michael. I'm glad to meet you."

We drove on a freeway around the city as we left the airport. We were soon going through a residential area where the houses were all very big. Judging by the people I saw on the street it looked like a heavily Italian neighborhood. We pulled up in front of a big house with a large steel gate in front. There was an intercom beside the gate and Michael announced us in Italian and the gate opened up.

It was beautiful inside with fruit trees and flowers all over the place. Up against the wall there were tomato plants that had to be 8 or 9 feet high and just loaded with tomatoes. We pulled in and parked in the parking lot where there were about a dozen cars already there. Every one was a shiny black sedan. Marie and Michael led me to a large wooden door that opened before we even had time to knock. A butler lead us through the house and into a big meeting room.

The room was already full of people. The table was full of food and drinks and we all sat down. I was given a seat at the head of the table, I guess because I was the guest. One by one each person stood up and introduced himself to me. I have never in my life felt more important.

There were so many courses of food on the table I couldn't sample them all. My head was feeling a bit weird with the jet lag and lack of sleep. There was lots of talking going on and everyone made a special trip to the head of the table to talk to me and welcome me to the family.

I sat there so stuffed I couldn't eat any more when the coffee and desert came out. In a situation like this in an Italian family the food is their gift to you. If you don't eat they will be insulted. It doesn't matter if you can't eat any more. You eat anyway. My stomach was already hurting as I sat there but there was no way out. After, as we sat around the table drinking coffee, some of the old timers started to talk. The more they talked the more their memories were unlocked and the talk became more and more about the old days. I was trying to stay awake but between the food and the weariness of the trip I seemed to fade into a zone where I could hear the stories but I was not there.........

Flashback

It's 1896 in Caraffa, Reggio de Calabria. Pasquale eked out a meager living out of his gardens on a two acre patch of dirt on the edge of town. People were poor in Caraffa, dirt poor. Pasquale and his wife Katerina had six children. Guiseppe was the oldest boy he was 10 years old. Then there were the four daughters, Angela, Fortunata, Pasqualina and Carmela. The youngest was Francesco who was just a baby.

Life was hard in southern Italy at that time. Pasquale had a couple of acres and a herd of goats and a vegetable garden that helped keep them alive. Many of Pasquale's friends had signed on to go on a ship and travel to the United States. Jobs were plentiful there. The American mining companies sent people to Europe and especially to Italy to recruit workers.

It was early in the morning one day when Pasquale's friend Dominic knocked on the door.

"Hey Pasquale," he yelled out pushing the door open.

"Comosta Dominic. Why you come banging on my door."

"Pasquale the miners are there in the square. They're signing people up to go to New York. If you sign they will give you 20 U.S. dollars."

"20 U.S. dollars, That's a lot of money."

"We better go talk to them."

"Yes, let's go" Pasquale shut the door behind him and he and Dominic walked toward the middle of town.

Guiseppe watched his father walk away. The two men walked down the main street to the square. They had a table set up and a few chairs around. There was a bit of a crowd around them and some of the men in the village had already signed to go.

Pasquale and Dominic walked up to the table where two men sat. One of the men looked directly at Pasquale and asked "You looking for work?"

"Maybe I am. Are you hiring?"

"Yes I'm hiring. I'm hiring men for the coal mines in Pennsylvania. We need men, Strong men and good workers and we're paying good money and a signing bonus."

"How much?"

"20 dollars U.S. a month and 20 dollars signing bonus."

Pasquale looked at Dominic. He made a gesture with his face. "You gonna sign?"

Dominic looked at Pasquale.

They stared at each other for a good long time and then Pasquale gave a quick nod and stepped up to the table and said, "Where do I sign?"

The man at the table pushed a piece of paper in front of him and pointed out the place he was to sign. Dominic pulled up beside him and signed too.

After they had signed the man motioned to another man to give them the 20 dollars. Dominic looked at the bill for a while before putting it in his pocket. That was the most money he had ever had at one time.

"When do we go?"

"Three days from now we meet here and get the boat at Samo to Palermo to Sardinia and to New York."

Pasquale and Dominic turned and walked back towards their home.

"Pasquale how does it feel to have 20 dollars?"

"It feels very good," he said taking the 20 dollar bill out of his pocket and holding it up to look at.

"Mine feels good too," Dominic said holding his up too.

They jostled each other playfully on the walk back home. About half way back Dominic stopped and grabbed Pasquale and looked him in the eyes. "I didn't think you would sign that easy Pasquale, you have a family, a big family. What will you do?"

Pasquale looked at Dominic for a minute as if it were the first time he had thought it out. "I guess I will send money home until there is enough to bring them over to America. That's what Salvatore Volare did a few years ago. I could have went last year too but now I see that he has brought his family to America and now I want to do that."

"That's good my friend," Dominic yelled and they pushed and pulled each other again and headed for home. But before they got back to Pasquale's house he stopped and grabbed Dominic and said, "Don't you say a word to Katerina. I will tell her when I am ready. Do you understand?"

"Yes Dominic, I understand but you should tell her soon."

Again they pushed each other around and continued on their way.

It was later that night when the children were all in bed that Pasquale told Katerina he had something to tell her. "I'm going to

America to work in the coal mines. I signed on today and got this money." He held out the 20 dollar bill. Katerina stepped forward and took the bill in her hand. She looked at it and then she looked at Pasquale.

"How long will you be gone?"

"Katerina, our life is poor here in Caraffa. It is a chance to have a better life in America. I will go and work and send money back to you for you and the children to join me. In a few years we will all be there."

Katerina was clearly stunned, maybe she would never see him again."Are we going to tell the children?"

"I will tell them Katerina," looking in her eyes,"I will tell them tomorrow." Katerina was visibly upset and held Pasquale close to her.

The three days went by fast. Before you know it Pasquale was saying goodbye to his family. The oldest boy Guiseppe was really upset that his father was going away. At ten years old he was now the man of the house. He would have to take over the work that his father had done in the gardens in order to keep the family fed. He had been working in the garden for a few years already so he knew what was expected of him.

Pasquale and the other men from the village traveled in a horse drawn wagon north to Reggio de Calabria and then in a small boat across to Messina. From there they boarded a larger boat to Palermo and a different boat to Poro Foxi on the island of Sardinia, where they caught the freighter to New York. There were about about 300 men making the trip. About 25 were from Caraffa. It was a long trip to New York across the Atlantic taking more than two months and several storms at sea to make the crossing.

New York was bustling with immigrants in those days with ships bringing people in every day to fan out into the country. Most of the immigrants were men who came to work and stay in New York for only a few days before going out to the mines and camps where they had jobs waiting. After arriving in New York Pasquale and the other men were taken to a warehouse where they stayed for a couple of days until they could get a seat on the train. The first destination was

Philadelphia, where Pasquale got off the train and boarded another going west and stopping in a mining town just east of Pittsburgh. About half of the men got off at Greensburg and the other half rode on to Pittsburgh. Pasquale and about 150 men were lead along a road close to the mine to a row of clapboard bunkhouses. They lined both sides of the road. Everyone was told to find a place for themselves. Just down the road there were another group of bunkhouses but these were all full with the mines existing workforce.

Pasquale and Dominic went into the second building and claimed bunks near the back of the room. There were about 20 beds in each bunkhouse. Within minutes all the bunks had been claimed. Most of the men in Pasquale's bunkhouse were from Caraffa.

It had been a long trip. Pasquale lay back on his bed and thought about his family. He had already been months away from them and he hadn't even started work yet. He felt sadness and excitement at the same time. Tomorrow work would start and he would begin making some money to bring his family over to be with him.

At the end of the row of bunkhouses was the cook house. Pasquale was falling asleep on his bunk when Dominic woke him up.

"Pasquale, Pasquale, wake up." Dominic said as he lightly shook him. "Mongha, come on we go eat."

Pasquale woke up and he and Dominic followed the others down the road to the mess hall. There was a man with a clipboard getting everybody's name as they came in the door.

"Your name" he hollered at Pasquale as he came through the door.

"Pasquale Marda vichi" Pasquale answered. And the man wrote on his list. Pasquale Marvici. Maybe it was the right spelling, we don't know, but that is what it sounded like. From that point on he was Pasquale Marvici. There were about 400 men that worked in the mine now with the new arrivals. The cook shack was very crowded. There weren't enough tables for all the men so they crowded together on the benches. And if you were done eating you had to get up and make room for somebody else. If you didn't get up on your own someone would give you a hand even if you didn't want one.

After dinner, Pasquale and Dominic went back to the bunk-house. Most of the men came back within a couple of minutes. There was a bit of a hierarchy that was developing in the bunkhouse. There were a few men from Catansero. One, namely Tony Galenta, was a big rough looking man with huge muscles on his arms. He was loud and a bit obnoxious and even though he was set up on the bottom bunk he had taken over the top bunk for himself as well. Pasquale looked over at Tony thinking 'That's a man that I should avoid. He looks like trouble.'

The work at the mine started the next day. A man came into the bunkhouse at five am and yelled at the men to get up, knocking the end of the beds with a wooden rod. The men filed out of the bunk-house and into the cook house and then back to the bunkhouse after breakfast. Then they formed a line outside to go down in the mine. Dominic and Pasquale rode the lift down the shaft with the rest of the miners. The mineshaft was dimly lit with coal oil lamps hanging on the wall of the shaft. It was hot as they went down deeper into the mine. The air was heavy and stagnant and filled with coal dust. Dominic and Pasquale wrapped their mouths and noses with a kerchief to keep from breathing too much dust. They soon arrived at the end of the shaft and were given a pick and shovel. There were several bosses among the men, and they split the crew into 5 smaller crews. Each boss led his men to a different part of the mineshaft.

Pasquale and Dominic ended up on the same crew. After they arrived at the end of one finger of the mine the boss turned and addressed the crew.

"O K listen up. My name is Nate Kellar and I'm your boss. I Expect you to do your work and do what I tell you. Now I want 2 on the picks and 2 on the shovels and 5 on the buckets. You load those cars,"he said pointing to a row of coal cars that were on a track in the main shaft. " Now get to work."

Pasquale and Dominic were the first with the picks. They were to pick the coal loose from the side and face of the shaft. There was just enough room in the shaft for two men to swing a pick at the same time. After loosening some coal they could step back and rest for a minute and while the guys on the shovels filled buckets and then the bucket crew took them out to the main shaft and dumped into the coal cars. There was a donkey winch cable system that pulled the cars to the surface when they were full of coal. It was grueling work, dirty and hot. Their sweat made the coal dust stick to them. They could feel the burning in their noses and heavy air in their lungs. The guys took turns on the picks, as that was the hardest job to keep up for long. There were no breaks, they worked straight through until six pm when Nate blew a whistle and yelled at the crew, "Quitting time, let's go." The men put down their tools and followed behind to the main shaft and the lift.

All the men were black from coal dust and hurried to wash the dust off their faces and hands and get into the cook house for dinner. It had been a long time since breakfast. Dominic and Pasquale fell into bed that night and before they knew it was time to get up and do it all over again. Twelve hours a day and seven days a week was the work schedule. Payday was at the beginning of the following month. The regular mine workers made 40 dollars a month but the immigrant miners only made only 20 dollars a month. And they were docked five dollars a month for their room and board, only ending up with 15 dollars.

The mine had a post office at the company store where you could buy stamps. Pasquale sent a letter to Katrina in Italy every month along with ten dollars. He kept $5 so he would have some money if he wanted to buy something at the company store.

Months went by and Pasquale lost count as all the days just melted together. He would get a letter from Katerina once a month as well. Things were going pretty good for her in Caraffa. Ten dollars a month was quite an ample amount of money in Italy at that time. The family wasn't hurting for anything. Guiseppe was doing very well with the garden and the goats and Katerina was starting to save a little money each month for the family to make the trip to America. As the years went by Pasquale and Dominic stayed working at the mine.

Pasquale had saved up a sizable sum of money over the years from the five dollars that he had kept each month. He had the money hidden inside of a tear in his mattress and had accumulated over $400. Nobody knew that Pasquale had that much money.

Over the years Tony Galenta had put together a protection racket in the mining camp. He usually picked on the smaller, weaker men in the camp and demanded part of their pay for protection. If they refused to pay he would arrange to have them beat up and after a beating or two they were convinced that giving him half of their $20 every month was good for their health. The men from Caraffa pretty much stuck together so Tony steered clear of that group for some time. He was getting protection money from over a hundred miners in the camp of 500. And he wasn't actually doing much work in the mine. Tony was getting fat and powerful among the miners. He was making a lot of money and could afford to buy anything or anyone he wanted. The men from Caraffa had eluded his protection racket and he wanted to get them paying too.

One night, Dominic was awakened by four men who held him down and whispered to him in the dark.

"You must buy protection. You're going to get hurt if you don't. Do you understand?"

Dominic nodded his head. Then the men slipped away in the darkness. The next day Dominic told Pasquale about this. Pasquale was a very proud man and would never pay protection and deprive his family in Caraffa any of the money.

In her last letter Katerina said that she had enough money to send Guiseppe to America and would be sending him soon. On his next payday Pasquale sent a letter to Katerina and he put the ten dollars that he always sent but then he put all the money he had saved except five dollars he kept. There was four hundred twenty five dollars in the letter. Katerina was surprised to open it and find so much money in it. Guiseppe had been wanting to go to America for a while and now Katherina would have enough money to send him.

A couple of months later Pasquale had a letter from Guiseppe. Guiseppe was in America. He had sent a letter from New York. He had a business opportunity out in California and was going to go there first. He was going out to invest in a vineyard and winery in the Napa Valley. He wrote that he would write again when he got out there and send a mailing address.

Guiseppe traveled by train to California. He was 20 years old and was bankrolled by his mother. He was to take a look at the investment in California and if it looked good then he was to buy it and go into business. After the business was his he would go to see his father and bring him to California to work in the vineyard.

While riding the train west, Guiseppe thought about all the things he would do now that he was in America. He had grown to be a big man, tall for an Italian man of that time at 5'7" with large shoulders and a barrel chest. And Guiseppe was a strong and rugged man and feared no one.

It would take a couple of months to look at the vineyard and winery to decide whether to buy it or not. Guiseppe wanted to make sure that it was a good business before spending the money.

Back in Caraffa, Katerina was doing pretty well. Francesco was 10 years old now and the girls were older. She had heard about the vineyard from an Italian man in Caraffa who had been to California. He could not afford to buy it himself so he passed the deal off to Katerina. The many years of getting ten dollars a month had given Katerina a small fortune in terms of the times. Then one day she received the letter from Pasquale with four hundred and twenty five dollars in it.

She had made up her mind that if Guiseppe bought the vineyard she would leave Caraffa and go to America. If Pasquale could send all this money back home to her then it must be worth it for everyone in the family to go over. She wrote a letter to Pasquale telling him of her decision. And then she wrote another to Guiseppe telling him that we will all go to America and bring Father to California after he hes bought the vineyard. It was a very exciting time for Katerina. She was finally going to go to America and see her husband who she had not seen for almost 10 years.

Meanwhile back at the mine in Greensburg, Tony Galenta was putting the pressure on the men from Caraffa to pay the protection money. He had a small army of loyal thugs that were exempt from paying for protection because they were the ones you had to pay to be protected from. Tony treated his thugs good, making sure they got tobacco and whiskey a couple times a week, and that if they were loyal to Tony he would make sure they did not have to work too hard. The bunkhouse that Pasquale and Dominic were in was about half the Caraffa men and half men loyal to Tony Galenta. Several of the other men from Caraffa had been wakened during the night and threatened with harm if they did not buy into the protection racket. Pasquale was not bothered but felt like it was just a matter of time before they got to him too.

The men from Caraffa met secretly behind the cook shack one night to talk about what they would do about the threats coming from Tony and his thugs.

"Galento and his thugs are collecting money from almost all the mine workers except us from Caraffa" Pasquale said softly so his voice wouldn't carry too far."What are we going to do, because I for one will not pay a cent to those thugs."

So far none of the Caraffa men had been beat up but several men had been threatened, including Dominic.

"We have to stick together if we are going to be safe," Pasquale whispered to his compatriots.

"We need to have a leader to be strong against them," said Rocco Marietti. "I vote that Pasquale be our leader."

Pasquale really didn't want to be the one that all the men would count on but there were many in the group that wanted him. And so they elected Pasquale to be the one that would keep them together and safe from the threat of the protection racket.

"I will stand with you and we will be strong, " Rocco announced before the meeting broke up and the men went back to the bunkhouses.

Tony Galenta and his thugs knew that something was going on with the Caraffa men yet they were determined to get these men to pay protection just like the rest in the camp.

The men from Caraffa always stayed close together. They made a point of not going anywhere without the safety of numbers. One night on the way back to the bunkhouse after dinner ten of them were attacked with clubs and beaten up pretty bad. Pasquale and

Dominic were already in the bunkhouse when the injured men started coming in.

"What the hell happened to you?" Pasquale said as he helped one of the men to his bunk.

"A mob got us," he said. " They attacked us with clubs"

"Who was it? Did you see?"

"No, they had their face blacked and they struck fast. "It was Galenta, wasn't it? It was his thugs."

"I cannot say Pasquale, but you are probably right."

The bunks were filling up with men who had been injured in the attack. Pasquale walked around and tended to a couple of the men. Just then, Tony Galenta walked in. The room was silent as Tony looked around the room. He went over to his bunk and several of his men came in and went to their bunks too.

"What happened to you men?" Tony said after laying down on his bunk.

"You know damn well what happened," Pasquale said forcefully.

"What are you talking about, Pasquale?"

"You are the reason my comrades are beat up."

"I am not the reason Pasquale. I am the man that protects them when they pay me. If these men had paid me for protection, I would have protected them from the mob, and I will protect you too but you must pay."

Pasquale got up and walked up to Tony. "I spit on you and your protection. You are a maggot compared to these men. I will never pay you protection money. I will die first." Pasquale went back over to his bunk in the back of the room near the wall and lay on his bunk. He was fuming.

Tony Galenta got up from his bunk and went outside his men following right behind. There was a young Italian man from Selerno who had just come over to America and had been working at the mine for about six months. His name was also Tony, Tony DeAngelo. He hit it off with Galenta and they became good friends. He was especially impressed by Galenta's protection racket. 'What a novel idea' he thought . Men pay so you won't beat them up. Galenta knew that if he got rid of Pasquale he would get the rest of the Caraffa men to pay the protection money. Pasquale was the most stubborn of them all and he was also their leader.

Galenta was already hot about Pasquale's tirade at him earlier. He invited DeAngelo to come out and talk to him.

"Eh Tony, how would you like to make $500."

"What are you kidding, sure I would like to make $500. Who do I have to shoot?" he said jokingly.

"Funny you should ask me that. Because I want you to shoot Pasquale."

"Pasquale eh! When do you want me to do this?"

"I want you to do it tonight."

"Tonight!"

"Yes, I want you to shoot him while he sleeps."

"Do you have a gun for me?"

"Yes I do." Galento slipped a 25 caliber pistol out of his pocket and gave it to DeAngelo. "I do not want him to make it to work in the mine tomorrow. A man like that could turn all the men against me and ruin my business. When he is dead then I will give you the $500."

The two men parted and Tony Galenta went back to the bunkhouse and lay down in his bed. A few of the men were already sleeping, and Tony lay there unable to fall asleep, knowing what was going to happen. He lay there for hours and the only noise he could hear was men snoring and groaning. Tony DeAngelo was in the bunkhouse next to the one Pasquale and Tony were in. He got up in the early hours of the morning and quietly made his way to the door and went out. He got to the back door of Pasquale's bunkhouse and slowly opened the door. Pasquale's bunk was in the corner about 4 bunks from the door. Tony walked silently up to Pasquale's bunk. He had a pillow with him and the gun inside the pillow. He came close to Pasquale and saw that he did not even budge. Pulling the gun up and getting it close to his head, he let two shots go. The sound was quite muffled by the pillow. The only other person to hear the shots was Tony Galenta, who still lay awake.

Tony DeAngelo then quietly went back to his bunk and went to sleep.

It was about five am, just before the wake up man went around to the bunkhouses to get everyone up when a huge explosion rocked the camp. The explosion was in the mine and killed or trapped the entire night shift down in the shaft. The camp soon turned to pandemonium, with people running all over the place. Everybody in every bunkhouse was up and outside to try to cope with the disaster. Dominic was the only one who noticed that Pasquale hadn't moved. He went over to his bed to give him a shake, and saw the bullet holes in his head. Pasquale had been shot. There was no one left in the bunkhouse except Pasquale and Domonic. Dominic lifted his friend's head to his chest and held him. His dearest closest friend had been killed. Dominic knew this was the end for the men from Caraffa. Galenta would have them all paying him for protection now.

The explosion wreaked havoc in the camp. There were 150 miners trapped underground, or dead. Some of the dead and injured were not far down in the mine and men went down and brought some of them out. There were a few injured but most of the men who were brought out were dead. They were lined up on the ground near the cook shack and covered with blankets. Tony Galenta saw this as an opportunity and had a couple of his men take Pasquale out of the back door in the bunkhouse and lay him out on the ground with the victims of the explosion.

Nobody saw them or knew that Pasquale was dead except Dominic. Dominic watched from a distance while Tony's men moved Pasquale's body. He wept for his friend.

Chapter 2

It was late in the fall when Guiseppe got off the Illinois Central Railroad in Chicago. It was a two-day wait for the train to the west coast of California. The Sante Fe Railroad took passengers to California from Chicago every two weeks. Guiseppe checked into the Brevoort Hotel on Madison Street in downtown Chicago. It was a new hotel that had just opened the year before. Chicago was a bustling metropolis with a lot of automobile traffic in the streets. It was one of the fastest growing cities in America in the early 1900's.

When Guiseppe was still in Italy he met a couple from Chicago who were acquaintances of his mother. Julia and Louis Guyon, were dance teachers in Chicago. They extended an invitation to Katerina and Guiseppe to visit if they were ever in Chicago.

After checking into his room and taking a short nap Guiseppe went out to find the Guyons.

Guiseppe went out on busy Madison Street and found a line of taxis outside of the hotel. He gave the driver the address and the driver took him to the Guyons house. It was a big house with a studio on the side where they gave dance lessons.

Guiseppe knocked on the door. He could hear activity going on inside the house and a minute later the door opened. It was Louis and he instantly recognized Giuseppe "Guiseppe, what a surprise, Come in."

The men shook hands and went into the living room. "Sit down Guiseppe, I will get us coffee." Louis came back a few minutes later with a pot of coffee and a couple of cups. He poured Guiseppe a coffee and sat down.

Louis asked about Pasquale and Katerina and what he was doing in Chicago. They talked for a while, catching up on the news about his father and mother. Guiseppe told Louis about going to California to buy the vineyard and winery. And once he bought it, his mother and sisters and brother Francesco would come from Italy and Father would come from the mines at Greensburg and they would run the vineyard together.

Chicago was in an era that was sometimes called 'Jazz Age Chicago.' Jazz music was becoming very popular and it invigorated public dancing during the early 1900's in Chicago. This led to the opening of dozens of dance clubs and dance halls in the city. Louis and Julie Guyon took advantage of this trend by offering dance lessons and promoting dances weekly. Business was very good with over 100 people in lessons and a dance every Saturday night. The Guyons dances had the reputation of being quite conservative. They shared the concern of many of the city's people that the "jazzier" dance music encouraged improper behavior from the young people that listened to it. The Guyons did not teach the Charleston or the fox trot but only the waltz and two-step. A lot of Chicagoans appreciated this conservatism and their dances were very well attended making them quite successful.

Guiseppe stayed a couple of hours at the Guyon's and then got a car back to the Brevoort Hotel. They had agreed that Louis and Julia would pick him up at the hotel in their car at 8 pm and they would go to a dance club.

They arrived right on time, Guiseppe was waiting for them in the lobby of the hotel. The Guyons were driving a new 1907 Buick touring car that had become the rage of the Chicago Jazz Crowd. Only the wealthiest were able to afford a car at this time in Chicago, or anywhere in America. Cars were still very expensive and were not affordable by to the common man yet. As America's auto industry developed there were many automakers that tried their hand in the business, with companies starting up and failing all the time. However Henry Ford was having a lot of success with the model 'B' which he personally piloted to a new land speed record of 91 miles per hour in 1904. By driving and racing his cars himself he gave his automobiles exceptional credibility for performance, which made them extremely popular with the American car buying public. Auto manufacturing was a highly competitive industry at that time with at least 240 firms established in the industry between 1904 and 1908 in America alone.

Louis parked outside the hotel and he and Julia went into the Lobby of the Brevoort Hotel and found Guiseppe waiting. While he was waiting Guiseppe had met a young Italian woman who was staying at the hotel. Angelina Volare had been living in Chicago for about a year and had recently moved into the hotel. She came from a wealthy family from Milan in the north of Italy.

Guiseppe told her that he was waiting for friends to go to a dance club and asked if she would like to come along. She was very attracted to Guiseppe and agreed to accompany him.

When Louis and Julia showed up, Guiseppe introduced Angelina and they all went out to where the Buick was parked. Julia and Angelina got into the back seat and Louis and Guiseppe rode in the front seat as was the custom of the times.

They first drove north of town to Clark Street where the 'Roadhouse' that had once been a resting place for weary travelers had recently been converted to an entertainment spot boasting a beer hall, bowling alley, outdoor dance floor and several stand-alone refreshment centers.

This was the first time Guiseppe had gone to a dance club such as this, though Angelina and the Guyons were familiar with this kinds of entertainment spot. After a quick walk around the establishment they took a table near the outdoor dance floor. A jazz band of colored musicians was playing and the dance floor was crowded. After settling in at the table and ordering drinks Louis and Julia took to the dance floor leaving Angelina and Guiseppe at the table talking.

It was no secret that Louis and Julia were expert dancers and loved to dance. They stood out on the dance floor. They danced just about every dance, only stopping to encourage Angelina and Guiseppe to have a dance. When they could not get them to dance together, Julia grabbed Guiseppe's hand and Louis took Angelina's and led them out on the dance floor. Guiseppe had only danced at weddings in the past and was usually quite intoxicated when he did.

Julia was a good teacher and soon had Guiseppe two stepping right along with her. Angelina had been to dance clubs in Chicago before and proved to be a pretty good dancer, to Louis's delight.

After spending several hours at the 'Roadhouse' Louis suggested that they go to the Princess Ballroom. They departed the 'Roadhouse' and drove across town to the Princess. The Princess was a huge ballroom with a dance floor that could accommodate more than a thousand people. It was one of the largest of the Chicago dance halls at that time. The dance floor had tables all around the edge and Louis managed to find an empty one. They ordered drinks and shortly afterward Louis and Julia went out on the dance floor.

"So tell me, why are you in Chicago?" Angelina asked Guiseppe.

"I am waiting for the train to California," he answered. "It's leaving the day after tomorrow. I am going to buy a vineyard and winery in Napa."

"Oh that sounds ambitious."

"Yes, my mother and my brother and sisters want to come to America after. My father is already here but he is working in the mines in Pennsylvania. He will come to California too."

They talked for a while and it was no secret that Angelina had taken a shine for Guiseppe. "Now that you are in America I want to call you Joe," she said.

"If you want to call me Joe then I am Joe to you," he answered.

When Louis and Julia returned to the table, Angela announced, "In America Guiseppe is not Guiseppe anymore. He is Joe." They all laughed and from that point on Guiseppe Marvici would be known as Joe Marvici.

It was very late when Louis dropped Joe and Angelina off at the Brevoort Hotel. Joe walked Angelina to her room and after opening the door she invited him in for a drink. She knew that she was not just inviting him for a drink but rather to spend the night with her and he accepted.

The next morning Louis came to the hotel and found Joe sitting in the Hotel restaurant with Angelina.

"Hello Guiseppe." Louis greeted him and extended his hand to Joe.

"He's Joe now, not Guiseppe. Don't you remember, we are in America now," Angelina spoke up.

"Alright he's Joe. Now I want you both to come to dinner at my house tonight."

"What time do you want us?" Joe asked.

"You come at six o'clock. I can pick you up with my car if you want."

"Don't worry we can find our way."

"Oh good, it's settled. Then I will see you at six," said Louis and he bid farewell to his friends.

Joe and Angelina spent the day together taking in the sights of the city. Angelina knew her way around Chicago and proved to be an excellent guide.

Later that afternoon they hired a car to take them to the Guyon's house, arriving right on time. The Guyons had invited two other couples to dinner as well. John and Gina Bregoli and Al and Rita Spatini were all students in the Guyon's dance studio. The conversation soon turned to the dance craze that was sweeping Chicago and across America.

"There is a lot of money to make in dance halls. I want to build a very large dance hall, that can accommodate four thousand people. There is a fortune to be made, just waiting for someone to do it.

Guiseppe, I mean Joe, you should stay here in Chicago and invest in a dance hall."

"Well it sounds good but I got to do what I started out to do first and then if it doesn't work out, then I might have to come back here. I thank you for the offer but I think I better catch the train tomorrow."Joe said, and then laughed.

It was a nice evening and a wonderful dinner of wine, lasagna, chicken cacciatore., veal scallopini, several different salads, complete with dessert, spumoni, and Italian coffee and a bottle of anisette (a licorice flavored liqueur).

Joe had been traveling for a few months and this was his first opportunity to relax with Italians and even be in the company of a beautiful Italian woman.

Joe and Angelina returned to the Brevoort Hotel and spent a second night together. Angela had hinted at going with Joe to California but he discouraged it.

"I will go now and do what I came to do and if I want you to come out to California, then I will send for you."

Angelina accompanied Joe to the train station the next morning and they said goodbye.

"If I did not have this task to do I would stay here in Chicago," he confessed before getting on the train. Angelina stayed on the platform and watched as Joe took a seat near the window. Their eyes locked and they smiled at each other as the train pulled away. She gave a short wave and Joe tipped his hat and then he was gone. Joe knew that he would not be sending for Angelina for she was not from Calabria. Even though she was from the north of Italy it was custom in Calabria that men would marry Calabrais women.

Chapter 3

Italy 1907

Katerina had been to the post office to check for mail from Pasquale several times but there was no letter. Pasquale always sent the money every month and it always arrived in Samo at the same time every month and had done so for more than ten years. It was very unusual that Katerina would not get a letter. After a month had gone by and there was still no letter from Pasquale she sent a letter to Guiseppe in California telling him what was going on.

It had been a long time since Katerina and Pasquale were together yet she was loyal to him, the same as if he was still at home in Samo. Funny thing with some Italian women, they are like the Canada Goose that never takes another mate after the death of the first. She had a feeling that Pasquale was dead but she knew that she would not give up hope until she was sure.

After expelling the French from Rome in1870, Italy maintained a strong military. In 1882 they formed an alliance with Germany and Austria-Hungary against the threat of attacks from the French. Every Italian man was obliged to do his tour in the military. Most tours in time of peace were only two years and in war 4 to 5 years.

Guiseppe had avoided going in the Italian military because he was the only man in the house and was allowed to defer to take care of his family. After he went to America the Italian military wanted him to come back to Italy and do his duty. They paid frequent visits to Katerina asking questions about Guiseppe and hoping to find him there. They made certain that Katerina understood that they would be watching Francesco to make sure he didn't slip away to America also.

Francesco was doing most of the gardening work and caring for the goats these days while each of the girls had some kind of job they could make a little money with.

Katerina took in laundry and worked as a cleaner in Samo, sometimes taking one or more of her girls with her to help. She was a very thrifty and frugal person and managed to save most of the money that Pasquale sent and even reluctantly loaned money to Guiseppe several times to do some real estate deals in Caraffa. Fortunately Guiseppe sold the property just before going to America, made a lot of money and paid his mother back with interest. Before he left for America she loaned Guiseppe a thousand American dollars to go to California and buy the vineyard. Even so, life was comfortable for Katerina and the children in Samo. Maybe she would go to America and maybe she would just stay in Samo. If Pasquale was indeed dead then she might just stay right where she was. Francesco was already 12 years old and was growing to be a tall boy. Katerina felt certain that Francesco would not leave her and go to America like Pasquale and Guiseppe did.

Her oldest daughter Angela was going to get married next summer to a man from Caraffa. That was just one more reason that Katerina did not want to leave Samo to go to America. Though she was sad about Guiseppe because he might not ever come back to Samo without the military grabbing him and making him do his tour of duty. She was also concerned about Guiseppe finding the right girl to marry. In her world if you were a Calabrase man you should marry a Calabrais woman. It was not good to marry outside of this tradition and she was worried that being in America that he might not be able to find the right woman. Even women from the north of Italy or from Sicily were not acceptable.

America 1907

The train pulled into San Francisco late at night and Joe had to wait until the next afternoon to catch the train to Napa. He checked into the newly rebuilt Fairmont Hotel. The Fairmont had been one of the many casualties of the San Francisco Earthquake of 1906.

It was on April 18, 1906 that the earthquake struck. The earth cracked in a swath 50 to 60 miles wide and over 400 miles long with thousands of side cracks all along the main one. Over 3000 people were killed from fire and collapsing buildings in San Francisco. The earthquake was felt from Coos Bay, Oregon all the way to Los Angeles. There was an aftershock three hours later that brought down many of the damaged buildings that didn't fall the first time. But the greatest damage was done by the fire that burned for four days following the earthquake. The U.S. Army ordered all available troops to San Francisco to help in the emergency.

At 10:05 a.m. a wireless telegraph station in San Diego radioed reports of the disaster to the "U.S.S. Chicago" which then steamed full speed to San Francisco. It was the first time that wireless telegraph was used in a major natural disaster. The "U.S.S. Chicago" participated in the largest rescue by sea in history by rescuing over 20,000 people from the pursuing fire.

The fire burned for four days engulfing most of the city. Thousands of volunteers, firefighters and soldiers put up fire lines and tried to stop the fire without success. They even dynamited mansions on the ritzy Van Ness Avenue in an attempt to build a fire break. It was unsuccessful and ended up sending the firefighters running in panic.

When the fire was finally under control on the fifth day later, buildings that were still standing but badly damaged were dynamited to bring them down.

By April 23 the fire was over and the same day the Governor of California announced "The work of rebuilding San Francisco has begun." And he went even further to announce, "I expect to see an new metropolis replaced on a much grander scale than ever before."

The Fairmont Hotel was located on Mason Street, which had been totally destroyed. The Mason Street buildings were one of the first areas to be rebuilt. The Fairmont was a new building that had opened for business only a few months before Joe arrived there. The city was still very much under construction and had the look of a new city. From Joe's window he could see San Francisco Bay and the rolling hills across the water.

The Sante Fe Railroad had a spur line that went out to Sacramento twice a week. It was the mail train that stopped in every little place along the line picking up and dropping off mail, passengers and freight, and picking up and spotting rail cars in sidings. The closest you could get to Napa on the train was Vellejo, which was about 18 miles away.

Vellejo was named after a Mexican General that was given the job of enforcing Mexican land holding laws in the mid 1800's. Mexico had decreed that a person who was not Mexican could not hold title to land in California at this time. General Vellejo established Fort Vellejo and used it as his base for enforcing these laws while at the same time acquiring huge tracts of land for himself totaling over 100,000 acres. This changed when the American Army took the fort and expelled the Mexican Army in Northern California in the late 1800's.

Joe arrived in Vellejo and and rode the horse drawn stagecoach the 18 miles to Napa. It was a long, dusty and bumpy ride along the hard packed dirt road. Johnny Paluchi, the owner of the vineyard knew that Joe would be showing up in Napa soon and had been checking on the stage arrival every day. So when the stage pulled into Napa, Johnny was there to meet the stage and Joe. They had met years ago in Samo and recognized each other right away.

"Welcome, my friend, to California," Johnny said while offering his hand. Johnny was driving a Ford model "B" pick-up truck that wasn't much different from a horse drawn wagon except it lacked the horses. It was one of the first trucks built in the new age of automobiles and was still called by many "The Horseless Wagon".

It took about 15 minutes driving north of Napa to reach the "Monte Vista Winery." The vineyards and the winery was on 40 acres of rolling hillside that were covered in grapevines. Johnny had been here for twenty five years and had developed the land, planting most of the grapes that were growing there himself.

Johnny pulled the truck up in front of the main house and Regina and their two daughters, Maria and Frederica came out of the house and greeted them.

Johnny introduced his wife and daughters to Joe and then invited him into the house for lunch. And of course they had to try a few of the different wines that they produced at "Monte Vista."

It was a long lunch with lots of conversation and a lot of wine and of course Johnny and Regina wanted to know all the news from Samo and how Joe's father was doing. The house was a large house built out of adobe bricks and lumber. A room in the house had been kept for Joe. There were usually 10 to 12 workers working the vineyard and winery most of the time and the hired workers stayed in a bunkhouse that was close to the winery building.

After catching up on the news Joe was shown to his room in the back of the house. He was tired from the long trip and lay down and rested for about an hour or so before Johnny knocked on the door and offered to show Joe around the winery. They walked out in the vineyards first, which had already been harvested a month before. Johnny talked about all the work it had taken to get the vineyard to produce the finest wine making grapes. Then they went into the winery building. The building itself was built out of adobe and wood, the same as the house, but had a huge cellar underneath. The main floor was about half full of empty grape boxes and several large vats and presses used for pulping the grapes and pressing them into juice. The entire crop of grapes had already been pressed and put into barrels in the basement for fermenting. In the basement under the winery there were two huge rooms. One of the rooms was lined with 25 gallon oak barrels that were full of fermenting wine from this year's crop. There were four rows of barrels with about 30 barrels to a row situated on racks that made the barrels sit on their side and off the floor a couple of feet making it easy to tend to. After a couple of months fermenting in the barrels, the wine was put into bottles and stored in another room in the basement in racks that reached all the way to the ceiling. The wine was separated into the years that they were bottled with the oldest being sold first, except for a small amount that was aged longer and fetched a higher price.

Because of Joe's arrival late in the season, with the wine making already done, the main business was marketing the wine. Several buyers from San Francisco and the east coast came to Napa every year to buy their supply of wine for the year. One such buyer was Joe Parisi and his brother John who had several restaurants in Connecticut and Massachusetts. They routinely went to California and bought enough wine for their restaurants to last the whole year.

The Parisi family was from Caraffa. The brothers had opened their first restaurant in New Haven, Connecticut in 1902 and had expanded to Hartford, Waterbury and Springfield, Massachusetts in just a few short years. A couple of months after Joe arrived in Napa, the Parisi Brothers came out from the east and checked into the Alexandria Hotel in Napa.

Some of the young boys in town would hang around the hotel with their horses and run messages out to the wineries when prospective buyers would show up in Napa. One day one of the young boys brought a message from the Parisi Brothers that they were coming to buy wine. Johnny took Joe with him to the Alexandria Hotel to meet the brothers. The brothers were in the bar when they got there.

Johnny walked in the door and stopped and looked around. The Parisi brothers saw Johnny walk in and waved at him. He and Joe walked over to the table and sat down.

"How are you, Joe," Johnny said extending his hand and turning to John, "And how are you John. And this is Joe, Joe Marvici, he's Calabrias."

"Calabrais eh! What town you from?"

"I'm from Samo"

"We are from Caraffa. What did you say your name is?"

"It's Marvici," Joe replied.

"I think my father knew your father."

They sat in the bar and talked about the old country for hours, eventually going back to the winery to drink some more and talk about buying wine. The Parisis were one of John's best customers over the last few years and usually bought around 500 cases of various wines of several different years. They shipped the wine back east on the railroad and made a point of not leaving for the east themselves until all the wine had been loaded on the train.

The Parisis extended an open invitation to both Joe and John to come and visit them if they were ever in the east.

It was shortly after the Parisi Brothers had left Napa on the train accompanying their wine back to the east coast that Joe received the letter from his mother telling him of the loss of contact with his father. He wrote back to his mother right away and promised he would go to Pennsylvania and find out what had happened to his father.

He also wrote a letter to his father hoping that he would get a reply and find out that everything was alright.

A couple of months went by and there was still no answer from his father. Joe talked the situation over with Johnny Paluchi and they agreed it would be better to go during the winter while work was slow in the winery and vineyard.

Johnny took Joe to Vellejo where he caught the Sante Fe Railroad for the long trip back to the east, stopping again in San Francisco and Chicago. The two day layover in Chicago gave him time to visit Louis and Julia Guyon and look up Angelina Volare who was still living at the Brevoort Hotel. This time Joe stayed with Angelina instead of getting a room of his own. The Guyons were close to opening their own dance hall not far from where they lived and had the dance studio. Joe and Angelina spent part of the evenings with their new friends each night before going back to the Brevoort.

Once again they all said goodbye as Joe caught the Illinois Central Railroad going east. Angelina wanted to go with him again but Joe once again discouraged her and promised he would be back through Chicago in a month or so.

Joe rode the train to Cleveland and then to Pittsburg where he got off the train and got a hotel for the night. He would catch the local out to Greensburg the next day, arriving around noon. Then entire town was the mine, even the wooden shacks of some of the miners who worked in the mine and the rows of bunkhouses of those miners who lived there. The store belonged to the company, and of course the presence of the mine itself, with the above ground buildings and office, led one to think Greensburg was the epitome of an American coal mine town.

Joe followed the road up hill to the office, opened the door, and went in. A woman approached him. "Hello, what can I do for you?"

"Hello to you," Joe said. "My name is Joe Marvici and my father was working in this mine and we have lost contact with him. I have come here to find out where he is."

"Okay, what was your father's name?"

"Pasquale Marvici,"

"Oh yes, he worked here a long time."

"Yes it was over 10 years."

"Just a minute," she said and went into one of the offices in the back of the room. A minute or so went by and she came out followed by a man.

"Hi I'm Bill Richardson," the man said extending his hand.

"Joe Marvici," Joe replied as they shook hands.

"Please come in my office." He motioned for Joe to follow him.

Richardson closed the door behind Joe and invited him to sit down.

"Joe, I have bad news for you. We had a coal dust explosion in the mine last fall and a lot of men died. I'm sorry to tell you that your father was one of the dead."

Joe was dazed by the realization that his father was dead, though he was not surprised. "Where is my father buried?"

"He's buried in the mine cemetery, down the hill towards the rail."

Joe left the mine office. He walked out on the road and stopped and looked back. 'So this is where my father has been for so many years,' he thought. Then he turned and walked down the hill to the cemetery to visit his father's grave and pay his respects to him. Joe walked up and down the rows of wooden crosses. Each one had a miner's name painted on it in black paint. Finally there it was, a wooden cross that read 'Pasquale Marvici died Sept 1907.' Joe wept at his father's grave. After saying a prayer and bidding farewell to his father Joe left the cemetery and walked back up towards the mine. He had a couple of hours to kill before the local train came back through Greensburg on its way back to Pittsburg.

Joe was curious if Father's friend Dominic was still at the mine or if he perished in the explosion as well. After asking a couple of mine workers he finally found an Italian man that knew Dominic and pointed out the bunkhouse where he stayed. Joe walked over to the bunkhouse and went inside. About half of the miners in the bunkhouse were working the day shift in the mine and the night shift guys were either sleeping or lounging around.

The first miner Joe talked to Joe was Tony Galenta.

"Hello, I'm looking for a friend. He's a Calabrais man, his name is Dominic. They said he lived in this bunkhouse."

"Oh Dominic, yes he's in here. Hey Dominic!" Tony yelled out looking towards the back corner of the room. "There's someone here to see you."

Dominic was half asleep on his bunk and rolled over. Opening his eyes, he looked over towards Tony and Joe. Joe started weaving his way through the bunks back towards where Dominic was. As he got close he said, "Dominic, it's Guiseppe, Pasquale's son. Do you remember me?"

Dominic got right up and approached Joe, shaking his hand and embracing him. "Guiseppe, my goodness you look good. How is your mother?"

"Dominic, my mother is well. I came to find my father. How are you?" Joe asked with a concerned tone as Dominic did not look well. The mine had taken its toll on Dominic's health over the years. Years of coal dust in the lungs had turned his skin a grey color and made his breathing quite laborious.

"Not so good Guiseppe, my health is failing and I will go to the city soon because I am not well enough to keep working here. Did you find your father?"

"Yes Dominic, I did find my father. I just came from his grave. Now I know where he is and what happened to him."

Dominic looked over at Tony Galenta who was watching and listening closely to the two men. After Pasquale was killed, Galenta had his way with the rest of the men from Samo. Dominic and the others were all frightened of Galenta and his thugs and were afraid to say too much in fear that they would be made to pay for it.

Dominic thought about telling Joe about the murder of his father but out of fear he did not say a word. He knew that Joe would not let it rest if he knew and both of them might end up dead so he kept quiet.

They sat around and talked in the bunkhouse for a little while and then Joe mentioned that he was going to catch the train. Dominic decided to walk to the train with him. As they were leaving the bunkhouse Tony Galenta, Tony De Angelo and a couple of Tony's thugs all offered their condolences to Joe, each reaching out and shaking hands while doing so.

Joe had no idea that he shook hands with his father's killers although Dominic knew and even though he would like to kill them at that moment, he said nothing.

Joe and Dominic followed the road down the hill to the railroad station and waited on the platform for the train to come. They talked a lot about the old country and both men felt homesick. Joe told Dominic all the news about his travels in America thus far before they noticed the train approaching.

"Dominic, you take care of yourself."

"You take care of yourself too and I wish you all the best in America," Dominic said while shaking his hand. "Maybe we will meet again. And you say hello to your mother for me when you talk to her next."

"I will Dominic. "Joe said and then embraced his father's friend.

Joe turned towards the train that was pulling up to the platform and Dominic reached out and grabbed his arm. He wanted to tell Joe about his father's killer but as he looked him in the eyes he just could not say it. Instead he said, "goodbye Guiseppe."

"Goodbye Dominic," Joe said as he stepped on to the train and disappeared inside. Dominic stayed on the platform until the train pulled away. As he turned to walk away his eyes welled with tears. He wasn't sure if the tears were for Pasquale or Joe or just for himself.

Joe got off the train in Pittsburg, not sure what he was going to do now. He could catch the next train west back to California, or catch the next train going east to New York and go back to Italy and take his chances with the Italian military, or he could go to Connecticut and visit the Parisi Brothers. Joe decided to think about it for a day or two and checked into the Hotel Victoria on 6th and Pennsylvania Avenue in Pittsburg. He took three days to make up his mind and finally decided to catch the train to Connecticut. He thought that he could make one of the other choices, be it Italy or California, after he had gone to visit the Parisis.

Chapter 4

The train pulled into the station in New Haven, Connecticut in the mid afternoon. The weather was cold and there was some snow on the ground. Joe remembered the name of Parisis restaurants because they were named after a town in southern Italy. Catenzaro was a coastal town on the instep of the boot in the south that looked out on the Ionion Sea. There were four Catenzaro Restaurants, one in New Haven and one in Waterbury, Connecticut which Joe Parisi looked after, and one in Hartford and one in Springfield, Massachusetts that John Parisi took care of. The brothers were making a lot of money from the four and a lot of that money came from the large amount of wine they brought in from California.

Joe got a cab at the train station and just told the driver "Catenzaro Restaurant." It was a short drive to the Catenzaro and Joe was soon walking through the door.

The restaurant was mostly empty, with just a couple of tables with people at them, since it was right between the lunch and dinner crowds. Joe Parisi was at the till by the door taking care of some customers who were paying. He did not recognize Joe and asked him if he wanted a table.

"I didn't come all the way from Napa to stand up and eat," Joe said with a smile.

"Joe Marvici," he said recognizing him and coming around the counter to shake hands. "When did you get here?"

"I came in to New Haven today, just a little while ago."

"Come on with me," he said as he led Joe to a big table near the kitchen. "Sit down my friend, I will be right back."

Joe Parisi came back in a few minutes with a couple of glasses and a bottle of Monte Vista Wine. He already had the cork pulled and poured two glasses. "Salut," each man said, as they clinked glasses and toasted each other's health.

They sat around the rest of the afternoon talking, interrupted only by customers coming in or leaving. Every once in a while someone came in that Joe Parisi knew. They came over to the round table by the kitchen where the Joes were sitting. After a bit of small talk they passed a paper and some money to Joe Parisi and then got up and left shortly afterward. After about the third time this happened, Joe asked him about it.

"What's going on there Joe?" he said.

"What with these guys giving me money?" he said with a laugh. "Joe, I'm going to tell you something. Everybody wants to give someone their money. All the people they make money and they don't save nothing, they give it all to somebody. Why not me?"he said, laughing again .

"Yeah, but why are they giving their money to you? They don't just give you money for nothing."

"They are playing the numbers."

"What's the numbers?"

"Didn't you play the numbers in Samo?"

"No, I don't know what numbers are you talking about?"

"It's the numbers at the track. All the Italians play it around here. The races in Boston, the horses. It's how they pay that determines the numbers. You see on the payout always the 4th race. The payout is in the paper on Sunday."

He got a newspaper and flipped to the racing page, sliding his finger down the page until he got to the 4th race. It read: Win 13.37

Place 5.01

Show 2.35

"This would signify the payout on a one dollar bet.

The number would be in the 1 dollar column. So the number that week was 352. And the odds are 450-1, so a dollar bet if it wins is going to pay $450."

"I like this game already but why do they give the money to you?"

"Because somebody has got to take the bets. So I take the bets and when somebody wins I have to pay them. But as long as they don't win, they pay me," Joe Parisi laughed.

It was well known in the Italian community that Joe or John Parisi would take bets on the numbers at any of their restaurants and a lot of people bet the numbers. As a result the Parisis made a lot of money on it.

The restaurant became busier later in the afternoon as the dinner crowd came in. Joe stayed at the big table by the kitchen until Joe Parisi's cousin Vinnie came in to relieve him. Joe Parisi had to have someone he could trust to run his restaurants. The person, whoever it was, had to be not only taking care of the restaurant business but also taking bets on the numbers as well. Managers had to be loyal to Joe, and he would pay them very well, but God help them if they stole from him. It was common for Italians to use members of their family or friends they had known all their lives for these positions.

After Vinnie showed up Joe Parisi could leave. Vinnie had been working for Joe for about three years even before he had the other restaurants and he generally worked the night shift.

After leaving, Joe Parisi drove his Ford Model "T" to his house just a few blocks from the Catenzaro. It was still early in the day and Joe Parisi suggested that they drive up to Waterbury to the Waterbury Catenzaro. It was at least a two hour drive, sometimes more from New Haven. Joe Parisi had another house in Waterbury where he stayed when he was there. The restaurant in Waterbury was not quite as large as the New Haven Catenzaro but was still quite a busy place.

The restaurant was managed by another cousin of Joe Parisi. Joe had brought Serafino over from Italy to manage the restaurant even before he opened it two years ago and he proved to be an excellent manager. Unless Joe Parisi was out of town doing business he made a point of going to Waterbury at least once a week to pick up the numbers racket bets. The numbers was a profitable business for the Parisis, usually collecting much more money than what they were paying out.

The two men took a table in the back of the restaurant and sat down to have some dinner. Serafino brought them a bottle of wine and glasses and sat with them between taking care of customers coming in or leaving. By the time their food was served the restaurant was very busy and the two men sat alone at the table.

"Tell me Joe, why did you come here from California?" Parisi asked.

"I came to look for my father. He was working in the mine in Greensburg, Pennsylvania."

"Did you find him?"

"Yes, I did." Joe turned his head and looked him in the eyes. "He is dead."

"I'm sorry to hear."

"There was an explosion in the mine. It killed a lot of men."

"So what will you do now?"

"Well, my plans are up in the air. I was going to bring my father to California after I bought the Monte Vista Winery. Then my mother, brother and sisters could come to America too. But now my plans have been changed with my father's death. I don't know if my mother will still want to come to America."

"I would like to bring my family to America too. My mother and three sisters are still there in Caraffa. Maybe next year they will come to America."

"And what about your father?"

"My father is dead too, he was killed in Italy. He was in the Italian Army and was killed near the French border in a skirmish with the French."

"How long you been here, in America?"

"About six or maybe seven years."

"I've been here not even a year."

"So what are you going to do?"

"I told Johnny Paluchi that I would come back, so I will have to go back there."

"You will buy the winery and vineyard?"

"That was my plan before my father died."

"Do you think your father would tell you not to buy the winery if he died?"

Joe looked at Parisi. "No he would tell me buy the winery."

"Then why would you not buy it?"

"My mother, she is still in Italy. She has already said to me in a letter that she may not come if my father is dead. She also told me that the army has been to the house looking for me a few times. That means that if I go to Italy they will probably find me and I will have to go in the army."

"Do you want to go in the army?"

"No, of course not."

"Then I suggest that you buy the winery and I will buy my wine from you."

"I'm not sure about the money, I am buying it with my mother's money. If my mother doesn't come to America. I'm not certain that she will give me the money."

"Listen Joe, every year I buy a boxcar load of wine from California. Much of it comes from 'Monte Vista.' We make a lot of money from the California wine. If you need a partner to buy the winery then maybe John and I would like to invest in it. Then we would be assured of having a guaranteed supply and we could ship all of the wine back here."

Joe looked up at Joe Parisi. This was a new idea and he had to think about it for a minute. It would depend on what his mother wanted to do. He would have to contact her and find out, but this would mean that all the wine produced at 'Monte Vista' would have a guaranteed buyer every year.

"Tomorrow we will go to Springfield and talk to John about this. But I already know that this would be a good deal for us and for you."

The two men talked and drank another bottle of 'Monte Vista' before leaving the Catenzaro. Joe Parisi had a small two story brick house on Banks Street in Waterbury just a couple of minutes from the restaurant. The Parisis had a house in every city they had a restaurant. The house in New Haven was Joe's main house and the one in Springfield was where John lived. Both Hartford and Waterbury had smaller places where the brothers stayed when they were in those cities.

They got up the next morning and talked some more over coffee before leaving for Springfield and stopping in Hartford on the way. They drove for a little more than an hour before arriving in Hartford. Joe drove through the city to the Hartford Catenzaro in the north end of town. The two men went inside and were greeted by another cousin of the Parisis. Romano Bambino, who managed the restaurant in Hartford, was quick to speak up when Joe Parisi walked in the door.

"Hello Joe, how are you?" Romano said in a loud boisterous voice. He was a big man over 6 feet tall, tipping the scales at about 280 pounds. He came towards Joe with hand extended and the two men shook hands.

"This is my friend Joe Marvici. He's a Calabrais."

"Good to meet you," Romano said with a smile and shook his hand also.

"I'm going to Springfield and we just want to stop and have a bite to eat and see if John is here."

"John was here yesterday, he went back to Springfield," Romano said while leading them to the table by the kitchen. They sat down and Romano brought them a bottle of wine and glasses. The restaurant had a few people having lunch but was rather quiet.

After eating lunch they were sitting having coffee when Romano came out from the kitchen and sat down at the table. There were no customers nearby but he looked around anyway before taking two Colt 45s from under his jacket and putting them on the table.

"Joe, look at these."

Both guns were brand new from the Colt Firearms plant in Hartford and both guns had a shoulder holster. Romano pushed one of the guns over in front of Joe and the other one over to Joe Parisi. Both men took the guns out of the holsters and looked at them closely. The 45 automatic was a relatively new model. Colt had been making the 38 automatic for some years but the 45 had only been manufactured for the last four years. The 45 automatics, like the 38s, were smaller flatter guns than the older revolvers. They were excellent for concealing under clothing. These guns were military issue only until the last year when a few were being sold to the public.

"How much?" Joe Marvici asked Romano.

"Twenty five dollars and a dollar a box for bullets."

Joe took his wallet out of his breast pocket, counted out twenty-six dollars and passed the money to Romano. Romano put it in his pocket and tossed Joe the box of ammunition. He looked over at Joe Parisi and Joe picked up the 45 and put it in the pocket of his over coat. He then looked at Romano and held out his hand without saying a word and Romano put a box of ammunition in his hand, which he slipped into the another pocket.

They left for Springfield shortly afterward. Joe took his gun out in the car and took off his coat and jacket to put the shoulder holster on. The gun made him feel empowered. It was something that could even the score no matter how big and powerful his opponent was. He felt instantly powerful, self-confident and untouchable.

The drive from Hartford to Springfield took about an hour and a half. Springfield was a hub of western Massachusetts in 1908, a city of 85,000 people located on the Connecticut River about ten miles north of the Connecticut border. The Hartford, New Haven, New York Railroad came through from north to south and the Boston, Worcester and West came through east to west.

There were four bridges across the river in the Springfield area. The first bridge coming from the south, was 'The South End Bridge.' Next was the new magnificent '9 Pillar Bridge' just completed earlier in the year. The new bridge cost $3,000,000. and it was built on the site of the old toll bridge that had burned several years earlier. At the north end of town was the bridge called appropriately the 'North End Bridge.' Lastly about 6 miles north in Chicopee, was the 'The Chicopee Bridge.'

The city's economy was based mostly on manufacturing, a large part of that being the production of arms. The Springfield Armory was a massive producer of guns, notably the Springfield Rifle. The Colt Firearms Company also had a plant in Springfield and was in the process of moving its Hartford plant to Springfield as well. At this time in history motorcycles had become as popular as cars, but noticeably less expensive and more affordable. A man named George Hendee saw an opportunity and opened up a plant in 1902 in Springfield to produce a motorcycle that was invented the year before by a man named Oscar Hedstrom. He called it the "Indian."

Springfield was also the birthplace of basketball. A Canadian named James Nessmith, who was working in the Sports Department at American International College, invented the game. The first game of basketball was played there in 1886.

Joe Parisi drove downtown to the Catenzaro Restaurant. After he parked the car, the two men walked to the front door. Joe could feel the weight of the 45 around his shoulder. They walked through the door and Joe Parisi led the way towards the back of the restaurant and into a small hallway and through another door into a back room. There were four men sitting around a table playing cards. There were piles of money in front of each man and what looked like quite a large pot in the middle of the table. Each man was concentrating on the game and only John made a gesture towards them and then turned back to his cards.

Joe poured a couple of glasses of wine and handed one to his friend while the poker players finished the hand. Almost every night there would be a card game here. The players finally laid down their cards, breaking the tension. John ended up winning the pot with a full house. At that point they took a break in the game to talk to Joe and find out who Joe's friend was.

John got up from the table and approached Joe with his hand out and shaking hands with his brother, he said, "Joe Marvici, it is good to see you. How are you?"

"Hello my friend." Joe replied. " I'm doing fine."

"These are my friends Salvatore Mauro, Pasquale Lucariello and John Masalino."

Joe stood up and shook hands with each man. "It's good to meet you."

After a few minutes of small talk the men got back to the card game. Both Joe Marvici and Joe Parisi took a seat around the table and got into the game. The game lasted late into the night and ended with no clear winner. It was as much a social event as anything else.

The card game finally ended just after midnight. The six men stayed around the table in the back room talking for about half an hour before before leaving and going home. Joe and Joe Parisi followed John across the city and over the 9 Pillar bridge into West Springfield. West Springfield was known as 'Mudtown" in those days mainly because all the streets were dirt and when it rained they turned to mud. The streets were marked with ruts from the narrow tires of the early automobiles. West Springfield was sparsely populated compared to Springfield, Which had streets lined with houses and hardly a vacant lot in the city. The houses in West Springfield were much more spread out and most lots were several acres.

John had a big house that sat on 5 acres on Merrick Street close to the center of West Springfield. After parking the cars and going inside John poured a glass of wine for his brother and one for Joe, before pouring one for himself. The three men sat around the kitchen table talking. Joe Parisi brought up the subject of buying into the 'Monte Vista Winery' in California. The Parisi brothers agreed that it would be good business to own a vineyard and winery that could supply the Catenzaro Restaurants. They stayed up late into the night discussing the subject and decided that they would do the deal with Joe Marvici. He could be the winery manager and the Parisis Brothers would be silent partners. This would greatly benefit the Parisis in their restaurants and if the supply exceeded their need they would sell the extra wine in the east. Joe shook hands with the brothers and clinked glasses in a toast to finalize the deal.

Communication systems around the world and especially in America were developing rapidly at this time. For years messages were being sent by wire using Morse Code which was a series of dots and dashes for each letter of the alphabet. Thus a message could be spelled out and sent across the wire for great distances. Since Alexander Graham Bell's invention of the telephone in 1875 communications systems had been continually improving. Yet by 1900 there were only 56,000 telephones in America and they were handled by many independent companies. Because of this the systems were very restrictive where in most cases one telephone could not talk to another telephone in a different telephone company. It was not until 1907 that Theodore Vail, who had been involved with the telephone 20 years earlier and then went on to do different things, came back to the telephone business to establish a truly national system from coast to coast in America. Vail and the Bell System boasted of having 11 million miles of wire and ten million poles. In 1907 there were 410,000 telephones that had been linked by wire to Bell. In 1908 there were another 310,000 added giving them close to 800,000 in all. In the year 1907 Bell reported earnings of $13,715,000 and over $18,000,000 in the Bank. It also reported that it had enough to continue to expand for two years without having to borrow any money.

The invention of the switchboard and the resulting army of female switchboard operators made communication much easier. There were phones in Springfield, much of Connecticut and New York City for about ten years before this took place.

The telephone also played an important part in the numbers racket. People would routinely bet the numbers over the phone and be required to pay for it later. Sometimes there were people who, being heavy betters and convinced that they were going to win, would over extend themselves and get into trouble by not being able to pay for their gambling loses. This could have become a big problem for the Parisis. If they were to let anybody get off, not paying, it could have an effect their business. Their policy was, nobody gets off. They would break fingers or arms or just beat them up and in extreme cases threaten them with a gun. "I cannot get money from a dead man. That's why I'm going to let you live," Joe Parisi would tell a man while he shoved a gun in his face. The brothers were tough and they had to be that way to survive in the world they were living in.

The police in Springfield turned a blind eye to the Parisis numbers racket. A few Italians on the police force even played the numbers themselves and police could eat in the Catenzaro for free anytime that they wanted.

That was the policy for all the Catenzaro restaurants and the police pretty well left them alone.

Joe Parisi had some business to take care of so they stayed another day in Springfield. It was early in the afternoon and Parisi was waiting for a call before going to the restaurant. The phone rang and after a brief conversation the men left. They headed toward Springfield and then Joe Parisi veered off on the road towards Agawam.

"I got one thing I got to do,"he said.

He pulled the car onto a side road and into a vacant lot. Another car was parked there with four men inside. He pulled up beside them and Joe Parisi motioned to Joe to come with him. The men got out of the other car and they met behind the cars.

"Mario, Mario, how are you?" Joe Parisi said to one of the men. Joe just looked on. Apparently Mario Hebert had a little gambling problem and was into the Parisis for more than $100 dollars which was rising all the time due to the 50% a month interest charges. The other men were friends of Joe Parisi, who he treated very well to help him enforce his 'pay up' policy.

"Give me some money Mario."

"Here," he said as he pulled $16 dollars from his pocket and handed it over to Joe Parisi.

"Give me some more."

"That's all I have."

Joe grabbed Mario by the hand and twisted his hand getting a grip on three of his fingers.

"Do you want me to break your fingers, Mario?"

"No,no ,please ," Mario pleaded.

He dragged him by his fingers over to Joe.

"I'm giving you one more week to pay, Mario. Then I'm going to have my friend put a bullet in your head." Looking at Joe he said, "Show him your gun."

Joe looked at Mario with a cold stare. Mario's face had a look of fear. Joe, with his left arm, pulled his coat back exposing the Colt

45 he had in the shoulder holster. Not a word was spoken as Joe continued to look at Mario and who looked back in fear. A feeling of power from having the gun overtook Joe. It made him feel so good that he looked at Mario and smiled. A look of extreme fear penetrated Mario's face.

Joe Parisi pushed Mario away from him. "Next week, Mario you're going to pay."

Joe Parisi gave a nod to his friends and they got Mario back in the car and took him back to the city.

They waited for the other car to leave before getting back in the car and heading for the Catenzaro.

"Sometimes, you got to get tough with people, otherwise they will walk all over you," Joe Parisi said looking over at Joe. Joe just smiled.

"I like you Joe. I think you are going to be a good partner in the winery. I wanted to see what kind of a person you were in a situation like this. That's why I brought you with me. I hope you understand."

"We will see if he pays you," Joe laughed.

After arriving at the restaurant they went right to the back room, stopping at the front long enough to order a bottle of wine and spaghetti and meatballs. It was late afternoon and none of the guys had arrived for the nightly card game when the two men sat down around the big table.

"We'll go back to New Haven tomorrow," said Joe Parisi.

"Yes it is probably time to go back to Napa. The season's work will be starting soon and there is a lot to do."

"Yes and you're going to buy the Monte Vista Winery."

The Paluchis wanted $2200 for the winery, vineyards and land. That would mean they would have to put up $733 each to purchase it. Joe always kept his money in a money belt under his clothing and had been traveling with a lot of money on him. Most of the money was his mother's but he had $500 dollars of his own on him as well. Now that Joe had the Colt 45 under his coat he was not the least bit worried about carrying so much money.

The money that the Parisis wanted to invest in the winery was money that they had made from the numbers racket. All of the money that came in that way was cash and it added up to a lot of money. It was not unusual to rake in over $2000 a month but it was unusual to have more than one winner in all. Even though the payout was paid at 450-1 the chances of winning were much higher at 999-1.

Joe Parisi handed over $1500 dollars in cash and another $100 travel expenses to Joe that evening.

"Remember Joe, we are silent partners, that means we are keeping silent about it. Just between us," he looked at Joe squarely and shook his hand.

He put the money into his money belt. The money belt was well concealed being sewn into the waistband on his trousers. His mother had worried about the money and sewn the secret pockets up for him before he left Italy. As a matter of fact she fashioned a secret pocket in each pair of trousers he had so that he would not be caught without one.

They left the next morning, stopping in Hartford and again in Waterbury before getting back to New Haven. Joe Parisi made the trip to all of the Catenzaro Restaurants every week so that he could pick up all the money from the numbers. Each manager was allowed to keep $1000 on hand for paying off the winners and the rest of the money came to Joe Parisi to take care of.

The two men stood on the platform at the New Haven train station. The train would be leaving in a few minutes and Joe and Joe Parisi had their last conversation.

"I hear that the telephone, is going all the way to California soon. Maybe I will be able to call you in Napa soon."Joe Parisi said."

"Yes my friend, That would be good, but even so I will keep in touch and I will see you in Napa in the fall."

The two men shook hands and hugged each other and Joe got on the train.

He changed trains in New York City, catching The Illinois Central to Chicago. While riding the train he thought it might be a good time to write to his mother. At least now he knew what happened to his father and he knew what he was going to do next, unlike when he came out east a few weeks before. He wrote to Katerina about all that had happened to him and all that he found out about his father. He told her that America was truly the land of opportunity, that he could make his fortune here and he did not want to come back to Samo. He wanted her and Francesco and the girls to come to America as soon as he was settled in California. He told her about the Parisis buying into the winery and that he still needed some of her money but he was going to send the rest of her money back to Italy. Instead of sending it all at once and take the chance it could all be stolen from the mail, Joe decided to send her $100. at a time. He would send more money to her when he got a letter from her telling him she had received the last $100. He mailed the letter to Katherina when he reached Chicago giving the letter a kiss and seeing his mother in his mind as he pressed the letter against his forehead before giving it to the mail clerk.

The train ride was long and tedious much like it was on the way out. There were long layovers in Harrisburg, Pittsburg, Cleveland and Toledo. He got to Chicago on the sixth day after leaving New Haven. It was another two day layover in Chicago as well. Joe looked up his friends the Guyons and Angelina who was still staying at the Brevoort Hotel.

"There's something about room service," Angelina said about it.

Joe and Angelina went with the Guyons once more to the Princess Ballroom. Louis Guyon had started building a new dance hall that he was going to call 'The Dreamland.' He had just acquired the property on the corner of Van Buren and Paulina on the city's west side. He took Joe and Angelina for a drive by the new property and passionately explained what he wanted to do.

A couple of days later once again Joe left Angelina on the platform at the Chicago Station and got on the Sante Fe to San Francisco.

Joe arrived back in Napa in the early spring. There was a lot of work to do in the vineyards when he arrived. He worked in the vineyard with Johnny Paluchi through the spring and summer. There was a crew of farmhands numbering from 2 to about 10 that worked in the vineyard too. Their numbers increased with the work throughout the season with the harvest of the grapes demanding the largest number of workers.

The wine making began shortly after the grape harvest started. This was no doubt the busiest time of year at the Monte Vista.

Chapter 5

Italy 1908

Katerina and Francesco were working in the garden in the afternoon when the mail came. There was only one letter that came that day. It was a letter from Joe in America. She had been expecting the letter from Joe as the last time she heard from him he wrote and told her that he was going to try to find out what happened to his father. She realized that the letter could be really upsetting so she did not open it right away. She retreated to her house and went into the bedroom, closing the door. Katerina hesitated in opening the letter and spent a minute staring at it. She finally opened it and read:

Dearest Mother,

I hope this letter finds you doing well. I have gone to the mine where father was working for so long. I am sorry to tell you but father has passed away. There was a terrible explosion in the mine last September that killed many miners. Unfortunately father was one of the dead. I visited his grave in the cemetery there in Greensburg and said a prayer for father, one for me and a one for you. I am very sorry to have to bring you this sad news and ask that you try to be strong…………

The letter went on but Katerina was overcome with grief and could not read any more after that. She fell upon her bed and cried for her Pasquale. Her thoughts quickly changed from herself to concern for her children. Katerina was a very unselfish person, caring more for the needs of others than herself. It was important to her to talk to her children and not put it off. Her concern for the feelings of the children was very important and she put her own grief aside until she knew that the children were going to be alright. She left her bedroom and went out to where Francesco was working in the garden. Two of the girls, Carmel and Pasqualina were playing down the street and Fortunata was still in the house. She called all the children together. The only one that was not there beside Joe was the oldest girl Angela who was married and lived in Caraffa.

Katerina gathered the children in the living room and waited for them all to sit down.

"I got a letter from your brother Guiseppe today. He gave me some sad news."

One of the girls whimpered when she said that, sensing that it had some thing to do with father.

"He went to the mine where your father worked and he found out that your father has been killed." She could barely get out the words but at the same time knew that she needed to be strong for her children's sake.

"There was an explosion in the mine and many died."

Fortunata was 19 years old and still remembered her father well. She started to cry. The three other children were very young when their father left and their memories were not as strong. But they knew of their father well and were aware of what it meant that he was dead. Katerina called the children to her and put her arms around them, holding them for a long time and trying to be strong at the same time. It was difficult not to break down and cry but Katerina was able to hold it back.

That night after she went to bed Katerina cried for her husband. This was something she felt she had to do away from her children and she did every night for a week or so and then a little less often after that. She felt it was her duty to go to Caraffa and tell Angela as soon as she could. Caraffa was not that far away so it was possible to go there and get back in the same day.

It was the next day before she finished reading Joe's letter. He wanted her to go to America but she wasn't so sure that she wanted to go. Katerina decided to think about it for now though Joe was not settled in California yet and she was not ready to go now anyway.

America 1908

Joe worked in the winery during the summer and into the fall. Johnny Paluchi wanted Joe to take over the business in the fall after the harvest. He reasoned that the sale of wine from the stocks in the cellar would keep some cash coming in and now that Joe has spent the last year here he knew what he was doing. Johnny and his wife were anxious to go back to Italy and wanted to close the deal. When the harvest was complete, Joe and Johnny did the deal, paid the money and signed the necessary papers. Johnny, Regina and their two daughters Maria and Frederica left for Italy a few weeks later.

Many of the workers that worked at the winery had worked for Johnny Paluchi for many years. That experience made taking over the business a lot easier for Joe.

One of those workers was Renoldo Ruiez, a short stocky man of Mexican descent who lived in the Napa Valley since the time of General Vellejo. He had been working for the Paluchis for more than ten years and had proved himself to be a loyal employee. Johnny entrusted him with the position of field boss in the vineyard. After the grapes were harvested and the wine making began he also took on the job of wine making boss, overseeing the wine making process. He maintained his position as the top employee in the operation even after Joe bought the business. Renoldo seldom ventured away from the winery and was left in charge any time Joe had to leave for any reason, proving himself to be very trustworthy, someone that he could count on to look after his interest.

The harvest came in with no problems and the grapes were squeezed and the wine put in barrels and bottled just like it always was done. The Parisis came out to California in the late fall and bought a large volume of wine. It was Joe Parisi that brought up the idea of expanding the operation, noticing that there was room in the cellar to put even more barrels for fermenting wine in. The wine was usually sold the year after it had been bottled except for a small amount that was held longer.

Joe suggested that they could increase the amount of wine that they were making by buying grapes from other vineyards and adding some more barrels to the fermenting area. He also suggested that the Parisis come out and buy wine a little earlier in the year before the wine was bottled so that they could empty the bottle storage area to make room for the extra wine.

The three men talked it over and the Parisi brothers provided another $500 to cover the cost of expanding. They also paid the full price for the wine that they bought, being more concerned with having a secure supply than a saving a little money.

The brothers bought more wine than they had ever bought before for shipment back to Connecticut. It took a couple of days to truck the wine to Vellejo and get it loaded it onto the train. The Parisis once again rode the train with the wine until it reached New Haven safely. There was too much money involved for them to trust the safe passage across the country to anyone else. After arriving in New Haven the wine was divided up and a supply of wine trucked to each of the Catenzaro Restaurants. There was not enough storage space in any one of the restaurants but if the wine was divided up they could accommodate the entire shipment.

During the time Joe had been at the Monte Vista most of his time had been spent on the winery land. Since the Paluchis had moved out Joe became acquainted with a few of the local people that were in the same business. After the decision had been made to buy more grapes he contacted a few of the neighbors to inquire about finding someone who was interested in selling their extra grapes or for that matter their entire crop. Some of the vineyards in Napa did not have a winery operation but were just involved in growing grapes. One such neighbor was a beautiful Spanish woman named Carmen Louisa Matendo Garcia. Carmen was a widow who had lost her husband several years before. Martin Garcia died during a bank robbery in Vellejo when a stray bullet shot and killed him as he was driving by the bank. He had been driving a wagon pulled by a team of horses when the bullet hit him in the head, killing him instantly. The bank robbers got away but were later cornered and apprehended by the U.S. Army north of there near, Santa Rosa.

The Garcia vineyard had been in the family for many years and was one of the few that survived the American Army expulsion of General Vellejo and the Mexican Army from northern California in the late 1800's.

Martin's father had cultivated the land and planted the vineyard himself. It was one of the oldest, most established vineyards and winery in Napa at the time. Even though the family was able to hold on to the vineyard and land, the winery that existed there was burned to the ground during the struggle. After that the Garcias just grew grapes and sold them to other wineries for wine production.

There were a few other Italians growing grapes in Napa at that time. One such family was the Copa family. Savako Copa had come from the north of Italy just outside of Naples. He, like Joe, came to the Napa Valley a single man and after getting into business he met a Spanish woman and got married. Rosita Ayenda Copa was a friend of Carmens. They had known each other for many years.

While canvassing the other vineyards in the area for more grapes to buy, Joe met and became friends with Savako and Rosita Copa. Their vineyard was across the valley only a few minute's drive away from the Monte Vista. Joe visited the Copa's on a regular basis and met Carmen on more than one occasion.

On one of those meetings Carmen invited Joe to her house to talk business. She knew that he was looking to buy more grapes the following season and wanted to talk to him about buying her crop. A relationship developed quickly between Joe and Carmen. She was quite beautiful, short and very well built, and they started to spend more and more time together.

Again Joe knew that he could not marry a Spanish woman, as his mother would not ever approve. For that reason Joe kept the relationship from getting too serious. They did spend a lot of time together and every few months traveled together to San Francisco for a few days.

Over the next few years the business at the Monte Vista increased substantially. Joe was able to buy grapes from several other vineyards as well. He had added many more fermenting barrels to his cellar and the Parisis showed up a month earlier in Napa just like they said they would and took more and more wine back to Connecticut with them every year.

Joe kept in touch with his mother in Italy, writing to her often but still was not able to convince her to come with the rest of the family to America. Everything he told her sounded interesting and inviting but she was scared of the prospect of leaving behind all that was familiar and going to a new place that was not.

It was summer in 1910 that the telephones in Napa were finally connected to the Bell system and it was possible to talk to Joe Parisi on the phone. He had been able to call Joe Parisi when he was in San Francisco as the Bell system had made connections there several years before it did in Napa. He talked to Joe or John in Connecticut a few times every month after the Bell system arrived. Even though telephones had started to spread across Europe they still had not reached southern Italy and Sicily. It would be quite a few years before the telephones would reach Samo.

Some of the farmers in the Napa Valley had experienced the loss of some of their grapevines in the summer of 1910. For a reason that was unknown to them the grapevines were dying. It had been reported to Joe that some of the grapevines had died off at the Monte Vista and Carmen and Savako Copa had also had some of their vines die off. But by 1911 the problem had gotten worse and in 1912 the situation was getting quite serious. Some of the vineyards had lost up to 40% of their vines by the end of the summer. This was proving to be a disaster for the farmers in the Valley.

In 1912, the situation in the Napa Valley, caused the grape harvest and wine production to be greatly reduced throughout the valley. The effects of the reduced harvest were felt throughout the wine industry in the years following when the stocks from other years began to run out. Joe had not considered it a problem until 1912 when the grape harvest had been reduced to the point where he was not able to make enough wine to fill all the fermenting barrels even with the extra grapes that he bought. The vines continued to die off all throughout the summer and it looked like the epidemic was going to sweep through the entire Monte Vista vineyard and all of the Napa Valley.

The Parisis came out to Napa in the fall just like always. They became aware of the problem after walking through the vineyards with Joe. They had been buying hundreds of cases of wine every year and even though there was plenty this year, next year was going to be greatly reduced. It takes several years for grapevines, from the time they are planted, to get to the point where they are producing a large crop of fruit. This means that even if new vines are planted right away, it was going to seriously impact wine production for several years.

The threat of Prohibition in the United States was starting to gather some momentum as well. Anti-salooning laws had already been passed in several states and there was a lot of pressure for more states to join in. Many people in America were starting to believe that alcohol was the main reason for rising crime, corruption, poor health and social problems and the rising costs to the taxpayer created by prisons and poorhouses.

Some events in the world, specifically Europe and North Africa, were causing tensions over there.

Italy was engaged in war with Turkey during 1911 and 1912 in a fight over the Dodecanese Islands in the Aegean Sea and Tropoli/ Libya in North Africa. That left all of North Africa in European hands. The partition of Africa was completed at the hands of the Europeans leaving Ethiopia and Liberia the only countries that remained independent. International tensions were increasing rapidly. An alliance had been formed between Germany, Austria, Hungary and Italy on one side and Britain, France and Russia on the other. Tensions between these two alliances had been building for at least a decade and had reached an all time high.

Italy's military enterprises created a demand for more soldiers, leaving no doubt in Joe's mind that he would be given a gun and sent off to war if he returned to Italy. There were thousands of Italians in America that were in the same situation. Some Italian men who went back to Italy were taken into service as soon as the military knew they were there. This situation existed for the Parisi brothers and many of the Italians that worked for them as well.

Because of the threat of war in Europe, Joe Parisi was intent on bringing the rest of his family to America. His mother Columbina, and sisters Ralfael, Mary-Angela and Agatha were still in Italy in 1911. Joe Parisi arranged for their passage on a French ship in the winter of 1911-1912. They arrived in New York in mid January 1912. Joe and John drove to New York to pick them up. When they arrived at the docks in New York the brothers were surprised to see a young man traveling with the women. Rocco Silvatico was a young Italian man and had narrowly avoided the Italian military in Carrafa. His parents told the authorities that he had gone to America three years earlier when they came to look for him. Rocco and Ralfael had gotten married a year ago in Monaco where they had been living since. Columbina and the two girls traveled to Monaco by ship. There they met up with Ralfael and Rocco and they all traveled together to America.

Both Joe and John welcomed Rocco into the family and congratulated him on the marriage to Ralfael. The brothers had bought a house for their mother in West Springfield on Worcester Street, just a few blocks from John's house. It was understood that the house belonged to Columbina. Rocco and Ralfael would eventually move into their own house as soon as they could afford it and the other girls would eventually marry and move out too. But for the time being they would all live together in Columbina's house.

In Springfield almost all the neighborhoods in the city had electrical service. West Springfield was still a few years from having power in all areas. Kerosene lamps were used extensively wherever the power had not arrived and Columbina's house had no power at that time. They were all quite used to living with kerosene lamps, as that was the only light that they used while living in Italy.

It took a few weeks for Columbina and the children to get used to their new home in Mudtown. The name Mudtown suited West Springfield to a tee. The streets were muddy most of the time, drying up for a few months in the summer and then turning right back to mud again in fall.

Mary-Angela, who was 14, and Agatha who was just 13, enrolled in school right away. Neither of the girls could speak English when they first started school but there were a lot of Italian children going to the school, which made it easier for them.

Both of the girls were given chores to do when they got home every day. For Agatha it was to clean the globes and fill the kerosene lamps every day before it was time to light them. Mary-Angela's chore was to set the table before dinner and clear the dishes and clean the table after dinner.

They could not give their mother a house with no furniture so the brothers saw to it that the house was completely furnished with all new furniture before they got there.

John gave Rocco a job working in the Catenzaro Restaurant in Springfield right away. He wanted to see Rocco and Ralfael get a house of their own, and the sooner that they did, the better.

Business had been good for the Parisi Brothers since they had come to America. They had made a lot of money and owned houses and restaurants in four different cities and an interest in the winery in California. They also controlled the numbers racket in a strip that reached from the Springfield area all the way to New Haven and Waterbury and all the smaller towns in between. The numbers racket was the most profitable part of their business, though the restaurants were a necessary component of their operation.

Italian men were very secretive about the business that they did. They did not discuss their business with wives and family at all. It was none of their concern and everyone accepted it as so. When the men discussed business it was never in front of women or children. Only the men who were directly involved were allowed to be in the room. For this reason wives and children simply did not know what the men did and it was not their business to ask.

Rocco was quickly introduced to the numbers racket and was just the person that the Parisi brothers were looking for to expand the business northward to include Holyoke and Northampton. He was given the job of recruiting men to act as bookies. Bookies were guys who collect the bets and handed the money over to Rocco, who handed it over to the Parisis. You might think it would be easy for the bookie to rip off some of the money by keeping some of the bets but it would be a serious mistake if one of those bets won and the bookie had to pay the bet. It was also a dead giveaway that they were stealing money from the Parisis and that could result in some serious harm. Those were big deterrents for most bookies, who usually made 10% of what they collected. Each bet had to be written down and handed in or telephoned in to Rocco by Saturday afternoon before the race took place just to keep it on the up and up.

Both Joe and John Parisi kept Rocco close by for first first few days that he worked for them, constantly giving him instructions about how to get the numbers operation going in the towns north of Springfield. Bartenders or bar owners were the best people to recruit. It just added to their income and it was off the books. John gave Rocco an older model T for transportation to Northhampton and after a couple of days he was sent off to do the job. It was a good test for new brother-in-law.

Joe was still trying to convince his mother to come to America. The tensions over war were continually growing and Italy was right in the thick of it but his mother still refused to budge from her home in Samo.

By 1914 there were powerful alliances between the countries of Europe. The Central Powers of Austria-Hungary and Germany was formerly the Triple Alliance before Italy and Rumania pulled out.

The Allies of the Triple Entente were Russia, France and Britain and their empires that stood in defense of Serbia and Belgium.

On June 28, 1914 Archduke Franz Ferdinand, who was heir to the throne of Austria-Hungary, was visiting Sarajevo, capital of the annexed Bosnia-Herzogovina. Both he and his wife were shot dead by a student who was a member of the Serbian secret society. This event led to the start of World War 1 leading seven countries in Europe to go to war.

At the time Austria-Hungary declared war on Serbia, Italy remained neutral. By 1914 Italy had built a formidable naval fleet, and when they declared war on Austria in 1915 the Navy's first task was to join with the French to blockade the Austrian Navy in the Adriatic Sea. Italy deployed its army of 900,000 men stretching out for 300 miles on the Austrian front from the Swiss border to the Adriatic Sea. They fought the Austrians on this front for more than a year, losing some ground in the earlier battles and regaining it in later ones. More than 250,000 died during these battles with the Italians taking the heaviest casualties, losing more than 150,000.

Italians in America were anxious about the war and were hungry for information about their homeland. American newspapers were a good source of information but any Italian newspapers that were available were prized for their information and passed around in the Italian communities.

The situation in the Napa Valley was getting worse as well. The grapevine die off had gotten so extensive that many vineyards were forced to replant their entire grapevine crop. This reduced Napa Valley wine production to a fraction of its former level and gave no guarantee that the vines would not die off again. By 1916 the Napa Valley wine industry was starting to recover but was given another hit by the growing army of prohibitionists. Already more than twenty of the forty-eight states had enacted anti-salooning laws and the trend was to continue, leading to total prohibition across America.

Chapter 6

Circumstances had certainly changed since Joe came to California nine years ago. The first few years that he ran the Monte Vista Winery were very profitable and even after the cost of expansion Joe and the Parisis made a lot of money. But those days were gone now as the business was in a tailspin. They thought about selling out but the entire valley was in the same boat. There were simply no buyers for land in Napa unless they wanted to give the land away. After a lot of discussions between themselves they agreed that the best thing to do was to cut their losses by closing the operation down. It was not making any money in the last few years anyway. As Joe said to Joe Parisi on the telephone, "I'm wasting my time here if I don't make money. Time for me to do something else where I make lots of money."

Joe Parisi telephoned back a couple of days later. "Joe, I want you to meet me in Chicago next week."

"Yeah, I can do that," Joe said. "But why do you want to meet in Chicago?"

"You see what's happening all over America. They want to do away with our drink. It's already happening. What am I going to do in my restaurants if I can't sell wine? How can we sit down to eat with no wine on the table. I still have some wine in the basements of the restaurants but I don't want to wait until there is none left before I go looking for more. But we have to get the wine outside America because nobody will be able to produce it here. We go to Chicago and we find a supply of wine coming from Canada. I'm going to bring my brother-in-law Rocco with me."

"Okay, Joe I will see you in Chicago next week," Joe told him. "I'll be staying at the Brevoort Hotel."

After he made arrangements with Renoldo to look after the land and buildings. Though there was no market for the grapes, he gave him permission to harvest the crop and do what he wanted with it while Joe was gone. He had a feeling that his life was going in a different direction now and he may not come back to California for a long time.

It was difficult saying goodbye to Carmen. She had been the bright spot in Joe's life over the last few years. Joe had strong feelings for her and thought to himself many times, 'if only she was Calabraise.'

Savako Copa and his wife Rosita had been wanting to get out of the valley too. But they were not sure where they wanted to go. When Joe told them he was going to Chicago, the thought of going to Chicago sounded inviting to them. They had become very close friends during the time they were in Napa. It made a difference to Joe that Savako was Italian and he trusted him like a brother.

Carmen would have left Napa with Joe if he had asked her but in Joe's world he could not and would not go against his mother's wishes and marry a woman that was not Calabraise.

Just like he did to Angelina many years before, Joe said goodbye to Carmen on the platform in Vellejo and boarded the train with his friends Savako and Rosita, bound for Chicago. While saying goodbye Carmen embraced Joe on the platform and she felt the gun under his coat. It was the first time he wore the Colt 45 in a long time.

Carmen stood on the platform and watched the train pull away. She knew that she was not going to see Joe again. A feeling of sadness overcame her and she raised her hand and gave one last wave at the train as it got further and further from the station.

The layover in San Francisco was only one day before they caught the Sante Fe Railroad to Chicago. The long trip on the train finally came to an end as they pulled into the Chicago Station. It was late morning when the three travelers checked into the Brevoort Hotel. Joe asked the desk clerk if Angelina Volare was still living at the hotel, hoping to connect with her if she was still around. The desk clerk remembered Angelina as she had lived at the Brevoort for years. She had moved out of the hotel a few months earlier and had moved to Chicago's south side, going to work for one of Chicago's most notorious gangsters, Jim Colosimo.

Big Jim, as he was known by most of the underworld in Chicago, was predominately involved in whorehouses. Matter of fact, at this point in his operations there was no one else in Chicago that would even try to to open an establishment that would compete with Big Jim. Any brothels that attempted to operate in Chicago were quickly closed down and the owners murdered and the girls forced to work for him. Big Jim and his hoods showed no mercy to anyone that tried to compete with them.

Big Jim had become stinking rich from his Chicago operations, and even though he could see that the prohibition of alcohol would create an opportunity to make millions more, he did not see the need for more money, being a millionaire many times over.

Big Jim's fortune had made him lazy and he was looking for someone that he could trust to be his number two man and take over the day to day operations of his whorehouses.

In 1909, while attending the wedding of his niece, Big Jim met Johnny Torrio. Terrible Johnny, as he was then known, was a tough young gangster in New York City. Johnny was a leader in the notorious Five Points Gang and took part in a number of gang battles and murders in New York. Though he was very short at only about 5'2", his reputation as a cold, cruel and calculating hood with a natural meanness and affinity for murder made him one of the most feared underworld figures in the country.

Johnny Torrio had been trekking to Chicago from time to time to handle mob business for Big Jim since his marriage to his niece in 1909. In 1916 Big Jim brought Johnny to Chicago to work full time for him. Johnny was being investigated for a couple of murders in New York and felt it was a good time to get out and relocate in Chicago.

Before leaving New York, Johnny Torrio realizing that prohibition was on the way and that millions could be made from it, expounded on how it could be made into big business to those who would listen.

In a meeting with underworld figures in New York just before pulling up stakes and leaving for Chicago, Johnny met Joe Parisi. Joe Parisi and his brother John had built the numbers racket into a hundreds of thousand dollars a year business and was just starting to expand into other forms of gambling in several cities in Connecticut and Massachusetts.

Joe Parisi was well known to Frankie Yale, a powerful New York hood who had been partners with Torrio prior to his move to Chicago. The meeting in New York was organized by Torrio to talk about the potential profits that could be made off of prohibition. The meeting was held in a restaurant in Brooklyn and was attended by some of the underworld's most prominent and dangerous figures. Johnny Torrio was given the nickname "The Brain." With the help of two others, namely Meyer Lansky and Arnold Rothstein, he laid out the basic strategy for organized crime in America and where it was going as soon as prohibition laws were in effect.

Sitting at the table with Joe Parisi was a young bullying teenage hoodlum named Alphonsus Capone, who often worked for Torrio as a strong arm enforcer.

The discussions that took place at that meeting were directed towards setting up the infrastructure needed to be able to sell liquor after the Prohibition Laws kicked in. Torrio lectured the group about preparing for the inevitable situation by acquiring warehouses to store liquor and trucks to transport it. The legitimate saloon business was going to be closed down and would have to be replaced by secret locations selling booze to the public. These locations would later be known as 'speakeasies' or 'blind pigs' and could be hidden in basements and sometimes behind false walls in restaurants and in back rooms of residences or other front type businesses. There would be a lot of people out of work that were currently employed by bars, warehouses, trucking companies and other areas of the liquor business including distilling, wine and beer production. These people could be recruited to work in the illegal business that was soon to flourish in America.

This was truly a colossal undertaking and Johnny Torrio was the first major underworld figure to recognize that they had to prepare for prohibition well before it arrived and they would be able to make millions on it.

Joe checked at the hotel desk several times but there was no message from Joe Parisi. He decided to give Louis Guyon a call. Louis was glad to hear from Joe and invited him and his friends to his new dance hall that night. Louis had finally opened the dance hall that he had been talking about for years. The Paradise Ballroom on Chicago's West Side, it is said, was the largest dance hall ever built in Chicago. The Paradise dance floor could easily accommodate over 4,000 dancers at a time.

"I'll put your names on the guest list at the door," Louis said.

Joe, Savako and Rosita took a cab to the Paradise that night arriving about nine pm. There were a lot of people already there and you could hear the music coming from inside. There was a lineup at the admission booths at the entrance to the ballroom. Finally getting to the booth, Joe told the ticket lady that they were on the guest list.

"Oh yes you're Louis's friends. Go right in, the doorman has your names," she said and pointed towards the main entrance.

"Where do I find Louis?" Joe asked.

"Louis will be at the big table to the left of the stage," the girl replied.

Joe asked again as they passed the doorman and he motioned towards the stage. "The big table towards the left of the stage," he repeated.

Joe, Savako and Rosita weaved their way through the crowd towards where the band was playing.

The Paradise was a beautifully built dance hall with two rows of Gothic pillars running down each side separating the tables from the dance floor. Some of the tables against the wall had booths surrounding them on three sides and chairs on the fourth. The upholstery in the booths was red quilted leather, which matched the chairs around the outside. The ballroom had an elegant look to it and the dance floor was large and finely polished. There were two beautiful marble bars located along the wall at the far end from the band, one on each side. The band was playing on the stage at the far end of the dance floor with a backdrop hanging behind them that read, "D'Urbano's Eccentric Italian Band."

Louis spotted Joe and his friends and stood up, waving his hand back and forth to get their attention.

"Joe Marvici, how are you?" Louis said shaking Joe's hand.

"I am well," he answered. "These are my friends Savako and Rosita Copa."

"Come sit down my friend," Louis said as he motioned towards chairs that surrounded the big table. Julia Guyon and Alphonse and Rita Spatini whom Joe had met at Guyon's home many years ago were there at the table. Rita Spatini's two younger sisters Antonette and Alisia were also sitting at the table. Both the sisters were very interested in meeting Joe. It was especially noticed that Joe was not accompanied by a woman and this handsome Italian man perked the interest of the two women. Antonette was the first to introduce herself, standing and reaching across the table to shake his hand.

"Hello Joe, I am pleased to meet you," she said, "My name is Antonette and this is my sister Alisia." Alisia followed Antonette's lead and stood and reached out to shake hands.

Joe was very polite to the two women and introduced Savako and Rita before taking a seat at the table.

Louis motioned for one of the waiters that was working that section of the ballroom, to come over to the table.

"Bring these people whatever they want to drink," he said to the waiter. Most of the guests got their drinks by going to the bar but there were a few waiters and waitresses that took care of the tables that were along the outside wall of the hall. The table where Louis and Julia sat was considered a V.I.P. table and was always served by a waiter.

The Paradise had a reputation of being one of the most conservative ballrooms in Chicago. Louis and Julia shared the concerns of many of the city's social reformers who felt that some of the new 'Jazzier' dance music encouraged the youth who listened to it to engage in improper behavior and indecent dancing. Determined that his dance hall would not attract any lowlife or undesirables Louis regulated what type of music was played there encouraging, waltzes and two steps and looking unfavorably on some of the more modern dances such as the Charleston or the fox trot. The conservatism of the Paradise was well received and appreciated by it's patrons. It was also an opportunity for young people to meet other and often unattached West Siders.

The sheer numbers of people that Louis could get into the Paradise were the reason that the profits were huge. The admission and drink prices were kept low to encourage people to frequent the Paradise and rarely was the ballroom not filled to capacity.

The two sisters took turns dancing with Joe throughout the evening. They had both studied the art of ballroom dance with the Guyons and were eager to try it out on Joe and teach him some of the modern steps.

Louis and Julia were masters of ballroom dance and seemed to float across the dance floor like they were dancing on clouds. They encouraged Savako and Rosita to dance as well by asking them to dance and teaching them some dance steps.

It was two am when the music finally stopped and the Paradise started to empty out. Louis invited the party at the V.I.P. table back to his house for more socializing and conversation. It was there that Louis and Joe retreated into Louis's study with their drinks and had a chance to talk privately.

Joe brought Louis up to date on the problems he had been having with the winery in Napa, and why he was in Chicago.

The conversation found its way around to the subject of the coming prohibition. Louis admitted that it was going to affect his business at the Paradise if he were to stop selling alcohol there. It would more than likely not close the ballroom though because he still was making a fortune on admissions every night. However it was noted that there was a lot of money that could be made on liquor if the prohibition went through and he intended to take advantage of it, if and when it happened.

Joe was hearing the same thing from other people. It was the same thing that Joe Parisi was saying. But if liquor was illegal how could a person get away with selling it without being arrested? In despair he had just walked away from the winery because of the problems selling the wine. Joe was an intelligent man who listened keenly when people talked. Sometimes he didn't say very much but he was always listening and absorbing information. He knew that he wanted in on the money that could be made from selling liquor but wasn't sure how to go about getting into it, though he was determined to find out. He wasn't sure why Joe Parisi wanted to meet him in Chicago but did suspect that it had something to do with liquor and the looming prohibition and maybe it would lead to an opportunity for him to get involved.

Joe Parisi and Rocco Savatico arrived in Chicago the next afternoon. They had driven Joe's new car, a 1916 Willy-Overland touring car out from New Haven. They found the Brevoort Hotel, checked in and went looking for Joe.

Joe and Savako were in the hotel bar when Joe Parisi and Rocco walked in. Rosita remained in the hotel room while the men did business. Joe Parisi and Rocco looked a little ragged from the four-day drive out from Connecticut. After shaking hands and introductions, they all moved from the bar where Joe and Savoko had been sitting, to a table towards the back of the room.

Joe Parisi had met Savako several times out in California and even bought wine from him in the past. This was the first time that Joe or Savako had met Rocco. They started the conversation off with small talk before getting down to the serious business of why Joe Parisi wanted to meet in Chicago.

Joe Parisi leaned forward in his chair and began to speak. He talked in a low voice causing the others to lean forward as well, in order to be able to hear him. "Okay you want to know why we are meeting here in Chicago? Well last month I was at a meeting in New York with some very important and powerful people. The subject of this meeting was getting ready to make money when the prohibition sets in. One of the things we have do to be prepared is to secure a supply, and that is why we are here in Chicago. We are going to meet people, Canadians that can supply us with liquor. Now is the time to start bringing it in and stockpiling it because by the time it becomes illegal it will be too late. Those that prepare now will have their area, where they will sell, already established. If we don't move on this now we are going to have to fight for our territory later. So you see my friends we have no choice, others are moving ahead and we don't want to be left behind."

Joe Parisi turned his glass up and finished his drink holding the glass up towards Rocco and signaling to get him another. Rocco went to the bar and came back with four drinks. He passed one to each man, as Joe Parisi continued to talk.

"There are a couple of things that I want you to understand. Number one, this is going to be a very dangerous business. Because of the money that would be made on liquor we are going to be dealing with dangerous men that will have no trouble to kill you if you cross them. Each one of us is vital to the survival of the others. You make sure you are packing a gun with you, it might save your life or even mine."

"Number two is, from now on all of you are working for me. I will pay you very well and you will all be rich men in the end but this is my business. I need people that I can trust and I don't want you to ever give me a reason not to trust you." Joe held up his glass for a toast, "Salut." The glasses clinked together and an alliance was born between the four men. What Joe Parisi didn't explain right away is that his brother John was not interested in getting involved with the liquor. He was quite happy to run the numbers game and the restaurants and was making plenty of money. So in order for Joe to get into selling liquor he needed to put a mob together to do it. Joe Parisi was big on the family and favored Rocco because he had married into the family. But Joe and Joe Parisi got along very well and had been business partners for eight years. Savako was the least known to him as far as taking him into this enterprise was concerned, but he was willing and he was Italian, even if he was from Naples.

From this day on the four men would become partners and it was decided that this partnership would be known as "The Familia Group," their operation would be called "A Casa de Familia." They all joined hands in the center of the table. "Fotunato" each man repeated and lifted their glass and toasted to "The Familia."

John Torrio had turned his New York operations over to his partner Frankie Vale shortly after the meeting in New York and moved to Chicago to go to work for Big Jim Colosimo. He had been talking to Big Jim trying to convince him expand his operation into the liquor business but Big Jim, the same as John Parisi, was not interested. He had already made millions from the whorehouses that he controlled all over the city and did not see the need for more money. Johnny Torrio had to be discreet in his efforts to expand into the liquor business without Big Jim's approval. The meeting in Chicago had to be viewed as a fact-finding meeting whose purpose was to show Big Jim that getting into liquor was a smart thing to do. He gave his approval to Torrio to put the meeting together and talk about it with others who wanted to get involved. Torrio had to be careful that this did not look like an attempt to undermine Big Jim's operation, which could be trouble for Torrio.

The meeting was held a couple of days later at the Metropole Hotel conference room. It was attended by around 40 people from around the country and several suppliers from Canada including two brothers Edward and Thomas Seagram whose family had been producing Canadian Rye Whiskey for several generations. The two brothers had taken over their father's company in 1915 and had been following developments in the United States over the past year. The Temperance movement was active in Canada as well as the United States. Some of the provinces had been declared dry for many years until finally in 1915 and 1916 prohibition was imposed on all the provinces. However the Canadians were not as zealous when it came to enforcing the prohibition laws. Production of alcohol was for the most part still legal and so was consuming alcohol in your own home. It was just illegal to sell or distribute alcohol in the province where it was produced, however it was legal to ship it to another province for sale and distribution. This was especially true in Quebec where the prohibition laws were short lived and poorly enforced.

The meeting was also attended by Fred Morris, Alexander Laural and Joseph Bassett who were wine makers from British Columbia. The situation was the same in British Columbia as in eastern Canada. Producers were allowed to make wine and only sell it outside the province.

On the other side of the table was Pat Thomas, a cowboy from Havre, Montana that had already been shipping whiskey north to the dry prairie provinces in Canada and was anxious to reverse the trend and import liquor to the much larger U.S. market. Thomas had already established a maze of trails and roads crisscrossing the border used for transporting booze north. He encouraged family farms to set up stills and make moonshine and succeeded in having an army of producers all over the state. Farmers in Canada were no better off than the ones in Montana and Thomas was confident that he could get the Canadian farmers to make booze for the U.S. market.

Another person of note at the table, was Carlo Sinafaldi from Worcestor, Massachusetts. He had been running the rackets and gambling around Boston ,Worcester and Providence, Rhode Island for a long time.

Besides Joe Parisi and his group there were others from Detroit, Indianapolis, Milwaukee, Toledo and the Chicago area.

In the conference room was a long table lined with chairs on both sides and one chair at each end. The number one man and number two man of each group sat at the table and the others stood behind them. Johnny Torrio took a seat at one end of the table and Big Jim Colosimo sat at the other end. Big Jim had come to the meeting at Torrio's request for the purpose of listening to what the other men had to say. He was still less than enthusiastic about getting involved in liquor but he wanted to know what Torrio and his friends were planning to do. He sat at the end of the table and said very little but paid close attention to the discussions that were going on.

"Gentlemen, Gentlemen," Torrio said standing up and lifting his hands up. "I am glad to see you all here. I brought you here to Chicago to talk about Prohibition. Let me tell you what I see. I see

Prohibition as a potential for the biggest windfall of money that I have ever seen. I want to be ready when it happens because I intend to get rich from it.Maybe you do too. There are some people here that are going to want to buy liquor. And there are some people here that are going to want to sell liquor. I brought you all together so that you will be able to do business."

"What's in it for me you might ask," said Johnny, "because you all understand that I am a businessman and I have to make a profit too. So here is how we will do business today. You will all talk and exchange information and contacts today and tomorrow you will start doing business. Whatever business you do as a result of this meeting will go through me. You buyers, you will buy through me. And you sellers, you will sell through me. I hope we understand each other because if you cheat me I will kill you." Johnny Torrio looked around the table slowly looking each man in the eye with a cold stare.

Acting upon Torrio's instructions, each number one man of each group introduced himself and told where he was from and if he was a buyer or a seller and what he was selling. The meeting went on late into the night. Caterers brought in food and the bar was open with free drinks for everyone.

The deals made that day would make every man around the table rich. Torrio, acting as the middleman, intended to make a fortune.

Following the meeting with Torrio, Joe and his friends stayed a couple more days in Chicago. The men talked extensively about the connections they made there and how they could use them to benefit the Familia when Prohibition came to pass.

It was clear that Torrio was a tough customer and smart too. This meeting allowed him to get his hands in the pockets of every-one who attended. And it was also clear that he was not someone to double cross, as his reputation as a tough and brutal hood stuck fear into the minds of anyone who might think about it.

The four men discussed the meeting several times at a corner table in the hotel bar. Rosita waited for them in the hotel room as always, she was not allowed to sit at the table when the men were discussing business.

The night before they left for Connecticut Joe took them all to the Paradise Ballroom to meet his friends Louis and Julia Guyon. "D'Urbano's Eccentric Italian Band" was still playing there and the ballroom was packed with people. They found Louis, Julia, Alphonse and Rita Spatini and her two sisters Alisia and Antonette sitting at the same round table to the left of the stage.

"Hello Louis, hello Julia," Joe said as they approached the table. "I want you to meet my friends Joe Parisi and Rocco Silvatico."

Louis stood up and extended a hand to both Joe Parisi and Rocco. "A pleasure to meet you," he said. "And this is my wife Julia and our friends Alphonse and Rita Spatini and Rita's sisters, Alisia and Antonette." Everyone shook hands and then sat down. The two sisters immediately turned their attention towards Joe and it wasn't long before Antonette had him out on the dance floor.

This was the first visit to a dance hall for everyone except Joe, Savako and Rosita who were just here a few nights ago. Joe Parisi was impressed by the large number of people that were there. He and Louis Guyon hit it off immediately and was very interested in the dance hall operation and had a lot of questions for Louis about it. Especially after Joe informed him that Louis and Julia owned the Paradise.

Seeing as how Antonette had moved in on Joe, Alisia turned her attention towards Rocco and was trying to get him to dance with her. Rocco might have been quick to respond to a beautiful young girl's interest in him except he was married to Joe Parisi's sister and Joe was sitting there at the table. Rocco was explaining to her that he was a married man and where he came from married men do not dance with women other than their wives. But Alisia would not give up and kept trying to convince him that he should dance with her.

Finally Joe Parisi spoke up, "For Christ sake Rocco, go dance with the woman will you."

Rocco looked over at Joe and he motioned for him to go.

"Yea Rocco come on and dance with me," Alisia said as she pull him by the arm towards the dance floor.

The night at the Paradise was a fitting night for their last night in Chicago. Joe Parisi was intrigued by Louis's business at the Paradise and asked questions about it constantly until Louis said to him, " Enough questions Joe. It is time for you to dance with my wife."

At first Joe Parisi declined but Julia wasn't taking no for an answer and managed to get him out on the dance floor with him.

The night ended with everyone having a good time and Joe Parisi quite impressed by the dance hall business.

"You be sure and stop and visit us again next time you're in Chicago," Louis said shaking hands with each of them as they departed back to the hotel.

Chapter 7

When they left Chicago the next morning the weather had turned colder. It was late in the fall and winter was definitely in the air. It was a four day drive from Chicago to New Haven. Joe Parisi's Willys-Overland touring model was an open vehicle with a windshield but with no roof. In order to stay warm each person had to wear a heavy coat and even with that the cold seeped in throughout the day. By the day's end everyone was starting to feel the cold. About the time the sun went down they had enough of the cold and stopped for the night at a hotel.

They arrived in New Haven on day four and drove directly to the Catenzaro Restaurant.

Vinnie was working the front when they walked in.

"Hello Joe," said Vinnie. "And how was your trip?"

"Hello Vinnie," answered Joe Parisi. "The trip was good, just a little cold on the drive." Joe walked directly to the table by the kitchen and the rest of the group followed and pulled up chairs around the table. Vinnie came around with a couple bottles of Monte Vista wine and poured everyone a glass and then himself one.

They made a bit of small talk and ordered something to eat. After eating Joe Parisi invited Joe to go outside on the smoking deck so he could smoke a cigar. He liked smoking these little twisted and kinked 'perogi' cigars. It took a lot of matches to keep one lit as it would go out after nearly every puff. Joe Parisi looked up from lighting his cigar and said, out of the blue, "I think you should marry my sister."

"Why do you think that?" Joe replied a bit surprised.

"Well, I would like it if you were in the family. I like you Joe, you have been a good business partner and we are still in business. I like to keep business in the family."

"And who is this sister. I have not met her."

"I told you about my sisters and my mother who were in Italy and now they are living in West Springfield. She is 16 and it is time for her to get married and move out of her mother's house."

"Okay, well.... I will let you know."

"We will go to West Springfield and you can meet her." Pausing for second to think, he then looked up at Joe, "You can live in the house in Waterbury and maybe Savako and his wife can stay there with you for now."

After eating they all went to Joe Parisi's house in New Haven where they stayed the night. Joe Parisi took a couple of bottles of wine with him from the restaurant and closing the door to his office, the four men had drinks and talked for several hours.

"We have a lot of work to do my friends," Joe Parisi addressed the group. "But for now we will take a few days to rest up. And then we're going to get to work."

The next morning they drove Joe Parisi's Willys-Overland to Waterbury. The first stop was at the Waterbury Catenzaro Restaurant, arriving late in the morning. Serafino was just opening up when they parked the car in front of the restaurant. They went inside and sat at the same table as always. Serafino brought a bottle of Anisette Liqueur to the table and a large pot of expresso. There were no cus- tomers in the restaurant yet and the kitchen staff had just arrived and was getting ready for the lunch crowd that would be coming in soon.

Serafino was meeting Savako and Rosita for the first time. Joe Parisi introduced them.

"Savako, Rosita and Joe are going to be staying in the house on Banks Street for a while," Joe Parisi said to Serafino. "Joe and I are going to Springfield today and Savako and Rosita are going to get settled here while we are gone. We will be back in a few days and I want to to make them feel welcome and see that they get everything they need. In other words look after my friends, okay."

After having some lunch Joe Parisi drove Savako and his wife over to the Banks street house and let them in and showed them around.

"Make yourself at home and we will see you in a couple of days," Joe Parisi said as he, Joe and Rocco got in the car and left for Springfield. It was a cold ride to Springfield that day in the open touring car. It was starting to feel like winter with a few snowflakes in the air.

Joe Parisi noticed that there were more cars on the road than he could remember. The automobile had certainly caught on in America and the number of cars on the road was increasing every day. 1916 was the first year that automobile production in America had surpassed a million cars. The majority of those were Ford Model T's, at 734,800 cars sold that year. One of the reasons for Ford's success was the moving assembly line, which allowed them to produce more cars and lower the cost. A couple of years earlier Ford introduced the $5 work day which was twice as much as workers in other factory jobs were getting and served as a way to create a market for his cars. By 1916 the price of a Model T touring car was $360, and the runabout model was priced at $345. New car lots were springing up all over the country to accommodate the sales of cars and especially the Ford Model T. They had passed a couple of lots while leaving Waterbury, and while passing through Hartford a large sign on the side of the road caught Joe's attention. The sign said 'Special Sale New 1917 Ford Model T $340'

"Hey Joe, let's stop here for a minute, I want to look at this car."

Joe Parisi pulled the car into the lot and they all got out. There were two rows of Model T's, about 20 cars to the row. The row closest to the road was all touring cars. The other row was Model T's with a roof. The four door models were known as 'Roadsters' and the two door models were known as 'Coupes."

Joe had accumulated more than enough money over the years in California and could afford to buy a new car. He had been driving the old Model T pickup truck in California for quite some time and it proved to be quite a reliable vehicle for many years. He even knew a little about the mechanics of it, which helped to keep it running.

Having just driven from Chicago in the open touring car, Joe was more interested in the models with the roof.

The salesman came out from the sales office building and seemed really eager to sell Joe a car.

"Hello, hello my friend. What can I do for you today?" he said enthusiastically. As soon as Joe showed interest in the 'Roadster" model he started in with a monologue that covered all the good points there were in buying a Ford Model T.

"Well my friend, you have chosen the right vehicle. Three quarters of the nation is driving the Model T. It's the most popular car on the market and the most dependable. Many of the very first cars produced and are still running and on the roads today. You will find no better company for supplying repair parts than Ford. The Model T Roadster will seat six people and it gets 20 miles to the gallon of gasoline. Look at these new modern tires that it comes with. "Drawing Joe's attention to the tires the salesman kicked the tires a couple of times, "These tires have been developed to last more than two years, not like tires in the past that only lasted for about 6 months." Then he invited Joe to get in and start it up. "Come on now, give it a try," the salesman said while opening the door and looking at Joe.

Joe looked at him and turned his head towards the other cars and walked down the line of cars stopping at one black Model T that he liked.

"I want to try this one," he said pointing at the car.

The salesman closed the door in the other car and came over to where Joe was. "This is the one you want to take for a drive?" he asked.

"Yes, this one."

"Alright then, let's go," he said, opening the door and getting in and starting the car. He moved over to the other side and motioned for Joe to get in behind the wheel.

Joe Parisi and Rocco walked around the lot looking at the other cars while Joe took a ride with the salesman. They were only gone for ten or fifteen minutes before driving back into the car lot.

He stopped the car in front of the office and shut it off.

"Come on into my office and let's make a deal on this car," the salesman said to Joe.

"There's no need to come in your office," Joe said. Looking over at Joe Parisi he said "Joe how long are we going to be in Springfield?"

"Just a couple of days."

"Okay, I'll be back in a couple of days and pick up the car," he said. "I'll come into your office then."

The salesman seemed a little surprised but he took Joe at his word and the three men got back in Parisi's car and pulled out onto the road going north to Springfield. They arrived in Springfield and went right to the Catenzaro and into the back room. The poker game was just getting started. Rocco decided not to sit in on the game and got a ride to West Springfield from a friend who was having dinner in the restaurant. He had been gone for a couple of weeks and was anxious to get home to his wife Regina. Joe Marvici and Joe Parisi sat in on the game. John Parisi, John Masalino, Pasquale Lucarielo and Joe Popsadoro were the other men at the table that night.

After playing for poker for several hours they wrapped up the game and ordered some food from the kitchen. Everyone at the table knew that Joe Parisi and Joe Marvici had just returned from the meeting in Chicago and wanted to hear the news of how the meeting went. Even John who had made it clear that he did not want to get involved in the bootlegging of liquor was interested.

"The meeting was very productive. We met a lot of important people who have the same idea as we do. It is certain that the prohibition of liquor is going to happen and we can make our fortunes selling it to people who want it. But what we have to establish first is the supply routes to buy it so that we can keep selling wine and liquor in our restaurants." Joe Parisi went on to say, "John Torrio and his boys in Chicago have connected us to Canadians who can supply us. Now that we have made the connection to Canadian booze it's our job to set up the transportation people and routes to get the booze from Canada to our restaurants. In Chicago we met a man by the name of Pat Thomas. He has been sending booze north into Canada for a few years now. He has recruited many poor farmers to make the booze going north by setting up stills to make whiskey as well as making wine. There are a lot of poor farmers here in the east too, so we can do the same thing that he's doing, except instead of making the booze we want them to drive to Canada and bring the booze to us. But first we have to acquire warehouse space to store it. We want to have warehouse or maybe more than one or two warehouses, in Springfield, in Hartford, in Waterbury, and in New Haven. It important that we don't keep everything in the same place but rather have several places in each town to store the booze. That way if the police get on to us they won't find all of it."

"We need to organize this transportation as soon as we can," Joe Parisi continued. "I want all of you to meet me in New Haven next week and we will lay out the plans to transport the booze from Canada to us."

Though John Parisi was there at the table he had made it clear that he did not want to get involved with the bootlegging. He was okay with selling wine and liquor in the Catenzaro Restaurants but that was as far as he wanted to go. The numbers racket and the restaurant business was making enough money as far as he was concerned.

The meeting broke up around midnight and and John closed the restaurant and the three men went to John's house in West Springfield for the night.

The next morning the subject of conversation shifted to Joe Marvici and Parisi's younger sister Agatha's prospective marriage. The Parisi brothers were very much in favor of bringing Joe into the family and this was a way to do it. The family was an institution that would guarantee trust and protection. It was a way of assuring each other that members of the family would stand behind each other in a crisis of any kind and define whose side they would be on. Joe Parisi liked Joe and wanted to be able to afford him the trust that being a member of the family would bring. He and his mother Columbina had talked about it prior to his going to Chicago. It was not unusual for young Italian girls to be married by the time they were sixteen years old and Agatha even wanted to get married.

The first meeting was in the living room at her mother's house. She and Joe sat on sofas opposite each other. Agatha was very pretty with dark hair and dark eyes. She was short, only five foot even and petite. She wore a crocheted hairpiece on her head, which covered her hair and hung down below her ears and earrings. She wore a modern style dress with a silky type fabric that was outlined by tassels around the neck and again around the bottom of the dress around her ankles.

Joe was just about thirty years old and looked very handsome sitting across from her. He made a habit of dressing in a suit all the time since leaving California. At 5 foot 7 inches and 200 lbs he had very broad shoulders and looked to be a formidable man.

Though they talked to each other, that was the closest they got to each other that day .

The next time they met it was for a ride in the car. Both Joe and Agatha sat in the back seat and Joe Parisi drove with his mother sitting beside him. It wasn't until their third meeting that they actually got to talk together without anyone else around. It was in the afternoon on the third day after they met that they went for a walk down main street to the North End Bridge. They walked about half way across the bridge and stopped in the middle. Joe was leaning on the railings looking over the river when he turned to Agatha.

"Agatha, you look very beautiful."

"You look very handsome too."

"Tell me, do you want to get married?"

"Yes, I do Joe. I'm old enough and I have been looking for the right man."

"How do you know that I'm the right man?"

"I'll tell you what Joe. You look like the right man."

"I look like the right man?" he laughed.

"Yes Joe, you look like the right man."

"So if I'm the right man then ......does that make you the right woman?"

"Yes it does," she laughed back at him. "My brother has told me about you Joe. He says you are a good man. And when I look at you now, I think my brother is right."

"Your brother has told me about you too. Maybe your brother is right." Joe took her hand and pulled her near to him. "Maybe your brother is right." He said again looking at her when he talked.

"We better go back before they come looking for us," Joe said to her and they started walking back to her mother's house. It was about a ten minute walk back to her mother's house. There was closeness that started that day between Joe and Agatha. It wouldn't be long before it seemed like they were destined for each other.

He said good bye to Agatha the next morning before they drove back to Waterbury. It seemed that she had touched his heart because he thought about her a lot after that.

They drove together as far as Hartford when Joe stopped and picked up his new car. The car salesman was thrilled to see Joe come for his car. He pulled the Model T that Joe had chosen up to the front of the office and invited him in fill out the papers. He was paying cash for the car and he got the registration and license plate right there at the dealer. After leaving the car lot Joe followed Joe Parisi back to Waterbury in his new car. This was the first new car he had ever owned and it felt good. It gave him a feeling of independence and importance not unlike he felt when he first started to carry a gun.

Joe went to West Springfield to see Agatha about every two weeks after that until just after Christmas 1917. They were married in the All Souls Parish in Springfield on Saturday January 13 in the new year. Even though his mother was not there when they got married, Joe felt like his mother would approve of this marriage, because Agatha was both Catholic and Calabraise.

It was a big wedding with people coming in from Connecticut, Massachusetts and New York. Louis and Julia Guyon showed up from Chicago as well. Agatha looked beautiful that day and had a beautiful wedding dress and veil. Her oldest brother Joe Parisi walked her down the isle. The couple escaped on the train to New York while the wedding party was still going strong. They spent the week in New York City for their honeymoon. When they left New York the following weekend they were very much in love with each other.

On January 17, 1917 the Volstead Act, prohibiting the manufacture, sale and transportation of intoxicating liquor, was introduced as the 18th amendment to the Constitution. On that day it came before the U.S. Senate and was passed by a one-sided vote after only 13 hours of debate. It passed the House of Representatives a couple of months later after occupying only one day of debate. The amendment would still have to be ratified by state legislatures but was well on its way to becoming law in the U.S.

Up until this point and even for months afterwards it was still possible to buy alcoholic beverages but the writing was on the wall that it was going to dry up soon.

Agatha and Joe moved into the house on Banks Street, in Waterbury after getting back from New York. Savako and Rosita found another house a couple of blocks away and moved out of the Banks Street house while Joe and Agatha were in New York. The first few days Joe stayed around the house with Agatha but there was a lot of work to do and Joe realized it was time to go to work.

Joe Parisi called a meeting at his house in New Haven to set business in motion. Rocco Silvatico, John Masolino and Salvatore Mauro drove down from Springfield. Romano Bambino and his cousin George DeMaria came from Hartford and Savoko Copa, Serafino Parisi and Joe Marvici came from Waterbury. They met at Joe Parisi's house on January 24th. Joe and Vinnie Parisi were at the house waiting when Serafino and Joe Mavici showed up. Within about a half hour the other men arrived. Joe Parisi had circled ten chairs around a large oak table in the dining room. The dining room and the living room were one large room that was defined only by the furniture. Joe Parisi sat down at one end of the table but most of the men pushed their chairs back away from the table in order to all fit in the circle. The table had two coffee pots and coffee cups for everyone and several bottles of wine with glasses for each. Vinnie's wife Paulina had come to Joe Parisi's house about an hour before the meeting was to take place. She made coffee and set the table with wine and glasses and cups. She also made up some cold cut sandwiches and meat and cheese trays for Joe's guests. The men made small talk and delayed getting down to business until Paulina finished her work and left the house.

Joe Parisi poured himself a glass of wine, took a drink and looked around the room. He paused for a minute, the others turned their attention to him. He had spent many hours thinking about how he was going to go about setting up the liquor ring. Parisi was a take charge guy. If something was going on, he had to be in charge of it. If you asked him about it he would tell you, that's the way it is.

"I'm sure you've all heard the news just last week. The prohibition laws are coming and pretty soon selling whiskey and wine is going to be against the law. That's why we are getting in this business. I will continue to sell wine and whiskey at all the Catenzaro Restaurants just like I always have. And every other restaurant that's selling wine now is going to want to sell it later too. There are ways, there are ways, my friends. We have to find the products to buy and we're going to find them out of the country, mostly in Canada. A few of us met with people in Chicago and made some connections in Canada. So what we have to do is to set up routes to transport our product." Joe Parisi went on, "We have the numbers racket from Bridgeport right through to Springfield and just recently as far as Northhampton and we want to be the one selling our product in the same area. In other words we have to go sign up our customers."

Joe Parisi had been in contact with the Seagram brothers in Canada following the meeting in Chicago. The Seagram's distillery was in Waterloo, Ontario, making it quite a distance to ship the product to Connecticut and Massachusetts. The Seagram brothers had met a man, namely Samuel Bronfman, who had been in the hotel business in Winnipeg and had recently moved to Montreal. From his years spent in the hotel business he realized that there was a lot of money to be made in distribution of alcohol. Bronfman wanted to set up a distribution business in Montreal and had cut a deal with Seagram's to distribute their product in Quebec. He was aware of the booming business potential that loomed from selling whiskey and wine to the east coast states across the border.

Bronfman had acquired a warehouse in Montreal in which he stored most of his product. He also had set up a string of smaller warehouses in small towns closer to the U.S. border to make it easier for his U.S. customers to buy his products. One such warehouse was in a small town in southern Quebec that was also called Waterloo. It was this warehouse, that was actually a barn, that Joe Parisi was directed to bring his trucks. The farm was owned by a man named Claude Hebert, and was located a few miles outside of Waterloo.

Though Joe Parisi had talked to Sam Bronfman on the telephone, he had not met him in person. Just in the name of being careful he decided to send Joe and Rocco to Quebec and case the situation out by finding the warehouse and meeting the people they would be dealing with.

He looked up and then pointed to Joe, he said, "Joe, you and Rocco are going to go to Quebec. I want you to check everything out, you know, look at the product and find out where we can pick it up. Make sure we can acquire wine as well. I want you to make a deal with these guys, okay. After you make a deal, then we'll send the trucks."

"Yea, Joe I can do that." Joe nodded.

Looking over at Bambino, Joe Parisi said, "Bambino, I want you to start signing up customers. You take George and Savako with you. You convince people, that they want to buy from us, you no what I mean?"

"Yea, I know what you mean."

"Serafino, I want you to find warehouses and trucks. You go up in Vermont and go talk to farmers who have trucks and maybe they want to make some money. You find some who know the back roads over the border, small business people, you know what I mean?"

Serifino nodded.

"We want to have many warehouses, maybe ten or twenty and they must be spread out so that if we lose some we still have the others. I want you to scatter these warehouses throughout this area," he pointed to a map on the table that showed Connecticut and Massachusetts. "You take John and Salvatore with you."

Joe Parisi had done quite well in the restaurant business and the numbers racket but he saw this as the potential to be much bigger. Joe got Vinnie to hand out envelopes to each man containing $250 in cash. Joe received a second envelope with the money to make the first deal. Joe Parisi had prepared the envelopes prior to the meeting.

Then he went on to say, "We put our hands together in Chicago to form a bond of honor. And now we must do it here. We can own this part of the world and get rich doing it. But we must trust each other. That' what it means for you to sit around this table."

Picking up his wineglass, he held it in the air and each man followed suit. "Salut, fortunato A Casa De Familia."

After that the meeting loosened up with people talking among themselves and having some sandwiches and coffee. It appeared that Joe Parisi picked the men that he wanted to be the boss in each area. It was Joe on the dealings in Quebec and Bambino would be the main muscle man for insuring that they had plenty of customers and Serafino was the logistics man. Each one of them was related to Joe Parisi. He was also acutely aware of the fact that there were other people with the same idea as he had out there and the possibility of clashing was very real. It was important to get your territory established and then hold on to it. By afternoon the meeting broke up and everyone left for home.

Joe and Rocco left on Monday morning for their Wednesday afternoon meeting in Quebec. Though the rest of Canada was moving towards prohibition like the United States was, in Quebec it never really caught on with the people. Many farmers in Quebec were housing liquor in barns and underground cellars like Claude Hebert was.

They had directions to the Hebert farm and found it easily. They were met by Sam Bronfman and Claude Hebert when they arrived. After a short tour around the farm and warehouse, they went into

Claude's office to talk business. Sam broke out a bottle of whiskey and and four glasses and poured a drink for everyone.

Over the last few years the Seagrams brothers had realized that this prohibition across the border could be an opportunity to make a lot of money. They had already started increasing production at the plant in Ontario, to fill the need and welcomed Sam's effort to get their whiskey to the United States.

"And can we get wine as well,"Joe asked?

"Yes, we can sell you wine too. We will bring it in from Montreal. How much are we talking about anyway," said Bronfman.

"We will start out with five trucks a week, half whiskey and half wine. What can we put, maybe forty cases on a truck?" The whiskey was packed in wooden boxes with eight bottles to a case. Straw was packed around each bottle to protect them from touching and breaking during transport. Each case was covered by wooden slats nailed over top. The wine was packed the same way, distinguished by a printed 'W' on the top of the box. Otherwise the boxes looked alike.

"Yeah, that's about right. So when will you start to pick up?"

"Pretty soon, maybe next week. I'll let you know."

"And how are we going to be paid for this. We want to get paid up front. Besides, you never know, it could sell to the highest bidder unless you've already paid for it, you know."

"I will pay you up front," Joe said looking over at Bronfman. I'm going to pay for the first months supply. And every month I'm going to come here and pay you. It's either going to be Rocco or myself that will come with the money. One of us will be looking after the shipments. We will come up here with the trucks for the first few trips anyway, until you get to know the drivers.

"Okay, you want five trucks of forty cases, that's two hundred cases a week and eight hundred a month. And at $8 a case for the whiskey and $3 for the wine and one hundred cases of each that's going to be $1100. You got $1100?"

"Yeah, of course I got the money," Joe answered reaching in the breast pocket of his jacket and pulling out an envelope. He opened it and counted out $1100, handing it to Bronfman. The four men shook hands and the first deal was done. "It's a pleasure doing business with you Joe," Bronfman said, as they shook hands, "but Claude will be taking care of business with you from here on."

Bronfman gave Joe a couple of bottles of whiskey and a couple of bottles of wine as samples to take with him. They left that afternoon for Connecticut, crossing the American border late in the day and driving to Newport, a small town in the north of Vermont. They stopped at the hotel and got a room for the night.

Joe and Rocco opened a bottle of wine and talked about their mission going so well.

"This prohibition, I think it's not a bad thing," Joe said as both men laughed about it.

Hartford was familiar territory to Romano so he decided to start signing up customers there first. His message was simple, if you want to sell alcohol in this town you're going to buy it from him. Armed with the telephone list he worked his way around Hartford visiting one establishment after another accompanied by George and Savako. They liked to pay visits to businesses in the morning or early afternoon when it was likely they would find the owner there. Many of the bars in Hartford were already taking bets on the numbers so Romano already knew many of the owners.

Romano walked into one such establishment, the Padilla Bar, with George and Savako behind him. He took a seat at the bar. There was nobody else in the bar except the owner, who was working behind the bar..

"Louie, how are you?" he said to the man behind the bar. George sat on one side of him and Savako on the other.

"I'm good Romano. What brings you here?"

"I just come down to talk to you."

"You want a drink?"

"Yes, and my friends."

"So what do you want to talk about?" Louie said as he poured four drinks on the bar in front of them.

Romano took a drink and then looked up at Louie.

"Pretty soon this is going to be illegal," Romano said holding his glass up in front of him. "You know that, don't you?"

"Yes I know."

"So what are you going to do? Are you going to keep selling it?"

"Well I would like to but how am I going to do that."

"Well as far as selling it, my friend, you will have to use your imagination. But if you want to sell it then you have to buy it from me. You know what I mean?"

"Well right now I can still get what I need from my regular supplier. I don't know how long before it starts to dry up."

"When your supply dries up, then you have to go underground if you want to sell booze. When you do that, it means that your regular supplier is out of business too. That's when you're going to need me, but by then it's going to be too late. You got to start buying from me now, then you will be assured of being in business later."

Louie paused for a minute thinking about what Romano was saying. He had been in business at the Padilla Bar for nearly ten years and the new prohibition laws threatened to put him out of business. This sounded like an interesting proposition to him even though it might get him in trouble with the law.

"I would like to stay in business but maybe I'm going to have to do my business through the back door," he said pointing to the back door of the bar that opened into the alley behind the bar.

"Now you are catching on," Romano replied. "Me and my friends, we are going into business. We are going to help businessmen like you to stay in business. But we want you to start now to buy from us. We have Canadian whiskey and wine to sell to you. I want you to give me a small order to start out and then start to cut your Boston orders back. You know, and gradually shift from your current supplier to us. You know what I mean?"

Louie quickly realized that this wasn't a choice but it was more like an ultimatum. The two men sitting beside Romano at the bar enforced this idea in his mind.

"I want to put you down for five cases of whiskey and five cases of wine." He said looking Louie straight in the eyes. It didn't look like much of a choice for Louie if he wanted to stay in business. It went without saying that both he and his business could meet an unfortunate accident if he decided not to go along with Bambino and his friends. He agreed to start buying from Romano right away with the first shipment scheduled to be delivered within two weeks.

The same conversation was repeated many times over to owners of other establishments that sold liquor, and with the same result. The orders were quickly adding up and soon Romano had orders for half of the first shipment of two hundred cases. However many customers of the drinking establishments were young men and millions of them were over in Europe fighting the Germans. For that reason business had dropped off at most bars and restaurants over the last year. Everyone hoped the war would be over soon and the men would be coming home.

Al Fina was a farmer who operated a vegetable farm a few few miles outside of Westfield on the Woronoco Trunk Road. His family had owned the land for three generations and had built a successful produce business supplying fresh vegetables to the Union Street Produce Market for distribution to grocery stores and restaurants in Springfield. Fina and his wife had ten children between the ages of three and sixteen. Every summer he alloted a piece of land to each of the older children to grow vegetables on. Each one looked after his patch of ground and was allowed to sell his crop to the produce market and keep half of the money made on the crop. Al was able to keep the kids interested in the farm that way because each one of them would end up with cash of their own at the end of each season. The children that were old enough to grow a crop helped with preparation and packing of all the produce produced on the farm, including their own crop which was prepared for sale right along with the rest. Aside from the main vegetable barn where all the produce was prepared for sale, there was a large underground root cellar in which the root crops such as potatoes, carrots, beets and cabbage were stored and sold during the winter and spring.

John Masalino had known Al Fina since he was a young man. His father had an interest in the Union Street Market and John had worked there when he was younger and met Al on many occasions.

It was John's idea to drive out to the Fina Farm and talk to Al about warehousing liquor in one of his buildings. It was the off season on the farm and Fina had been selling the root crops out of the root cellar for several months and had created a lot of free space in the underground cellar. The root cellar was built with a loading ramp and dock that allowed trucks to back down to the level of the cellar to load or unload. Fina was quick to make a deal with the Masalino and his friends and even contract his two Model T trucks to haul the product from Canada.

Al knew a woman in Vermont that would probably be willing to supply the extra trucks and drivers that they needed to move the liquor. She was in a little town situated between Burlington and Montpelier, Vermont. Interestingly enough the town was named Waterbury. Apparently many of the early pioneers were from Connecticut and in fact Waterbury, Vermont took its name from Waterbury, Connecticut when it was first established in 1763.

The woman was Antonette Spencer, sometimes known as 'Toni' or 'Nettie.' She was quite a controversial personality. She was known to smoke cigarettes and even chew tobacco on occasion. She married Albert Spencer, who became a millionaire in the rubber business, owning several factories in Burlington. They lived an affluent lifestyle, even having houses in New York, Newport and London, England. Albert Spencer died in London in 1907. He was getting on in years by that time and rumor had it that Antonette poisoned his soup, a rumor that was never proved.

A short woman, high spirited woman with a large nose and high cheekbones, she always wore her hair in a bun. She was not well liked by the other women of Waterbury. Part of the reason was the luxurious way in which she lived, with furnishings of Victorian elegance and a maid and a butler looking after her. She did have a reputation of being a wild woman and that reputation followed her in stories about her. One was about her running a brothel in Cleveland and another having an unacknowledged child. Of course some of these stories could have been fabricated by some of the Waterbury ladies who despised her so, mostly out of jealousy or envy. After her husband's death she moved back to Waterbury and turned the house into an inn.

But her real passion was cars. She bought all the new models of the fastest and most powerful cars as soon as they came out. Though she didn't often drive them, she ordered the drivers to "Step on it" and if they drove too cautiously she'd tell them, "I'm paying for it so you'll drive as fast as I want you too."

Al Fina knew Toni before she married Albert Spencer. In fact, she went to school with him for a few years as a teenager.

Serafino, Salvatore, Al Fina and John Masalino drove up to Waterbury, Vermont the next day to meet with Toni Spencer. She was a person who liked excitement, and the idea of trucking bootleg liquor from Canada really piqued her interest. She already owned three trucks and was prepared to buy more if she needed them. Toni was like a woman on fire, full of enthusiasm while they were talking about it.

The furniture in the rooms at the inn was imported from Europe and beautifully decorated. Each of the four took a room in the inn for the night though they all stayed up quite late drinking and talking downstairs in the sitting room.

Percy Jones was a colored man who worked for Toni for many years as her butler and sometimes her driver. He was tall, a little over six feet and always looked very proper and neat. Percy looked after many of Toni's affairs including her banking and collecting rents from her many properties in Burlington. He also hired the other people who worked for her, such as maids, gardeners and drivers. Wherever she went you would find Percy standing quietly nearby just in case she might need him. It was rumored that Toni and Percy had an intimate relationship as well. He was the key to finding the back roads into Quebec.

However a black man driving a nice car around in the country-side by himself would look very suspicious. But if he was driving Toni around it would not look suspicious at all.

The next morning it was decided that Toni would go with Percy to find a back road across the border. The other four went first back to Al's farm and then to Springfield where John and Salvatore lived. Serafino kept driving straight through to New Haven, he wanted to report in to Joe Parisi. Though the telephone was available and some times was used in a pinch, Joe Parisi insisted that his people report to him in person. He didn't trust the telephones much when it came to talking about business.

It was late and the Catenzaro was getting ready to close when Serafino got to New Haven. Joe Parisi was not there, he had gone home an hour earlier. Serafino got an order of pasta to take with him and drove to Joe Parisi's house.

"Serafino, it's good to see you, come in," said Joe Parisi greeting him at the door.

They went into the living room, and pouring a couple of glasses of wine, Joe Parisi asked, "How did it go? Did you find some trucks?"

"Yes, we did. I think we are ready to do the first trip."

"With how many trucks?"

"We can go with five just like you wanted."

"Ahh, that's good. I have heard from Joe and he is on his way back too." Parisi said. "How about warehouse. Did you find a warehouse?"

"Yeah, it's one of the guys with trucks, Al Fina, he lives on a farm on the way to Woronoco. He has a big underground root cellar. It'll hold lot cases of booze."

"And Bambino, he's got some customers already so we can move some of the product right away. We just wait for Joe Marvici to get back here and we can get going."

Joe and Rocco stopped and stayed the night at Rocco's in Springfield. The next morning they telephoned New Haven to let Joe Parisi know where they were. He wanted them to pick up Masalino and Mauro and bring them down to New Haven with them. Romano and George were driving down from Hartford and Savako from Waterbury as well. They all met that afternoon at Joe Parisi's house in New Haven.

Bambino had already found customers ready to take 50 cases of wine and 50 cases of whiskey right away, which was half of the first shipment. But they still needed to find a warehouse in Connecticut that was closer to the New Haven, Hartford and Waterbury market. After listening to everyone's information Joe Parisi had a plan.

"First Vinnie, you're going to stay here and look after the numbers. Bambino, you and George keep getting the customers but first I want you to find a warehouse somewhere around Waterbury. John and Salvatore you're going to drive two of the trucks. How many drivers do we have?"

"We have two drivers. There is the farmer Al Fina and the woman in Vermont. I think she is going to have her butler drive one of the trucks."

"Salvatore, you are going to drive one too. Me, Savako, Joe and Rocco are coming along too in another car. This is the first trip and I want to be there and see that it goes according to plan."

"Joe," he continued, "I want everybody carrying a gun. We leave tomorrow morning." Looking over at Serafino he said, "You take John and Salvatore with you now and we will meet you in West Springfield on the way through."

Shortly afterward Joe left for home. He had not seen Agatha for almost a week. She met him at the door after hearing the car pull up in front of the house.

As he opened the door Agatha was there to greet him. "I am so glad to see you my dear," she said as she kissed him.

Joe was very tender and loving towards Agatha and was generous with money, giving her free rein to decorate the house or to go shopping however and whenever she wanted. But Joe was there only for the night, as he had to leave on business the next morning. They made love that night and that's when she told him that she thought she was pregnant. They were both overjoyed at the prospect of having a child. Joe had proved to be a kind and caring husband and Agatha was sure that he would make a good father.

The next morning Joe kissed Agatha goodbye and picked up Savako and drove to New Haven. There he picked up Joe Parisi and drove up to West Springfield. Rocco got in the car with Joe and John, Salvatore and Serafino drove in another car. They went first to Al Fina's farm where Al was waiting with the two Model T trucks gassed up and ready to go. John Masalino drove one of the trucks and Salvatore rode with him while Serafino rode with Al Fina who was driving the other truck. It was pretty well an all day drive to cover the nearly two hundred miles on roads of varying conditions. Some times the road was smooth and sometimes they could only be navigated at slow speeds. They rolled into Waterbury, Vermont in the late afternoon on this winter day. The sun was already getting close to the horizon. The three vehicles pulled up to the rear of the inn so as not to attract too much attention. Al Fina led everyone into the inn through a rear entrance.

Always aware of what was going on at the inn, Percy met the group as they opened the door." Good afternoon gentlemen," he said. "Come this way."

He led them into a spacious living room that had five couches and several stuffed easy chairs. A few minutes later Toni came into the room.

"Hello, hello, hello," she said leaving no doubt of the excitement in her voice. "Yes, we had to drive back and forth across the border a few times to find the best way but we have a couple of routes we can take. You know there's snow on some of the roads that's too deep to drive through right now, so we had to do a bit of searching to find a plowed road." Tony unfolded a map and laid it out on one of the coffee tables. The men gathered around while Tony pointed out the route". One that we found takes off from Norton and comes out just north of Stanhope and on the road to Coaticook. But we got to wait until after dark to be coming and going from here. Don't want to get the townspeople knowing there's something going on."

By six o'clock it was as dark as it was going to get and the convoy of five trucks and one car headed north towards the Canadian border. Percy and Toni were in the first truck leading the way. She looked out of place in the front of a truck with her fancy dress and a bonnet on her head, though somehow it looked believable because of her colored driver.

Vermont, oddly enough, had gone through almost fifty years of prohibition that ended in 1903 and was brought back again in 1915. The act that outlawed liquor the second time provided for a statewide referendum that happened on March 7, 1916 and was defeated by over 13,000 votes. The result was that the statewide prohibition law was repealed on January 23, 1917 or just four days after the

Volstead act prohibiting liquor passed in the Senate. Vermont was one of the states that never ratified the 18th amendment before it became law.

They took a back road around Norton so as to not pass right through the middle of town and then went east for about five miles and then north onto a dirt road. The road was up and down as it followed Avrill Creek down to the Norton River. They had crossed the line into Quebec by this time. A few miles later the road connected to the highway to Coaticook. Turning west at Coaticook it was about an hour and a half's drive to Waterloo. It was about a four-hour drive altogether to get to from Waterbury, Vermont to the Claude Hebert's farm in Waterloo, Quebec.

Claude was waiting for the trucks to arrive at the and had all of the cases pulled out on the dock and ready to go. It only took about fifteen minutes to get the trucks loaded and they were on their way back to Vermont. Joe, Joe Parisi and Rocco all talked with Claude Hebert briefly before they were back on their way.

The trip came off without a hitch as they followed the same route back to Vermont and then Waterbury. It was very late when they got back to Waterbury and they decided to stay at the inn until the next day and leave for the Al Fina's place after the sun went down. Toni rode in the truck with Percy all the way not wanting to miss any of the action.

It was about ten o'clock in the morning when they got to Al Fina's farm and off loaded the trucks. The first trip was a total success with no problems occurring either way. After all the cases were stored away in the cellar they opened a couple bottles of wine and had a drink on the loading dock. Joe Parisi paid Al Fina $40 for his two trucks and Toni $60 for her trucks before she and Percy drove back to Vermont. She decided to leave the other trucks at Fina's and the guys would drive them up to Waterbury and do it all over again next week

John, Serafino and Salvatore drove back to Springfield in the car that they drove to Fina's. Joe Parisi headed back to New Haven with the others dropping Rocco off in West, Springfield. Joe's car was at Joe Parisi's and he and Savako then drove back home to Waterbury.

Chapter 8

After that first trip the routine was set. Every Tuesday morning John, Salvatore, Serafino and Rocco would leave from West Springfield and meet Al at his farm. They would drive the four trucks to the Inn in Waterbury, Vermont, arriving after dark. Percy and Toni would join the group and they all would take off from there to the border and Waterloo. They made it back to the Inn at three or four in the morning. After resting up for a few hours they took off again before daylight, unloading at Fina's and then driving back home. Rocco actually went along as the trigger man if they needed it but there were really no problems during that first year.

Bambino had signed up quite a few bars and restaurants to buy their products from him but drinking establishments weren't very busy these days. The young men were still away at war and the women were working a lot. A lot of people looked favorably on prohibition in the very beginning thinking that it could be a good thing and less people were drinking because of it. That led to cases of whiskey and wine building up in the two warehouses as only about half of the loads were getting sold. Even with the amount of liquor that was sold in that first year, it generated enough profit to keep everyone in the 'Familia' living quite comfortable.

The numbers racket also expanded as Bambino convinced more establishments to do business with him. As far as the family was concerned though, Joe Parisi was still the money man or Number One. He only showed his face in those really stubborn cases where some extra muscle was needed. He was a huge man with shoulders about three feet wide. A frightening figure when he wanted to be, but he always talked calmly, with a cigar hanging out of one side of his mouth. If he took that cigar out of his mouth that probably meant somebody was going to get walloped. But for the most part Joe Parisi was the general who called the shots and controlled the money.

Aside from doing a few errands for Joe Parisi and showing up sometimes to put some pressure on somebody who couldn't seem to pay his bills, once a month Joe Marvici accompanied the trucks to Quebec and took the money to pay for the next four week's shipments. Joe and Rocco rode together following the trucks to Quebec.

At home Agatha got bigger throughout the summer and on October 19 she had the baby. It was a baby boy, born with a full head of hair and dark eyes. It was Italian custom to name your first born son after your father so Joe wanted to name him Pasquale. And so he was baptized a few weeks later, Pasquale Fortunato Marvici. A family friend, Joe Popsadoro, was asked to be his Godfather and Mary-Angela, Agatha's sister, his Godmother.

On the international front, America had gotten fully into the war in Europe by the end of 1917, and the draft was taking lots of young men to fight in Europe. Joe, like Joe Parisi and like many other Italians, just didn't bother to sign up and was able to stay out of the war.

Business continued at about the same level it had been the year before. It was still affected by so many servicemen being overseas and then was further hampered by the 1918 flu epidemic. In America alone the flu killed 548,000 people. More and more people were afraid to go out because of fear of catching the flu. Restaurants and bars were hurting for business because of this.

The writing was on the wall as far as the prohibition laws were concerned, but Joe Parisi was starting to wonder if the plans to capitalize on it weren't going askew. He had been building up a supply in the warehouses in Connecticut and Massachusetts for a year and a half and the situation had not changed that much. By the summer of 1918 there were over two hundred businesses signed on to buy liquor from The Familia. Yet they were still only selling half of the two-hundred cases a week that were coming from Quebec.

However the numbers racket had expanded considerably during that same time. Bambino's efforts to sell liquor had spilled over into the numbers as far south as Bridgeport and encompassed many small towns between there and Northhampton, Massachusetts. By that summer the Family controlled the numbers and liquor sales in every town in the Connecticut River corridor of western Connecticut and Massachusetts. It was because of the profit on the numbers and the small liquor sales that Joe Parisi was still able to finance stockpiling of liquor in the warehouses.

The first sign that things were about to change was in the late summer as reports came from Europe that the Allies had the Germans on the run. Finally on November 11 the Germans surrendered and the war was over.

Just a month before Savako and Rosita received a letter from Carmen Garcia who was still in Napa. Apparently the grape harvest that year very good. She and Renoldo had put their efforts together to harvest the crop on her farm, Savako's farm as well as the Monte Vista. All the grapes were squeezed and put into the fermenting barrels and were almost ready to bottle. They had over two hundred barrels of wine fermenting which was about three thousand five hundred cases or enough to fill two boxcars.

Savako talked to Joe Marvici first and then they both went to Joe Parisi with a plan to get the wine back east while they could still ship it legally. The smuggling operation out of Quebec was going fine and Parisi saw this as an opportunity to make a lot of money especially now that it looked like the war was going to be over soon and rumor was that it wouldn't be long now until alcohol was illegal.

"Offer them two dollars a case. If they accept it, and they will, then you two go to California and bring it back."

Carmen gave a telephone number in the letter to get in touch with her and Savako called her from Parisi's. Joe Parisi was right, she accepted the two-dollar offer and Joe and Savako were going to California.

The trip to California was probably going to take Joe away from home for about three or four weeks. Pasquale was a year old now and Joe had been able to spend a lot of time around home to up to now. This would be the first time that he would be gone for this long. Rosita moved in with Agatha to help her out when the men left.

Joe and Savako took the same familiar train that Joe had taken several times before, back to California. The same two day layover in Chicago and out on the town with his friends the Guyons. Joe did not let on in any way what they were going to California for, telling them that he was selling the Monte Vista instead. By this time Louis Guyon had become a very rich man. The dance hall business had been very good to him. He was still selling liquor in the dance hall bars and making a fortune at it but doing it legally was not going to last long now.

They caught the train the next day, changing in San Fransisco and finally getting off at Vellejo. Carmen and Renaldo were waiting at the station when the train came in.

Carmen had already arranged for the two boxcars to be spotted on the sidetrack. They drove by to look at the cars and be sure they were there and were going to be easy to load.

During the last couple of weeks Carmen and Renoldo had gotten the wine out of the barrels and into bottles and then cases, so that they would be ready to ship when Joe and Savako got there. Using four trucks to transport the wine to Vellejo, they got the two boxcars loaded in three days. Each run they made they all traveled together from Napa to Velleho and unloaded the trucks together. Rosita, Renaldo, Savako and Joe each drove one of the trucks, each accompanied by a worker that helped with the loading and unloading. The boxcars were loaded with one door closed and piled right to the roof of the car and straight up at the other door, which was then shut and both doors padlocked. The total amount loaded into both cars came to 3800 cases, more than expected. There were actually about two hundred cases still back at the Monte Vista that they wouldn't fit in the boxcars.

It was a complicated formula paying for the wine off of each farm, as it was all sold together. Carmen had kept track of how much wine came from each farm and the costs associated with the harvesting and making and bottling. The two dollar price per case was lower than it would normally sell for but took into consideration that both Savako and Joe and his partners were the owners of the wine making operation. Also, Carmen's vineyard only grew the grapes and was not set up for making wine. The boxcar loads of wine when sold in the east would return quite a large profit even after paying for the shipping. Joe had brought enough cash with him to pay for the entire shipment and left it up to Carmen to take care of the costs associated with it and pay Renoldo and the other farm workers.

The boxcars were picked up and added to a freight train bound for the rail yards in San Francisco. There they became part of a freight train that was bound for Chicago. In Chicago the cars were sorted and the ones going east were added to an Illinois Central freight going to New York. Finally they were shipped out of there on the New Haven Railroad and spotted on a side track in New Haven. The whole trip took just about two weeks before the boxcars reached New Haven.

Joe and Savako returned to New Haven on the passenger train leaving the day after the cars were picked up in Vellejo. As usual they stopped in Chicago for a couple of days and got to New Haven almost a week before the wine did. When it finally arrived, it was imperative that they move the wine from the boxcars into the warehouse in Waterbury as quickly as possible. This whole operation was cutting it really close as far as the prohibition law was concerned. Many of the states had already ratified the 18th amendment and as soon as the two-thirds majority was reached it was set to become law.

Joe Parisi went to the Fina farm when the weekly shipment arrived from Quebec. He organized the trucks to come to New Haven as soon as they were unloaded to help move the wine from the box-cars to the warehouse in Waterbury. Even Percy and Antonette participated. It was the first time that they had ever been in Waterbury, Connecticut. The operation was conducted in the middle of the night, the first trucks arriving at the railroad siding after ten o'clock and working all night.

Everyone in the Familia was moving cases of wine that night, even those who had cars were loading the trunks and back seats with boxes. Joe Parisi parked his Willy-Overland near the boxcars to keep an eye on them and make sure that his guys were the only ones taking wine from the boxcars. Vinnie Parisi was at the other end overseeing the unloading at the warehouse in Waterbury. They even filled the storerooms at the Catenzaro Restaurants to the brim, both in Waterbury and in New Haven. By the time the sky started getting light at about 7a.m. the last truck was loaded and one of the boxcars had been emptied.

Joe Parisi, concerned about the second boxcar, made sure that it was guarded during the day, until they could get it unloaded the following night. Bambino and DiMaria parked Bambino's car near the boxcar during the day. They stayed some distance away, just enough to keep an eye on the load without being too conspicuous. They took turns catching up on some sleep with one person staying awake.

About three in the afternoon George was sleeping and Romano noticed a car pull up to the two boxcars. The locks had been put back on the empty boxcar, so you could not tell that there was any difference between the two.

Four men got out of the car and walked around the two boxcars. They were checking the tire tracks on the ground in front of the door of the first one. After a few minutes they all got back in the car and drove away. Romano woke up George as soon as the car stopped and the two of them both watched. Romano got out of the car and walked a couple of blocks to where there was a telephone. He called Joe Parisi.

"You better get down here," Romano said.

"Why, what's going on?"

"I'll tell you when you get here."

"Be right there," said Parisi. He took Joe and Rocco with him. They left his house and drove to where George and Romano were parked.

Romano got out of the car and went over to Parisi's car. "There was a car with four guys in it, they stopped by the boxcars and were looking around."

"When was this?"

"Just a few minutes ago."

"Hmm!" Joe Parisi said, putting his hand to his chin to think. "Okay, Joe you and Rocco stay here with Bambino. Maybe we'll start early tonight moving this stuff."

Joe Parisi went back to his place and called Vinnie. "Vinnie, I want you to get down to the siding. It looks like we had some visitors. Bring Savako and Salvatore with you."

"Who's the visitors?"

"I Don't know. I want you to tell Toni and Al that I want their trucks at the siding as soon as it's dark. We are going to start early."

"I'll be there in a few minutes," said Vinnie. He, Salvatore and Savako were on their way in a couple minutes. They all kept off in a distance keeping an eye on the boxcars. If someone stopped to check them out now the boys would be moving in on them. Joe Parisi stopped and checked up on things shortly before dark. He picked up Joe to drive his car and Salvatore to drive the last truck.

The days were short this time of year and it was dark by six pm when the first round of trucks showed up. There was a sense of panic on this second night that wasn't there the night before. This time they loaded all the cars and the five trucks, putting on all they could take in each load. The vehicles were loaded down to the point that any more would have surely broken the springs. By three o'clock in the morning the boxcars were empty, the locks put back on and the ground brushed over to obscure the tire tracks, making it look like nothing had happened there.

At about 6a.m. the next morning just a few hours after the boxcars were emptied they were descended upon by a mob that came in four cars and ten trucks. They cut the locks off the boxcar doors with large bolt cutters, and to their surprise found the cars empty. It was Enzo Fatini and his gang out of East New York, who somehow got a tip that there were two boxcars full of wine in a siding in New Haven. He could only surmise that there was something going on in New Haven, and that was the reason this wine disappeared. Enzo decided to keep an eye on the goings on in New Haven and see if he could figure out who the wine belonged to.

The huge shipment of wine filled every available storage space that Joe Parisi had, in fact when the trucks went back to Fina's farm they were loaded. Some of the wine was dropped off at the Catenzaro Restaurant in Hartford and more in Springfield. This also meant that they would probably stop buying wine from Canada and take take their orders all in whiskey now. The fact that the war was over and millions of servicemen would now be returning to America gave Joe Parisi some hope that accumulating such a large quantity of whiskey and wine would pay off. At this point he was stretched almost to his limit and hadn't paid Torrio any money either. Sooner or later he knew that Torrio was going to come looking for it. The cost to carry such an inventory had built up to the point where it had to start selling soon. Even the numbers racket couldn't support it any more.

A little more than six weeks after the wine came in from California, just two months after the end of the war, the required number of state legislators ratified the 18th amendment and prohibition in America became law. Restaurants and drinking establishments all over the country had big parties to celebrate the last legal day to drink alcohol. All of the Catenzaro Restaurants had such a party and they were packed with people not wanting to miss that last night. And then at 12 o'clock midnight January 19, 1919 it finally happened.

Within a few months legal drinking establishments were closing by the thousands and restaurants found it harder and harder to get liquor legally, so they turned to the suppliers of bootleg liquor. Fortunately for Joe Parisi and the Familia their customers were already in place by that time.

It was the bars that had to reinvent themselves and go underground, creating the 'speakeasies'. Restaurants could get away with quietly selling a customer a bottle when they came in. Then the customer could order a soft drink or coffee and spike his drink unnoticed while sitting at the table. Some restaurants had a bar attached or off to the side of the dining room. In most cases the bar was shut down but they still served wine with the meal. That's the way it was at all of the Catenzaro Restaurants. It was poured in the back room and brought out in coffee cups instead of wineglasses. To all appearances they they were complying with the new law. There were signs on the wall stating that no alcohol will be served on the premises. Another sign at the front door said that this establishment is complying with the 18th Amendment. The bar was still there but a sign hung over it that said, 'Bar Closed.' So it certainly looked like they were in compliance yet it was anything but.

Because the larger quart bottles of whiskey were hard to conceal, the whiskey was put into half-pint bottles call 'mickeys.' These bottles cost a dollar and held about four drinks. There were eight of these mickeys in a bottle of whiskey which means that each case sold this way sold for $64 while costing only $8 giving 800% markup. The profit on the wine was almost as good. A bottle of wine that cost 37 cents could be sold for 50 cents a glass and fetch $2.50 a bottle from it.

As soon as the prohibition law was passed the price to the restaurants and speakeasies for the wine and whiskey went up. Joe Parisi wanted to make sure that he could sell as much as possible to his customers at all their restaurants. So when selling it to other establishments the price was always higher and that made sure that they had to sell it for more. Once the word got around, the Catenzaro Restaurants were full to capacity every night.

After putting money into buying liquor and wine for the last two years, Joe Parisi finally started to see money coming his way. Just the value of the inventory that was in the two warehouses and in storage in the restaurants was close to half a million dollars. At the end of the first three months of prohibition it became apparent that they were selling more than the five trucks a week that were bringing in from Quebec. It was time to double up the amount of trips and start adding a few more trucks as well.

Toni and Percy engineered a pyramid scheme where their drivers found other trucks and drivers and capitalized on them, giving them the opportunity to do the same thing to trucks that they signed up. By this time Toni and Percy would only take a trip once in a while and skimmed four dollars a trip off the other trucks. They in turn could skim a couple more dollars off the next trucks and so on. The last trucks down the line might be making only ten or twelve dollars a trip which was still good money at the time.

Toni was generous with the drivers that were driving her three trucks, paying them four dollars a trip. They took over the Quebec to Fina Farm run and Al Fina's trucks were busy transporting whiskey from his farm as far south as Bridgeport and moving cases of wine as far north as Northhampton. All of the movement of liquor took place under the cover of darkness.

For the next year business greatly increased and the Familia was making a lot of money. Prohibition also changed the way people drank. They switched from drinking wine and beer to drinking hard liquor because it was easier to conceal. The mickey-sized flask was very popular and commonplace and with the servicemen coming back from the Europe it seemed like everyone wanted to get in on the action now. People patronized illegal drinking establishments like never before. Even those people who didn't drink much before the 18th amendment were going out and drinking after it was law.

The war for territory in New York City among the different gangs became brutal after the prohibition laws were enacted. Enzo Fatini and his partners George and Frank Grazia were trying to get control over the eastern New York suburbs around New Rochelle, White Plains and Stamford, Connecticut. The fight for New York became intense between the rival gangs trying to carve out territory and resulted in Fatini's partners being shot dead in a battle in Yonkers. Capone was suspected in having a hand in the murders and kept one step ahead of the New York Police who were investigating. He was tipped off by a member of the police, and advised to get out of town. Johnny Torrio wanted Capone to come to Chicago and help him get the liquor business going there and this seemed like a good time to make the move.

Fatini was apprehensive about trying to penetrate too close to New York again and decided to turn his attention to the south coast of Connecticut. It was he and his friends who were in New Haven cutting the locks off the boxcars of wine from California. They had given up on New York and had taken over the business in Greenwich, Stamford, Norwalk, and Fairfield, Connecticut. Joe Parisi had gotten word from some of the businesses in Bridgeport that someone else was trying to sell booze to some of his customers and strong arm them into paying protection. This kind of invasion on territory could not be tolerated and Joe Parisi had to act to protect his business.

Parisi took Joe, Savako and Vince with him and went to Bridgeport to confront the situation. One customer who played the numbers was Sonny Jordan, who used to have a bar on Main Street in Bridgeport. He was forced to close when the prohibition laws were enacted. After he closed his bar he opened two illegal establishments and had been doing a pretty good business. Buying his booze from Joe Parisi had a fringe benefit of putting Sonny under his protection too, and Sonny didn't want to mess with that by not being loyal to him. Sonny had been approached by Fatini and told Joe Parisi about it. He agreed to let Joe know when Fatini and his boys came back so that Joe could catch them in the act.

They went around to some of his other customers and it turned out Fatini and his people had been putting pressure on a lot of them to buy their booze from him. The situation was starting to look like it could get nasty as there was no way that Joe Parisi was going to let anyone muscle in on his territory. All of the other customers that they talked to agreed to let him know when these guys came around again.

They went back to New Haven that afternoon and Parisi put the word out that everyone should be ready to go on short notice. He decided that as soon as he got the first tip that Fatini and his boys were back in Bridgeport trying to sell their product, they would mobilize and go to Bridgeport in force. Besides the original ten members there were six more added to the group-Antonio Rizzo, Alphonso Valo, Pasquale and Ermindo Licariello, John Bregoli and Armondo Marcotti.

Fatini and his guys worked mostly in the afternoon when the businesses were not that busy. Joe Parisi had all his men hang around his house or the Catenzaro Restaurant in New Haven, every day until he got the call. It was just about noon one day when Sonny called from Bridgeport.

Parisi went to Bridgeport with sixteen men in four cars all armed with handguns and machine guns and a couple of shotguns. The more menacing they appeared to their adversaries, the more chance that they would scare them off, or at least that's the way Joe Parisi thought about it.

One of Sonny's speakeasies was located in the basement under a clothing factory. There were some concrete steps going down to a steel door that led into the basement. Once the steel door was closed you could not detect any noise, making it possible to have bands and dancing. The patrons were all let in between eight-thirty and nine at night every night. At nine o'clock the doors were locked, the alcohol started to flow and the band started to play. If you didn't make it by nine then you wouldn't get in and in order to leave you had to go through a one way door that locked behind you and follow the hallway upstairs and through the clothing factory.

Fatini and three of his friends showed up at Sonny's speakeasy before Joe Parisi and his men arrived there. Their car was parked next to the building and there was one guy at the car. Joe Parisi's cars pulled up and he was surrounded by men with guns before he knew what hit him. Rocco grabbed him and stuck a gun in his face. He looked over at Parisi who made a motion with his hand to take him around the side of the building. Rocco led the man off with the gun still pointed at his head.

There was no way to break into the steel door, it had to be opened from the inside. Parisi and his men stayed just out of sight of the door so that Fatini and his guys would come out on their own and let the door slam behind them. That's exactly what happened except, the first guy coming up the stairs didn't recognize the guy at the car as anyone he knew. He stopped and thought to himself for a second and quickly realized that something was not right.

"Wait a minute," he yelled. "Enzo look out……….."

Immediately there were a dozen guns pointed at him. He reached for his gun and Bambino threw off the overcoat he had draped over his shoulders and pointed a shotgun at him as he walked forward. The man stopped dead and put his hands in the air. Fatini made one last grab for the steel door to keep it from closing but couldn't hold on to it, as Sonny was pulling it closed from the inside.

They had Fatini cold. There was no getting away now. Rocco brought the first guy from around the corner and put him with the others. He frisked all of them and got all of their guns. Then Joe Parisi went down the stairs and knocked on the steel door and Sonny opened it up. He ushered Fatini and his guys inside and Joe Marvici, Rocco, Vinnie and Bambino followed them in.

"You are Fatini?" Joe Parisi asked.

"Yes, I am Enzo Fatini."

Joe Parisi motioned for Fatini to sit down.

"Enzo, why are you trying to take my business?"

"I'm sorry, I didn't know it was your business. I've been pushed this direction by the big bosses in New York."

"Well you're going to be pushed back by us little bosses here in Connecticut." Joe Parisi paused for a minute. "I'll tell you what Enzo. Let's me and you make a deal today."

"What kind of a deal do you want to make?"

Joe Parisi took a map out of his overcoat and put it on the table. He drew an outline with his finger around the area that he controlled right now.

"If you want to sell liquor, you can sell all that you can, as long as you do it outside of this area," pointing to the map again.

Enzo studied the map for a minute. He was already selling his product in the towns west of Bridgeport and it looked like he could move into Danbury, as that was outside Parisi's area.

"I'm only going to talk to you about this once, you understand. If there's a next time you and your friends will end up dead."

"Yea! I understand."

"Okay, so you and your friends you gonna leave now and I don't want to see you around here again. Now get out."

"Are you giving us back our guns?" Fatini asked.

"No, now get out," Joe Parisi said with a cocky attitude. They went out the steel door and walked up the stairs right by the others who were waiting outside. The five got in their car and left. It left an impression on Fatini just how much power Joe Parisi had in this area.

"Sonny, I think we got that problem straightened out. How about a drink?"

Sonny brought a bottle of whiskey to the table and a tray full of glasses. He poured a drink for the five men and himself.

"Salut!" they all repeated as they clicked glasses with a toast.

Joe Parisi knew that sooner or later he was going to have to deal with Johnny Torrio about the 10% commission that he was supposed to pay him for all the liquor from Canada. But Torrio was caught up in business in Chicago that was keeping him really busy. He had brought Capone to Chicago to help him handle business there and had just recently taken over Big Jim Colosimo's operation due to the man being mysteriously assassinated.

Torrio was a friend of Carlo Sinafaldi. Sinafaldi worked in eastern Massachusetts in the Worcester and Boston area and bought all his liquor in Canada too. However he had control over the docks in Boston and was able to get liquor coming in from Nova Scotia. Sinafaldi was in Chicago and he and Torrio were talking one day when Torrio mentioned that he'd never collected anything from Parisi yet and figured that he must owe him ten or fifteen thousand by now. Torrio wanted Sinafaldi to buy the debt from him and collect it himself. He was in the east and it would be easier for him to look after it than Torrio in Chicago. They argued about the price of the debt while having a few drinks and finally settled on five thousand dollars. That five thousand not only bought out the debt but also gave Sinafaldi the right to collect the 10% on everything that Joe Parisi bought from Canada in the future too. They shook hands on it and Sinafaldi returned to Torrio's that night and paid him off in cash.

After getting back to Massachusetts Sinafaldi paid a visit to Joe Parisi in New Haven to talk to him about paying up. He and several thugs from his Worcester operation drove down to New Haven to meet with Joe Parisi.

The first year of prohibition had turned out very good for Parisi. Money had been coming in by the suitcase full and paying the 10% commission on the liquor from Canada was peanuts as far as he was concerned. He met Sinafaldi in the Catenzaro Restaurant in New Haven. While Sinafaldi's thugs waited outside, he and Parisi sat down in the restaurant and talked over a few glasses of wine and and a nice meal of pasta and veal scallopini. Joe Parisi had kept track to the penny how much he owed Torrio over the last three years and some. He had it figured out that he had bought one hundred and sixty thousand dollars worth of wine and whiskey from the contacts that he made at the meeting in Chicago. After they had eaten and talked for a while Parisi summoned Vinnie to the table to deliver the money. Vinnie left out the back door of the Catenzaro and came back about ten minutes later with a briefcase containing sixteen thousand dollars in cash. He put the briefcase on the table in front of Parisi who then clicked the snaps open and opened the case to reveal sixteen stacks of bills. Each one was wrapped with a band of paper with each stack containing a thousand dollars. Joe Parisi counted them out on the table and then put the money back in the briefcase and pushed it across the table to Sinafaldi.

Sinafaldi was impressed. It looked like his five thousand dollar investment was already paying dividends. But what really made an impression on him was the amount of liquor that Joe Parisi bought, because if he was buying it, that means he was selling it too.

Sinafaldi and his thugs left New Haven and went back to Worcester feeling confident that Parisi was going to be on the up and up on the 10% commission. He couldn't help feeling envious of the business that Parisi was doing. On the drive back to Worcester, Sinafaldi was conniving just how he could take over business in the area that Parisi was controlling. The percentage that he was getting on the Canadian sales was small potatoes compared to the overall business. Sinafaldi figured that he must be doing close to a million dollars a year in liquor and even more when you considered the numbers racket too. Parisi's operation in the corridor of western

Massachusetts and Connecticut had to be doing as much if not more than he was doing in Worcester and Boston. Sinifaldi could see that Parisi was well organized and it was not going to be easy to take any business away from him.

The first year of prohibitions everything had gone perfectly according to plan. Joe Marvici was still making a trip once a month to Quebec with cash, to pay for the whiskey they were getting from Waterloo. By 1920 the amount of whiskey coming over the border between Vermont and Quebec was staggering. Smaller distilleries were starting up all over the place in Quebec. There were literally hundreds of trucks crossing the border every night.

Toni and Percy had built up a fleet of twenty trucks that made the trip twice a week. They had heard about some of the other trucks having trouble with hijacking but none of their truck drivers had gotten bothered up to now.

Joe got to spend a lot of time around home in Waterbury. Little Pasquale was walking around and getting into mischief the way babies do, and Joe was enjoying family life. Agatha was pregnant again and they were both excited about having a new baby.

Agatha adopted a family tradition that her mother had carried on at home when she was growing up. The family dinner on Sunday afternoon had been a tradition in the family for a long time. Every Sunday she would make a big meal and invite anyone who was a friend or family who could make it. There were usually at least ten or fifteen people around the table at Joe and Agatha's house every Sunday. Sometimes Columbina and Mary-Angela would come down to Waterbury and help with dinner. Joe Parisi drove from New Haven almost every week as well. A real sense of family developed because of the Sunday dinners, especially with little Pasquale.

Every Sunday was like a ritual where guests descended on Joe and Agatha's house about one o'clock in the afternoon. All the women collected in the kitchen and helped prepare the food. There were always multiple courses. It was not uncommon to have a main course of chicken Cacciatore, another of lasagna, another of roast pork, along with stuffed green peppers, spaghetti with meatballs, with squid on the side. This was all preceded with Tortellini or/and escarole soup, home baked bread, and finished off with three or four different kinds of pies or cakes and finally Spumoni ice cream and coffee. Even the spaghetti was homemade. If you arrived there early the strands of homemade spaghetti would be drying, draped over racks and chairs all over the kitchen.

While this was going on the men stayed out of the way by hanging out in the living room talking and drinking wine. When dinner was nearly ready they moved into the dining room with the big table but just stood around while the women filled the table with the many courses of food they had prepared. When all the food was on the table the men sat down. It was always another five or ten minutes before all the work was done and the women could all sit down.

After Joe said a short blessing everyone dug in. It was quite a feast every week and had the effect of producing a great deal of cohesion. These Sunday family dinners at Joe and Agatha's created a home life that was central to the family.

Because of Joe's family life, Joe Parisi kept his workload small. He was making his sister happy and only giving Joe one trip to Quebec a month and a little help collecting money sometimes. He knew that he could always count on Joe if he really needed him and considered him to be the most loyal and trustworthy of the whole group.

Joe still kept in touch with his mother in Italy and sent her money on a regular basis. He realized at this point he was not going to get his mother out of her home in Samo short of kidnapping her or some other radical move. She kept him informed about what was going on with his sisters and Francesco, who was twenty-four now and still living at home. Joe wrote to his mother about little Pasquale too, and that Agatha was having another baby soon. How he missed his family in Italy and often thought about going back to see them.

Chapter 9

Enzo Fatini was in a barber chair getting a shave in Greenwich, Connecticut, one afternoon. Through the door walked six thugs with guns drawn. Two of Fatini's men were sitting in the barbershop as well. Nobody had a chance to resist.

"What the hell!" Fatini exclaimed as he started to get up and then settled back into the chair. "Not again," he said thinking that he'd let someone get the drop on him again. "You," said a man called Bruno pointing at Fatini, "you're coming with me."

They hauled him out of the barber chair making sure the other two didn't follow, and squeezed him in the back seat of a car, between two of the thugs. Fatini was blindfolded and they drove for hours, before pulling up to the back of a house in Worcester, Massachusetts. They walked him into the house with the blindfold on, only removing it after he was in a room standing in front of Carlo Sinafaldi.

"Enzo Fatini, am I right?" said Sinafaldi.

"Yes, you're right. Who wants to know?"

"I am Carlo Sinafaldi. I am glad to meet you," he said extending his hand. Fatini shook hands with him. Still feeling a little puzzled by what he was doing here he said, "What do you want?"

"I want to know what you know about Joe Parisi."

"You want to know about Joe Parisi?"

"That's what I said. What do you know about him?"

"Why should I tell you about Parisi?" said Fatini.

"Look Enzo, Parisi is doing a lot of business in Connecticut and Massachusetts. I think it could be in your interest to tell me what you know. Maybe he's got to have a little competition. Now I know you got a small operation. Maybe you want to expand." Sinafaldi paused for a minute to light a cigar. He took a puff of his cigar and blew out the smoke and continued. "So come on Enzo, what do you got to tell me?"

"Well, I did have one run in with Parisi."

"Okay, why don't you tell me about it."

"Okay, okay, we had a little trouble with him in Bridgeport. Luciano and his Cosa Nostra muscled me out of New York. I have a very small area in southwest Connecticut where you found me, you know, Greenwich, Stamford and Norwalk. After being chased out of New York I went to Bridgeport to try to do some business there. Unfortunately Parisi and his men got the drop on me and my guys, while we were working that town. I guess they could have killed us but he made it clear that Bridgeport was his town and I better get out of there if I wanted to live.

He showed me on a map where he was doing business and he told me I could sell all the booze I wanted to as long as I did it outside of his areas."

Sinafaldi opened a drawer in his desk and took out a map of New England and opened it up on the desk. "Come here Enzo," he said motioning to him. "You show me where he told you he was doing business."

Enzo looked at the map and drew an oblong line from Bridgeport to Northhampton, Massachusetts including Waterbury, Hartford and Springfield.

Sinafaldi was impressed by the size of the area reaching one hundred twenty miles long and about twenty-five miles wide.

"How is he able to control such a big area?" Sinafaldi asked.

"He's got quite an army of thugs. There was at least fifteen of them when they got the drop on me in Bridgeport."

"What do you know about his supply routes?"

"I don't know anything about where or when he's getting his product. But I got a tip from a friend who works in the rail yards in the city last year. He said that there was a couple of boxcars of booze sitting on the siding in New Haven. Me and my boys went to New Haven and found the boxcars but when we opened them up they were empty. I think we got there too late."

"Where did they come from?" Sinafaldi inquired further.

"I'm not certain but my friend said they came from Chicago."

Sinafaldi paced back and forth for a minute. He was wondering if Torrio knew anything about it or if Torrio was playing both sides. Sinafaldi knew that booze was coming from Quebec as well because of the payoff that he collected from Parisi.

Sinafaldi paced back over to his desk and took a bottle out of the drawer and got a couple of glasses and poured drinks. He gave one to Fatini and took one himself.

"Enzo, I want you to work for me and put a little squeeze on Parisi's operations in Bridgeport. Just enough pressure to make him turn his attention that way. If you need a little help, I can give you some help."

"He's a very powerful man. He told me that me and my boys would end up dead if he caught us doing business in his territory again."

"His territory is getting too big. We have to clip his wings. You join up with me now and I will make it so you get more territory for yourself later. So what do you say?"

Fatini looked at Sinafaldi and paused a few seconds to think. He wasn't sure if he trusted him all that much. Sinafaldi was a much bigger and more powerful hood than Fatini. Maybe he had a chance to wrestle territory away from Parisi. What did Fatini have to lose? He realized that if he didn't go along with Sinafaldi that there was a good chance that Sinafaldi would take over his small operation anyway. It came down to that. Fatini didn't really have much of a choice.

Sinafaldi promised Fatini a couple of shipments of whiskey every week as long as he was trying to sell it in Bridgeport or somewhere in Parisi's territory. They shook hands on the deal to join forces against Parisi. After the meeting was over Sinafaldi's thugs blindfolded him and drove him back to Connecticut.

Sinafaldi's plan was to interrupt business for Joe Parisi by ambushing the trucks bringing booze south from Quebec. The problem was there were so many trucks coming across the border from Quebec that it was hard to figure out which ones belonged to Parisi. If he could stop the supply from Canada then he might be able to make Springfield vulnerable to being taken over due to lack of product. To Sinafaldi, taking Joe Parisi on with just muscle was too dangerous and could end in failure.

Sinafaldi assembled an army of hoods to patrol the northern part of Vermont and New Hampshire, ambushing convoys of booze coming from Quebec. Every time they took a convoy over it took a few days to escort the trucks to Worcester and unload the booze in Sinafaldi's warehouses. This was turning out to be a windfall for Sinafaldi but was creating other enemies in New York State and New Hampshire because he was hijacking trucks that belonged to other people instead of Joe Parisi.

Because of this, some of the convoy drivers were starting to arm themselves quite heavily and the hijackings became intense gun battles and no longer such easy pickings. Because of such intense resistance Sinafaldi began heavily arming his hijackers. In spite of the rumors that were going around about convoys getting hijacked, Toni's trucks carrying Parisi's booze had not yet had any problems.

This had been going on for several months. Sinafaldi's men couldn't seem to find Parisi's convoys, still running twice a week from Quebec to the Fina farm. Sinafaldi was also running into intense resistance from the convoys that they were targeting. Many times the fire power coming from the convoys was too intense and Sinafaldi's thugs were driven off.

After about four months of attacking booze convoys and not being able to get one of Parisi's shipments, Sinafaldi realized that his plan was not working and decided to abandon it. He was making more enemies than he wanted doing it this way. He needed to get someone inside Parisi's operation to be able to pinpoint the right trucks.

The Familia was a tight knit group that was not going to be easy to penetrate. They gathered for Sunday dinners in Waterbury and they were all making a lot of money and living very good. Up to this point there hadn't been any real problems and business was running smoothly.

Back in Worcester, Sinafaldi was sitting alone at his desk. He sent his men outside his office so he could think about what to do to accomplish his purpose of getting Parisi's business. He raised his hand to his chin and closed his eyes and then it hit him. He opened his eyes and said, "blackmail," and then smiled. The logical thing to do was get somebody who was already there, on the inside, and blackmail them into working for him. He picked up the telephone and called Johnny Torrio in Chicago. "Hey Johnny, I want to black-mail somebody. Can you find me a girl, you know, a nice girl, good looking and maybe if she likes dope, that would be good?"

"Yeah! I think I can find someone."

"Oh yeah, if she's got a kid, that's even better. Okay?"

A couple weeks later a young woman named Paula and her six year old daughter, Katherine, got off the train in Boston. Sinafaldi met her at the station and they drove back to Worcester

Paula was a heroin addict who worked for Torrio as a high priced call girl in Chicago in order to support herself, her daughter and her habit. Sinafaldi set her up in an apartment in Springfield and gave her a generous amount of spending money and supply of heroin. An older woman named Marie, who lived in the same build-ing was hired to be the babysitter for Katherine whenever Paula had to go out to work. Paula took care of her appearance and was a pretty nice looking woman. It was important to keep her looks up in her line of work in order to bring in the high priced business.

This job however, was to target one of two men who worked for Joe Parisi. One was Salvatore Mauro and the other John Masolino. Both were bachelors and both could be occasionally found around Springfield's dance clubs or the Catenzaro Restaurant in Springfield. Sinafaldi had men watching both Salvatore and John in order to track their movements so that they could arrange an accidental meeting with Paula.

Finally one day around lunch time, after a tip by one of Sinafaldi's men, Paula went into Benny's Cafeteria on Worthington Street. Standing in line waiting for a sandwich was Salvatore Mauro and she got in line behind him. Pretending that she thought he was someone else she touched his arm and said,"Oh hi."

Salvatore turned toward her and she puts her hand across her mouth leaving the impression that she had made a mistake and then said, "Oh, I'm sorry I thought you were someone else. Forgive me."

"That's quite all right Miss," Salvatore said with a smile.

A few words went back and forth as the line moved along. After paying for his sandwich Salvatore sat at a table and when Paula was finished paying she took a few steps as if she was deciding where to sit, when Salvatore looked up at her.

"Do you mind?" she said motioning towards his table.

"No, not at all," he replied. "Sit down."

"Hi I'm Paula," she said, extending her hand.

"I'm glad to meet you Paula," Salvatore answered and took her hand. "I am Salvatore."

They politely shook hands and Paula let his hand go very slowly and seductively.

"You are a very handsome man Salvatore," she said. "And I'm amazed how much you look like my friend John," she lied to him.

"You are a very beautiful woman," Salvatore replied.

"Why thank you."

They talked over lunch and Paula really turned on the charm, careful to seem a little cautious so as not to give away the motive for her interest in him.

"I'm new in town and I don't know anybody around here." she confessed. "Would you like to show a lady around?"

"I would be quite happy to show you around the city."

"Do you have an automobile?"

"Yes I do. Would you like to go for a drive?"

"Oh that would be wonderful, that is if you don't mind."

They left Benny's Cafeteria and walked about half a block to Salvatore's car and went for a drive. Salvatore drove her around the Springfield area for an hour or so when she suggested that they go to her place for a drink.

Even though Paula was just in her early twenties she was a master of seduction and in short order had Salvatore eating out of her hand. They continued to see each other every day after that for the next several weeks. Paula was able to hide both her daughter and her heroin addiction from him during that time.

Every few days one of Sinafaldi's hoods slipped an envelope under her door with a few more day's supply of heroin in it. After she was convinced that Salvatore was totally taken by her she introduced him to heroin. Sinafaldi was sure to give her the purest heroin that he could, knowing that it would be highly addictive.

It was in Paula's apartment after they had just made love that Paula brought out a flap of dope. She looked over at Salvatore and asked, "have you ever tried this?"

"What is it you have there darling?" he asked her, looking closely as she unfolded the flap.

"It's heroin," she said. "Come have a look."

Salvatore moved over towards her and looked closely at the flap of dope.

"Want to try some?"

Salvatore was just a little suspicious and answered, "after you."

"Alright," she said and then took a bit from the flap and put it in a spoon and mixed it with a small amount of water. Then striking a match she heated it until it started to bubble. She then reached into the drawer beside the bed and got a piece of cotton and a hypodermic needle. After putting the cotton in the spoon she drew up the liquid through the cotton into the needle.

She wrapped a scarf around her arm and pulled it tight. "Do you want to help me?" she asked.

Salvatore held the scarf tight as she worked the point of the needle into a vein in her arm. She drew the needle slightly until some blood appeared in the needle and then she injected the heroin into her arm.

"Let go of the scarf," she said.

Salvatore let it go, allowing the heroin to flow in her veins. Paula let out a slow low moan as she got off on the dope. It was a minute or so before she stabilized and turning to Salvatore, she said, "alright now it's your turn."

She repeated the process and then wrapped the scarf around Salvatore's arm. He was a little nervous about it, having never done this before. She found a vein with the point of the needle and after drawing a small amount of blood into the needle she shot the dope into his arm and then let go of the scarf. The rush to Salvatore was immediate and caused him to lay back on the bed. He could feel the heroin race through his veins to every part of his body. He lost track of where he was and was totally overcome by the drug. Salvatore let out a low moan and then a smile came across his face. The feeling was complete and total pleasure through every inch of his body and it was growing by the second becoming increasingly more intense for a couple of minutes. Salvatore lay back on the bed with his eyes closed.

Paula wasted no time putting the needle and spoon away and then started performing oral sex on him. A feeling of total body orgasm had taken over Salvatore's body made even more intense by Paula and giving him the most intense orgasm that he had ever felt. He climaxed with such intensity that he let out a loud low pitched howl that was so loud that Paula had to cover his mouth with her hand. Afterwards Salvatore just lay there on the bed with a smile on his face. He had lost track of his surroundings for a few minutes, being totally consumed with the high he was feeling.

Salvatore's limbs seemed heavy and his mind was clouded and his thoughts seemed confused as he lay there. The only clear thought he had was about the orgasm he just experienced, and the wonderful feeling that he was feeling now.

Paula laughed quietly as she kissed him all over his body as he lay there seemingly paralyzed.

While he was under the influence of the drug, Paula subtly tried plying him for information about his work. Salvatore was not easy to get information out of, even when high on heroin. Keeping a tight lip about business was something that was deeply entrenched in all of the Familia. Talking about business with a woman was unheard of within the group and Paula wasn't able to get much out of him.

Even when he left to take care of business he wouldn't tell her anything about where he was going and what he was doing. Salvatore was still unaware of Paula's daughter. She brought her daughter home to stay with her only after Salvatore left her apartment, and was careful to make sure she was at the babysitters whenever he was around.

A couple of weeks went by and Paula was still unable to get Salvatore to talk about business but by that time she had managed to get him heavily addicted to heroin. The question of why Paula always seemed to have a supply of heroin crossed Salvatore's mind, but after she shot him up with it, the question faded from his thoughts.

Sinafaldi paid a visit to Paula one afternoon while Salvatore was not there.

"What did you find out?" he asked her.

"Nothing, he's not talking. I tried to get him to talk but he's not telling me anything."

"Is he hooked on the dope yet?"

"Yes, I would say that he is."

"Do you know what chloroform is?" Sinafaldi asked.

"Yes I've heard of it."

Sinafaldi took a small bottle of it out of his pocket, "I want you to wait until he is sleeping and soak a cloth with this and hold it over his nose. It will put him out for a couple of hours and we can take a picture of him with your daughter. Don't worry, we won't harm her, we just to have a nice picture so that Salvatore will tell us what we want to know." He then took a flap of heroin out of his pocket and gave it to her. "After he tells us what we want to know you and your daughter can go back to Chicago."

Sinafaldi gave her a telephone number to call as soon as she managed to put him out with the chloroform.

Salvatore showed up at Paula's apartment every day knowing that he could get a fix there. By this time he was hooked on Paula and on the heroin. She was very affectionate towards him so as not to let on what she was about to do. It was a couple of days after Sinafaldi had given her the bottle of chloroform that she found a chance to use it on Salvatore. It was the in early morning hours when Salvatore returned to her apartment after driving one of Fina's trucks with a load of whiskey to New Haven and returning the truck to the Fina farm.

Paula made a habit of fixing the dope and shooting him up every day as soon as he arrived at her apartment. She shot Salvatore up and then herself. She made sure she gave him a good hit that afternoon. He laid back on the bed with his eyes closed after she administered the fix. Paula was a little nervous about what she was going to do as she prepared a fix for herself. After she shot herself up, her mind cleared so that she was focused on what she had to do.

While Salvatore was lying on the bed with his eyes closed Paula went into the bathroom where she kept the bottle of chloroform. She soaked a washcloth with the liquid and slipped it into her panties. Then she quickly went into the bedroom and climbed onto Salvatore in a sixty-nine position straddling his face with her crotch and pressing herself against him. She was nervous that he would catch on to what was happening and distracted him by performing oral sex on him. Salvatore never knew what hit him and in his enjoyment of the heroin and the sex he breathed enough of the chloroform to knock him out.

When Paula was sure that he was out she phoned the number that Sinafaldi had given her. A voice from the other end said they would be there in ten minutes. Paula gave Salvatore a few more sniffs while he was passed out just to make sure he wouldn't wake up.

A few minutes later there was a knock on the door and Paula opened it. There were two men at the door that she hadn't seen before and one of them had a camera.

"Hello Paula," said one of the men. "Where is he?"

"In the bedroom," she answered pointing in the direction of the bedroom.

"Where is the child?"

"She's downstairs in another apartment."

"Go and get her," one of the men instructed her.

Paula went downstairs and knocked on Marie's door. After a couple of minutes Marie answered the door.

"I'm sorry to bother you at this hour Marie but I came to get Katherine."

"Yes, I knew you were coming. I got a call from Sinafaldi a little while ago." Marie led Paula into the bedroom where Katherine was sleeping. She picked her up and carried her upstairs. Katherine stirred a little but did not wake up.

When she got to her apartment one of the hoods motioned for her to bring Katherine into the bedroom. Salvatore's naked body was on the bed and Paula lay Katherine, who was still asleep, next to him. She carefully took off Katherine's pajamas as she positioned her naked body on the bed.

Paula paused for a couple seconds quite aware that this was her daughter and not wanting to take this thing to far. She looked back at the man with the camera.

"Don't worry my dear, we are not going to hurt the little girl. We just want to get a photograph that will make our friend talk. So come on and help your friend look like he's having a good time." Paula sat next to Salvatore on the bed and started to play with him in an effort to arouse him for the photo. Between the chloroform and the heroin Salvatore was not easily aroused. After a couple of minutes, one of the men positioned Katherine next to Salvatore in a way that looked like he had been having sex with the child. The camera man took six pictures, moving Katherine around slightly between each photo. As soon as they were done they left the apartment and Paula brought Katherine back down to Marie's.

When she got back Salvatore was still passed out. She climbed into bed with him and went to sleep just like nothing had happened.

Salvatore woke up the next morning unaware of what had happened to him the night before. He did feel a little groggy but thought nothing of it. They both did another fix before Salvatore left for the day. He drove to Woronoco to the Fina farm again that afternoon.

Paula called Sinafaldi shortly after Salvatore left the apartment.

"Alright Carlo, it's done, now I want to get out of here," she told him.

"Yes Paula, you done good. I have the photographs right here in front of me. They are very good. I'm going to have a car come and pick you up. Will you be ready to go in an hour?" he asked.

"Yes I can be ready."

"Okay, they will pick you up and take you to Boston, where you can catch the train back to Chicago. I'll see you in Boston and I'll square up with you there."

The car with Sinafaldi's hoods was there right on time and Paula and Katherine were whisked away. They were in Boston by the afternoon where she met Sinafaldi in a downtown hotel. Sinafaldi gave Paula a train ticket to Chicago, along with a large bag of heroin and $500 in cash for her trouble. He also sent one of his men back to Chicago with her just to be sure she got back safely.

Salvatore, on the other hand, was completely unaware of what happened and what was about to happen to him. He finished his run to New Haven and returned to Paula's apartment. The door was locked when he arrived and so he knocked on it. As the door opened two of Sinafaldi's thugs came up behind him and the door opened with two more inside with their guns pointed at Salvatore. One of the men behind him stuck a gun in his back and pushed him inside the apartment. They pushed Salvatore up against the wall and frisked him, relieving him of his gun.

"We have a car downstairs and we are going to walk down to the car and get in and we are going to take a drive. There is somebody who wants to talk to you. I don't want to shoot you, so you just come along with us and no funny business and you won't get hurt. Understand?"

Salvatore nodded a yes and down to the car they went. He was trying to piece the whole thing together in his mind while they began driving west. Why were they in Paula's apartment and what happened to her? The thugs in the car wouldn't answer any questions so Salvatore stopped asking.

They drove west for about an hour and stopped just outside of Ware, Massachusetts. They pulled the car onto a side road and drove up the dirt road for about a half-mile and stopped. Sinafaldi showed up about ten minutes later in another car.

Sinafaldi's thugs got out of the car and motioned for Salvatore to get out.

"Salvatore Mauro," Sinafaldi said. "I am Carlos Sinafaldi. So we finally meet face to face."

"What's this all about?" Salvatore asked.

"It seems that we have a mutual friend."

Oh yeah, who is this mutual friend?

"It is your girlfriend Paula."

"What girlfriend? I don't have a girlfriend."

"Oh yes you do. As a matter of fact you have another friend too. Your other friend is heroin, isn't it?"

Salvatore was surprised at what he was hearing and was trying to think fast, trying to put the events together. The mention of the word heroin caused a sensation in his mind reminding him that he was going to need a fix soon. He was beginning to grasp what was going on. It looked like he'd been set up.

"I want you to look at these photographs," Sinafaldi said and then passed him copies of the photographs they had taken of Salvatore and the little girl on the bed.

Salvatore looked in disbelief. "What the hell!" he said surprisingly. "Where the hell did you get these?" It was unmistakably Salvatore in the photos, with a child that he'd never seen before. Each photo was a different pose with the child in a sexual position with both the child and Salvatore naked. The stigma attached to photos like this was extremely bad. Even looking down the barrel of a gun or a severe beating by Sinafaldi's thugs could not be any worse. These kinds of photos could completely ruin his reputation even with his friends and associates. Salvatore was stunned realizing that he had been double crossed by Paula.

"You take a good picture my friend," Sinafaldi smiled at him. "These photographs can be just between you and me if you want to co-operate."

"What do you want?"

"I want to know about Parisi's booze shipments. When and where they are being shipped and the location of his warehouses. And I want you to tell me."

"And you're going to blackmail me with the photographs?"

"Yes, I am. And if you don't agree to work for me now then maybe you will feel differently after the heroin wears off." Sinafaldi smiled and took a flap of heroin out of his pocket and waved it in front of Salvatore's face. "So do you tell me now and I have the boys take you back to Springfield and you co-operate with me or do we take you someplace and watch you cold turkey off the dope and look death in the eye. Because to me it makes no difference, you're going to come on our side sooner or later and you can save yourself a lot of trouble by doing it now instead of later."

Salvatore knew that he was in big trouble. No matter what he did he was screwed. Even among the underworld there was integrity and honor and sexual photos of someone exploiting children was enough of a reason to be gunned down. But he was equally fearful of co-operating with Sinafaldi as that could get him killed too.

"Fuck you, I'm not going to turn against my friends."

"That's too bad Salvatore, because we are going to have to see how strong you are now." Sinafaldi motioned to his thugs to get him back in the car. They grabbed him and forced him back into the car and followed Sinafaldi's car towards Worcester They drove about fifteen minutes and turning onto a dirt road that led to a farmhouse. Sinafaldi got out and unlocked the front door and motioned for his thugs to bring Salvatore inside. Salvatore was led into a back bedroom and handcuffed to the metal bed frame.

"I'm going to come back tomorrow and see if you're feeling any different by then," Sinafaldi laughed at Salvatore. "Don't worry my friend, when you decide to talk to me I have something for you," he smiled and waved the bag of heroin at him. Salvatore looked at Sinafaldi with a menacing glare as he turned and walked out of the room.

"I will see you tomorrow," he said to one of the thugs he was leaving there to watch Salvatore. Sinafaldi got in his car and drove back to Worcester

Sinafaldi left the four men that had kidnapped Salvatore at the farmhouse with him. They made themselves at home, making some coffee and sitting around the table playing cards while they waited.

Salvatore lay there on the bed his hands handcuffed over his head to the iron bed frame. The heroin was beginning to wear off and he was starting to feel uncomfortable and a little sick to his stomach. Salvatore had been high on heroin every day for almost a month and had managed to keep from feeling sick from withdrawal by always having another fix available. This was the first time that he felt any symptoms of withdrawal. By the next morning Salvatore felt much worse. His guts felt like he had swallowed a bucket of glass and it was making its way through his intestines. By the next afternoon Salvatore was in so much pain that he could not keep from moaning in agony. After two days with no heroin Salvatore was in really bad shape. The pain in his entire body had intensified and he felt like he was going to die.

That afternoon Sinafaldi showed up at the farmhouse to see how Salvatore was doing.

"Are you ready to talk to me yet?" Salvatore looked up at him from his position handcuffed to the bed. There were no blankets on the bed, just a mattress and frame. He looked like he was ready to die, but with a hard look on his face he still shook his head no.

"I have something for you," Sinafaldi said and motioned for his men to help. He took a hypodermic needle out of his coat pocket and passed it to one of his thugs. One of his men held Salvatore's arm while the other stuck the needle in his arm and shot him up. The relief for Salvatore was immediate as the heroin took effect. Sinafaldi had given him a small fix of uncut heroin. It would give him some relief for a little while but eventually he would go back into withdrawal that would be even more brutal than he'd already been experiencing. After a few minutes Sinafaldi had the men take off the handcuffs and bring Salvatore into the other room. He sat down across the table from him.

"Salvatore, why do you want to put yourself through this if you don't have to?"

He slowly looked up at Sinafaldi, "because they are my friends and I honor them."

"Do you think they are going to honor you when they see these photographs?" he said, taking them out of an envelope and putting them on the table and spreading them out so Salvatore could see them. The photographs were bad and could get him killed if Joe Parisi's boys saw them, but double crossing them would certainly get him killed.

"I'm going to visit you tomorrow," said Sinafaldi. "Maybe by then you will feel differently." He motioned to his men to take Salvatore back and handcuff him to the bed. Sinafaldi left for Worcester

Salvatore felt okay for a few hours before the heroin started to wear off and withdrawal symptoms started to set in again. Salvatore's spirit was starting to break down as he started to feel sick. No doubt that Sinafaldi had him over a barrel, he thought as his condition got worse by the minute. The small dose of uncut heroin served to give him relief for a little while but then it caused his body to react even more violently as withdrawal set in again.

A few hours later Salvatore thought that he was going to die. He felt much worse than he had the night before. The small fix of heroin had only served to make the craving more intense causing Salvatore to cry out in pain and twist himself around on the bed. His wrists were starting to bleed from the handcuffs as his body shook uncontrollably. He was making so much noise that Sinafaldi's thugs closed the door, letting him suffer in the dark room overnight. By morning Salvatore felt like he wanted to die to put himself out of his misery. His clothes were soaked with sweat and he could get no relief from the pain that felt like crushed glass going through his veins.

By the time Sinafaldi showed up the next day Salvatore had enough. He would do anything at this point to not have to go through this anymore.

"Salvatore, how are we feeling today," Sinafaldi said as he entered the room. Salvatore looked up at him with glassy eyes that looked like death. He was so weak that he could hardly speak at this point. Again one of his thugs poked a needle in his arm administering another fix. Within a few minutes Salvatore's eyes began to focus and the pain subsided as the rush of the drug flowed through his veins again. He was still in a bit of a daze when they brought him out to the table in the other room again.

"Salvatore, are you ready to co-operate with me or do we let you have another night handcuffed to the bed?"

Salvatore's mind was beginning to clear and looking down at his bleeding wrists he realized that he would probably die if he spent another night handcuffed to the bed. He looked up at Sinafaldi and slowly nodded, indicating he was ready to co-operate.

"Oh good, you are finally coming to your senses," Sinafaldi chuckled. Salvatore just stared back at him. "Now tell me Salvatore, I want to know about Parisi's shipments of booze."

"What do you want to know?" Salvatore said looking up at him.

"I want to know how many shipments he gets every week and what days they come in on."

Looking down at the table Salvatore answered slowly, "The shipments come in twice a week. One on Monday and on on Thursday."

"And where do they cross the border?"

Salvatore hesitated for a minute and then looked down at the table knowing that giving up this information could get him killed. "They cross at Norton, Vermont," he said reluctantly.

Sinafaldi spread a map out on the table. "Here, you show me where."

Salvatore looked at the map in front of him. It took a few seconds to focus on it and for his mind to absorb what he was looking at. He scanned the map and slowly pointed to Norton, in the north-east corner of Vermont.

"Where do the trucks start out from and whose trucks are they?"

Salvatore looked at the map again and this time pointed to Waterbury, Vermont.

Sinafaldi looked closely at where he was pointing to on the map. "Right here?"

Salvatore nodded.

"In Waterbury?"

Salvatore nodded again.

"Whose trucks are they?"

"They belong to the woman who owns the Inn in Waterbury," Salvatore answered.

"How many trucks do they have?"

"Twenty," Salvatore looked weary under the questioning. He knew that he should not be giving Sinafaldi this much information but he didn't think he would live through another night drying out, handcuffed to the bed.

Sinafaldi kept up the questioning until he felt like he had gotten the information he needed to be able to find Parisi's liquor trucks. However Salvatore managed not to disclose any information about the warehouse on the Fina Farm.

"Take him back to Springfield," Sinafaldi said to his thugs, throwing a flap of dope on the table in front of Salvatore and turning to walk out the door and return to Worcester

They drove Salvatore back to Springfield and dropped him off at the Catenzaro Restaurant. The heroin was the only thing that was keeping him upright. He had not eaten for four days and the physical effects of drying out were brutal and lingering. Salvatore stumbled inside the restaurant. John Parisi was at the front desk and saw him coming in.

"Salvatore! What the hell happened to you?"

Salvatore hesitated answering him. It was obvious that something had happened by his appearance, but he surely didn't want to tell John about it right now.

"Where have you been? People have been looking for you."

"John, I just need a ride to my house. Can you give me a ride?" Salvatore asked, wanting to delay having to explain what happened until he could think of an explanation that wasn't going to get him killed.

"Yeah, sure," said John. John still asked questions about what had happened but Salvatore didn't have any answers for him right now. John dropped him off in West Springfield and then went back to the restaurant and called Joe Parisi in New Haven to tell him what had just transpired with Salvatore.

"Hello Joe, John calling."

"Hello, what's going on."

"Salvatore showed up at the restaurant this afternoon."

"Did he tell you where he's been for the last four days?"

"No he didn't. I just got back from giving him a ride home. He did not look very good and he didn't want to tell me anything."

"Where is he now?" Joe Parisi asked.

"I just dropped him off at his house."

"Okay, I'm going to pay him a visit and find out what's going on."

"So we will see you today?"

"Yes, I will see you later." Joe Parisi hung up the phone and then called Joe Marvici.

"Joe, I want you to come with me to Springfield today. I just got a call from my brother. Salvatore showed up at the Catenzaro. I want to find out where he's been for the last four days."

"You coming right away?"

"Yes, I'm leaving right away. I'll come by and pick you up."

Joe Parisi picked Joe up in Waterbury and drove north, stopping in Hartford to talk to Bambino.

"Romano, what are you doing? Are you busy?"

"I'm always busy. Why do you ask?"

"We are going to Springfield. Salvatore has been missing for the last four days. He missed a couple of runs and I want to find out why."

"You want me to go with you?"

"Yes, I want you to come with us. I don't know what's going on but this is the first time anything like this has happened with any of our guys. I want to find out where he's been."

After John dropped him off at his place Salvatore went to bed. He hadn't slept for the last four days and was still sleeping when Joe Parisi, Joe and Bambino knocked on his door later that day. Salvatore woke up slowly, hearing the pounding on the door. He lay there for a couple of minutes feeling too wiped out to even get up out of bed. He finally got up to answer the door. He could hear Joe Parisi yelling on the other side for him to wake up and answer the door.

The door opened and the three men came in. Salvatore was still in a daze and not quite with it yet.

"Salvatore, you are here," said Joe Parisi, sounding almost surprised.

Salvatore was feeling a little unsteady and took a seat at the kitchen table. The other men pulled up a chair at the table as well.

"Salvatore, where have you been? You missed a couple of runs. We were looking for you. You want to tell me where you've been and why you didn't show up for work." Joe Parisi leaned across the table towards him.

Salvatore's mind was clouded and confused. He knew that this would be a good time to try to think clearly before answering. He looked at Joe Parisi and then at Joe and Bambino.

"Well, are you going to talk?" Parisi snapped at him.

"I was with a girl, and we were doing some dope. I guess I got carried away and lost track of the time." Salvatore answered, trying to think of a way to explain himself without letting on what really happened.

"And who is this girl?"

"Her name was Paula, that's all I know."

"And where is she now?"

"I don't know. I think she was just passing through town and she's gone now."

"And she was the reason that nobody seen you for the last four days?"

"Yes she was. Her and the dope." Salvatore took the flap of heroin from his jacket and threw it on the table.

Joe picked up the dope and looked at it. He looked over at Parisi and asked Salvatore, "Are you hooked on this stuff now?"

"Yes, I think I am," Salvatore answered sheepishly.

Joe grabbed Salvatore's arm and brought everyone's attention to his wrists, which were scabbed over from the cuts.

"What's this all about?"

Salvatore looked at Joe and lied, " that was the girl, she liked to handcuff me while we were screwing."

"This does not look very good for you." Parisi said, pausing for a few seconds then turning to Joe and saying, "What do you think we should do with Salvatore?"

"I don't know Joe," he answered. Probably best thing is to get him off the dope. If he's on dope he's no good to us. He's too vulnerable. He becomes our weak spot and we don't want to have any weak spots."

The part about getting off the dope made Salvatore a little nervous.

Joe continued, "There's only two ways to get him off dope. One way is to shoot him right now or, he can kick it, starting now."

He looked over at Salvatore. "So which one is it Salvatore? Do I shoot you right now or do you come with us and and get off the dope?"

"It's really not much of a choice is it? I guess I'm coming with you."

Salvatore took a minute to change his clothes and bring a suitcase with a few things with him and they left in Parisi's car and drove to Connecticut.

"Hey Romano, don't you have a cousin who's a doctor," Joe turned and asked Bambino who was sitting in the back seat with Salvatore.

"Yeah, my cousin Luigi Patzino is a doctor. He lives in Bristol," Romano answered.

"We stop in Hartford and you give him a call, okay. Make sure you tell him that we will make it worth it for him to take Salvatore for a week or so or until he's better and off the dope."

The talk of drying him out was starting to make Salvatore nervous. The shot of heroin that Sinafaldi's boys had given him in the morning was starting to wear off and he was starting to feel the withdrawal symptoms again.

Joe Parisi pulled the car up in front of the Catenzaro Restaurant in Hartford and Romano got out and went inside to make a phone call to his cousin in Bristol.

Romano got his cousin on the phone "Hello Luigi, this is Romano. I got a favor to ask of you."

"Hello Romano, what do you got to ask me?"

"I got a friend he's very sick and he needs to be in the care of a doctor for about a week, maybe more. I want to know if you can take care of him for me."

"What's wrong with him?"

"He's got a problem with dope. He needs to get off the dope."

"Oh man Romano, I'm just a family doctor what I want to get mixed up in that for?"

"He's a friend of mine. It's either he gets off the dope or I got to kill him. Come on I need you to help me. I will make it worth it for you."

"Oh yea, how much?"

"You take him for a week and I will pay you a hundred dollars."

"Okay, when are you coming with him?"

"I'll be there in less than an hour."

"Okay, I'll be waiting. You come around to the back door."

"Okay, I see you soon." Romano went back to the car where they were waiting for him.

"It's all set," Romano said. ""He's going to take him for a week. It's costing us a hundred dollars."

"We are going to leave somebody there to keep an eye on things. Romano he's your cousin so I want you to stay close by and let me know what's going on. You take your car and we will follow you there. And Joe I want you to drive to Bristol every day and check up on things," said Joe Parisi.

They followed Romano to Bristol, which was about halfway between Hartford and Waterbury. Luigi was waiting for them and had a room in the basement of his house ready for Salvatore. Though he was a bit reluctant to get involved with getting people off heroin, but he had looked after addicts before who were trying to kick and the money was good. Besides the fact that it was his cousin asking for a favor.

Salvatore was already going into withdrawal by the time they got there. They took him down to the room in the basement. The bed, bedding and a small table was all that was in the room. This time Salvatore was going to be looked after and would not be hand-cuffed to the bed.

Joe Parisi gave Romano the flap of heroin before leaving telling him, "Just in case he needs it to get through this."

Romano stayed behind to keep tabs on things. Joe and Joe Parisi only stayed long enough to have a few words with the doctor and give him the money before leaving for Waterbury.

On the drive to Waterbury Joe and Parisi talked about the situation.

"What do you think is going on here?" Parisi asked.

"Do you think he's telling us the truth?" Joe asked.

"Well maybe, but missing for four days has got me worried."

"Yea, that seems like it could be a problem but what about the girl?"

"Did you see a girl? I didn't see a girl. Maybe there was a girl and maybe there wasn't. That's why I want you to keep an eye on him too. I got a feeling that there's more going on here than he's telling us."

"Yeah, I see what you mean. Everything has been going pretty good for us, so if suddenly we start having some trouble then we have to look towards Salvatore. Look, up to now nobody has given us any trouble except that little mosquito Fatini. And I don't think he wants to bother us any more."

Joe Parisi looked over at Joe. "Joe, I want you to keep an eye on this situation. Maybe it's nothing and maybe it's not. You look after it. If you think Salvatore is stabbing us in the back and he needs to be,.......... dead or whatever, you take of it, okay?"

"Don't worry about it. I got it," Joe answered.

Joe Parisi dropped Joe off at his house in Waterbury and continued on to New Haven.

There were three children at the house now since Agatha had just given birth to twins a few weeks ago. Columbina had come from West Springfield and was staying with her to help out with the children. Joe walked in the door and little Pasquale came running up. Joe scooped him up in his arms and carried him upstairs to the bedroom where Agatha and Columbina were taking care of the twins, Frank and Ermindo. The two boys were very large babies and Agatha was a small woman. Her womb had been very crowded with two large babies and though Frank developed just fine there were some problems with Ermindo. Ermindo's legs did not develop properly. Because of the crowded space the blood flow to Ermindo's legs was restricted causing his legs to under develop. They were not sure that he would be able to walk as he grew up or thought that at the very least he would walk with a limp.

Joe greeted Agatha with a kiss, and with little Pasquale in one arm, he leaned over and tickled baby Frank as she was breastfeeding him. Columbina was holding Ermindo and he turned his attention to him wanting to be sure and give equal attention to both. Columbina loved helping them take care of the babies and always told Joe, "these twins look like you and they are going to grow up to be big handsome men like you, Joe."

The next morning Joe drove to the doctor's place in Bristol to check up on Salvatore. Romano had stayed at the doctor's house overnight keeping an eye on Salvatore. By this time Salvatore was suffering the withdrawal symptoms quite intensely, much like he was when he was handcuffed to the bed at the farmhouse. The difference was having the doctor there to mopping up the sweat that was pouring out of his body and giving him a lot of water to drink to help flush out the drugs. The doctor also gave him some low level pain killers which did not stop the pain but did make it slightly more bearable.

Joe stayed around for the day, giving Bambino a break and a chance to go to Hartford for the day. Bambino returned later that evening. Joe drove back home to Waterbury and returned the next day and relieved Bambino again.

It wasn't until the third day that Salvatore started to show any improvement. The thing about a drug like heroin that is so intensely addictive, especially in the uncut form that Sinafaldi was supplying, is that as it starts to leave the system it becomes more intense. It is almost like it has a mind of its own, causing it to hang on for dear life when it is finally getting ready to let go. Salvatore was sick in every molecule of his body just before the drug released its hold on him. This was the point at which Salvatore felt like he was going to die. Just when he thought that he couldn't take it any more a warm feeling came over him. Relief started in his toes and produced a warm tingling feeling similar to the way he felt when he first shot up. This feeling spread very slowly up through his legs and then into his groin and abdomen and finally throughout the rest of his body. Salvatore knew that what he was feeling was the heroin finally letting go. The actual process of letting go took not more than half an hour. He still felt totally worn out and beat up but the feeling of letting go left him feeling strangely refreshed.

It was over. With the help of his friends and the doctor he had kicked it. The only danger was the lingering craving that was still present in his mind and could lead him back to using it again. Some say that it takes years to get rid of these cravings but for now he had kicked.

When Joe arrived in Bristol on the fifth day Bambino and Luigi were having coffee with Salvatore in the doctor's dining room. Salvatore still looked in rough shape but he felt like he was ready to go home.

Joe followed Bambino to Hartford and then the three men drove together to Salvatore's house in West Springfield.

"I want somebody to stay with you for a few days Salvatore," Joe told him. "I don't want you to stay alone right now. I'm going to call John Masalino. I want him to keep you company."

Masalino came right over and Joe explained the situation to him in detail. "Don't let Salvatore out of your sight for the next couple of weeks John," Joe told him. "If you see anything suspicious, I want you to let me know right away, understand?"

Masalino kept Salvatore with him for the next couple of weeks and even had him staying at his house. Every day Salvatore looked a little better and he resumed his job driving the trucks twice a week from the warehouse at the Fina Farm to the one in Waterbury. After a couple of weeks John Masolino telephoned Joe in Waterbury to let him know that he thought the situation with Salvatore had gotten back to normal.

"I think that he's okay now. We always trusted him before and I think he's going to be okay," he told Joe on the telephone.

"Okay, you can stop babysitting Salvatore but I want you to keep an eye on him, you know, just in case he wants to go back on the dope. Maybe he was telling us the truth and maybe there was a girl that got him into it, just like he said. You just watch out and let me know if there's anything funny going on."

Chapter 10

Sinafaldi's plans to muscle in on the Familia's business in Springfield were starting to develop. He had sent a car with four of his thugs to Vermont to check out the situation there. They were posing as real estate developers looking to acquire some property in Waterbury. This was a business that Sinafaldi was in before prohibition, having been involved in real estate development in the Boston/Worcester area for years. While they were snooping around in Vermont, Sinafaldi himself was looking for real estate deals in the Springfield area, in order to get a presence established there.

Sinafaldi's men checked into the Inn in Waterbury and met Toni and Percy. The Inn was crowded every day with the many truck drivers who were bootlegging booze over the border. Every night, just after sundown when the trucks left for their midnight run into Quebec, the town and the Inn emptied out. It was startlingly obvious when, besides Percy and Toni, Sinafaldi's men were the only ones in the Inn for the night. Even the street had very few vehicles compared to earlier in the day when the town was packed with cars and trucks. This was still forty to fifty miles from the Canadian border depending on where one crossed over. There were many trucks using Vermont routes to get their booze into places in New England

and New York and further. It was the job of Sinafaldi's men to find Parisi's trucks.

They all made small talk around the Inn that night. Bootlegging was talked about, as it would have been odd not to mention it. Still, neither Toni or Percy said anything about their own involvement, other than mentioning the added business that it brought to the Inn.

In the early morning hours when people at the Inn were still asleep trucks started showing up back in Waterbury. By the time the sun came up in the morning the Inn was full again and the streets were crowded with trucks and cars. Sinafaldi's men could easily figure out that a lot of bootlegging was based out of Waterbury, but it was going to take more digging to be able to pinpoint the Familia's trucks.

While talking to Toni over breakfast, Sinafaldi's men told her that they were going to drive to Burlington check out a couple of real estate deals. They visited the Real estate office in Waterbury before leaving town in order to give their story credibility.

They drove out to Burlington and spent a few hours there before heading back to Waterbury late in the afternoon. They wanted to arrive in Waterbury after dark or about the time the trucks were leaving for the midnight run across the border.

They parked the car in a dark alley about a block away from the Inn. From there they had a view of the row of trucks that were parked behind the Inn. About an hour after dark the first of the trucks started up and started to pull out onto the road. Within five or ten minutes all the trucks had left from the back of the Inn and were on their way. The car with Sinafaldi's men filed right in behind the last truck and followed them. They left Waterbury taking a dirt road north towards Hyde Park and then west to Johnson and then northeast to Newport, continuing east to Norton, and ending up only about five miles from the border. They followed the caravan of trucks north from Norton onto a well traveled dirt road that led to the border.

Sinafaldi's men decided not to cross the border but to wait until the trucks came back and follow them to see if they were going to Springfield.. They parked the car on a side road and laid in wait for the caravan of trucks to return. A few hours later, as they waited in the car, the clouds were lit up from the headlights of the trucks coming towards them. They waited for the trucks to go by and pulled out behind the last truck and followed quite a way behind. It was not hard to figure which way they went with the lights of the trucks lighting up the night sky.

Toni had developed quite the trucking business over the last couple of years. Her trucks were making two trips a week for the Familia but they were also making two trips a week to Manchester, New Hampshire and another two trips a week to Albany, New York. This particular night the trucks were going to Manchester with their cargo. Sinafaldi's men thought that they were following the Familia's trucks until they crossed the Connecticut River at White River Junction and headed east toward Concord and Manchester.

They followed the trucks into Manchester where they all disappeared behind a large metal door into a large brick warehouse in the industrial area. The trucks were quickly unloaded and the door opened again a short time later and the trucks came filing out in single file heading back the way they came.

Sinafaldi's men realized that they followed the wrong trucks and weren't sure if there were other trucks going to Springfield or if these trucks were hauling their load to different places each night. In order not to arouse suspicion they followed the trucks back as far as Montpelier and stopped at the Inn at Montpelier, on Main Street in that city. Many of the inns and hotels that catered to the bootlegging trade were open for business all night, especially in the early morning hours when many of the truck drivers were looking for a room. Sinafaldi's men stayed there and slept during the day and again drove to Waterbury arriving there just after dark to once again, lie in wait for the exodus of trucks.

They didn't wait very long before the procession of trucks pulled out from the Inn and headed north to Canada again. Again Sinafaldi's men followed the trucks to Norton and onto the dirt road to the border. Again they waited for the trucks to come back across the border. This night's shipment was going to Albany and the trucks took a different route coming back across the border, crossing at Richford, Vermont, about forty-five miles west of Norton. Sinafaldi's men waited in the car for the trucks to return until well into the morning hours and, finally realizing that they weren't coming back the same way this time, they left and drove back through Waterbury on their way to Montpelier. As they passed through Waterbury they could see that the caravan of trucks were back there parked behind the Inn.

They did it all over again the following night again, waiting in Waterbury for the procession of trucks to leave and following them again. This time they decided to follow them over the border into Quebec and to Waterloo. They waited by the road not far from the Hebert farm and slipped in behind the line of trucks as they left the plant for the journey south. The convoy of trucks crossed over the border in Norton this night and proceeded south on the same route that they took to Manchester, only this time they passed the Connecticut River, crossing at White River and proceeding south towards Massachusetts. As they crossed into Massachusetts Sinafaldi's men were sure they had the trucks going to Springfield until they turned off of the main road to Springfield in Northhampton and took a back road towards Woronoco. The trucks turned into the drive to the Fina Farm, which was about two hundred yards long, with its buildings hidden by trees between the main road and the farm buildings.

The trucks were quickly unloaded, the men having done this many times before, and were back on the road to Waterbury within the hour. Sinafaldi's men were not sure if this was the Familia's shipment or if there was going to be another run the following night. They followed the trucks back to Vermont and stayed at Montpelier again.

Sinafaldi's men followed the trucks for the next week, discovering a pattern that mixed up the days that the shipments went to each destination. Toni's trucks ran every day hauling booze to the three destinations so that each week the day of the week for delivery changed by one day. The convoys going to Springfield would go on Monday and Thursday one week and Sunday and Wednesday the next and so on.

They also figured that the trucks were hauling to the Fina Farm but were never able to get close enough to see the underground root cellar that it was being stored in. When they figured they had enough information for Sinafaldi to be able to hit the trucks going to Springfield, they went back to Worcester and reported to Sinafaldi what they had found out.

Sinafaldi and a few of his men spread a map out on the table in his office in Worcester and set about making plans to ambush the Familia's booze shipments. His plan was to hit the convoys only on the days they were going to Springfield. If he could cut off the Familia's supply of booze then it would open the Springfield market up to him and maybe be more effective than just fighting it out for the Springfield business. He decided they would hit the trucks in Northern Vermont shortly after they crossed the border so that it would not be too obvious who was doing it.

Sinafaldi decided that they would hit the convoy near the Bluff Mountains along a sixteen mile stretch between Norton and Island Pond. As the trucks were traveling in a convoy of twenty, with an armed driver in each one, it would take quite a few men to be able to take over the trucks and hijack their payload of booze. Sinafaldi decided to send twenty trucks of his own carrying two men armed with machine guns to a truck, to intercept the convoy. The plan was to fake a broken down truck in the middle of the road after half of the convoy went by, thus cutting the number of trucks in half. To the drivers the line of Sinafaldi's trucks look like another convoy heading north to pick up booze from Canada. It was not unusual for them to pass someone else's trucks doing the same thing as they were doing. After the trucks were stopped Sinafaldi's men swarmed the trucks laden with booze and removed the drivers at gunpoint and disarmed them. One of Sinafaldi's men then got in the truck and drove away, leaving the drivers on the road on foot in the middle of the night. On the road ahead the first ten trucks were stopped in the same way and the drivers removed and disarmed. These drivers were on foot on the road as well when the hijackers and the hijacked trucks drove by.

They pulled the trucks off on a dirt road a few miles out of Island Pond and transferred the booze into Sinafaldi's trucks. Abandoning the other trucks they headed south towards the

Massachusetts line crossing over the Connecticut River into New Hampshire at Woodsville. They followed the river south on the New Hampshire side turning southeast through Keene proceeding across the Massachusetts line to Worcester. They unloaded at one of Sinafaldi's warehouses just outside of Worcester. Sinafaldi came down to the warehouse when the trucks arrived to oversee the unloading of the eight hundred cases of booze. The first hijacking was a success and he hoped that it would hit the Familia hard, especially if he continued to hit their trucks and affect their supply to the Springfield area.

The drivers of Toni's trucks walked for a few hours towards Island Pond before coming upon the dirt road where the trucks had been abandoned. There were lots of tracks where the trucks had turned off the road. A few of the men walked down the road for a couple hundred yards following the tracks and found the trucks abandoned and emptied of the load of whiskey. The drivers of the first group of trucks drove back looking for the others who were still walking and picked them up and drove them back to their trucks.

Having no payload they drove back to the Inn in Waterbury arriving there pretty close to the time they normally did after delivering and unloading their load. Toni heard them drive in and come in to the Inn. There was more commotion than usual coming from the drivers which caused Toni to get up and investigate. As she walked into the main room in the Inn one of the drivers spoke to her.

"Toni, we've been robbed."

"What!" she replied surprised. "How and where?"

"We were hit just outside of Norton."

"Who hit us?"

"I don't know. They didn't say. But they got the whole shipment."

"Everything?"

"Yes everything."

"Tell me what happened."

Several of the drivers crowded around to tell her the whole story of how they ambushed the trucks with men with machine guns after splitting them up.

"They only wanted the booze. They left the trucks for us to find only they were empty when we found them."

After getting all the details from the drivers Toni woke Percy and recounted the story to him. Then she made a telephone call to Joe Parisi in Connecticut. Joe was still asleep when the telephone rang. The phone rang quite a few times before he got up to answer it.

"Hello," he said, wondering who would be calling him this early in the morning.

"Hello Joe, this is Toni Spencer."

"Toni," he paused for a few seconds. "What's going on?"

"Joe we've got a problem. Somebody has hijacked our shipment."

"What! Tell me what happened."

"Just as I said, somebody has hijacked last night's shipment."

"They got it all?"

"Yes they got it all." Toni paused. "I think you better come up here. We have to figure out what we're going to do about it."

"Okay, I'll be leaving as soon as I can. I'll see you later today." Joe Parisi hung up and called Joe in Waterbury.

"Hello Joe. We've got a problem. We've got to go to Vermont. I'm leaving right away and I'll come by to pick you up."

"Why, what's the problem?" he asked.

"I'll tell you when I pick you up. I want you to telephone Bambino and tell him to be ready to go when we pass through Hartford. Tell him to bring get hold of George too. And you get hold of Savako. I'll be leaving right away. Make sure all of you are packing some extra hardware."

"I'll be ready," Joe said before hanging up the telephone.

Parisi left New Haven and picked up Joe and Savako in Waterbury and Bambino and George DiMaria in Hartford. They arrived at the Inn in Waterbury, Vermont in the early afternoon.

Toni, Percy and several of the drivers were waiting at the Inn when the five men arrived there. They all went into the study and Percy closed and locked the door behind them.

"Tell me how this happened," Joe Parisi said looking over at Toni.

She pointed at Brett Wilson, one of the drivers in the lead truck. "Brett, tell these gentlemen what happened last night."

"We were just outside of Norton, driving south, when we came upon two trucks in the road. One of them had the hood up. It looked like the one with the hood up was broke down. There were three men looking into the engine. It appeared that one of them was working on it. The trucks were side by side in the road and there was no room to get by. I slowed my truck down and before I was completely stopped the three turned around facing me. All three of them came towards me and had machine guns pointing at me. Before I knew what was going on somebody opened the door on the passenger's side with a gun pointing at me and told me to get out with my hands up. There was nothing I could do without getting shot. I got out and went to the side of the road with the guy following me with a gun at my back."

"What about the other drivers behind you?" Joe Parisi asked.

"They were all out of their trucks too and had a gunman behind them."

"Did you get a look at the guy behind you?"

"No I didn't get a good look at him but they made us walk back past the last truck and I did get a look at a few of the other gunmen."

"Could you recognize them if you seen them again?" Joe Marvici asked.

"I think I might be able to recognize a couple of them." Brett answered. "But all the trucks weren't there. Only about half of our trucks were behind my truck. Somehow they got us separated from the other half of our trucks."

Joe Parisi sat back in his chair and let Joe Marvici ask the questions. "Any of you gentlemen driving in the other trucks?"

"Yes, I was," a man stepped forward.

"What's your name?"

"My name is Bill Murray." "Tell me what happened."

"Well," he started to explain. "There's a few one lane bridges that we have to cross. I stopped at one of the bridges because there was a truck coming across towards me. Before he was even across the bridge I had a man with a gun at the window of my truck. He had the drop on me before I knew what was going on. It's the same as Brett said. He ordered me out of the truck and walked me back past the end of the last truck with the other guys. And then they took off with our trucks."

"Did you recognize any of them?"

"No I didn't." he said. "I don't think they were from around here."

"Why, what makes you think they weren't?" Joe asked.

"It was the license plate on the truck that crossed the bridge towards me. I could see that it was from out of state. I wasn't sure where it was from but I know it wasn't a Vermont plate. Maybe it was New York or Massachusetts. All I know is it wasn't a Vermont plate."

Joe sat back in his chair. It was the only clue they had at this point about who might have been responsible for hijacking this load of booze. There were several drivers in the room and Joe wanted to hear from each one of them, hoping that one of them would be able to give him another clue. Their stories were all the same and didn't shed any new light on the hijacking.

Joe Parisi just listened as Joe questioned the other drivers. After he had questioned them all they sent them out of the room and talked among themselves about what they were going to do to protect their trucks from getting hijacked again.

Joe turned to Toni and asked, "When is our next shipment?"

"Day after tomorrow," she answered. "But our trucks are hauling to Manchester tonight and Albany tomorrow."

"Have you had any trouble with those routes?"

"No not yet, but then we haven't had any trouble with any of our routes until last night."

"Then we should wait and see if there's going to be any problems with those routes. And then day after tomorrow when we run our next trip we send some extra people to protect our trucks," Joe looked over at Joe Parisi and nodded.

Joe Parisi nodded and then said,"Yea that's a good idea but I want to know who was it that hit our trucks. I don't like to be robbed. We got to find who did it. Until we find out, first thing we do is protect the trucks by having more guns along for the trip. Maybe we going to send two men in each truck instead of just one."

Parisi looked over at Joe and gave him a nod. Joe paused for a second and then turned to Bambino, "Bambino, I want you to round up some more men to ride with the drivers."

"Yeah sure Joe, I can do that," Bambino replied.

"The next shipment to Fina's is the day after tomorrow. I want you to get them together for that shipment. Make sure they have guns. We don't want to lose any more booze."

"Yeah sure Joe."

"And listen, we not only have to make sure we don't lose any more booze, we got to catch at least one of these guys, so we can find out who's doing this to us."

"Yeah sure Joe," Bambino said again.

"Maybe we got to have a lead car or maybe a couple that stays a mile or so ahead of the rest. What do you think Joe?" he said looking over at Joe Parisi.

Joe Parisi nodded his approval.

"It's been a while since Percy and I went on one of the runs. Maybe this would be a good time to start going again," Toni piped up looking over at Percy. Percy looked over at Toni. His eyes lit up and he smiled and he nodded his head. He and Toni had things pretty quiet lately with all the runs to Quebec going quite smoothly for a long time until now and they were both up for a little more excitement.

"If you and Percy go in the lead truck," Joe said turning to Toni," then I'll take a car with some of our men and stay a couple of miles ahead. Then if I see anything suspicious like a lot of vehicles on the road going the other way or stopped on the road, then we will check out what they're doing." He turned his attention to Bambino. "Bambino, I want you to follow behind the pack with a car with at least four or five men and make sure that we don't get hit from behind."

"Yeah, sure Joe I can do that too," Bambino raised his hand indicating he understood.

Joe got up and paced around the room looking at each person in the room. "Okay, we meet here day after tomorrow in the afternoon. Everybody has a gun and a backup gun in each truck. We will give them a surprise that they're not expecting if they try to hit us again. And Toni you let us know right away if you have any trouble with your other hauls. And one more thing, we don't know how these people found out when and where our trucks would be, so what goes on in this room stays with the people in this room. The other drivers, they don't have to know nothing more than they are driving the trucks, that's all." Joe paced around the room looking each person in the eyes and lastly at Joe Parisi who nodded his approval. "And Toni, I want you to keep your eye on these drivers when you are doing your other runs. Look for anything that seems suspicious. We don't know right now but one of them could be somebody that we should worry about."

"I'll keep an eye on them Joe," she answered with a nod. As she was saying that she suddenly recalled the four real estate developers that visited the Inn a couple of weeks ago. Toni thought about it for a minute as Joe and the others talked among themselves.

"There was something I should mention to you Joe. A couple of weeks ago a car showed up at the Inn with four men. They stayed here at the Inn. They said they were looking to buy some real estate here in Vermont. I didn't think too much of it at the time. They only stayed one night here and then they went to Burlington."

"Do you know who they were. Did they tell you their names?"

"Well, only one of them signed the register but there were four of them." Toni thought hard to recall something about them. "I could look in the register," She said and went to get it. She came back quickly with the Inn register and flipped through the pages and ran her finger down the column until she came to a signature that she thought was the man who signed for the rooms.

"Yeah here it is," she studied to make out the signature. "It looks like........ Eugene Grazia, though the signature is not real clear."

"Had you ever seen these men before?" Joe asked.

"No, I never seen them before and they never stayed here before."

Percy spoke up, "as I recall one of them went by Billy and another was called Bruno. I don't remember the last ones name but we did spend some time visiting with them."

"Would you remember what they looked like if you seen them again?"

"Yeah, I would remember them if I seen them again," Percy said.

"What do you think Joe?" Joe said to Joe Parisi."

"Hmm," Joe Parisi said, "could be something to it."

"You let us know if these guys come back or if you see them again, okay."

The meeting broke up and the five headed back south to Connecticut. They talked among themselves on the drive back.

"Who do you think might be hitting our trucks Joe?" Parisi asked.

"I don't know right now but I got a feeling that whoever it is they want more than just the one shipment. I guess we gonna find out if I'm right or not. I will bet that they are going to get greedy and do it again, and then we going to catch somebody and find out who's behind it."

They dropped Bambino and George DiMaria off in Hartford and continued to Waterbury. After dropping Joe and Savako off at Joe's house, Joe Parisi drove on to New Haven by himself. Even though he was carrying a gun, he felt a little uneasy that day on the way home. It was the last time Joe Parisi made the drive by himself. The hijacking in Vermont had left him with a feeling that it might not be safe to travel alone any more. From that point on Vinnie rode with Joe Parisi anytime he went anywhere.

Bambino had rounded up an army of men to protect the next shipment. They met at the Fina farm in the morning the second day after their meeting at the Inn. There was a man with a machine gun for each of the twenty trucks and at least three men with machine guns in the car that led and the one that followed the pack. Joe Marvici drove the lead car and Bambino drove the car that followed.

Salvatore Mauro was among the army of men. He said nothing of course but was quite aware of the hijacking and the part that he played in it. Though he normally drove one of the trucks, on this trip he was one of the men riding in the last car with Bambino.

The procession of trucks left the Fina Farm that afternoon and arrived at the Inn at Waterbury just before dark, pulling in behind the Inn and parking. They stopped at the Inn for an hour or so until the sun set and they could travel under the cover of darkness. The trucks followed the lead car driven by Joe and began the run to the Canadian border as usual.

Toni drove the first truck that followed Joe's car full of men. Percy rode with her and carried a shotgun and a machine gun. The rest of the trucks followed closely, careful not to get spread too far apart. Joe took notice of every car or truck that they passed on the road on their way north to Canada this time. The trip north went smoothly as it had many times before, as the convoy crossed the border back into the United States, heavily laden with the cargo of whiskey on the back road just east of Norton.

They were about twenty miles into Vermont when they first encountered vehicles going the other way on the road. The approaching vehicles pulled over to the side of the road to let the convoy go by.

"We are going to stop and find out who this is," Joe said to the others in the lead car. Joe pulled the car up close to two trucks that were stopped on the side of the road appearing to be going right by and then quickly stopped beside them. The doors to Joe's car opened quickly as he stopped and the others jumped out of the car with guns drawn. The men in the trucks were taken by surprise as two men approached each one with machine guns drawn and aimed at the driver and passenger. Joe got out of the car and opened the door of the first truck.

"Get out," he ordered the men in the first truck. They got out with their hands in the air as Joe went to the next one and ordered them out.

Rocco searched the men and took pistols from from hidden holster beneath their coats.

"What are you doing on this road?" Joe said to the four men.

"We are going to Montreal," said one of them.

"Why do you travel in the middle of the night?"

The procession of trucks with Toni and Percy in the lead truck approached the cars stopped on the road. Joe held up his hand, signaling for them to stop. One by one the trucks came to a stop.

Joe walked around to the front of the first truck and read the license plate. They were both Massachusetts license plates.

"Where are you coming from?"

"Boston," said one of the men after Rocco pressed a machine gun into his side.

Joe walked back to his car and motioned for Toni to come. She and Percy got out of their truck and walked to Joe's car.

"I don't like the looks of this," Joe said to Toni. "Come out here and look at these guys. Tell me if you recognize any of them from the Inn."

Toni and Percy went over and looked at the four on the side of the road not saying anything as they studied their faces.

Percy whispered in Toni's ear, "That one on the right, I think he was at the Inn"

Toni motioned for Joe to come over beside the car and talk.

"One of them that looks familiar," she said and then turned to look back at them.

"The one on the right. He looks like one of the men who stayed at the Inn."

Joe looked at the man and turning back to Toni asked, "Are you sure you seen him at the Inn?"

"Yeah Joe I think he was there with the real estate developers. Go and ask him."

Joe turned again towards the men, but as he started to approach them he saw lights from a number of vehicles coming around the corner towards them.

"Get these guys off the road," Joe ordered. "Toni get the drivers to shut the lights off." Toni went back to her truck and sent Percy down the line of trucks ordering them to shut their lights but keep the motor running.

Savako poked one of them with his gun and motioned for them to get off to the side of the road. The four men marched off the road into the brush with their hands in the air.

"Fool around and you're gonna be dead," Savako said as he stopped them in the brush.

The vehicles came closer and started to slow down as they approached. As the vehicles came closer the two trucks on the side of the road became visible in the lights. Joe's car continued to run with it's lights on, blinding the drivers of the approaching cars so that they were not able to see the long line of trucks that were behind.

The gunmen in each of the cars had come up to the front of the line and were scattered across the road with their guns drawn on the approaching vehicles. Bambino, who was driving the last car, realized that something was going on at the front of the line and pulled out beside the line of trucks and drove to the front of the line. He noticed that the trucks all had their lights turned out as he sped down the road beside them. The other men in Bambino's car had their guns at the ready. As he got closer to the front of the line he could see lights from the vehicles that were approaching. He brought the car to a stop beside Joe's car leaving his lights on and blocking the road. Then Bambino and the other four got out and took positions around the car with guns pointing toward the approaching vehicles.

As they approached they slowed down and stopped. There were five trucks and they were quickly surrounded with guns drawn. Their drivers were made to get out of the trucks. The men were then herded down the road to where the others were being held at gunpoint and searched. Each of the men was armed with handguns, and machine guns and shotguns were found in the trucks.

"Who of you is the leader of this bunch?" Joe said to the group of men. A man stepped forward announcing that he was the leader.

Joe motioned for Toni and Percy to come closer and to look at the man to see if they recognized him as having been at the Inn.

Percy spoke up right away. "Yea Joe, he was there. I remember him well."

"He was with the real estate developers?" Joe asked to be sure.

"Yes, he was. I remember his face," said Percy.

Joe turned to Bambino. "Bring him here," he said, and walked over toward his car. Bambino stuck a gun in the man's back and pushed him in the direction of Joe's car with the barrel. The army of guns was kept pointed at the others as Joe interrogated the man.

"What is your name?"

"Eugene Grazia," he answered begrudgingly.

"And who are you working for?"

"Nobody, I work for myself."

Joe wound up and hit him in the face. Grazia staggered backwards and put his hand to his face.

"Now who are you working for and what are you doing on this road tonight?"

Grazia just stared at Joe. He hit him again this time knocking him to the ground.

"Get up. Now are you going to answer my question or do I get my friend here to blow your head off?" Joe nodded and looked at Bambino. Bambino put his shotgun against Grazia's head and cocked it. The sound of the gun cocking brought a look of fear to Grazia's eyes as Bambino smiled at him as if he was going to enjoy blowing his head off.

"Should I kill him?" Bambino said to Joe.

"Yea, kill him," Joe said and started to turn away.

Bambino looked Grazia in the eye and smiled, "goodbye my friend."

"Okay, okay, I will talk to you, just don't shoot me."

Joe turned back towards Grazia and motioned to Bambino to hold off.

"Who are you working for?"

Grazia looked at Bambino who still had his gun trained on him, then, looking at Joe again, he said, "I am working for a boss from Boston. We are picking up booze from Quebec and delivering it to Worcester."

"Who are you delivering it too?" Before Grazia could answer Toni called to Joe. She had brought a couple of the drivers that were hijacked the week before over to Joe. She had them look over the men that were being held at gunpoint and they recognized a couple of them as being involved in the hi-jacking.

"Joe I think this is the gang that got our load last week," she said. "Bernie says he recognizes a few of these guys." Toni motioned to Bernie to come forward.

"You seen these guys before?" Joe said.

"Yeah, these were the guys that got us last time we came through here," Bernie said to Joe looking right at Eugene.

"You're sure about that?"

"Positive," Bernie said in response.

Joe turned back to Eugene, "So you want to steal our booze again."

Eugene did not respond.

"Who's your boss?" Joe said motioning for Bambino to prod him with the gun again.

"Sinafaldi."

"Carlos Sinafaldi?" Joe was surprised that he recognized the name. "He sent you and this gang to rob our booze?"

"Yes," Grazia was saying as little as he had to say, as Bambino kept poking him with his gun.

"And he is responsible for hijacking the shipment last week?"

Eugene didn't answer right away until Bambino jammed the gun in his ribs with some force.

"Yes," he said as he looked at Bambino who was starting to get impatient with the answers coming slowly and reluctantly.

"And you planned to hijack this shipment tonight?" Joe said getting in Eugene's face.

Eugene just stared back at Joe.

Bambino slapped him in the face. "Answer the question," he said as he stuck the gun in his face this time.

"Yes."

"You were going to hijack this load with just these men and these few trucks."

Eugene was reluctant to answer and Bambino was getting very annoyed with the slowness of his answers. This time he hit him across the face with the gun barrel opening a cut across his cheek.

"I want to hear you answering the questions otherwise I'm just going to shoot you. Understand?" Bambino shoved the gun in his face again.

"The other trucks are up ahead."

"How far ahead?" Joe questioned him further.

"A few miles."

"And why are you and these men on the road going this way? Why are you not on the road ahead with the others?"

"They are going to stop your trucks, while we turn around and get behind you."

"And how many trucks are waiting for us ahead?" Bambino wound up as if he was going to crack Eugene in the face again.

He answered quickly when he thought he was going to get cracked with the gun barrel again. "There's twenty trucks altogether."

"And the rest of them are waiting for us up ahead?"

"Yes."

How does Sinafaldi know this is our shipment?"

Eugene didn't respond right away and Bambino jammed the gun in his ribs again.

"Okay, okay," he said to Bambino, then looked at Joe. "He got some information from someone in your organization."

"Who did he get information from?"

"I don't know."

Bambino put the gun against his head.

"I don't know who, I just know that it's somebody inside your organization."

"Bambino, we're going to take this one with us," Joe said referring to Grazia. "Make sure these trucks don't move again."

Bambino shoved Grazia towards his car and opened the door and pushed him inside. He left one of his men to to guard him and then ordered the others to disable the seven trucks on the side of the road while Sinafaldi's men looked on. A barrage of gunfire opened up on the trucks, shooting them full of holes. After a couple of minutes every tire was shot up and all the glass was shattered. Gas was pouring out on the ground and a couple of the trucks had small fires burning under them. The trucks were pretty well destroyed by the time the shooting stopped.

Joe looked on from the driver's seat of his own car and then ordered everyone into their vehicles. They pulled away leaving Sinafaldi's men on the side of the road with no guns and all the trucks disabled.

Grazia was sandwiched into the back seat of Bambino's car as they drove away. Joe, leading the pack, stopped his car a few miles up the road and sent a man back to Bambino's car.

"Bambino, go up and talk to Joe" he said. He then went to Toni in the lead truck and gave her the same message. Bambino got out and went to the driver's window in Joe's car. Tony was there right away too.

"Here is what we are doing," Joe announced to them. "We are going to run into the other trucks ahead looking to ambush us. They don't know that we already took the others out of the picture. Bambino you and your men are going to stick with me. We going to clear the road for our trucks and open up on them. Toni, I want you and Percy to lead the trucks right through and don't stop. We will keep them pinned down. You get our trucks through while we fight it out. When the last truck goes past us we are going to follow right away. We have surprise on our side. They don't know that we know they are there." Joe looked at Toni, "make sure your guys are shooting at them when you passing them."

Toni nodded indicating she understood the plan. "I'll give you a minute to get the word to the other drivers before we go."

Toni and Bambino went back to their cars. Toni told Percy what they were going to do and he went back along the line of trucks giving brief instructions to the others. Toni blinked her lights when

Percy got back to her truck and Joe pulled away with the others following.

They drove for about 20 minutes and after rounding a corner Joe noticed some vehicles with their lights out along the road ahead.

"The fun begins," he said as they approached the trucks waiting for them. He slowed the car down and instructed his men to get their guns ready. Bambino and the men in his car got ready with their guns as well. Grazia was sandwiched in the back seat of the car between the gunmen with his hands bound. He was ordered to get his head down between his legs.

As they approached the trucks the doors opened and men started to get out. Joe could see that they had guns and were attempting to block the road and stop the trucks. It was hard to see the first two vehicles in the approaching line because of the headlights. Sinafaldi's men were taken by surprise when the guys in both Joe's and Bambino's car opened fire.

Sinafaldi's men scattered when the shooting began, running off the road and taking cover behind their trucks. Joe kept the car moving until he was right beside the first trucks. The men in Joe's and Bambino's cars opened the doors and stood on the running board shooting over the roof of the car. Guns blazed out the windows on the left side. Sinafaldi's men were pinned down and taken by surprise. It was difficult to return fire with the amount of fire that was coming their way.

There was still enough room on the road for Toni's truck and the other trucks to pass. She never took her foot off the gas and went speeding by. The right hand side of the truck was dangerously close to the ditch on the right side. Toni could feel the truck lean slightly as she roared past Joe's and Bambino's cars with the other trucks following close behind. The bullets were flying in both directions as they passed. Percy was hanging out the window shooting as they passed the last of Sinafaldi's trucks when a cluster of bullets hit the side of the Toni's truck. Toni was startled as she heard the bullets slam into the truck, and stepped on the gas. There was a blast of steam as a couple of bullets hit the radiator. A fine spray of water came out of the radiator and started to create a mist on the windshield.

Toni floored the gas pedal and the truck roared away from the shooting. She drove at top speed a few miles down the road. Her truck was losing water from the gunshot through the radiator and was starting to heat up.

"Percy, climb back and get a case of whiskey," she yelled.

"Why do you want a case of whiskey?" Percy asked.

"Just get back there and get one," she ordered.

Percy wasn't going to argue and climbed out on the running board while Toni sped along the road. He climbed into the back of the truck and grabbed a case of whiskey as Toni told him to and climbed back to the front of the truck.

"Open the case and give me a bottle," she ordered.

Percy did what she asked, handing her a bottle.

"Take the wheel and keep this truck moving."

She climbed out of the driver's seat on to the running board, keeping one foot on the gas until Percy took over for her. As he slid over into the driver's seat Toni climbed out across the hood of the truck with the bottle of whiskey in her hand. She made her way to the radiator and twisted off the radiator cap and threw it away. There was a lot of steam and the cold wind was blowing in her face as she uncapped the bottle and poured the whiskey into the radiator. When the bottle was empty she tossed it on the side of the road and reached back for another. Percy handed her another bottle and she poured it into the radiator too.

The road was bumpy and Percy kept the truck traveling as fast as it could go. Toni was bouncing up and down, sprawled across the hood and hanging on for dear life as she poured the second bottle into the radiator.

Behind them the sound of the gun battle could be heard over the roar of the motor. The other trucks tried to keep up the pace and stay close to Toni and Percy.

As the last truck sped past Joe's car he stepped on the gas and took off after it. Bambino followed Joe. The guns were still blazing out the windows and over the roof of the two cars. The bullets slammed into Sinafaldi's trucks as they pulled away, smashing glass and tires and disabling many of the trucks. The men did not expect to meet such resistance and remained pinned behind their trucks as Joe's and Bambino's cars sped away, spraying machine gun fire at them until they were well past and down the road.

Toni's truck had taken the worst damage of any of the trucks but that was not going to stop her. She rode sprawled across the hood keeping the radiator full of whiskey until she poured the last bottle in. She then crawled back to the cab of the truck and had Percy go into the back and bring up another case of whiskey while she drove the truck. She then crawled back onto the hood and poured that case into the radiator, as the truck kept moving. Toni repeated this for a couple of hours and managed to get the truck all the way back to the Inn in Waterbury. Joe noticed that the trucks had detoured off their normal route towards the Fina farm and had taken the road towards Waterbury. The trucks were spread out by this time and he was unable to overtake Toni in the lead truck because of the speed that they were traveling.

By the time she got back to the Inn she had poured about five cases of whiskey into the radiator. The drivers of the two or three trucks that were directly behind Toni and Percy could see that something was going on with the lead truck. They could see the bottles and wood from the whiskey crates that Toni was throwing to the side of the road. And sometimes when they got close they could see Toni climbing around on the hood of her truck. Nobody in the other trucks had any idea that Toni had been doing this as her truck was leading the pack and the others were finding it hard to keep up.

Normally the trucks would bypass Waterbury and head straight to the Fina farm but this night Toni and Percy led them right into town and pulled up at the rear of the Inn. Tony had climbed back into the the driver's seat a few miles from the Inn. It was one o'clock in the morning when they finally got there. The other trucks lined up behind Toni, as Joe and Bambino pulled up alongside them wondering how come they detoured to the Inn.

After pulling up to the back of the Inn and shutting the motor down Toni climbed out of the truck. She looked pretty ragged after riding on the hood, keeping the radiator full of whiskey for the last eighty miles. She smelled heavily of whiskey and her face and hair looked quite wind blown.

Joe pulled his car up beside her. She and Percy were standing beside the car.

Toni approached the window on the driver's side.

"What in the hell happened to you?" Joe said as she came up to the side of the car.

She had dirt streaked all over her face and her clothes looked like they hadn't been washed for a week.

"We had a little trouble with the truck," she said. "We took a bullet through the radiator and I had to pour a few cases of whiskey into it to keep us moving."

Joe got out and walked around to the truck. It was still steaming and smelled heavily of whiskey, which was still dripping out of the radiator.

"We should load the rest of the cases in the other trucks and send them to Fina's," Toni said as Joe stood in front of the truck trying to get the picture of what had happened.

"How did you get the whiskey into the radiator?"

"I had to climb out on the hood of the truck and pour it in," she explained.

"While you were moving?" he asked with a smile.

"Of course I was moving. You didn't see us stop the truck did you?"

Joe just looked at her with a smile on his face. He shook his head in disbelief as he understood that she had climbed across the hood of the truck and poured whiskey into the radiator for the last eighty miles.

"Okay boys let's get this load off of here and into the other trucks," he said.

Savako motioned for a couple of the trucks to pull up beside Toni's truck and the men unloaded what was left of Toni's load onto the other trucks.

"Send them to Fina's," Joe ordered Savako to instruct the drivers. "And keep an eye out for trouble."

Savako sent the other trucks off to Fina's and Joe's car and Bambino's car took off for Connecticut. Eugene Grazia was still handcuffed in the back seat of Bambino's car. Salvatore Mauro was one of the men guarding him. The two men knew each other as Grazia was present when they had kidnapped Salvatore and blackmailed him into telling them about the trucks hauling booze. Salvatore's recollection of those events was quite clouded because of the state he was in but he did suspect that Grazia was present and could rat him out.

Salvatore looked at Grazia suspiciously and thought that if he made any attempt at making a run for it he would be the first one to want to shoot him. 'A dead man won't talk' thought Salvatore.

After the trucks pulled away from the Inn, Joe and Bambino pulled out and headed south to Connecticut with their prisoner.

Chapter 11

The Familia had left Sinafaldi's trucks in pretty bad shape on the side of the road. The first seven trucks were all shot up too badly to be able to go anywhere. Four of the other thirteen had too much damage to move again but the other nine trucks were still able move. None of the men had been injured in the gun battle with the exception of a few flesh wounds. They all piled into the remaining trucks, leaving the damaged vehicles on the side of the road, they drove north until they found the rest of the men walking on the road.

They picked up the other men and drove back to Worcester. Sinafaldi was livid when he found out what happened and that the trucks returned without any of the whiskey and only nine of his trucks.

He was called to the warehouse early in the morning after the trucks got there to meet with the drivers.

"They were waiting for us," one of his men told him. They must have been expecting us to hit them again."

"And what was the matter with you? You could not fight back?" he yelled at his men.

"They got the drop on us pretty quick. And they had a couple of cars with guns traveling with them. There wasn't much that we could do."

"They got Grazia too. They took him with them."

Sinafaldi was disgusted at his men for letting themselves be beaten so badly. He called off the hijacking plan for the time being. He thought that there had to be another way to cripple the Familia's business in Springfield.

Sinafaldi met with some of his top men to talk about how they could proceed from here. He had no intention of giving up the idea of taking over the Springfield business. He was a little worried about Grazia though. He was usually pretty tight lipped but Sinafaldi knew that the Familia had ways of making people talk, the same way that he did.

"It is probably not a good idea to try to attack their whiskey trucks again," Sinafaldi said, pacing back and forth as he addressed a few of his top men. "It seems that Parisi will be sending gunmen along to protect them. We can only assume that the guns are going to be there on every trip that he makes to Canada. We have to go to another plan and we know that he is warehousing his booze at the farm in Woronoco. And we know that he's bringing three shipments a week to the farm. What we don't know is how well protected his operation on the farm is." He looked around the room at his men while he pondered the idea of hitting the farm. "How are we going to find out if he has guns at the farm except to hit it and see?" Again Sinafaldi scanned the faces of his men as he thought about his question.

One of his men started to say something and then hesitated.

"You got something to say Benny?" Sinafaldi said.

"Well yea, Boss. They got Eugene. Don't you think we ought to wait until they turn him loose before we try to hit their operation again?"

"That's exactly what they'll expect us to do. That's why we got to hit them again right away."

"But Boss if we do that they might just kill him."

"And what's to say they are not going to kill him anyway?"

"But Boss, he's one of us. Are we going to take that chance. If we hold off they might let him go."

"And what happens if he talks? Then we might have to kill him ourselves and we will lose the advantage that we have right now. Nobody will expect us to hit the farm while Eugene is still being held." Sinafaldi looked across the room with a sinister look on his face. He made it clear that he was willing to sacrifice Grazia in order to cripple the Familia's business in Springfield. None of his men were willing to argue the point with him.

Sinafaldi spread a map out on the table and started to talk about how they were going to pull off the job.

"We are going to need more trucks to be able to handle a lot more booze. This is not just one shipment in that warehouse," Sinafaldi said while pointing at the location of the warehouse on the map. He looked up at one of his men. "Tommy, how many trucks and men can you round up in the next few days?"

"How many do you want?"

"I want enough to carry maybe two thousand cases. If there's that much in that warehouse, then I want to get it all."

"Let me check with my brother down at the docks in Boston. I think he can help us out with some heavy trucks. We're going to need some heavy trucks to be able to carry such a large load of booze."

Sinafaldi looked over at Tommy. "I want those trucks to be here, ready to go, tomorrow morning. Parisi's trucks will be making another run to Quebec tomorrow and I want to hit the warehouse while they are making their run. They will have their guns with the trucks and that's when we hit."

"That's swell Boss, but I don't know if I can get that many trucks together that quickly."

"Did you hear my plan?"

"Yea, I heard your plan," Tommy answered.

"Then you will get the trucks," Sinafaldi growled at him. He turned to the others in the room and said, "I want the Springfield business and I'm going to get it. Parisi and his boys will not be able to hold on to it if we hit them hard right now. And we are going to hit them. I don't want to hear any excuses. Now get out of here all of you, and get your work done. We are leaving from here tomorrow morning and you better be ready."

He went to the door and opened it. The men filed by, passing in front of Sinafaldi on their way out . He stopped one of his men as he was leaving and told him to wait. After everyone was gone Sinafaldi closed the door and sat down at the table.

"Sit down, Dominic. I want to talk to you."

Dominic sat down at the table across from Sinafaldi.

"Dominic, tell me, what do you think, is Eugene going to tell them about Salvatore Mauro? Do you think he will rat him out to Parisi? Or do you think he will be tight lipped about it?"

"That's hard to say. He might depending on how hard they press him."

Sinafaldi paused for a minute and then said, "I want you to get hold of Enzo Fatini in East New York. I want you to get him to leak information to Parisi that it is Mauro who is betraying him. Let him know that I want Parisi to get word that Mauro gave us the information we needed to be able to hit his trucks. If Grazia doesn't tell him I want him to find out. This way it will cause some shit in his organization when we hit his warehouse."

"Okay Boss, I'll get right on it."

"Now get out of here," Sinafaldi ordered and Dominic got up and left.

Bambino followed Joe towards Springfield after leaving the Inn at Waterbury. A few miles after leaving the Inn Joe pulled his car over to the side of the road and got out. Bambino pulled over beside him and got out of the car to talk to Joe.

"Let's let Grazia ride in the trunk the rest of the way," Joe said. "He's already seen enough and I don't want him to see anymore."

He and Bambino went back to Bambino's car and got Grazia out of the back seat. As Grazia looked at Salvatore as he got out of the car. Their eyes met for a second. A rush of fear passed through Salvatore as if Grazia had said something to him with the look. Salvatore recognized him from the ordeal in Worcester but acted like he had never seen him before. He knew that Grazia could talk and if he did it could be the end for him.

Bambino opened the trunk and ordered Grazia to get in. He looked at Bambino as if he didn't want to get in. Joe grabbed him and pushed him forcefully into the trunk. He landed with his head against the floor of the trunk as his hands were handcuffed and he could not use them to soften the fall.

"Have a nice ride my friend," Joe said before closing the trunk.

"Bambino, I want you to follow me to Waterbury. We are going to let the boss talk to this guy and see what he wants to do with him."

They got back into the cars and went directly to Waterbury, Connecticut. They took all of the gunmen with them including Salvatore.

Salvatore was thinking all the way about how he was going to keep Grazia from talking. If he got the chance to be alone with him he would have to kill him, but it was possible that he wouldn't get the chance.

The two cars pulled up in front of Joe Parisi's house in Waterbury later that morning. Joe Parisi answered the door and invited both Joe and Bambino inside.

"How did it go this time?" Parisi asked.

"They tried to hit us again but they didn't succeed. We managed to fight them off and took out quite a few of their trucks.

"Tell me what happened," Joe Parisi ordered and Joe recounted the attempted attack on the trucks. "We brought one of them back with us. Toni recognized him as one of the real estate developers that stayed at the Inn a few weeks ago. His name is Eugene Grazia."

"Did you get any more information out of him?"

"Yea, he admitted that he was working for Sinafaldi and it was Sinafaldi that hit our trucks."

"Sinafaldi, that son of a bitch, I should have known it was him. What else did you find out?"

"We brought Grazia back with us," Joe said with a smile. "He's in the trunk of Bambino's car. You can ask him some questions yourself."

"Good work boys. Maybe we'll take him to the docks tonight and see if he wants to tell us some more about Sinafaldi."

"One more thing Joe," Joe looked at Parisi very seriously. "He told us that Sinafaldi has got someone on the inside who gave him information."

"What do you mean on the inside? One of our boys?"

"Yes, one of our boys. That's how he found out about our trucks. That's how he knew when we were moving booze."

"Did he say who it was?"

"No not yet but I think he might tell us if we ask him again. You know, persuasively."

"Bring the car around back and bring him inside," Joe Parisi ordered. "Bring him in the basement door and we'll see if he wants to tell us who it is."

"Okay," said Joe, nodding to Bambino to bring him around. Bambino went out to the car as Joe and Parisi went down to the basement and opened the door from the inside. The four men stayed with Joe's car in front of Parisi's house while Bambino drove around to the back alley and parked in front of the cellar door. Salvatore was with Bambino's car and realized that they were going to interrogate Grazia further when they opened the trunk and got him out. The cellar door opened from the inside and Bambino dragged Grazia down the stairs into the basement.

"Over here," Joe Parisi said, motioning for them to bring him over to the coal bin. Grazia's hands were still handcuffed behind his back and he looked the worse for wear after being beat up before he was put into the trunk and being in there during the trip from Vermont. Grazia did not know where he had been taken but he knew of Joe Parisi and knew it was him he was facing now.

Bambino uncuffed one hand and stretched his hands over his head cuffing him to the cross members in the floor joisting. Eugene was stretched out, standing on a small amount of coal, just enough to prevent him hanging from the cross members. The handcuffs were cutting into his wrists and causing them to bleed slightly.

"My friends tell me that you are Eugene Grazia," said Joe Parisi.

"That's right," Grazia answered.

"And you work for Sinafaldi."

"That's right."

"You and a mob of Sinafaldi's men hijacked one of my booze shipments last week."

Grazia nodded his head this time.

"And you were trying to hijack another one when my boys got you."

This time Grazia just stared at Joe Parisi, not saying or doing anything.

"Did you think I was going to let Sinafaldi have my booze without a fight?"

Again Grazia didn't respond, but just looked at Parisi.

"Okay Eugene, you look like you want to be a tough guy and now I'm going to ask you some questions and I want you to give me some answers. Then we are going to see how tough you are."

Grazia just stared back at Parisi, albeit with a look of fear was in his eyes.

"My friends tell me that you said that Sinafaldi had information from inside our organization. Is that true?"

"Yes that is true."

"And who is that information coming from?"

"I don't know who, I just know that the information came from inside."

"You don't know or you don't want to to tell me?"

"I don't know."

Joe Parisi wound up and punched Grazia, landing a hard punch to the ribs. Parisi was a big man with a powerful punch and hit him in the ribs with such force that he broke one of his ribs with the punch.

Grazia moaned in pain from the punch.

"Now, I want to ask you again, who is it that Sinafaldi is getting information from."

Grazia looked at Parisi and shook his head indicating that he didn't know. Parisi proceeded to punch him in the mouth.

Grazia's mouth was filling with blood from the punch. He looked at Parisi and spit blood at him. Joe Parisi hit him again to the ribs, this time on the other side. Grazia winched in pain trying not to cry out. More blood filled his mouth.

Joe Parisi turned to Bambino. "Romano, take the shovel and move some of that coal out from under his feet."

Bambino shoveled coal until Grazia was hanging by his hands with his feet dangling in the air. The handcuffs cut into his wrists further and blood dripped from his mouth. Parisi administered a hard punch to his crotch and Grazia cried out in pain. Joe Parisi hit him again to the crotch. He cried out again and Parisi hit him again.

"Now, are you going to tell me who Sinafaldi is getting information from?"

Grazia shook his head and murmured a low pitched "no."

"You know if you don't tell me you're going to end up dead, you know that, don't you?"

Grazia opened his eyes and looked at Parisi. It was difficult to talk but he said in a low voice, "Go ahead kill me, because if I tell you who it is and you don't kill me then Sinafaldi will. So I'm telling you nothing."

"Okay my friend, if you don't want to talk to me now then maybe we'll see if you want to talk to me after you hang here for a while. And if not then we are going to have to kill you," Joe Parisi said calmly, as a matter of fact.

Joe Parisi turned to Bambino, "Romano, put a man down here to keep an eye on our friend today and we'll take care of him tonight."

"Okay Joe," Bambino answered, and went outside to get George. "George, I want you to keep an eye this guy today. You stay with him and I'll send some food and coffee down for you."

Bambino went upstairs and brought a chair down to the cellar for George. He went back upstairs and sat down with Joe and Joe Parisi. Parisi made some coffee and the three men talked among themselves.

"Do you think he is telling us the truth about someone inside giving information to Sinafaldi?" Joe Parisi asked.

"Yeah, I do. And I think that we have to find out who it is," Joe answered.

Parisi looked over at Bambino, "Who do you think it is?"

"Well let's say that it is true that someone inside has given him some information. What we know so far is that someone has told him about when and where our trucks would be coming in from Quebec. That could be any number of people. Maybe it's somebody close to us or maybe it's one of Toni's drivers."

"What do you think Joe," Parisi turned to Joe.

"I think he will he will tell us. He just has to endure a lot more misery first. I never met anybody who would rather be dead than talk. He will tell us who it is."

"Let's take him down to the docks tonight and build him some concrete shoes. . Maybe then he will tell us," answered Parisi.

"We got to be careful who we trust now until we find out who's been talking to Sinafaldi. Tomorrow we go back to Quebec and they could try to hit us again. This time if they do they will be more prepared. I don't think that they were prepared for us to have our trucks protected like we did. Maybe we should change the route we take back. Let them try to find us again."

Joe Parisi agreed but added, "Do you think Sinafaldi is just wanting to get our booze or do you think he wants something else. He's already got an operation around Boston and Worcester. Why would he be trying to hijack us?"

"Are you still paying him the 10% that he bought from Torrio?" Joe asked Parisi.

"Yes I was, but now that I know what he's doing here I don't think I'll be giving him anything more."

"If we get in a war with Sinafaldi, we might have to deal with the Chicago mob too," Joe reasoned.

"It's possible, but they are a long way from here and that's the reason that Sinafaldi bought the contract from Torrio anyway."

They talked for a good hour in Parisi's house. The others still waited outside by the cars. One in the back alley and one in front of the house.

George stayed in the basement keeping an eye on Grazia while Parisi, Joe, Bambino and the rest of the men went to the Catenzaro to get some breakfast. The restaurant wasn't open yet as the men went in through the back door and took a seat at the big table towards the kitchen. One of the cooks was already there and Parisi ordered coffee and breakfast for everyone. He then telephoned Vinnie from the restaurant and asked him to come down to join then.

It had been a long night for them, getting close to twenty-four hours since they had left Connecticut the day before to accompany the trucks to Quebec. There was some talk around the table about Sinafaldi and how Grazia had told them that there was someone inside who had given him information. Salvatore tried to act calm when the subject came around to this but it was making him nervous. He was thinking about how to get close enough to Grazia to kill him before he talked.

Though Joe remembered when Salvatore disappeared for several days he somehow discounted him as a suspect. But even so he thought it was a good idea not to leave him alone with Grazia, just in case. Salvatore had been with the Familia right from the beginning and was a trusted member of the group.

After breakfast Bambino took some food to George and then drove back to Hartford with Salvatore and John Masalino and a couple of the others. Joe and Savako went home to Waterbury to catch a few hour's sleep, returning later that afternoon to Joe Parisi's. Bambino showed up at Parisi's shortly after Joe. He brought Salvatore and John back with him.

Joe Parisi and Vinnie visited the docks in New Haven during the day and arranged for a fork lift and a section of the docks to be opened to them that evening. They were selling a lot of booze to the longshoreman at the New Haven docks and had a little muscle and influence there.

After the sun went down and everyone met at Parisi's. They got Grazia down from the ceiling of the coal bin took him down to the docks. The section of the docks they were going to would be deserted. They opened the chain link gate that closed it off and went onto the docks, locking the gate behind them.

They drove the two cars right to the end overlooking the water and into a large warehouse and parked the cars. They dragged Grazia out of the car. Vinnie opened the trunk of his car and took out four bags of cement and a round washtub. He ripped open the bags of cement and emptied them into the washtub. There was a hose nearby and Vinnie started to add water to the cement. Salvatore had a shovel and was mixing up the cement as he added the water. The cement filled the washtub right to the top and spilled over the sides as Salvatore mixed it.

"Bambino get the forklift," Parisi said.

Bambino went around a corner and came back driving a forklift. He drove the forklift close to the washtub full of cement. Vinnie and Salvatore grabbed Grazia and shoved him towards the forklift and the cement as Joe and Joe Parisi looked on. They raised Grazia's hands over his head and Bambino lifted up the forks and ran one of the forks right between Grazia's arms and lifted it up picking him up by the handcuffs. Grazia cried out in pain as he was lifted up. The handcuffs cut into his wrists as Bambino lifted him up and moved him over the tub of cement.

Grazia was lowered until his feet were touching the cement. Slowly Bambino lowered him into the tub until his feet touched the bottom. The cement came half way to his knees and was already getting thick and heavy. Grazia started to kick his feet, trying to pull them out of the cement, but it was too heavy and in his position hanging from the forklift he tired out quickly and soon gave up trying.

Joe and Joe Parisi watched and came closer to Grazia as he stared back at them.

"Eugene do you know what this means?" Parisi said to him.

Grazia was in a lot of pain and anguish hanging there with his feet buried in the tub of cement. He looked at Parisi and said, "fuck you, fuck all of you." He tried spitting at the two men standing in front of him but he could not muster enough strength and the spit ran down the front of his jacket.

"I'll tell what this means," Joe Parisi said to him. "This means that you are going to sleep with the fish. We are going to drop you off the end of the dock with your new shoes. And you are going right to the bottom. Nobody's ever going to find you and the fishes and the crabs will take care of you."

Joe poked the cement with the shovel to see how hard it was getting. It was starting to set up but he wanted to make sure it was hard enough so that when they picked him up again his feet would not pull out of the cement and the sheer weight of it would pull Eugene's arms right out of their sockets.

Joe got close to Grazia and whispered in his ear, "Do you want to tell us who the inside man is, or do we drop you off the dock with your secret?"

Grazia remained stubborn and refused to say anything. Joe Parisi waved his hand at Bambino giving him a sign to lift the forks up a little. Bambino raised the forks until Grazia was stretched out. The weight of the cement was so great that the handcuffs cut into his wrists, causing them to drip blood. There was no way his body could support the weight without ripping his shoulders and wrist right out of their sockets. The pain was excruciating and Eugene cried out again and started to lose consciousness.

Parisi motioned to Bambino to lower him. Grazia sagged as Bambino lowered him. He was barely conscious as Parisi asked him again if he wanted to talk yet. Eugene looked at him and this time was unable to answer.

Parisi waved his hand at Bambino again indicating to pick him up again. This time Bambino lifted him off the ground. The tub of concrete lifted up with him. Grazia cried out in pain as his shoulders dislocated from their sockets and his wrists continued to drip blood.

Joe Parisi turned and walked toward the edge of the dock, and Bambino followed him with Eugene hanging from the forklift. The tub of concrete bumped into the front of the forklift as it dragged across the dock. Eugene was barely conscious and moaning as Bambino approached the edge of the dock. He stopped and let him down enough so that Parisi could look him in the eyes.

"This is going to be your last chance to tell me who it is," Joe Parisi said to him. Grazia slowly shook his head no. Parisi stepped back and waved at Bambino to go ahead. Bambino moved the forklift to the edge of the dock and tipped the forks forward lifting Grazia up enough so that he slid off the forks. As soon as the handcuffs slid off the forks he dropped like a ton of bricks, hitting the water and disappearing instantly. A few bubbles came up to the top of the water and soon stopped. The six men watched the water for a few seconds until the water stopped bubbling and then turned and walked back to the car. Bambino returned to forklift to its parking area, wiping the blood off the forks before he returned to his car.

They left the dock, locking the gate again as they left, and drove back to Joe Parisi's house in New Haven.

Chapter 12

Joe and Savako left for Waterbury to spend the rest of the day at home. Joe had been spending a lot of time away from home with all the happenings going on around the Familia since the hijacking the week before.

Agatha wanted him to spend more time with the family. She was pregnant again with their fourth child. Pasquale was already five years old and the twins Frank and Ermindo were turning three soon.

It was a Sunday and Agatha had prepared a big dinner. There were a lot of people at the house when Joe and Savako arrived. Mary-Angela had come from West Springfield to help Agatha with the dinner preparations. Rosita was also at the house when they arrived.

Serifino Parisi showed up right after Joe and Vinnie. They joined the other men who were sitting in the living room drinking wine while the women were preparing dinner.

Joe Parisi had received a phone call from Enzo Fatini before leaving his house in New Haven that morning. Fatini told Joe Parisi that he knew that someone in the Familia had betrayed them, leaking information to Sinafaldi about the booze runs. Joe Parisi was surprised that he was hearing from Fatini about it. He questioned Fatini about why he knew anything about it.

At first he was skeptical about Fatini knowing anything about it, but after talking to him for a while he thought that he might be telling the truth. Fatini told him about Salvatore Mauro being blackmailed by Sinafaldi with drugs and about the photos with the child.

Suddenly Joe Parisi remembered the incident with Mauro disappearing for a few days a month or two ago and then showing up addicted to heroin. Fatini had some copies of the photos of Mauro with the little girl and offered to deliver them to Parisi. Before leaving for Waterbury, Joe Parisi went to the Catenzaro Restaurant and waited for one of Fatini's men to deliver the envelope containing several of the photos of Mauro and the little girl. He brought the photos with him to Waterbury.

It all made sense to Joe Parisi after seeing the photos. Sinafaldi had blackmailed Salvatore Mauro with heroin and photos of him and the little girl. He remembered questioning Salvatore after the incident, telling him that it was a woman that got him on the heroin.

After coming in and sitting down with a glass of wine Joe Parisi asked Joe to close the doors in the living room so they could talk in private.

He broke the news to Joe, Vinnie, Serafino and Savako as they sat there. He passed around the photos that he had received from Fatini. And after discussing it they all agreed that Salvatore had become a liability and would have to be removed from the Familia. They would be making the next trip to Quebec for booze the next day and Salvatore would be among the men that would be riding in Bambino's car guarding the shipment.

Joe Parisi did not usually go with the trucks but decided that he would go this time and deal with Salvatore himself. It bothered him that Salvatore, who had been with the Familia right from the beginning, would betray him. There was no doubt that Salvatore would have to go. He was present that morning when they dropped Grazia off the dock and if he betrayed Joe Parisi once he was likely to do it again. They could not take the chance.

Parisi ordered the men present to keep this information to themselves and only after Salvatore was dealt with would they tell Bambino and the others about what had happened.

The next morning Joe and Vinnie Parisi left New Haven meeting up with Joe, Serafino, and Savako in Waterbury and drove north to meet Bambino and several gunmen that he had hired to ride with them to Vermont. They stopped in Springfield and picked up John Masalino, George Di Maria and Salvatore Mauro. Joe Parisi wanted Mauro to ride in his car to Vermont with Vinnie, Serafino and himself. Salvatore was expecting to ride with Bambino as usual until Parisi ordered him to get in his car.

The three cars headed north with Bambino's car in the lead on the way to Vermont. Parisi's car followed Bambino, and Joe followed him. Shortly after crossing the border into Vermont, Joe Parisi drove off the main road onto a dirt road. Joe followed him and they drove for about fifteen minutes along the dirt road coming to a bridge across the Saxutte River. Bambino had gone ahead for a few miles, not noticing the other cars were not behind him.

The two cars stopped on the bridge and the men got out of the cars. Salvatore had no idea what was going on and got out with the others.

Parisi went over to Joe and told him to get Salvatore's gun from him.

"Salvatore," Joe said as he approached him with Savako and Serafino beside him. "Give me your gun."

Salvatore was taken by surprise. "Why do you want my gun, Joe?"

"Just let me have your gun."

Salvatore reached into his coat and took out the gun and handed it to Joe. Joe turned and gave the gun to Joe Parisi who handed it to Vinnie. Vinnie gave Parisi the envelope with the photos. He opened the envelope and took the photos out first looking at them and then showing them to Salvatore.

"Salvatore, I received these photos yesterday and I also was told that you were being blackmailed by Sinafaldi." He looked at Salvatore with an intense look on his face. "Is there something you want to tell me about it?"

Salvatore was stunned. He thought when Grazia was dropped off the dock and had not said anything that his secret was safe. He looked at Parisi with a look of fear, knowing that this was the ultimate betrayal and would more than likely result in his death.

Salvatore looked at the photos. His hands were shaking as he looked up at Parisi. "There was a woman and I didn't know that she had a child too. I have never seen this child in the photos. I was unconscious when these photos were taken."

"You have seen these photos before?"

"Yes, Sinafaldi showed then to me."

"And you gave information to him about the liquor shipments?"

Salvatore didn't say anything.

"And he was giving the dope to you?"

Salvatore's voice had the sound of desperation. He knew he was in big trouble. His voice quivered as he answered, "Yes, he was shooting me up while his thugs held me down. Then he handcuffed me to the bed and let me dry out. I thought I was going to die."

"And then you told him about the shipments?"

"Joe, they did this to me many times. I did not think I would live through it."

"And what else did you tell Sinafaldi?"

Salvatore thought about it for a second. He was not really sure what else he had told Sinafaldi. He could not remember much due to his state of mind at the time.

"I'm not sure if I said anything else to him. I was pretty bad shape at the time," Salvatore spoke slowly knowing that the situation was serious.

"Salvatore, I cannot let you get away with this. You have betrayed all of us in the Familia and now we cannot trust you." Joe Parisi turned towards Joe. "What do you think we have to do with Salvatore, Joe?"

Joe looked Salvatore in the eyes as he answered, " I think we do not have a choice. We can't have people around that we cannot trust."

Joe Parisi pulled a gun out from under his coat and shot Salvatore. Salvatore fell to the ground, looking at Parisi with pleading eyes as he fell. Joe Parisi pumped three more shots into him.

"Take his wallet and throw him off the bridge," he ordered as he put his gun away and walked back to the car.

Vinnie rummaged through his pockets and found his wallet. Then Serafino and Vinnie picked up Salvatore's body and dropped him off the bridge into the river. It was a long drop to the river. The current quickly took him away down stream as they watched from the bridge. Vinnie, Joe, Serafino and Savako all watched Salvatore hit the water and each one of them made the sign of the cross as the current swept him away. Joe Parisi got back in his car and the others followed. They turned the cars around and drove out in the direction they came.

When the two cars hit the main road Bambino was waiting there in his car. Joe Parisi turned right on to the main road and kept going north towards the Inn in Waterbury. Joe followed him, neither one of them stopping to tell Bambino what was going on. Bambino pulled out behind the other two cars and followed them wondering what that was all about.

They arrived at the Inn about mid afternoon and it was then that Joe Parisi told Bambino what had transpired on the road with Salvatore. Bambino reacted by looking up and making the sign of the cross also. This had been the first member of the Familia that had been killed. Salvatore had been with them right from the beginning and they all felt a certain loss in losing him this way. Joe regretfully filled Toni and Percy in on what had happened prior to heading off to Quebec that afternoon. He explained that Salvatore had ratted them out to Sinafaldi, that was the reason that Sinafaldi had found the trucks and attacked the liquor shipments.

Salvatore's body was washed down the Saxutte River and into the Connecticut River and washed up on shore about ten miles down river from Brattleboro. His body was found by a couple of young boys who were fishing in the river a few days later. The Brattleboro Police were called out and the body retrieved and brought to the Vermont Coroner's Office. It was apparent to the Police that the man had been shot several times. He had no identification on him so they were not able to identify the body. The Coroner took a photograph and published it in the Brattleboro newspaper a few days later. When no one called to identify the body the photo was published in the paper in Montpelier, Vermont and Springfield, Massachusetts and the following week. The body was finally identified by a neighbor of Salvatore's a few days later. The photo was also brought to the attention of Sinafaldi by one of his men after it was published in the Springfield newspaper.

Joe Parisi led the train of trucks north to Quebec that afternoon. The trip went off without a hitch on the way north and it seemed like everything was going smoothly on the way back until the trucks got within a half hour from Woronoco and the Fina farm. Joe Parisi was still leading the pack when he came across a roadblock. The Northhampton Police and the FBI had the road blocked off with cars. They had men with guns behind the cars and tried to stop the caravan of liquor trucks. Sinafaldi had tipped off the cops that Joe Parisi and the liquor trucks would be coming through with a load of booze early in the morning in an attempt to further disrupt the supply to Springfield.

Parisi stopped his car for a minute when he saw the roadblock up ahead. He studied the situation and then turned to the men in his car, "Get ready boys, we're going through."

He signaled to Joe in the car following to come ahead and drive his car right towards the roadblock. Parisi didn't realize that they were cops at first and thought it was Sinafaldi's men trying to hijack the shipment again. His men opened up on the cops with guns blasting out the windows of his car and the car following. He didn't realize that they were cops until they swung around the side of the roadblock and went by them, noticing some of them were in uniform. By this time it was too late, the shooting had begun.

Parisi stopped his car and Joe stopped behind him and opened up with machine guns on the cops while the trucks laden with booze roared by with Toni in the lead. Bambino's men joined the fight, shooting over the roof of the cars and keeping the cops pinned down while the trucks escaped into the night. When the last truck went by Parisi took off after it with Joe and Bambino following. Men were hanging off the running boards and shooting out the windows until they were well away from the cops. Some of the trucks were leaking booze from bullets that had penetrated the cases. The cops got into the cars that were not damaged from the gunfight and went in pursuit. A few of the Familia's trucks had been damaged as well and did not make it very far from the roadblock. The men in those trucks were standing in the road when the three cars came by and were picked up, leaving the damaged trucks on the side of the road.

Toni led the pack at full speed running as fast as she could to the Fina farm, with the line of trucks and the three cars full of gunmen following.

There were five or six cars full of cops in pursuit. Parisi went around a corner and stopped his car. He motioned for the other cars to stop and set up waiting for the cops to come around the corner. When they did they opened up on the cops again catching them by surprise and disabling a couple more of their cars before taking off again. This time the cops did not follow and they thought that their troubles were over for the night.

Toni's truck was the first to pull into the Fina farm, with the rest following. Something was different this night. Usually Al Fina would be out right away when he heard the first truck come in.

Sinafaldi had descended on the Fina farm hours before with an army of trucks and men. Al Fina came out when he heard the trucks coming down the driveway thinking that it was the regular shipment, arriving early. Sinafaldi and his gunmen in the lead car greeted Al Fina with guns drawn. They forced him to open the warehouse and drove the trucks inside loading them up with booze. Sinafaldi had arrived with over fifty trucks and proceeded to load one right after the other. The warehouse had several thousand cases of booze inside, more than they could haul in one night. The loaded trucks took their cargo to a warehouse in Holyoke. They made several trips back and forth with each truck but were not able to empty the Fina warehouse. Sinafaldi stayed at Fina's for several hours while his trucks came in and left loaded with cases of booze.

After a couple of hours Sinafaldi left following the last truck to Holyoke. He had managed to get more than half of the stockpile at the farm. Al Fina was tied up and left inside the warehouse, which is where they found him when they arrived later that night.

Toni drove her truck up the driveway and to the warehouse. As she approached she noticed that the door to the warehouse was swung wide open. This was unusual as Al normally went in front of the trucks and unlocked it when they arrived.

She cautiously drove her truck inside and shut it off, sensing something was not right as the other trucks pulled in behind them. The warehouse looked unusually empty compared to the last time they had been there. On the floor was debris scattered about from the cases of booze being loaded in a hurry.

Toni and Percy got out of the truck and looked around the warehouse as more of the other trucks were pulling in.

Percy heard noise coming from the rear of the warehouse and went to investigate. He came upon Al Fina bound to a post and gagged. Percy hurried to untie him and remove the gag.

"What the hell happened here Al?" Percy asked.

"Sinafaldi showed up here with a bunch of trucks and they hijacked a lot of the booze. I thought it was you guys coming in early. They caught me by surprise."

Al told Percy what had happened while Percy untied him.

"Toni, come here, over here," Percy yelled as he got the ropes off Al Fina.

Toni and a couple of the other drivers came running around the boxes. Percy had Al untied by the time she got there.

"What the hell," Toni exclaimed as she came up on them.

Percy looked at her. "Sinafaldi again. Looks liked he hit us here."

"Why that son of a bitch," said Toni. " Parisi's going to be pissed."

The trucks were all parked in the warehouse by now and they could hear Joe Parisi's car and the two following cars driving into the warehouse.

"Come on, we better tell the boss what happened." They walked around the boxes of booze back to where the trucks were parked.

Joe Parisi got out of his car and started to look around, realizing that something was wrong. Joe pulled his car up behind Parisi and Bambino was behind him. All of the gunmen were getting out of the cars when Toni, Percy and Al Fina came out from behind the boxes.

"Sinafaldi hit us here Joe," Toni said to Joe Parisi and the others.

"What?" Parisi exclaimed. "Why that son of a bitch. When did this happen?"

"A couple of hours ago." Al Fina answered. "He was here with a bunch of trucks and they got away with a lot of booze."

Joe Parisi was fit to be tied. He paced back and forth in front of Toni, Percy and Al Fina.

"Sinafaldi, are you sure it was him?"

"Yes, I'm sure, he told me his name was Sinafaldi when they got the drop on me," Fina said nervously.

"That son of a bitch," Parisi repeated. "I'm going to have to kill the bastard. If he thinks he's going to keep this shit up I'm going to kill him. First he hijacks our trucks and now this."

Joe Parisi was ripping mad. He paced back and forth while he was thinking about what to do now. After a few minutes he called Joe, Bambino, Vinnie and Toni to one side to talk the situation over with them.

"Okay, we got to figure out what we do now. We can't leave this shipment here. If we do Sinafaldi might be back for the rest. And we got the cops out there, maybe we outran them and maybe they're waiting for us. What do you think Joe, what should we do with this booze?"

Joe thought for a minute before answering, milling over the situation and the possibilities around in his head.

"It would probably not be a good idea to take these trucks back on the road with their load right now. Like you say we could have the cops on us and our troubles might be worse if we did that." Joe paced as he thought about what to do. "I think we might be better off to stay here with the booze for now. If Sinafaldi comes back we will be here to protect our business. Then maybe tomorrow we can start to move the booze from here to Waterbury until we can find another warehouse closer to Springfield."

"What if we were to stock our customers in Springfield and fill the storage room at the Catenzaro. Then we could move the rest of the booze." Joe Parisi suggested.

"That would help us but that still leaves a lot to move all the way to Waterbury," Joe answered.

"What about you Toni? You got any ideas?" Parisi asked. "Bambino, what about you?"

Bambino spoke up before Toni had a chance to speak. "Yea Boss, I think Joe is right, We better stick around and protect our interest for now."

Toni started to speak and then hesitated. Joe Parisi looked at her waiting for her to speak up when she stopped.

"Come on Toni, what do you want to say?"

"Well you know Joe, some of these guys are just drivers. They aren't gunmen. I think we should get the drivers out of here for now. Leave the guns here to protect us from being hit again. Then we bring the trucks back in a day or two and move everything out of here."

"She's got a point Joe," Joe said to Parisi. "That will give us a few days to find another place to store everything. We can leave men here to keep our booze protected while we do."

Joe Parisi turned to Vinnie, "Vinnie get Al Fina over here."

Vinnie walked over to where the other were milling about and yelled for Al Fina, motioning for him to come with him. " The boss wants to talk to you Al." Al followed Vinnie back to where Joe and the rest were talking.

"Al, I want to leave some men here to protect our product for a couple of days. I want you to take care of them, you know, feed them and give them a place to catch up on some sleep. We think it might be too risky to try to move everything right away. We'll come back in a couple of days and move everything to a new location."

"Yeah sure, I can do that." Al answered. "I got another barn that we might be able to use. It's not quite as big but it'll probably hold most of what we got left here."

"Where is it?" Joe spoke up.

"It's about a quarter mile up the road. Do you want to go take a look?"

"Yes, let's go look at it," Joe Parisi said, motioning for the others to came along. They got into his car and drove out of the driveway and drove down the road onto a dirt road. They followed the road around a few corners and came upon the barn. Al got out of the car and unlocked the large front doors. He swung them open and Joe Parisi pulled his car inside. The main part of the barn was completely empty except for a few pieces of farm machinery. Al stored some hay in the upstairs loft, which was still about half full of hay bales.

Joe Parisi, Joe, Bambino, Vinnie and Toni all got out of the car and looked around.

"This would work for right now," Parisi mumbled to himself. "We could unload the trucks here and move the rest of the booze over here pretty fast. The only thing I don't like about this is it's not close to your place Al. Do you think you can keep an eye on it over here?"

Before Al had a chance to answer Joe spoke up. "Joe who's going to know we moved it here unless somebody tells them. We got to move it, we got the trucks here now, so let's move it. It's going to be safer here than where it is now. For all we know Sinafaldi put the cops on to us and who's to say he's not going to send the cops over there after the rest of the booze. We got to move everything and this is our best bet to get it moved. So let's do it."

Joe Parisi looked at Joe and pondered what he was saying for a minute. "Okay let's do it. We can get half the men here with guns to help unload and the other half stay over there and help load the trucks."

They drove back to Al's and sent the trucks with Toni to the barn to get unloaded. It was only a few minutes between the two buildings. The trucks went back and forth moving just over thirty five hundred cases in a couple of hours. Al calculated that Sinafaldi hijacked about forty five hundred cases the night before.

After all the booze had been moved Toni took the trucks back to Vermont. Joe Parisi decided to leave a few guns at the Fina farm just in case Sinafaldi came back again. He was more worried about Sinafaldi forcing Al to tell him where the booze was than he was about him finding it on his own. Al had a bunkhouse behind his house that he used for farm workers that the men could stay in. Serifino and six other men stayed behind at Fina's.

It had been a long night and previous day as the three cars headed south to Connecticut early in the morning.

Business had been booming for the illegal booze that the Familia was bringing into Massachusetts and Connecticut. They had been bringing booze over the border from Quebec for several years and had quite a stockpile, counting the warehouse at Fina's, the one in Waterbury and the storage rooms in the Catenzaro Restaurants in four cites. The sales at the speakeasies and many small retailers that purchased their booze from the Familia had been steadily increasing and the money was pouring in.

The hijacking of the trucks and the raid on the warehouse at Fina's were the first setbacks in the business since the beginning.

Sinafaldi had managed to upset the business to some degree but still had not affected the sales of booze in any of the cities that the Familia was operating in. The Familia's customers were mostly Italians who had been dealing with them from the beginning and remained loyal to them throughout.

It would take more than just one raid and a hijacking to affect the stock in such a way that they would not be able to supply their customers.

Chapter 13

Joe Parisi called a meeting between his top men in the Familia at the Catenzaro Restaurant in Hartford a couple of days after getting back from Vermont. Joe Marvici, Romano Bambino, Vinnie Parisi, Savako Copa, Rocco Sivatico, John Masalino, George DiMaria and Serafino Parisi were all there. They met at Bambino's house in Hartford on the Sunday after Easter in April 1924. The purpose of their meeting this time was to find a way to assassinate Carlos Sinafaldi. Sinafaldi had gone too far in trying to take over the business in Springfield. The hijacking of trucks coming from Quebec was only the beginning. After the failed hijacking and the tipping off of the cops about the trucks near Woronoco and the raid on the warehouse at the Fina farm, Joe Parisi made up his mind he wanted Sinafaldi dead.

Sinafaldi had not stopped there, he continued to try to take over the Springfield business by threating the owners of the underground dance clubs, speakeasies, restaurants and bootleggers operating out of their houses and small shops that sold booze for the Familia around Springfield. Many of the business owners had been approached by Sinafaldi or his men and been threatened with trouble if they did not drop the Familia and use him as their supplier.

Joe Parisi had influence with the cops in the Connecticut towns but lacked the connections to get the cops over on his side in the Springfield area of Massachusetts. Sinafaldi on the other hand paid kickbacks to the cops in the Worcester area and was connected to some of the cops around Springfield and Holyoke, Massachusetts. Springfield was populated heavily with Italians, who because of the power struggle between the two bootleggers, seemed to change sides easily according to who they felt was the most threating to them. The Springfield and West Springfield cops who were loyal to Sinafaldi started to give the bootleggers who were not with Sinafaldi a lot of trouble, raiding their businesses and arresting some operators and their customers, sometimes involving the F.B.I. as well.

The Familia could have just pulled out of Springfield and relinquished it to Sinafaldi and just operated in Connecticut, but there was no guarantee that Sinafaldi would not try to move in on their business in Connecticut after he took over Springfield. It was also a matter of principle. Nobody would want to retreat to Connecticut and just let Sinafaldi have the business without a fight, especially Joe Parisi.

The men all gathered in the dining room at Bambino's. His wife and her sister brought food and wine to the guests at the table and then left the room closing the doors and leaving the men alone.

Joe Parisi stood up and the rest of the men quieted down and turned their attention to him as they waited for him to speak. There was a pause for a few seconds as Parisi collected his thoughts.

"I want Sinafaldi dead," He said in a loud voice pounding his fist on the table. He hit the table with such force that the wine glasses and the silverware and plates rattled on the table. The wine rippled in the glasses and a silence fell across the room.

"I have had enough of Sinafaldi. This is a matter of business and pride and he is trying to destroy both in this organization." Joe Parisi looked around the room with a scowl on his face.

"It is time for us to kill him and get him off of our backs for good."

The other men murmured about it in the silence that followed.

"I want to hear your ideas about how we are going to get him." He looked at each man at the table one by one.

Joe Marvici spoke up first. "We got to find out about his movements, where he goes and where he goes to eat,"

"How do we do that?"

Bambino stood up to speak. "We have to get somebody on the inside. Somebody that Sinafaldi will trust to tell us where we can find him. Somebody that will let us know when he is vulnerable."

"And who can do this for us?" Parisi asked.

"Joe started to talk slowly, "What about Enzo Fatini. Do you think we can get him to work for us? Maybe we have to make him the right offer. It seems like he might be able to get close to Sinafaldi."

"Is Fatini somebody that we can trust? Or can we make him somebody that has to do what we want him to?" Joe Parisi asked.

"Fatini has a very small operation and I'm sure would like it to expand. Maybe we can help him to expand his business if he were to help us get the drop on Sinafaldi," Joe suggested.

Vinnie stood up and everyone turned towards him waiting for him to speak up. "Just remember boys, that Fatini has worked with Sinafaldi before and if we want him to do what we want, we are going to have to have something on him. Something else besides a promise to just give him more business. Don't forget Sinafaldi can offer him more business too."

"Vinnie is right, we got to get something on him. Something to make sure he's going to be on our side," Joe reiterated.

Joe Parisi sat back in his chair and put his hand to his chin while he thought about it. The rest of the men murmured among themselves around the table.

Joe Parisi stood up again and hesitated for a few seconds before speaking. "Okay I want a meeting with Fatini. This is what we are going to do. We are going to offer him business with us in exchange for information about Sinafaldi. If he accepts our offer we are going to blackmail him with it and if he doesn't well we will say that he has and blackmail him anyway. We tell him that either he helps us or we will leak information to Sinafaldi that he has been working for us. I don't think Sinafaldi is going to take a chance with him no matter what his story is, whether he is is working for us or not. Fatini is not stupid. He will know that Sinafaldi might not believe him and there's a good chance he will kill him anyway."

The men talked among themselves about Joe Parisi's idea for a minute.

"Joe, I want you to take Bambino and George with you and pay a visit to Fatini." Joe Parisi continued, " Set up a meeting with him tonight in New Haven. You can tell him that it will be worth his time to meet with us. Then after we meet with Fatini I want to see all of you here tomorrow. We can plan how we are going to get Sinafaldi."

The meeting broke up and Joe, Bambino and George DiMaria drove to New York to meet with Fatini. They met with him in a restaurant in Westchester, just outside of the city. Fatini showed up for the meeting accompanied by three of his hoods. The purpose of the meeting was to get him to meet with Joe Parisi in New Haven. Fatini was suspicious of the three men from the Familia and at first was reluctant to agree to a meeting in New Haven.

"What do you want with me?" he asked Joe.

"You know we are a small operation and these days it's hard to operate when you are small. There is a lot of big boys out there. Big and powerful and they are starting to swallow up small operations like us and you too for that matter. The only way we can hope to survive and be prosperous is to get bigger so we can defend ourselves from the big boys and keep our business secure."

Fatini took a drink and leaned forward in his chair, "Yea, I'm listening, go on."

"We want you to come to New Haven and meet with our boss. We think that you would be a benefit to us and we could help you too. After all it's all about business. The boss, he wants to talk to you about doing business with us. I think it will be worth your time."

"When does he want to talk to me?"

"Tonight, you come to New Haven tonight."

Fatini thought this sounded a little suspicious but he liked the idea of doing business with the Familia. Up to this point he had done very little with them.

"Okay I will come to New Haven and meet with your boss. Where does he want to meet me?"

"You come to the Catenzaro Restaurant at seven o'clock," Joe said. Fatini agreed and each man shook hands with him before getting up and leaving, driving back to New Haven. Fatini showed up at the Catenzaro on time with four of his own hoods. Joe Parisi was waiting for him at a table in the back of the restaurant. Fatini entered the restaurant with two of his men with him, the other two waited outside the door by the car. Joe and Bambino led them to the table where Joe Parisi waited. Joe Parisi stood up and shook hands with Enzo Fatini and invited him to have a seat. Joe and Bambino took a seat at the table along with the two men Fatini brought along.

Fatini introduced the other men to Joe Parisi. "These are my friends Angelo and Constantine." They each shook hands with Joe Parisi before sitting down.

"I think you have already met Joe Marvici and Romano Bambino." They shook hands with each other before taking a seat at the table.

Fatini started the conversation, asking, "Your men said that you wanted to talk to me about business. Do you want to do business together?"

"Yes, I think we can do business together. You know that this business is getting competitive. The big boys want to get bigger and squeeze out small operations like ours. I think we could benefit by working together and becoming stronger. What do you think?

Enzo looked at Joe Parisi a little suspiciously. He was not sure why all of a sudden Parisi wanted to do business with him.

"What's in it for me, Joe?" he asked.

"We both know that you have a small operation and you're being kept out of New York. We don't want to go there either but you can't expand into Connecticut without conflicting with our operation. Now I am offering you an opportunity to join our operation."

"I heard that your having some trouble in Massachusetts. Does this have anything to do with Sinafaldi giving you some trouble there?" Fatini asked.

"It is true that Sinafaldi is giving us trouble. He is trying to expand into Springfield and has hijacked some of our supply. We want you to help us send Sinafaldi back to Worcester and maybe take some of his business away from him. Anywhere that we take business from him we will give it to you. We want to put him on the defensive."

"How do you know that Sinafaldi hasn't made me the same offer about you?"

Maybe he has. But you would be foolish to join with him against us."

"Why is that?"

"If you join with him against us we will come after you first. We will take your territory and then we will kill you. Is that a good enough reason?"

Joe Parisi looked coldly at Fatini. "So what is going to be?"

Fatini sat back in his chair and glanced around the table. He leaned forward and rested on his forearms looking up at Joe Parisi. "So you're telling me that any of the territory that we take from Sinafaldi will be mine to control."

"Yes that's right. But you have to buy your booze from me. You do that and I will leave you alone."

"Alright I will help you." Fatini reached across the table and shook hands with Joe Parisi.

Joe Parisi motioned to Bambino to bring a bottle to the table and pour drinks for everybody. Each man picked up his drink and Joe Parisi toasted, "To a long and prosperous relationship between us, salut." They clinked their glasses together and repeated, "salut" before taking a drink.

Joe Parisi drank a toast and then leaned across the table again and spoke to Fatini. "Enzo, I want you to help me hit Sinafaldi. I want you to set a meeting with him in Springfield. You tell him that you have some information about us that you think that he might want to know."

Fatini leaned back in his chair. "What am I going to tell him about you? If I have a meeting I got to tell him something important."

"That just it Enzo. You don't actually have to meet him. You just set up the meeting so we know where to find him. We will meet Sinafaldi instead of you."

"Wait a minute. Wait a minute. If he thinks he's supposed to meet me and then you show up and try to kill him he's going to know I set him up."

"And you are going to set him up."

"And what if you don't kill him? Then he's going to come after me now, isn't he?"

Joe Parisi turned to Joe and motioned to him. "Joe, give me the money." Joe reached into his coat pocket and pulled out a stack of bills wrapped in a rubber band and handed it to Joe Parisi.

Parisi dropped the stack of bills in front of Fatini.

"Here's ten thousand dollars Enzo. When we get Sinafaldi there is another ten thousand for you and as soon as we start to take over some of his business, we will turn it over to you."

Fatini picked up the stack of money and looked over at Joe Parisi. "You want him pretty bad, I see."

"Yes we want him pretty bad."

Fatini put the money in his pocket. "Okay, I'll do it."

In his office in Worcester Massachusetts, Sinafaldi met with the Chief of Police in Springfield. Charlie Banister had been on the take for several years with hoods in the Springfield area and had met Sinafaldi through Bill Richardson who was the Chief of Police in Worcester. Richardson had been receiving money from Sinafaldi for a few years giving him a safe environment to conduct business in the Worcester area. Banister had been part of the police roadblock that tried to intercept the shipment of the Familia's booze near the Fina farm. Sinafaldi and a couple of his senior men met with Banister and Richardson about a week after the Familia had fought their way through the roadblock.

"This Joe Parisi and his organization are starting to get on my nerves," Sinafaldi addressed the men at the table. "How did they get past your roadblock?"

"They had a lot of guns with them. More than we expected," said Banister.

"Didn't you have guns too?" Sinafaldi asked.

"Yeah we did but we couldn't stop them. They shot our cars up and we had to stop following them."

Sinafaldi leaned over the table and was clearly agitated over the cop's inability to stop Parisi and his shipment of booze. "I told you when he was coming through with his booze and you didn't bring enough men with you to stop him."

Banister defended himself, "I told you he had more guns than we expected. You didn't tell us about that. Your information was that it was a shipment of booze. You didn't mention the army of guns protecting it."

"I'm telling you now, that Parisi and his organization are bad news. I'm missing one of my top men, Eugene Grazia. Nobody has found a body, but he hasn't been seen since Parisi's men grabbed him a couple of weeks ago. And the guy that was found floating down the Connecticut River in Vermont last week, he was Salvatore Mauro. I got some inside information from him about Parisi's booze runs and next thing you know he is dead. What do you think happened there?" Sinafaldi paused. "I'll tell you what happened. Parisi found him out and killed him and threw him in the river."

"Yeah, I seen his picture in the paper," Banister remarked.

"What are you going to do about that?" Sinafaldi asked."

"Are you sure Parisi was behind it?"

"What do you think? Of course I'm sure."

Banister took a drink and paused for a second and then said, "What do you want me to do about Parisi now?"

"I know he is still operating in Springfield. I want you to put the heat on his business there. You already know that he and his brother own the Catenzaro Restaurant. I'm sure they're running a booze operation from there. I think you can start by putting some heat on the restaurant. I know that they are selling booze to a number of speakeasies and bootleggers in Springfield and the towns around Springfield." Sinafaldi leaned across the table and spoke directly at Banister. "I want you do whatever it takes to put him out of business and send him back to Connecticut."

"He's got a lot of friends in Springfield you know."

"You can send his friends back to Connecticut too." Sinafaldi paused. "Look Charlie, I'll tell you straight. I want the Springfield business and Joe Parisi is standing in my way. I tried hijacking his shipments. I hit one of his warehouses. I have even got you and your boys to try to intercept a shipment of booze and so far I have not succeeded in loosening his hold on Springfield. I want you to help me chase him out of Springfield. If we get him out of here I'll make a rich man out of you. Do we understand each other Charlie?"

"Yeah we understand. I'll see what we can do to make his life miserable."

Sinafaldi reached into his pocket and pulled out an envelope full of money and slid it across the table to Banister. He picked it up off the table and took a quick look inside it before putting it in his pocket.

Sinafaldi leaned forward in his chair looking directly at Charlie Banister. "I'm not giving you this money for nothing, Charlie. I want to see Parisi and his Familia group chased out of Springfield. I want to see some results and I want to see it soon," Sinafaldi growled at him.

"Yeah, yeah, don't worry. I'll make sure he's feeling some heat very soon." Banister answered.

"And one more thing Charlie. Salvatore Mauro who's body was found in the Connecticut river. He had betrayed Parisi by giving me information about his booze shipments. Next thing you know he's found dead in the river. It only makes sense that Parisi found him out. I want you to look into it and see if you can tie Parisi to the killing. And I think he is responsible for the disappearance of Eugene Grazia too. Nobody has found his body but he hasn't been seen or heard from for a few weeks now. See if you can find out anything about that too. If you could get Parisi on a murder charge that would help get him out of the picture."

Yeah, yeah, I'll look into it. I'll see if I can connect him to one or both of those killings. We'll get right on it."

"Okay Charlie, get out of here. Stay in touch with me and let me know what you are doing and if you're getting anywhere investigating the murders." Sinafaldi stood up and shook Banister's hand as he was leaving.

The door closed behind Charlie Banister and Sinafaldi turned immediately to Bill Richardson. "Bill I want you to keep an eye on Charlie and make sure that he's doing what he's supposed to. It looks to me like he likes the money a lot and he might even be on the take from Parisi. Keep your eyes and ears open, okay."

"Yeah, Carlos, don't worry about it. I'll keep an eye on him."

Sinafaldi reached in his pocket and took out another envelope full of money tossing it to Richardson.

"Okay Bill you can get out of here too. And you keep in touch with me too."

After Richardson left the meeting Sinafaldi sat back in his chair, thinking about what had transpired. He turned to Benny Gallo who had taken over as Sinafaldi's second man after the disappearance of Eugene Grazia.

"What do you think Benny? Are these cops going to get Joe Parisi and his Familia or should we talk to John Torrio in Chicago about bringing in some muscle and getting rid of Parisi before he has a chance to hit us again."

"I don't know Carlos," answered Benny. "Why don't we wait a couple of weeks and see what the cops can do. We can always call Torrio later."

"Maybe you're right, but I'm telling you I want Springfield and Parisi and nobody is going to stand in my way."

A couple of days later Sinafaldi had a call from Enzo Fatini. Benny Gallo was in the habit of answering the phone for Sinafaldi and screening the calls before passing them on to Sinafaldi.

"It's Enzo Fatini on the phone Boss," Benny said while holding his hand over the receiver.

"What does he want?"

Benny uncovered the phone and asked Fatini, "What it's about?"

"I have some information about Parisi. I think he would like to know. I want to meet with him and discuss it with him."

"Just a minute," Benny covered the receiver again.

"He says it's about Parisi. He wants to meet and talk to you about it."

"Okay, give me the phone."

Benny passed the telephone to Sinafaldi.

"Hello Enzo. What is it you want to talk to me about?"

"I would rather not discuss it on the phone. Can we meet somewhere?"

"Where are you now?"

"I'm in New York."

"Where do you want to meet?"

"Can we meet in Springfield?"

"Okay, when do you want to do that?"

"How about tomorrow?"

"Yeah, okay. I'll meet you in the middle of the North End Bridge tomorrow at three o'clock. You wait in the middle of the bridge and I'll pick you up with a car."

"Okay, I'll be there."

"Are you going to be alone?"

"I want to bring my number two man with me."

"What's his name?"

"Demarco, Tony Demarco."

"Just two of you?

"Yes."

"Okay, I'll see you tomorrow at three."

Fatini hung up the telephone and immediately called Joe Parisi. Vinnie answered the phone. "Hello."

"This is Enzo Fatini calling. Let me talk to Joe Parisi."

Vinnie covered the phone. "Joe, it's Fatini. He wants to talk to you."

"All right," said Joe Parisi and he took the phone from Vinnie.

"Enzo, how are you doing today?"

"I'm doing okay Joe."

"What do you want to tell me?"

"I want to meet with you today. Can I drive up to New Haven today. We have to talk."

"What's this about?"

"It's about our friend in Worcester."

"Okay, I'll meet you at the Catenzaro at four o'clock."

"Okay, I'll see you there."

Fatini and three of his men left New York and drove to New Haven to the Catenzaro Restaurant. They entered the restaurant a little before four o'clock. Vinnie met them inside the front door.

"Hello Enzo. I can only let one of your boys come with you. The others will have to wait out at your car. Don't worry everything is fine, it is just a precaution."

Enzo motioned to Tony Demarco to come with him and for the others to go out and wait at the car. Vinnie led Fatini and Demarco towards the rear of the restaurant to the large round table where Joe Parisi always sat.

"Can I bring you something while you wait? The Boss will be here in a few minutes."

"Yea, you can bring us a drink."

Be right back." Vinnie said and then walked away and returned a couple minutes later with a couple of glasses and a bottle of wine. He poured the two men a drink and then left the table.

Vinnie made a telephone call to Parisi's. Joe Marvici answered the phone.

"Fatini just got here," Vinnie announced.

"Okay we will be right there."

A car pulled up to the rear entrance of the restaurant. Joe Marvici got out first and then Savako and Bambino. They were all brandishing loaded machine guns. Joe Parisi climbed out of the car and went into the back door. He walked through the kitchen and into the dining room to the table where Fatini was waiting. Savako stayed by the back entrance and Bambino watched the table from the kitchen door. The two Joe's approached the table and greeted Enzo and Tony Demarco before sitting down.

"What do you have for me Enzo?" Joe Parisi asked right away.

"I got hold of Sinafaldi and he wants me to meet him in the middle of the North End Bridge tomorrow at three o'clock."

"And what did you tell him?"

"I told him I had some information about you and I wanted to talk in person." "That's good. So he told you to meet him in the middle of the bridge at three?"

"He told me that I can bring Tony and that's all. I don't know if he is going to be in the car or if they are going to pick me up and take me to him."

"Hmm," Joe Parisi pondered the situation. "Either way we will know where he is if we follow you."

"You know Joe, if you start shooting right away, Tony and I could end up dead too. You got to give us a way out. Either you get him before we get in the car or if he's not in the car and you follow us then we got to know when you're going to hit him so we can get out of the way."

"Maybe we will have a few cars going back and forth over the bridge at three o'clock." Joe Parisi said. "He is going to stop and pick you up on the bridge."

"Yeah, that's what he said. We are going to park the car and walk over the bridge. We'll stop in the middle and wait for him to pick us up."

"You got guns Enzo?"

"Hand guns. Yea we got guns."

"What if we hit him right when he stops for you?"

"And what if he's not in the car?"

"You got to let us know whether he is or not.'

"And how am I going to do that?"

"We will have to give you something to drop off the bridge."

"What do you mean?"

"Something bright. Something we can see from the side of the bridge. Maybe just a rock that is painted red. When the car comes up to pick you up if you see Sinafaldi in the car as it approaches you kick the rock off the bridge. When we see it falling towards the water we know that he is in the car and we hit him right there. If the rock doesn't fall off the bridge then we follow the car and see where it goes."

"What if Sinafaldi sees me kick the rock off the bridge? It's going to spook him and maybe he'll shoot both of us."

"Then you have to be careful. You put the rock down when you get there. Put it on the edge of the bridge and turn your back to it and lean against the railing. If he's in the car kick it off with your heel. If he isn't in the car make sure you keep your bodies between the car and the rock so that they won't notice it before driving off."

"Yeah! Who is going to be watching for the rock?"

"We will have someone watching. As soon as you kick the rock someone will see it and signal us and we will be in motion."

"And then what happens? You will have to be fast so that Tony and I can get out of the way. We don't want to get in the car if Sinafaldi is in there and you're going to be shooting at him. If we hesitate too long then he is going to know something is up."

"You know what he looks like?"

"Yes, I know, we have met before."

"Then you got to kick that rock off the bridge as soon as you see he is in the car. If you wait too long then we will not be there quickly. Because as soon as we know that he is in the car we are coming out shooting. We are going to have to kill the men he brings with him too. You're going to have to get out of there and hope that they're too busy shooting at us to care about you."

"Sounds pretty risky."

"Yes Enzo, it's risky. But what isn't risky when you're in this business? And when Sinafaldi is dead, I give you the rest of the money."

"Okay Joe, I'll do it." Fatini reached across the table and shook hands on the deal.

"See you tomorrow Enzo," Joe Parisi and Joe Marvici followed Fatini and Demarco across the restaurant to the front entrance as they left. They then exited through the kitchen door and drove to Parisi's house. They all went inside and sat at the kitchen table. Vinnie poured a glass of wine for each man. Joe Marvici put a piece of paper in front of him and started to draw a rough diagram of the North End Bridge.

"Okay boys, lets make up a plan on how we are going to do this," Joe said as he pushed the drawing towards the center of the table. Each man leaned forward to get a good look.

"Okay, Fatini and Demarco are in the middle of the bridge when Sinafaldi drives up," Joe draws a circle in the middle and an arrow indicating Sinafaldi's car. "We can put a man down under the bridge to watch for the falling rock. As soon a he sees it he has to give us a signal that Sinafaldi is in the car. We got to have a signal but it has got to be a quiet one. We don't want any loud noise that would tip Sinafaldi off."

"Mirrors," said Joe Parisi. He got up and went into the bathroom returning with a small mirror. "Watch,"he said as he pointed the mirror towards the light and reflected an image of light against the opposite wall. "We put a man under the bridge with a mirror. When he sees the rock fall towards the water he can send a signal with the light beam from the mirror to someone on the end of the bridge. That person can send a signal to the cars the same way and then we attack Sinafaldi's car before Enzo can get inside."

Joe drew an X on the paper where the man with the mirror would be standing and estimated where someone would have to stand to see the signal. He showed the diagram to Joe Parisi. "Like this?"

"Yeah, that's right."

"We want to have cars on both sides of the bridge," Joe said looking at Parisi. "We got to be sure that Sinafaldi is not tipped off by seeing any cars hanging around the bridge when he goes by." Drawing on the paper again he points out possible ways Sinafaldi could approach the bridge. "If he comes from West Springfield he will be approaching from Park Avenue." Joe drew an arrow from the direction of West Springfield. "It's probably more likely that he is going to come from Springfield, this way down Main Street." He drew another arrow coming from the other direction. "We could have a couple of cars waiting by the park and watch for him to come by on that side of the bridge."

Joe Parisi studied Joe's drawing for a minute. "What happens if he comes down River Road and turns on to the bridge from there?"

"Yeah, I see what you mean. We will have to be closer to the corner of the park just in case he comes that way."

"We will put a hot dog vendor close to the corner." Joe Parisi pointed at the spot on the map. "Then it won't look out of place to have a couple of cars parked close by. We could do the same thing on the West Springfield side of the bridge too. If he comes from that direction we can pick him up there too."

"Do you think we could get to him before Fatini gets in the car?"

Joe Parisi looked up from the map. "I don't think it matters Joe, as long as we get him before he gets off the bridge."

"What about Fatini and Demarco?"

"What about them? They know what's going on. They are just going to have to keep their heads down when the shooting starts. We're going to have to move fast once we know that Sinafaldi is in the car. Fatini could hesitate getting into the car but if he waits too long it will probably tip Sinafaldi off that something is going to happen."

"Okay I would say that we need at least four cars with four guns in each to pull this off." Joe marked an X on the paper on each side off the bridge and another covering River Road on the Springfield side of the bridge and one more covering Main Street in West Springfield. "Then we need a man under the bridge and a signal man on each side of the bridge to signal the cars when they see Fatini kick the rock off the bridge."

Each man leaned over the table to get a good look at the map. "Joe, you and I will be in this car," Parisi pointed to the X on the map for the car that would be at the hot dog stand on the Springfield side of the bridge. "This is the most likely way that Sinafaldi will come. Bambino you will cover River Road and Vinnie you will be on the West Springfield side. We need one more car to cover Main Street in West Springfield. Vinnie I want you to get in touch with Rocco. Get him to meet us at the Catenzaro in Springfield tomorrow morning. Tell him he needs to arrange to have three more men in his car with him. Don't tell him about the details yet. We will go over it with everyone tomorrow before we go to the bridge and set up the trap for Sinafaldi."

Before the meeting broke up, they made plans with everyone who was going to be involved, to meet at the Catenzaro Restaurant in Springfield in the morning. Joe Marvici left Parisi's house and drove home to Waterbury. He got in touch with Savako and Serafino, telling them to be ready to go in the morning, that they had an important meeting in Springfield the next day. Bambino left for Hartford and notified George DeMaria and a couple of other hoods that he used occasionally when he needed some extra muscle.

"Vinnie when you talk to Rocco and John Masalino, tell them to have three more men each to ride with them and be ready to go in the morning. We will meet at the Catenzaro at eleven o'clock. Tell them to be there. Don't tell them what this is all about just tell them to be there."

"Okay Boss," Vinnie responded and then picked up the phone to make the phone calls.

The next morning, just before eleven o'clock, the Catenzaro Restaurant was still closed when cars started to pull into the parking lot behind the restaurant. The men went into the restaurant through the kitchen door and walked through into the dining room. There was a large table toward the rear of the restaurant that was large enough to sit twelve of the eighteen men. The rest of the men were standing around behind the seated men listening.

Joe Parisi spread out a paper with the map on the table and began to talk about the plan they had worked out.

"I hired two hot dog vendors to show up at the park this morning. It's my second cousin Antonio. He's going to set one up here and another here." He pointed to the two spots on the map, one on each side of the bridge. "Bambino who can we trust to be under the bridge and watch for the falling rock and signal with the mirror?"

"I got my sisters kid here. He's just turned nineteen and he's a pretty sharp kid. I think we can trust him to do the job." Bambino turned towards the kid, "Louie you think you can do this job.

"Yea, sure I can," Louie responded.

"All you got to do is to sit under the bridge and watch for a red rock to fall from the bridge." Bambino told the kid. "When you see it fall you flash Johnny with this mirror who's going to be standing right here waiting for your signal." He pointed to the map.

"Yeah, Uncle, I can do that. I'll do a good job, you watch."

"He'll do alright Joe. He's a good kid. Dependable and he knows how to follow orders."

"Vinnie, you and Bambino will be driving a car on each side of the bridge. If we get the signal that Sinafaldi is in the car, I want you guys to be sure he doesn't get his car off the bridge. You're going to block his way even if you have to smash into him." Joe Parisi paused and took a drink. He looked over at Rocco, "Rocco you're driving the car that's covering Main Street in West Springfield. You and your guys are going to back up Vinnie. I want you to park where you can see Vinnie's car. When you see Vinnie take off you follow him. If somehow Sinafaldi's car gets by him then it's up to you to stop him from getting off the bridge. If you have to smash into him then you do it."

Rocco nodded.

"Bambino, Joe and I will be backing you up. I'm telling you the same thing I told Vinnie. If he is coming your way after he picks up Fatini you make sure he doesn't make it off the bridge."

"Hey Boss, what do we do if he's not in the car. Are we going to follow the car?" Bambino asked.

"Yeah, we will follow them and let them lead us to Sinafaldi. He's not going to be far away," Joe Parisi answered. "We got to stay a ways behind so that they don't get suspicious." Parisi looked at everyone around the table. "Now does everyone know what they are doing and what car they are going to be in?"

Each man answered Parisi as he looked around the table.

"Okay, they are picking up Fatini at three o'clock so that means I want all of you at the bridge at two o'clock. I don't anyone to look obvious. I want you to look like you are doing something else. Bambino you get these kids some fishing poles. They will be hanging out under the bridge fishing. Vinnie you and your boys are parked at the hot dog stand. You make sure that it looks like you're just stopping for a hot dog. Bambino and your boys are doing the same thing. And one more thing, after this meeting is all over, I want everybody to go home. We are not going to meet anywhere. We are going to go home and keep a low profile, keep out of sight. It's going to look like we haven't done anything. Any questions?"

Parisi had made the plan to get Sinafaldi clear to everyone. Nobody had any questions.

"Okay, get out of here and we will see you at the bridge at two o'clock. Remember there is no need for anyone to talk to or have any contact with anyone in one of the other cars. It would make it look suspicious, like we were waiting for somebody. You all have your instructions and remember, there is no reason to talk to each other at the bridge. Got it?"

There was a murmur around the room indicating that everyone understood and the meeting broke up.

That morning at Sinafaldi's home, about the time that the Familia was meeting at the Catenzaro Restaurant, Sinafaldi was getting ready to leave Worcester and drive to Springfield for his meeting with Enzo Fatini. The telephone rang and Benny Gallo answered the phone.

"Hello, this is Benny," he answered.

"Hello, Can I speak to Carlos?"

"And who's this?"

"It's Bill Richardson, Benny. Let me talk to Carlos," he answered.

Benny covered the phone and asked, "Carlos it's Bill Richardson. Do you want to talk to him?"

Yeah, I'll talk to him," Sinafaldi answered and reached for the phone. "Hello Bill, what's going on?"

"Hello Carlos, how you doing today?"

"I'm doing just fine. What's going on?" he asked again.

"Well the reason I called is because I was just talking to Charlie Banister this morning. Him and his boys raided one of Parisi's bootleggers last night and they are going to hit the Catenzaro Restaurant in Springfield tonight."

"Well that's good news."

"Yeah Carlos, he wants to wait until tonight when they have a room full of customers to do the raid, you know with it being a Friday night, the place should be full of people."

Sinafaldi covered the phone, "Benny the cops are going to hit the Catenzaro tonight." Benny gave him the thumbs up.

"Well that's good news Bill. I'm going to Springfield today on business. Maybe I'll stay there tonight so I can get the morning paper and read all about it."

"That sounds like a good idea," Richardson replied. "I'll keep you informed if I hear anything."

"Thanks for the call Bill. And yea keep me informed if you hear anything else."

Sinafaldi hung up the phone and turned to Benny. "Benny, now the cops are going to start hitting Parisi's operation. They got one of his bootleggers last night. If we can keep the pressure on him we might be selling our own booze in Springfield pretty soon."

"We got to be careful Boss," Benny answered. You know he's not just going to just lay down for us because we are giving him some trouble. He's going to want to defend his territory. We don't want to underestimate him."

"Don't worry Benny, the cops are going to be his problem right now. We'll just wait for them to clear the way for us and then we will move right in. And besides that I want talk to Torrio in Chicago and see if he will send a gunman. Someone who will just come in and do the job and get rid of Parisi and go back to Chicago." Sinafaldi paused in thought for a minute and then said, "Matter of fact Benny I want you to get Torrio on the phone. Do it right now."

"Okay Boss," Benny picked up the phone and called Chicago. After speaking to several of Torrio's men he finally got John Torrio on the other end. "Just a second Mister Torrio," he handed the telephone off to Sinafaldi.

"Hello Johnny, this is Carlos Sinafaldi. How are you doing today?"

"I'm doing just great Carlos. What can I do for you today?"

"John you remember Joe Parisi?"

"Isn't he the guy whose contract you bought from me to collect my percentage?"

"Yeah, that's the guy."

"Yes I remember him. So what about him?"

"I'm having some trouble with him. I want to get him out of the Springfield Mass. area. I want to bring in a gun from outside to deal with him. I thought you might be able to help me out."

"Carlos, I can help you out, but it is going to cost you."

"Okay Johnny, what's it going to to cost?"

"Because I like you, Carlos, it's only going to cost you twenty five thousand for me and twenty five thousand for the gun."

"So fifty thousand dollars? That's a lot of dough, Johnny."

"Well how bad do you want to get rid of him?"

"Yea, you're right, I do want him out of the picture pretty badly."

"It's going to mean a lot more business for you isn't it?"

"Yeah it is," Sinafaldi answered. "So when can you get him up here?"

"When can you get the money to me?"

"How do you want me to do it Johnny?"

"Send your man to Chicago right away with the twenty five thousand for me and I'll send somebody to you. And you can pay them their twenty five thousand when they get there."

"Yeah, okay Johnny, I'll have somebody leaving for Chicago today."

"You do that Carlos and soon as they arrive with the money I'll send somebody to you. I want you to understand that it's all money up front. You pay him the money and he hits your man and then he gets out of there. He doesn't have to hang around and wait for you to pay up. Do we understand each other?"

"We understand, Johnny."

"Okay Johnny, your money will be on the way today. I'll talk to you later."

Sinafaldi hung up the phone. "Benny who am I going to trust to take twenty five thousand to Torrio in Chicago?"

"Just to go and make the drop and come back?"

"Yeah, just go give him the money and come back."

"Do you want me to take it, Boss?"

"Yeah, good idea. I'll leave you at the train station in Springfield and you come right back. I don't want you to go alone. Who do you want to take with you?"

"I'll take my brother-in-law, Tony."

"Okay Benny, you take Tony with you and we're leaving for Springfield in an hour. You and Tony get ready and I'll meet you back here in one hour." Sinafaldi looked at his watch then looked up at Benny. "Get going Benny."

Benny quickly put on his coat and left. Sinafaldi sat back in his chair thinking about the events that were about to unfold. With Joe Parisi out of the picture taking the Springfield business would be much easier. Maybe his meeting with Enzo Fatini that afternoon would help him to get Parisi and make it easier to take over the Springfield business. He had no idea and it had not even crossed his mind that Parisi would be gunning for him today. He trusted Enzo Fatini and thought him to have no love for Joe Parisi and his organization because of his run in with him a few years back. He would drop Benny and his brother-in-law Tony at the Springfield train station and then go to meet with Fatini. When the gunman arrived from Chicago that would be the end of Parisi and the cops would still be closing down any business that Parisi and his group controlled and then he would move in on the Springfield business and take it over.

It was an hour later when Benny and Tony showed up at Sinafaldi's home. Sinafaldi's driver Dominic and one of his body-guards arrived within a couple minutes to accompany him to Springfield and to the meeting with Fatini. Benny and Tony each had a small suitcase to travel with. Sinafaldi gave Benny the briefcase that contained the twenty five thousand dollars for Johnny Torrio.

Just before they left for Springfield Sinafaldi made another call to Torrio in Chicago letting him know that Benny and Tony would be getting on the train today and should arrive in Chicago on Sunday with the money.

After the phone call they all got in Sinafaldi's car and left for Springfield. They arrived in Springfield a couple hours later and went right to the train station. Benny and Tony boarded the train around one o'clock bound for New York where they would catch the train to Chicago later that day. Sinafaldi, his bodyguard and driver all went to an Italian restaurant on Main Street in the south end for lunch. It was about two thirty in the afternoon when they left the restaurant for the North End Bridge to pick up Enzo Fatini. Sinafaldi was a cigar smoker and had his driver stop at a smoke shop as they passed through downtown Springfield.

Chapter 14

It was just after two thirty when Joe Parisi arrived at the bridge. Joe Marvici was driving the car and Savako Copa rode in the front seat beside him. Savako carried a machine gun and Joe Marvici had a sawed off shotgun on the seat next to him. Both men were carrying handguns as well. Joe Parisi rode in the back seat with a machine gun also and he had a handgun in a holster under his coat. When they arrived at the bridge a hot dog vendor was already set up at the park. The park had a few people spread out around and there were a few cars parked near the hot dog stand and a small crowd of people around it.

"Take a drive over the bridge," Parisi said to Joe as they approached. Joe drove slowly by the hot dog vendor and gave the car gas as he went onto the bridge. The North End Bridge had a sloping shape as it arched over the Connecticut River. It was an uphill climb to the middle of the bridge and it was not possible to see the other side until the car got almost to the middle of the bridge. From the middle the slope was all downhill to the West Springfield side. Joe drove around the traffic circle on the West Springfield side and turned down Main Street. There was a second hot dog vendor at the corner of Main Street near the commons on Park Avenue. There were people out around the commons and a few gathered around the hot dog stand. Vinnie was parked at the hot dog stand and Rocco was parked around the corner on Main Street near Park Avenue. Joe followed the traffic circle around and back up over the bridge. It was still about twenty minutes before three when they got back to the other side.

Bambino had taken his nephew Louie under the bridge and showed him where to stand in order to see the red rock that Enzo would kick off the bridge if Sinafaldi was in the car. He showed Louie how to use the mirror to signal Johnny who was hidden from view of anyone crossing the bridge. Johnny would signal Bambino who would be parked at the hot dog stand. Joe was going to be driving back and forth over the bridge at three o'clock. Bambino would turn on his lights as soon as he got the signal from Johnny and proceed over the bridge to where Sinafaldi was meeting Fatini.

When Joe saw Bambino's car with the lights on either coming towards him or in his rear view mirror that was his signal to head for the middle of the bridge for the kill.

It was about ten minutes to three when Enzo Fatini and Tony Demarco arrived. They parked the car at the end of the bridge near the park and walked to the middle of the bridge. Enzo took the rock out of his pocket and set it under the railing an inch from the edge. He leaned against the railing with the rock right behind him where he could easily give it a nudge over the edge. The two men waited there making some small talk while they waited. It was a sunny day and there was a light wind blowing along the river.

The trap was set for Sinafaldi. They all waited for him to drive up. After taking a few minutes at the smoke shop to buy cigars, Sinafaldi arrived about five minutes after three. He was not suspecting any problems and was feeling pretty untouchable lately, having the cops in Springfield on the take. The West Springfield Police Station was only about a half mile from the bridge on Park Avenue as well.

Sinafaldi was smoking a cigar as his car came onto the bridge. He could see the two men waiting for him in the middle of the bridge as they approached.

Fatini was studying every car that came across the bridge and noticed a car starting to slow down as it approached. He squinted and strained to see if Sinafaldi was in the car. As the car got closer Fatini could plainly see that Sinafaldi was in the back seat.

"He's in the car," he said to Tony and kicked his foot backwards knocking the rock over the side and into the river.

Louie was sitting under the bridge with a fishing pole and was watching the time closely and kept his eyes open for the falling rock from about five minutes to three. It was five after three when Fatini kicked the rock off the bridge. Seeing the rock falling, Louie quickly flashed a beam of light to Johnny, who was up near the road.

Johnny quickly flashed a beam from his mirror at Bambino's car. Bambino immediately turned on his lights and revved the engine up and took off from River Road where he was waiting, toward the center of the bridge.

Joe, Savako and Joe Parisi were at the ready also. They had been cruising back and forth across the bridge and had just went around the traffic circle in West Springfield and were heading back across the bridge when they saw the car pull over at the center of the bridge where Fatini and Demarco were standing. As they drove towards them Bambino's car was just coming on to the bridge with lights on. That was the signal that they were waiting for. Both Vinnie and Rocco had taken off toward the bridge when they also saw the car stopping on the bridge.

Sinafaldi was still unaware that anything was going on. His attention was on Fatini and Demarco as his car pulled up to them. His driver stopped the car in front of them and they both approached Sinafaldi's car. Sinafaldi motioned for Fatini to open the door and get in. His bodyguard got out of the front seat and opened the rear door.

The three cars raced towards Sinafaldi's car from the West Springfield side. Vinnie's car sped towards them from the Springfield side. There was some other traffic on the bridge, though it was light. Joe sped past a few cars heading for Sinafaldi's car while Savako and Joe Parisi had guns ready.

It was Fatini's driver that first noticed that something was going on as he saw the cars speeding towards them.

"Boss, we got some trouble," he said to Sinafaldi.

Fatini was standing by the open door and was starting to get in. He looked up and seen cars coming at them then turned the other direction and Vinnie's car with lights on was speeding towards them too.

"Why, you son of a bitch," Sinafaldi snarled at him and pulled a handgun out of his coat pointing it at Fatini. Fatini quickly swung the door closed and dove towards the back of the car. Sinafaldi squeezed off a couple of shots at Fatini that missed him, popping a couple of holes in the car door. Tony Demarco jumped out of the way but was hit in the arm by one of the shots from Sinafaldi's gun. He dove to the ground and scrambled towards the back of the car holding his arm.

Joe Parisi and Savako started firing out the car window as the car got closer to Sinafaldi's car. Their machine guns riddled the car with bullets as Sinafaldi's driver stepped on the gas trying to get away. There was no place to go as they approached followed by two more cars driven by Vinnie and Rocco. Guns blasted out the windows of all three cars. Fatini and Demarco were on the ground behind Sinafaldi's car as the car pulled away leaving them unprotected on the bridge as bullets whizzed by.

"Let's get out of here," Fatini yelled at Demarco over the sound of gunfire and they both got up and started running away from the car.

The driver took a couple of rounds through the head and lost control of the car. The car hit the curb and bounced off, veering out to the middle of the bridge as he slumped in the driver's seat. Sinafaldi and the bodyguard kept shooting to no avail as the cars got closer to them and bullets continued to slam into their car. Suddenly Bambino slammed into their car from behind. Sinafaldi's bodyguard was hit and slumped in the seat beside the driver. Sinafaldi was surrounded with guns bearing down on him and had no chance of getting away. He raised up his hands and dropped his gun as he sat in the back seat.

Joe pulled the car up next to him and stopped. Joe Parisi and Savako had their guns trained on him at point blank range.

"Carlos Sinafaldi," Parisi said to him through the window. "You fucked with me for the last time."

"Parisi, I should have known," Sinafaldi answered back. Those were Sinafaldi's last words as Joe Parisi pulled the trigger and pumped several rounds into him. Sinafaldi's body jerked from the bullets and slumped in the seat.

"Step on it, Joe," Parisi ordered and the car took off for Springfield. The other cars quickly followed, leaving Sinafaldi's car crosswise on the bridge. Fatini and Tony Demarco were almost back to their car when the four cars sped past them. They got to their car, and took off toward Main Street heading toward downtown Springfield.

A passer-by, traveling over the bridge while the shooting was going on drove to the West Springfield Police Station. The shots could be heard at the police station only a half mile away from the bridge down Park Avenue. A couple of cops were walking up the steps of the station when the shooting began. They paused, stopping on the steps when they heard the first shots coming from the bridge, and listened.

"Is that gunfire I hear?" one asked.

"Sounds like it to me," the second cop answered. "Go tell the desk Sergeant, I'll wait here."

The first cop quickly ran inside the station. "Hey Sarge, we got gunfire out there. Sounds like it's coming from the bridge."

Outside, the passer-by stopped in front of the station where the other officer was standing in front of his car and listening.

"Somebody's getting whacked on the bridge," he yelled out of the window of his car.

"Don't drive off, friend. Go inside and tell the desk Sergeant what you saw," the officer said to him.

The man pulled his car over, parked it and went inside. The cops were scrambled and ran by him to their cars as he walked up the stairs.

The desk Sergeant reacted immediately getting on the intercom and scrambling all the available policemen in the station. Within minutes several cars were speeding towards the bridge with sirens going.

When the police arrived at the North End Bridge, Sinafaldi's car was the only one on the bridge. The car was sitting sideways with one wheel against the curb. The windows were full of bullet holes and the left side of the car was shot up pretty bad also. The windows had blood splattered on them and the three men were all slumped over in their seats inside the car.

Three police cars pulled up to the car and stopped. The doors flew open and in a matter of seconds the car was surrounded by cops. One officer opened the driver's side door and checked the driver's pulse. He had taken a few bullets to the head and had blood running down his face.

"This one's still alive," he said as he detected a pulse.

On the other side of the car another officer open the passenger side door and had to catch the bodyguards body as he started to topple out of the car. He shoved him back onto the seat and checked his pulse as well.

"He's alive too." he said. "Better get an ambulance down here."

Another officer opened the back door of the car where Sinafaldi lay across the seat. He checked him to see if he was still alive as well and was able to feel a slight pulse. Sinafaldi's body was covered with blood as well and he had also taken a bullet to the head. In spite of his injuries he was the only one of the three men who was still conscious.

"This one's still alive too," the officer said. Sinafaldi opened his eyes and looked at the officer. He tried to say something but was only able to barely whisper.

"I think this guy's trying say something," one of the officers said.

"Hey buddy, talk to me."

Sinafaldi looked at the officer. His eyes was glassed over and looked a little cloudy as he tried to speak. Blood was oozing out of his mouth and his coat was soaked with blood. His eyes were glazed but still open. One of the officers talked to him.

"Hey friend, can you hear me?" he said. "Who shot you?"

Sinafaldi tried to answer but he was unable to say anything coherent. The officer asked him again but to no avail. Sinafaldi passed out while the officer was trying to talk to him.

Within a few minutes two ambulances arrived and loaded the three men and headed for the Mercy Hospital in Springfield. Sinafaldi managed to live long enough to make it to the hospital but died shortly after getting there. Both the driver and the bodyguard survived the trip to the hospital although they were both barely alive. They were both rushed into surgery and had numerous bullets removed. It was a miracle that either one of them survived, considering the sheer number of bullets that they had taken. The driver had taken two bullets to the head and several in the chest and arms though they had missed his heart. After the surgery the doctors only gave him a slight chance to survive his wounds.

Sinafaldi's bodyguard fared a little better, having taken all the bullets through the upper body and also missing any vital organs. The doctors gave him a better chance to survive though he was still in pretty bad shape. Neither man regained consciousness for a couple of days in the hospital.

Because the shooting happened in the middle of the North End Bridge it was not clear if the West Springfield Police had jurisdiction over the shooting or if it was a matter for the Springfield Police. The Springfield Police got word of the shooting quickly and were on the scene investigating soon after the ambulances arrived.

The bridge was immediately closed off to traffic as the police tried to piece together what happened.

It was obvious that Sinafaldi's car had been shot at with automatic weapons by the sheer numbers of bullet holes in the car.

The passer-by who had stopped at the West Springfield Police station had been brought back to the bridge to talk to the Springfield Police.

"I was driving over the bridge on my way to visit my brother in West Springfield," he told the Police. "There was a car stopped in the middle of the bridge and there was a couple of guys on the sidewalk talking to the guys in the car. I didn't think too much of it until the shooting started."

"Where were you when you heard the shooting start?" an officer asked him.

"I had passed the car that was stopped on the bridge and was closer to the West Springfield side of the bridge when I heard the shooting start. I looked behind me towards the center of the bridge and I could see that several other cars were on that side of the bridge too. There was a lot of gunfire and I wasn't going to stick around so I drove to the West Springfield Police station right away."

"Did you recognize anyone?"

"No I didn't."

"Did you recognize any of the other cars or the guys talking to the guys in the car?"

"No I didn't."

"Do you think you would recognize anyone if you seen them again?"

"I don't think so, I wasn't paying that much attention when I drove passed them until the shooting started. They were just a couple of guys on the bridge, you know."

After a few more questions the police let him go with instructions that he was to get in touch with them if he remembered anything else about the shootings or if he saw any of the men again.

The cops questioned the hot dog vendors on either side of the bridge also but were not able to get any information from them either.

It was not long before Charlie Banister got wind of the shooting and came down to the bridge to have a look.

After looking the situation over, Banister paid a visit to the Chief in West Springfield. "I think I know who did this and I want to take jurisdiction on this one," he told the Chief. "Carlos Sinafaldi was a friend of mine and I want to make sure that his killers get what they got coming."

"You think you know who did this, Charlie?"

"Yeah, I think I know."

"Are you going to tell me who it is?"

"Yeah sure, I think it's Joe Parisi and his mob. Sinafaldi and Parisi have been at odds with each other for a while now. Sinafaldi has been feeding me information about Parisi and I think maybe Parisi found out about it."

"What kind of information?"

"One of his guys disappeared a few weeks ago, Eugene Grazia, and he thought Parisi was responsible. And you know about the guy they found floating in the river up in Vermont?"

"Yeah I heard about him."

"We ran his picture in the newspaper and he was identified as Salvatore Mauro from West Springfield. He apparently worked for Parisi and Sinafaldi had him on the take too. He figured that Parisi found him out as well.

"Have you got any proof that Parisi was involved?"

"No not yet. But maybe Sinafaldi's guys in the hospital will pull through and they will be able to tell us something."

"Okay Charlie, I give this one to you. You let me know if there is anything I can do to help you out with this."

Banister was pretty upset about Sinafaldi being killed. He had a good thing going with him and was going to miss the payoff money that he had been getting now that he was dead. Maybe someone in his organization would take over Sinafaldi's operation and continue to pay him off. This was the night he and his men were going to raid the Catenzaro Restaurant. Banister wanted to go through with the raid hoping that it would flush something out in Parisi's operation and maybe give him a lead in catching him or tying him to the shooting. The restaurant would be busy, tonight being a Friday night and Banister decided to go through with the raid.

He waited until about ten o'clock that night when the place was full of people before hitting the restaurant.

The police arrested about eighty people including the staff and John Parisi for selling illegal liquor. Even though John didn't want to be involved in the bootlegging business he had been selling booze in the Catenzaro right from the beginning. Because he had never been hassled or raided the entire time since Prohibition came in, he had become pretty relaxed about it.

The four cars that were involved in the Sinafaldi hit had successfully got out of Massachusetts without being detected, making it back to Connecticut later that day. Enzo Fatini and Tony Demarco made it to New Haven where they met with Parisi. Parisi got Joe and Savako to take Demarco to Doctor Luigi Patzino who could take care of Demarco who had been shot in the arm by Sinafaldi on the bridge. The doctor dug the bullet out of Demarco and patched him up before they went back to New York.

Early the next morning, Joe Parisi got a call from his brother John in Springfield. The cops had released him on bail after holding him overnight in jail.

"Joe, the cops hit the restaurant last night."

"They hit the restaurant?"

"Yeah, they came in about ten o'clock last night."

"The Springfield cops?"

"Yeah that's right. I just got out of jail this morning. We were full of people too and they arrested everybody who was there."

"What did they charge you with?" Joe asked.

"They got us for selling booze and they cleaned us out too. They were asking a lot of questions about you, Joe."

"What kind of questions?"

"There was a shooting on the North End Bridge yesterday. They were asking me a lot of questions about it. I guess they think you were involved."

"What did you tell them?"

"I didn't tell them nothing. I don't know nothing about it. But it's all over the newspaper this morning. Carlos Sinafaldi was shot and killed and a couple of his men are still in the hospital in pretty bad shape. Charlie Banister thinks you had something to do with the shooting. The cops been asking me questions about it all night."

"What hospital are they in?"

"They're at the Mercy Hospital Joe. I guess the cops have them under heavy guard right now."

"Well Sinafaldi had it coming. What did he think I was going to do just let him keep fucking with me? I'm glad that he's dead. I hope the other two die too."

"You better stay out of Massachusetts Joe. The cops are looking for you. They want to pin this on you."

"They got any witnesses?"

"Not unless Sinafaldi's guys pull through. But they got shot up pretty good and might not make it."

"Keep me informed John. If you hear anything about it." "Yeah, don't worry I'll let you know if I hear anything."

Joe Parisi got off the phone with John and called Joe Marvici in Waterbury right away.

"Joe, my brother just called me.," he said. ""He spent the night in jail last night. The Springfield cops raided the Catenzaro about ten o'clock last night."

"Oh shit. Is he still in jail?"

"No they let him go this morning. I guess the place was full of people too. They got about eighty people. Arrested them all. The cops were asking John a lot of questions about me. He said that they suspect me in the Sinafaldi shooting and want to pin it on me."

"Do they have any witnesses?"

"Just Sinafaldi's guys. They're still alive. They're in the Mercy Hospital under police guard. I guess it's all over the Springfield newspaper."

"Is there a chance we can get to them and make sure they don't survive?"

"I don't know Joe. Maybe you could take Savako and Bambino with you and go to Springfield and see if you can get near them and put them out of their misery."

"Yeah, okay, do you want me to go today?"

"Yeah Joe, I would go myself but John told me to stay out of Massachusetts, the cops are looking for me."

"Okay I'll get right on it," Joe answered and hung up the phone and called Savako and Bambino and arranged to pick them up later that day.

They arrived in Springfield about mid afternoon and drove by the Catenzaro Restaurant first. The place looked deserted. The parking lot was empty and the windows were dark. They drove by without stopping and then drove to the Mercy Hospital. There were Police cars at every corner outside the hospital and police at every entrance. It looked like the cops were keeping a tight watch on the hospital and Sinafaldi's men. Joe stopped at a news shop and sent Bambino in for a newspaper and a few cigars.

They looked through the paper looking for the birth announcements. Joe drove around the hospital and parked about a block away. They read in the paper about an Italian woman, Antonette Cordova had just had a baby the day before and Bambino went inside posing as her husband. He went to the front desk and asked which way to the maternity ward. Once inside Bambino did a quick check around the hospital trying to locate where Sinafaldi's men were being kept. He got to the fourth floor and was walking through the hall and turning a corner there was cops all over the place at the end of one of the corridors. Bambino ducked into a nearby room and peeked down the hall. That had to be where Sinafaldi's men were. There was no way he was going to get close to the room. He checked it out for a minute and casually walked back out into the hall and down the stairs and back to the car.

"I don't think we can get near them Joe, there's cops all over the place on the fourth floor."

"You think they're on the fourth floor?" Joe quizzed Bambino.

"Well the hallway was filled with cops and I presume that they're guarding Sinafaldi's guys."

A police car turned the corner in front of them and cruised through the parking lot nearby. As the police drove by them slowly the two officers in the car checked them out stopping in front of their car for a few seconds before they continued their patrol around the building.

"Let's get out of here before we end up having to talk to the cops," Joe said as he started the car and began driving away. As they were leaving they passed a couple more police cars that were patrolling around the hospital.

Joe drove to John's house in West Springfield to see if John was home and to use his telephone to call Joe Parisi in Connecticut.

"Hello Joe."

"What did you find out?"

"The cops are all around the hospital and there are quite a few around the room. I don't think we can get near Sinafaldi's guys right now."

"Where are you now?"

"We're in West Springfield at John's."

"When are you coming back to Connecticut?"

" I'll head back today. I'm going to stop over at your mother's place for a few minutes first and pay her a visit. We'll be back later today. I'll give you a call when we get there."

"Okay, I'll talk to you when you get back."

Benny and Tony Gallo arrived in Chicago on Sunday morning and Johnny Torrio had a couple of his men meet them at the train station. They took a car to Torrio's office in the south side. Torrio was insulated from meeting just anybody as a means of protecting himself from any harm. They were brought to his office and met with several others before they got to see Torrio. Al Capone was Torrio's number one man now and was gaining more power in his operation all the time. It was Capone that met with Benny and Tony first and arranged for the hit man to go to Massachusetts with them. They did meet Torrio briefly and turned over the twenty five thousand dollars to him before boarding the train back to Springfield.

Though they traveled on the same train Benny and Tony and Danny Montoya, Torrio's hit man, did not sit together on the train and acted like they didn't know each other.

They changed trains in New York and Benny had a chance to call ahead to Sinafaldi's in Worcester to let him know that they would be coming into Springfield later that day. Benny was the guy that usually screened the phone calls for Sinafaldi but because he was out of town Paulo Paziano who was another of his top men was looking after the phone.

"Hey Benny, how you doing?" Paulo asked.

"I'm doing alright. I'm in New York right now and everything has gone as planned. My train is coming into Springfield this afternoon. You can tell the boss to send a car to pick us up."

"Don't worry, we'll pick you up. Is Torrio's man with you?"

"Yeah, we made the delivery and he's on the train with me and Tony."

"Hey Benny a lot has happened since you've been gone."

"Oh yeah, well you can tell me about it when I get there."

"Well there's one thing that I better tell you now."

"What's that? It can't wait?"

"Benny, they got the boss."

"What do mean they got the boss? What are you talking about?"

"Parisi, he ambushed him on the North End Bridge. Carlos is dead, Benny."

"He's dead? Holy shit Paulo, when did this happen?"

"On Friday, the day you left for Chicago."

Benny paused for a minute. It came as quite a shock to him. "The boss is dead?"

"Yeah, that's right."

"Okay Paulo, pick us up at the train station and we got to have a meeting right away. We got to decide what we're going to do now."

"Okay Benny, I'll set it up and we'll have a car pick you up. You know...... that you're the top man here now. We need somebody to take over and I think everyone agrees that you're the man now."

"I'll see you this afternoon," Benny answered before hanging up the telephone. He stood by the phone for a minute or so, still shocked by the news, before making for the platform and the train to Springfield.

Benny got on the train and didn't say anything to Tony right away. He was still in shock about Sinafaldi's death and was trying to figure out what he would do now. Benny had been with Sinafaldi for the last six years and was highly regarded as his number two man.

He would have to take control of the operation quickly and ride out the plan to kill Joe Parisi and take over his Springfield operation.

Paulo came to the train station with two cars and several other gunmen to pick up Benny, Tony and Danny Montoya that afternoon. They drove back to Worcester where they met with some of the others in Sinafaldi's operation.

Benny decided on the drive to Worcester that they would carry out the plan to knock off Joe Parisi and take over his Springfield operation. Knowing that Sinafaldi had been set up by Enzo Fatini, Fatini was also going to be a target for a hit.

Benny assumed command of the operation at the meeting in Worcester and set out a plan to get revenge and drive Parisi out of Springfield.

Danny Montoya was set up at first in the Plaza Hotel in Springfield and given a car and driver. They knew that Joe Parisi was living in New Haven and had business in Waterbury and Hartford as well. A couple days later Montoya and his driver went to New Haven and checked into a hotel there. They started going to the Catenzaro Restaurant to eat every day in hopes that he would catch Joe Parisi there and get the chance to carry out the hit.

Back in the Mercy Hospital Sinafaldi's bodyguard and driver were recovering from their gunshot wounds and regained consciousness about a week after the shooting. The police guard was still around their rooms at the hospital. Charlie Banister was informed as soon as they regained consciousness. He went to the hospital to question the men as soon as they could talk to them.

Banister was pretty certain that Joe Parisi was responsible for the shooting but he needed a witness to be able to issue a warrant for his arrest and he hoped that one or both of the men could identify him as the shooter. Banister had found a photo of Joe Parisi in the police files and brought it with him to the hospital for the men to look at, hoping they would recognize him.

Both men were barely conscious when Banister went to the hospital and were not able to talk very much. Banister's questioning consisted of showing the photo to the two men and asking them to nod their head if they thought that the man in the photo was involved in the shooting.

Both men identified Joe Parisi as being one of the shooters in the car by nodding.

That was enough for Banister to issue an arrest warrant for Parisi. He doubled the guard around the men at the Mercy Hospital and issued the warrant that day. Banister contacted the police in Connecticut in hopes of getting Parisi picked up in New Haven and extradited to Massachusetts on the murder charge. The New Haven police began watching Parisi's house and the Catenzaro Restaurant. It was a couple of days before they finally caught up to him.

Joe Parisi showed up at the Catenzaro Restaurant for dinner that afternoon and the New Haven Police surrounded the restaurant and arrested him. At the same time the police were arresting Parisi, Danny Montoya was walking into the restaurant with the intention of carrying out the hit on Parisi. Montoya looked on as the police took him into custody and walked him outside into a waiting police car.

The New Haven Police drove Joe Parisi to the New Haven Jail where he was held until the following morning and then taken to court. The Springfield Police were notified the night before and they were in court the next morning to plead their case for extradition to Massachusetts.

Vinnie Parisi was working in the Catenzaro Restaurant the afternoon the police came in to arrest Parisi. Before the police had even gotten out of the restaurant he was on the phone with Joe Marvici.

"Hey Joe, this is Vinnie. I'm down here at the Catenzaro right now and the cops have just arrested the Boss."

"What are they arresting him for?"

"The cops said it was for Sinafaldi's murder."

"How can they arrest him in Connecticut for that?"

"I don't know Joe but we got to get in touch with a lawyer."

"Okay, I'll get in touch with a lawyer right away."

Joe got hold of Anthony Bono, a lawyer who practiced in New Haven and worked for the Familia on occasion. It was after office hours so Joe had to call him at his home.

"Anthony, this is Joe Marvici."

"What can I do for you Joe?"

"We need your help Anthony. The New Haven Police just arrested Joe Parisi." "What are they charging him with?"

"It might be something to do with a murder charge in Massachusetts."

"When did they pick him up?"

"Within the last hour at the Catenzaro restaurant in New Haven."

"Okay Joe, I'll get in touch with the cops and find out what's going on. I'll call you right back." Bono hung up the phone and phoned the New Haven Police.

"Hello, this is Attorney Anthony Bono. I would like to know if you are holding Joe Parisi."

"Yes we are," the officer answered.

"What charge are you holding him on?"

"He is being held on an extradition warrant," the officer.

"Extradition warrant, where is the extradition warrant for?"

"The extradition warrant is for a murder charge in Springfield, Massachusetts."

"Okay, I'll be coming down to the station right away. I want to see Mister Parisi."

"Okay Mister Bono, we'll be expecting you."

Bono phoned Joe back right away. "Yea Joe, they got him down there and they are holding him for extradition on a murder charge in Springfield. I'm going down there right away to see him. I'll phone you right after I talk to him."

Bono arrived at the police station about ten minutes later and was led to the cell where Joe Parisi was being held. The guard opened the cell door and let Bono in, locking the door behind him.

Hello Joe, how are you?" Bono said. "I'm Anthony Bono. Joe Marvici called me and asked me to look into this situation."

The two men shook hands. "Thank you for coming coming down here Anthony. Now how long before you can get me out of here?"

"I don't know Joe. They're are holding you on a charge of murder one and they want to extradite you to Massachusetts. I can't do anything for you tonight. You got to go before the judge tomorrow morning and we will see what happens then."

Joe got up and started pacing back and forth, "Listen Anthony, I didn't murder anybody. I want you to do what it takes to get me out of here."

"I'll do the best I can for you Joe but tell me what do you know about this Carlos Sinafaldi. He's the guy they are charging you with killing."

"Hey I didn't murder Sinafaldi."

"Do you know him?"

"Yeah I know Sinafaldi, but that doesn't mean I killed him."

"Where were you last Friday Joe?"

"Last Friday, I was with my brother-in-law, Joe Marvici. We were at his house in Waterbury."

"Will he testify to that?"

"Yeah of course he will."

"Okay Joe, I'm going to get in touch with him and I will see you in court in the morning." Bono got up to leave, shaking hands with Joe Parisi. He called for the guard to let him out. "See you tomorrow morning Joe," he said as he was leaving. When Anthony Bono got home he phoned Joe Marvici.

"Hello Joe, this is Anthony Bono."

"Hello Anthony. Did you see Joe Parisi?"

"Yes Joe I did. The police are holding him for extradition to Massachusetts as you told me. He is being accused of murdering a Massachusetts man, Carlos Sinafaldi. Do you know this man?"

"Yes, I have met him and I know who he is."

"Yes, well Joe, Mister Parisi says he was with you last Friday at your house in Waterbury. Is that true?"

"Yes it is."

"Are you willing to testify to that in court?"

"Of course I will," Joe answered.

"Okay Joe, Mister Parisi will be appearing in court tomorrow morning at nine thirty in New Haven. The Springfield police will be there stating their case. They will be trying to get an extradition order to bring him to Springfield and stand trial for the murder. I'll talk to the prosecutor tomorrow morning and find out what they have on him for evidence. Do you want to meet me in court in the morning?"

"Yeah sure I'll be there."

"Okay I will see you there."

Joe hung up the phone and immediately phoned Bambino in Hartford and then John Masalino in Springfield telling them both what was going on. They both agreed to meet him at the courthouse in New Haven the next morning. After talking to them he went to Savako's and talked to him as well.

Vinnie also showed up in court the next morning along with Joe, Savako, Bambino and John Masalino. Anthony Bono had already talked to the prosecutor before they got to the courthouse.

Anthony Bono came over to talk to them after they arrived. "Hi Joe," he said as he approached them. "Apparently there were several other men involved in the shooting and both were hospitalized with gunshot wounds and are expected to survive. They apparently identified Joe Parisi from a photograph as being involved in the shooting and are going to testify against him."

"Impossible, he could not have been in Springfield last Friday, he was with me at my house in Waterbury."

"Yes Joe, we can present that to the judge and maybe we can keep him from being extradited to Massachusetts. Is there anyone else that can testify that he was in Waterbury at your house?"

"Yeah, Vinnie was with us. We had a business meeting. Vinnie will testify too," Joe turned to Vinnie. "Hey ain't that right Vinnie?"

"Yeah, I was there too. I'll testify that Joe was in Waterbury with us."

"Alright, that's good," Anthony Bono replied. "Let's see what we can do."

They followed Anthony Bono into the courtroom and sat down. Within a couple of minutes Joe Parisi was led into the courtroom by two New Haven police officers. The Springfield Police were there too hoping to get the extradition order and take Joe Parisi back to Springfield to stand trial.

The judge came into the courtroom a couple minutes later and the hearing began. The New Haven Prosecutor opened the hearing presenting the case for extradition stating that Joe Parisi had shot Carlos Sinafaldi at point blank range in Springfield on the North End Bridge. The Springfield Police had statements from Sinafaldi's driver and bodyguard identifying Joe Parisi as one of the shooters. They were still hospitalized in Springfield in stable condition and were not able to make it to the hearing.

The prosecutor presented the case against Joe Parisi first calling several of the Springfield Police as witnesses. The police were very convincing and only had to present enough evidence to the court to show that they had a case against Parisi to warrant a trial on the charges against him.

After the New Haven Prosecutor presented the case against Joe Parisi, Anthony Bono had a chance to contest the evidence against him. "Your Honor, I have two witnesses that place Mister Parisi in Waterbury the day of the shooting. He could not possibly been in Springfield on that Friday as he was engaged in a business meeting at his brother-in-law's home in Waterbury."

"Are your witnesses present in the courtroom today?" the judge asked. "Yes your honor, they are."

"Would you like to call your witnesses this morning Mister Bono?"

"Yes your Honor, I would like to call Joseph Marvici as my first witness."

Joe got up and walked to the front of the courtroom to be sworn in by the clerk.

As he put his hand on the bible to be sworn in, the door of the courtroom opened and in came Benny Gallo with five of Sinafaldi's thugs. Among the five was Danny Montoya. They sat in the bench in the back row of the courtroom.

Joe was watching them as he listened to the clerk, "Do you swear the evidence you give will be the truth, the whole truth and nothing but the truth, so help you God."

Joe hesitated for a second, being distracted by Gallo and his boys and then turned to the clerk, "I do," he said.

"Take a seat," the clerk said to Joe as he withdrew to his own seat.

Anthony Bono stood up and walked towards the witness stand. "Mister Marvici would you state your full name please."

"Yes, my name is Joseph Marvici."

And how are you acquainted with Mister Parisi?"

"Joe Parisi is my brother in law."

"And where were you on Friday July 11th at approximately three o'clock in the afternoon?" "I was at my home in Waterbury."

"And what is the address of your home?"

" My address is number 8 Banks Street."

"And was anybody with you at that time?"

"Yes, I was with my brother in law, Joe Parisi and my cousin Vinnie Parisi."

"And what was the nature of your business with Mister Parisi?"

"We were having a business meeting."

"Is there any way that Mister Parisi could have been in Springfield on that day?"

"No, how could he be in Springfield that day? He was with me. Nobody can be in two places at the same time."

"Thank you Mister Marvici." Anthony Bono looked over at the Judge, "I have no further questions your Honor."

The prosecutor passed on asking Joe any questions and Anthony Bono called Vinnie Parisi next.

Vinnie backed up Joe's story that Joe Parisi was in Waterbury with them the day that Sinafaldi was shot. However the Judge still felt that the Springfield Police had enough evidence with the two witnesses identifying Parisi and granted the extradition warrant. Right after the Judge's decision Benny and Sinafaldi's men got up and left the courthouse.

Confident that Joe Parisi was going back to Springfield they left the courthouse and drove back. They were not going to get a chance to put the hit on Joe Parisi right now as long as he was in police custody. Joe Marvici and Vinnie were lying and Benny knew it. He had already paid Torrio and Montoya twenty five thousand each for the hit on Parisi and that seeing as though it was going to be hard to get Parisi now maybe he should get Montoya to go after Joe and Vinnie. If Parisi had no witnesses then he would surely be convicted of Sinafaldi's murder.

Joe Parisi was taken into the custody of the Springfield Police and transported back to Springfield that afternoon. Parisi was booked for murder and taken to the York Street Jail. Charlie Banister paid him a visit shortly after he got there.

The guard unlocked Parisi's cell and let Banister in. "Hello Joe, I glad to see you came back to see us. I'm Charlie Banister the Police Chief here in Springfield." Banister reached out to shake hands with Parisi but Joe did not offer his hand in return.

"What do you want coming here?" he asked.

"I just want to tell you that Carlos Sinafaldi was a friend of mine. We had a very good association between us you might say. And now, well he's dead and that really has messed up my association. You know what I mean?"

Joe Parisi looked up at Banister and didn't say anything.

"Okay Joe, maybe you and I should have an association. And maybe things will go easier on you if we did. You know what I mean?"

"Listen, I didn't shoot your boy Sinafaldi and I'm not going to be convicted of it. So whatever association you think you want to have with me, maybe you should stick it up your ass."

"Alright Joe, but you better have a good defense or you're going to be our guest here for a long time. Maybe you want to think about it for a while?"

Joe just looked at Banister, and then looked away.

Banister called for the guard to unlock the cell and then left.

Chapter 15

A couple days later Joe Marvici and John Masalino visited Parisi in jail. Banister was able to talk to Parisi in his cell but they were only able to visit him in the visiting area of the jail. It was up to Joe to look after the day to day operation of the Familia now that Joe Parisi was in jail. Parisi was still calling the shots even though he was in jail. He expected to be acquitted of the murder charge and be back out on the street again soon.

The Springfield operations had definitely suffered a setback between the raid on the Catenzaro Restaurant and the arrest of Joe Parisi. Toni Spencer was still hauling booze from Quebec up to this point but she was having some apprehension about it with Parisi in jail and there seem to be a great deal more heat on now. The raids on the booze shipments seem to be more frequent now ever since the raid on the warehouse. Banister had been tipped off prior to the Sinafaldi shooting and stepped up the raids since then, getting the federal officers involved as well. It was getting increasingly harder to get the booze shipments through and Toni was already pretty well off and did not really need the money. Up to this point she was only doing it for the excitement. By this time it seemed like everyone was involved in the liquor business one way or another. Toni decided about this time that she was going to put her money in other things.

Things that were legal. She started supplying less trucks for the liquor runs, even though there was no shortage of trucks wanting to work and make some extra money.

There was a feeling of uneasiness around Joe's home. His wife Agatha was worried about him. With the new baby Carmela and the twins John and Frank there were four children now. What would she do with four children if something happened to Joe? Men were killed and her brother was in jail for the killing. Agatha feared for her brother and her husband.

Joe Parisi's appearance in court on the twenty ninth of July gave reason for concern for Agatha. She pleaded with Joe not to go to Springfield for her brother's court appearance. She had a bad feeling about it and she told him so. "Joe, please stay home this time. Let the other guys go."

But Joe had too much pride and felt like he was obligated to be there. He left in a car with Vinnie, Savako and himself. They met up with Bambino, Rocco and Bambino's nephew Louie in Hartford and they drove together the rest of the way to Springfield.

Joe Parisi was scheduled to be in court about ten o'clock in the morning. They got to the courthouse just before ten and met briefly with Anthony Bono.

"What's it look like now?" Joe asked when they talked.

"Today is the arraignment, which means that the state is going to present the evidence that they have and try to convince the judge that they have enough to to take the case to trial. So let's go in there and see if they do and we will introduce your testimony about Joe being with you in Waterbury."

They went into the courtroom and and sat towards the front of the room. As soon as Anthony Bono came in and sat down Joe Parisi was brought out by a couple of deputies. A half dozen of Sinafaldi's faithful came into the courtroom, taking a seat in the back row just a few minutes before the hearing began.

Charlie Banister and a couple of his officers and several officers from the West Springfield Police who were there on the scene shortly after the shooting entered the courtroom as well.

As the judge came out from his chambers the court officer ordered everyone to stand and then be seated after the judge was seated at the bench.

"Will the defendant please stand," the court officer asked. Joe Parisi and Anthony Bono stood up as the charges against Joe Parisi were read aloud.

"The State versus Joseph Parisi on the charge of first degree murder. It is alleged that on Friday, July 11th, 1924 at approximately three o'clock in the afternoon, Joseph Parisi shot and killed Carlos Sinafaldi."

"The Judge turned to Joe Parisi and asked, "Mister Parisi, how do you plead?"

Anthony Bono responded, "Mister Parisi pleads not guilty your honor."

The judge instructed the two men to take their seat and addressed the prosecuting attorney, Steven Whitney. "Mister Whitney would you like to proceed?"

"Yes your Honor," Whitney responded. He proceeded to lay out the case against Joe Parisi, stating that the state had witnesses that were also involved in the shooting that would testify that Joe Parisi was the trigger man in the killing of Sinafaldi. At this point the driver and bodyguard were still in the Mercy Hospital in stable condition but had given evidence in the form of affidavits identifying Joe Parisi as the shooter. The affidavits also told about the meeting on the bridge with Enzo Fatini. At this time the police had not been able to catch up with Fatini and question him about it.

Whitney also intended to call Charlie Banister as a witness. Banister was to testify that he had met with Sinafaldi a few days before the shooting and Sinafaldi had told him that he thought that Joe Parisi was plotting to kill him.

The case against Joe Parisi was reasonably strong and in his summary to the court Whitney felt that he would prevail at the arraignment and get the case to trial.

When he was finished it was Anthony Bono's turn to offer a defense summary to the court. He began by stating that Joe Parisi couldn't have possibly been the shooter on that day. "Your Honor I have two witnesses that Mister Parisi was in Waterbury Connecticut at the time of the shooting. He was having a business meeting at his brother in law's home and had spent most of the day there. I will call Joseph Marvici and Vincent Parisi to give evidence that Joseph Parisi was in fact in Waterbury and nowhere near the North End Bridge in Springfield where the murder took place."

When Anthony Bono had completed his summary the Judge instructed the prosecution to proceed.

Steven Whitney entered the two affidavits of the driver and bodyguard into evidence giving copies to the Judge and to Anthony Bono. Then he called Charlie Banister to the stand to testify about the meeting with Sinafaldi a few days before the shooting. Banister also gave evidence that the Police were still trying to find Enzo Fatini in order to question him about his part in the shooting.

At this point in the case Parisi his associates were unaware that Sinafaldi had in fact hired Danny Montoya to come in from Chicago to kill Joe Parisi.

When the prosecution was finished Anthony Bono began to present the defense. He began by calling Joe and Vinnie to give evidence that Parisi was in Waterbury at the time of the shooting. This was pretty well the whole case for the defense. Without this testimony there was really no defense.

The Judge figured out that somebody was lying in this case in light of the conflicting evidence. It was either the driver and bodyguard or it was Joe and Vinnie. They both could not be telling the truth.

After about twenty minutes pondering the case in his chambers the Judge returned to the courtroom and rendered his decision.

"I believe that even though the evidence appears to be conflicting in this case that there is not enough evidence to warrant an acquittal. Therefore my decision is that I am binding this case over to Grand Jury for trial. And because Mister Parisi is not a resident of Massachusetts I order that he be held in jail in Massachusetts without bail until his court date."

Anthony Bono tried to argue the bail decision with the Judge but to no avail. The Judge had his mind set that he was not going to grant bail of any kind. This was obviously a bootleg war and the kind of thing that the police and the courts were trying to get under control. The Judge felt that releasing Parisi now would result in more killings and he refused to hear any arguments about it and got up and left the courtroom.

Sinafaldi's men got up right after the Judge made his decision and left the courtroom.

The court deputies took Joe Parisi into custody again and transported him back to the Springfield Jail.

Anthony Bono left the courtroom with Joe, Vinnie, Savako, Bambino, Rocco and Louie and they all walked out of the front entrance of the Springfield Courthouse. They were all talking among themselves when they walked out of the courthouse and down the long flight of concrete steps in front. Suddenly there was a blast of gunfire. Joe looked out to the street and saw a car driving by with several men firing at them out of the windows. Anthony Bono immediately got down to the ground as everyone else pulled their guns and started to return fire. Joe pulled his out his gun and started to shoot as the car roared off toward downtown. There were bullet holes in the walls in front of the courthouse and several bullets lodged in the front doors but miraculously no one was hit. Every bullet had missed its mark.

Joe mocked the shooters saying, "What kind of men do they send around to shoot at us. A bunch of amateurs and incompetents. All that shooting and they couldn't hit anybody."

Joe and Vinnie went with Anthony Bono to the jail to visit Joe Parisi after they left the courthouse. That was where Joe noticed a bullet hole in his coat sleeve where a bullet had narrowly missed him.

Bono was able to get in to see Joe Parisi in his cell but Joe and Vinnie had to wait and visit with him in the visitation room.

Anthony Bono was led back to Joe Parisi's cell where Joe was sitting on his bunk looking kind of dejected.

"Hello Joe," said Anthony Bono as the guard let him into the cell.

Joe looked up and answered, "hello Mister Bono."

"We had a little trouble getting here after court."

"Oh yeah, what do you mean?"

"We were shot at outside the courthouse."

"Oh really, who shot at you?"

"Well I don't know Joe but who ever it was I think that they wanted to get rid of your witnesses."

"What Joe and Vinnie? Was anybody hit?"

"No , they missed everybody.

"Well that's good," he chuckled.

"You know Joe, it looks like you've made a few powerful enemies here in Springfield. Police Chief Banister is one. He's got it out for you, you know."

"Yeah I know, Anthony. He paid me a visit the other day."

"Oh yeah, what did he want?"

"He told me that Carlos Sinafaldi was a friend of his and he was very upset that Sinafaldi was killed. I guess he had what he called, an association with him and he told me that if we were to have an association that maybe things would go easier on me."

"What did you tell him?"

"What do you think I told him? I told him to stick it up his ass."

"You think that he was looking for money?"

"Of course he was."

"That's too bad you feel like that Joe. You should think about reconsidering his offer."

"What do you mean. He and his cops raided the Catenzaro. I don't think I have enough money to get him on my side."

"Look Joe I don't know if it's him or Sinafaldi's guys but somebody is trying to kill your witnesses. If they are successful, then you don't have a case. The only thing you got right now that gives you a chance to stay out of prison is your alibi that you were in Connecticut when Sinafaldi was killed."

Joe Parisi got up and started to pace across the room.

"Look Joe, I'm on your side. And as your lawyer I have to give you advice. My advice is this. If chief Banister visits you again, then you should try to make a deal with him. If he wants an association that involves money or a cut of your business, I would take him up on it. It might be the only chance you got to stay out of jail."

"I don't trust him."

"Okay, so you don't trust him. But you should think about it Joe."

"Alright, I'll think about it."

Anthony Bono shook hands with Joe and slapped him on the back. "Okay, I'll talk to you in a couple of days." Bono summoned the guard to let him out and left.

A few minutes later the guard came in and led Joe Parisi to the visitation area where Joe and Vinnie were waiting for him.

He sat down at a long table where Joe and Vinnie were sitting on the other side. Several prisoners were visiting with people at the table and a guard stood at each end of the table watching.

"Hello Joe, hello Vinnie, how are you doing?" Joe Parisi greeted them.

"We're doing good," Joe responded.

"I just saw Anthony Bono. He just left my cell."

"Yea we know. We came over here with him."

"He told me that somebody was shooting at you when you left the courthouse today."

"Yeah a couple of guys in a car took a few shots at us. They were not very good shots though. They missed everybody except they got my coat, Joe laughed and showed Joe Parisi the hole in his coat. "What a bunch of amateurs."

"Jesus Joe, that was pretty close."

"Shooting a hole in my coat will not kill me," Joe laughed again.

They all had a laugh about it and then Joe Parisi got serious and said, "Anthony Bono told me he thinks Charlie Banister is out to get me."

"Oh yeah, what do you mean?"

"Banister came to see me in in jail a couple of days ago. He told me that he had an association with Sinafaldi and he was not happy about him being shot. It sounds like Sinafaldi had him on his payroll and he wanted to have an association with me which means that he wants to be on my payroll now."

"What did you tell him?"

"I told him to forget it. And now Bono tells me I should have been more agreeable and maybe went along with him."

"What? Paid him off?"

"Maybe I should. Bono thinks it might help me if I get him on my side." Parisi paused for a minute. "Bono said I haven't got a very strong case. Those guys in the hospital are going to testify against me. We still got to try to get to them and get rid of them. Might be good to hire somebody to knock them off. And Enzo Fatini, you know if the cops catch up with him and he talks to them then it's going to look pretty bad." Joe Parisi leaned over the table towards Joe and Vinnie. "I want you to find Fatini and make sure he won't talk to the cops. You know what I mean?"

"Yeah, okay Joe, I know what you mean," Joe answered.

About that time the guard signaled that the visiting time was over. Joe and Vinnie said goodbye to Joe Parisi and left the jail. They went the Catenzaro Restaurant to talk to John Parisi and fill him in on what was going on with his brother. John managed to get the restaurant open again but had taken a big hit on business since the raid by the Springfield cops. The cops confiscated a large amount of booze that was in the storage room in the basement when they raided the place. John had restocked the basement storage from the warehouse in Woronoco about a week after the raid but was having trouble getting customers back since then.

It was early in the afternoon when they arrived. There were only a few customers in the restaurant for the lunch hour. John Parisi and John Masalino were sitting at a table near the kitchen when Joe and Vinnie walked in.

They all shook hands and sat down at the table. John poured Joe and Vinnie a drink.

"We just came from the jail."

"How's Joe doing?" asked John Parisi.

"He's doing alright. But you know it doesn't look to good for him. Those guys in the hospital could cause him a lot of problems,"

Joe answered. "He still wants us to try to get to those guys and shut them up."

"That's not going to be easy Joe, the cops are watching them pretty close."

"I know, we already tried to get close to them at the hospital. The cops were everywhere around there."

"And how are you doing? John tells me that they were shooting at you at the courthouse."

"They just got my coat." Joe showed them the bullet hole in his coat.

They stayed at the Catenzaro for an hour or so, talking over lunch before leaving to go back to Connecticut. John Masalino left the restaurant with Joe and Vinnie. As they walked out the door and started to cross the street a black car sped around the corner, screeching as it came, heading straight for the three men. Joe could see the barrels of guns sticking out the window seconds before the gunmen opened fire. Bullets were spraying past them and slamming into the brick wall at the front of the Catenzaro. The three men drew their handguns and fired back at the car. At the same time they backed up into the front door of the restaurant as the car continued down Worthington Street.

John Parisi heard the shooting going on and hurried to the front of the restaurant finding the three men just inside the door with their guns drawn.

"What the hell is going on?" John shouted.

Joe turned towards John and said, "What do you think is going on John? Somebody is shooting at us again."

"Is everybody alright?"

Joe looked around at John and Vinnie. They both shook their heads indicating they were okay. "Yes, it looks like we're all okay. I think these guys are really bad shots," Joe laughed. "I think we are not in too much danger as long as these guys are the ones shooting at us."

Vinnie open the door and peeked out on the street. The car with the shooters was gone and the street was quiet. "It looks all clear," Vinnie said to the others. They went outside and looked up and down the street before crossing the street to Joe's car. They got in and drove out of town, headed for Connecticut.

It was obvious that somebody, most likely those loyal to Sinafaldi, was trying to kill Joe and Vinnie to keep them from testifying at Joe Parisi's trial.

Joe got home to Waterbury late in the afternoon after dropping Vinnie off in New Haven. Vinnie was staying at Joe Parisi's house while Joe was in jail in Springfield.

Agatha heard Joe pull up in front of the house and greeted him at the front door.

She embraced him, holding on to him for a long time. "Joe I'm so glad that you're home. I was worried about you all day today."

They went inside and Joe took off his coat and hung it up in the closet. Agatha noticed the bullet hole in his coat as he was putting it in the closet.

"Joe what's this?" She grabbed the coat and inspected the hole.

"That's nothing."

"What do you mean that's nothing? How did this hole get here in your coat?"

Joe didn't want to tell her at first but she kept pressing him until he finally told her.

"Somebody was shooting at us outside the courthouse today. A bullet got my coat. What can I say?"

"Oh Joe, you got to be careful. I don't want you to get shot. What's going to happen to us if you get killed?" Agatha was quite distraught and clung to Joe, not wanting to let him go.

"It's okay, I'm telling you it's okay, these guys can't shoot. They missed everybody. Don't worry my dear, I'm going to be alright."

Agatha gave Joe a long hug and then kissed him. She looked up at him and smiled asking, "How did it go with my brother?"

"He's going to go to trial."

"When is his trial going to be?"

"I don't know. They haven't set a date yet."

Agatha kept close to Joe the entire night. She was worried about him and had a bad feeling about the whole ordeal.

Vinnie phoned Joe early the next morning wanting to talk to him about Enzo Fatini. They had not seen or talked to Fatini since the day on the North End Bridge and felt it was time to deal with him. He could be a real problem if the cops were to get to him before they did.

"Joe I think we better go pay a visit to Fatini today," Vinnie said to him.

"Okay Vinnie I'll pick you up in an hour. Maybe you better give Rocco a call and

bring him with us."

As Joe left the house that morning for New Haven Agatha did not want him to go. She was terribly worried about him and told him so.

"Don't worry my dear. I'm going to be alright. I'm not going to get shot."

She waited at the front of the house, watching him as he got into the car and pulled away. Agatha made the sign of the cross and said a quiet prayer as the car pulled away.

Joe picked up Vinnie and Rocco in New Haven and drove to New York to meet with Enzo Fatini. Fatini based his operation in Westchester, just outside New York City. It was a small town on the edge of the city and Fatini was not hard to find. He based his operation out of the back room of a local pool room named 'Mickey's'.

They arrived in Westchester about ten thirty in the morning and drove by the pool room. It wasn't open yet so they went to a local diner just across the street and had breakfast while they waited. Joe, Vinnie and Rocco took a booth by the window so they could see the front of the pool room. They had been in there about an hour before they noticed someone unlocked the front door of the poolroom. Joe paid the bill and then they walked across the street and went inside. There were a couple of guys who had just started playing a game of pool. One of them put his cue down and walked to the counter.

"Hello gentlemen, what can I do for you?"

Joe answered, "We are looking for Enzo Fatini."

"He's not here right now."

"Can you get in touch with him?"

"Maybe I can, but who should I say is wanting to see him?"

"You can tell him that Joe Marvici is here to see him."

The man behind the counter picked up the telephone and dialed a number. "Hello Enzo, there's three men down here wanting to see you," he said under his breath as he turned away from Joe. "One says his name is Joe Marvici." He listened for a minute and then hung up the phone. "He says he'll be here in a few minutes. Why don't you fellas have a game of pool while you wait?"

The man placed a rack of balls on top of the counter. "Take table number three," he said pointing in the direction of the table.

Vinnie picked up the balls and they all went to the table and took off their coats, exposing their guns that were in shoulder holsters under their coats. "You guys play and I'll just watch," Joe said as he sat down at a table.

Vinnie racked up the balls as Rocco picked a cue off the rack.

About a half an hour later Enzo and Tony Demarco walked in the front door. They both stopped for a minute when they got inside and scanned the room. Enzo recognized Joe sitting at the table next to where Vinnie and Rocco were playing pool. He walked over to Joe.

"Joe, how are you doing? It's good to see you. Why don't we go in the back and talk."

"Yeah, let's talk Enzo," he said motioning for Vinnie and Rocco to come with them. They both picked up their coats and followed. Enzo led them through a narrow hallway into a small room at the back of the pool room. Enzo opened a cabinet and took out a bottle of liquor and a glass for each man and poured a drink for each of them. He put the bottle on the table and picked up his drink, holding it out. "Salut," he said as each one of them did the same and took a drink.

"What can I do for you Joe?" Enzo said after setting his glass on the table.

"I want to talk to you about Joe Parisi."

"What about him?"

"You know the cops have arrested him for Sinafaldi's murder."

"Yeah, I heard about it. That's too bad."

"You know his driver and bodyguard got shot up pretty good but it looks like they are going to live and they are going to testify against Joe. But here's the problem, Enzo. They know that Sinafaldi was meeting you on the bridge that day and they will probably tell the cops and the cops are going to want to talk to you."

"And so, I don't have to tell them nothing."

"That's good Enzo that you're saying that to me but I want to be sure that you're going to say that to the cops." Joe took a drink and looked back at Fatini.

"Don't worry Joe, I'm not going to tell the cops nothing."

Joe looked over at Demarco. He raised his hands, "Hey don't worry Joe, I'm not saying anything either."

"You got an alibi?"

"What do you mean?"

"If the cops question you, you better have an alibi. And you better have some witnesses that will say you were here in the pool room or something. It's not a good idea to try to come up with an alibi after they talk to you. You want to make sure you have it first before the cops want to talk to you."

"Yeah okay Joe, I'll make sure I have a few people that will say I was here that day."

"And Tony too. You have an alibi too. I don't know if the cops know about you but you want to be sure just in case they do."

"Sure Joe, I got an alibi," answered Demarco.

"Joe looked over at Vinnie and made a motion with his hand. Vinnie reached in his coat and brought out an envelope and handed it to Joe.

"Here's the other ten thousand Enzo," he said, tossing it down on the table. "And make sure you keep your mouth shut."

Fatini picked up the money and flipped through it like it was a deck of cards.

"Don't you worry. I'm not saying nothing." Fatini said as he put the money in his coat pocket and then poured them another drink. They downed their drinks and talked for a few minutes more before Joe, Vinnie and Rocco got up to leave.

"We'll be in touch Enzo," Joe said to them as he was leaving.

Fatini accompanied them as they walked back through the pool room, which was still deserted, and out to the front door. Joe stopped there and shook hands with him before walking out to his car. They got in the car and drove off. They had only gone a couple of blocks before Joe turned to Vinnie sitting beside him in the front seat.

"What do you think Vinnie, is Fatini going to keep his mouth shut?"

"I don't know Joe but are we going to take the chance with him?"

"Maybe not," Joe said and turned around the block and back towards the pool hall. He pulled the car into an alley right next to the pool hall where they could see the front entrance. Joe parked the car and shut it off and waited for Fatini to come out.

From where they were parked they could look right into the window on the alley side and had a clear view of the front entrance. They sat in the car for about ten minutes before Fatini and Tony Demarco appeared at the front door. Fatini's car was parked just outside the door and a little towards the alley. Joe started up the car and edged it forward until they had a clear view of Fatini and Demarco, who were on the sidewalk by now.

Vinnie and Rocco opened fire, pumping several rounds into them. Fatini didn't know what hit him until it was too late. Both he and Demarco dropped onto the sidewalk as Joe sped the car away with Vinnie and Rocco continuing to shoot as they raced by the fallen men.

They drove out of town and sped towards the Connecticut state line which was only a few miles away.

It was still early in the afternoon when Joe dropped Vinnie and Rocco off in New Haven. He drove back to Waterbury and was home by dinner time. Agatha heard his car pull up in front of the house and met him at the door.

"Joe I'm so glad to see you," she said, wrapping her arms around him and giving him a kiss. As she embraced him she could smell gunpowder on his coat. For a second she was going to say something about it but changed her mind and led him into the house without a word about it. She later confided in him but avoided bringing up the smell of gunpowder.

"Joe, I'm worried about you and I'm worried about my brother. I don't know what's going on but I'm worried that both of you could end up being shot. There's too much killing and shooting going on. I want you to get out of this business and do something that's safe."

"Listen my dear Agatha. I've worked with your brother for many years now. And now that he is in jail, I have got to look after the business. I can't just do something else right now. What would your brother think if I decided to just walk away from his business. He is counting on me to look after things until he is out of jail. I have no choice."

A couple of days later the news of Fatini's and Demarco's shooting was in the New Haven newspaper. Both men had died right there in front of the poolroom. The cops found the envelope with the money. The wad of cash in the inside pocket of Fatini's coat was unable to stop the bullets though there were a number of bullet holes in it. The police in Westchester had no leads on who might have shot them and it appeared that Joe had gotten away before anybody saw his car.

He visited Joe Parisi every week while he was in jail in Springfield. Joe Parisi was happy to hear that Enzo Fatini and Tony Demarco would not be talking to the cops and that his only problem was going to be Sinafaldi's driver and bodyguard. Without them the state would have no case against him.

"How can we get these two guys too?" Joe Parisi asked Joe while he visited him in jail.

The driver and bodyguard were both recovering in the hospital and were due to be released soon. Chances were that the police guard would be relaxed after they got out. Joe Parisi wanted Joe to wait until they were released from the hospital before he tried to get rid of them too.

The Springfield Police had got wind of the Fatini and Demarco shooting in Westchester and highly suspected that Joe Parisi and his group were responsible but had no evidence to tie them to it. They were trying to be very careful with the driver and bodyguard and watched them closely in order to keep them alive to testify in Joe Parisi's trial.

Meanwhile Danny Montoya was still in the area and Benny Gallo wanted him to stay and try to get the hit on Joe Parisi. It was going to be hard to get to him in the Springfield Jail. Gallo thought that if he were to have a meeting with Charlie Banister maybe he could persuade Banister to create an opportunity for Montoya to get a shot at Parisi. Banister liked the large amounts of money that Sinafaldi had greased his palm with in the past, and Benny thought it would be worth a try to offer Banister another payoff.

Joe Parisi had been in jail for more than a month and a half by this time and a trial date had been set for early October. Benny Gallo arranged to meet Charlie Banister in Sinafaldi's office in Worcester, where they had met quite a few times when Sinafaldi was still alive.

The meeting took place on a Sunday afternoon. Banister drove out to Worcester to Sinafaldi's office by himself, where he met with Benny Gallo and Danny Montoya.

"Charlie how are you doing today?" Benny asked.

"I'm doing pretty good. How are you doing Benny?"

The two shook hands and Benny turned to Danny Montoya, "Danny this is Charlie Banister. Charlie is the police chief in Springfield."

"Hi Charlie, good to meet you."

"Charlie, I'd like you to meet a business associate of mine, Danny Montoya."

Benny poured a drink for each of them and they all sat down around a table.

"So what can I do for you Benny?"

"Well Charlie, I know that you're holding Joe Parisi in jail in Springfield, waiting for him to go to trial for killing the Boss. The way I see it he just might beat the murder rap, you know, with some of his boys willing to testify that he was somewhere else."

"Well, he does have some witnesses that are saying that, but your boys in the hospital are saying that he was there and did the deed, and it looks like they are going to be alright and can testify in court."

"Yeah Charlie but I suppose it's all about who the judge believes. I mean Parisi could still walk away."

"Yeah that's true but I don't think he will."

"Well Charlie I would like to get a chance to make sure that he doesn't get away with it."

"What do you mean, kill him?"

"There could be a lot of money in it for you if you could arrange to help me out."

"How much money?"

"Twenty thousand."

"I don't know Benny. He's in the city jail. It might be hard to get him out of there to where you could get the chance."

"Charlie, did you hear about Enzo Fatini and one of his boys getting knocked off in New York last week?"

"Yeah I did."

"Fatini was the guy that the Boss was meeting that day on the bridge."

"Yeah, I just found out about that. It would have been good to get to him before he got knocked off."

"Well he's not going to tell you nothing now. Parisi's boys more than likely are responsible for killing him."

Charlie Banister leaned back in his chair and took a drink. He appeared to be thinking about it. "I suppose I could bring Parisi to the station and question him about it. If you knew when I was going to bring him in maybe you could get a chance then."

Benny reached into his jacket and pulled out a brown envelope and slid it across the table to Banister. He picked it up and put it in his pocket without opening it.

"I'll give you a call next week Benny, but why don't you try to knock off Parisi's witnesses. Without his witnesses he's going to jail for a long time."

"You give me a call, Charlie. If this doesn't work then maybe we'll do that."

Banister got up to leave, "I'll be in touch, Benny," he said as he was leaving.

Charlie Banister went to work Monday morning. He phoned the Chief of Police in Westchester, New York to see if they had any leads on Fatini and Demarco's murder. He found out that the Westchester Police were still investigating the murder but at this point they had no suspects. Charlie told the chief about the murders that took place in Springfield and about wanting to question Joe Parisi about what he might know about the Westchester killings.

The chief told him he wanted to send a couple of detectives that were working on the investigation up to Springfield to be present when they questioned Joe Parisi. Banister agreed to have the detectives present and scheduled them for the following Wednesday.

Banister waited until he got home from work that night before calling Benny and telling him it was going to be Wednesday. "I can't give you a time Benny but I don't want you to do anything before we get to question him. We will bring him to the station sometime in the morning. I don't know how long it's going to take because there's going to be a couple of guys from New York here for it. If you're going to hit him then I want you to wait until he goes back to York Street."

"How am I going to know when he's going back?"

"You'll just have to watch the station. They'll be bringing him in and out of the station by the side door. Just keep an eye on the side door. And don't shoot any of my officers."

"Okay, Charlie, thanks. I'll talk to you later."

On Wednesday the detectives showed up in Springfield about eleven o'clock in the morning. Charlie dispatched a couple of officers to go to the York Street Jail and bring Joe Parisi back to the station for questioning.

Joe Parisi was surprised when a guard came to his cell door and unlocked it.

"Parisi, come with me. There's a couple of cops here that want to talk to you."

The guard led Joe through a couple of locked doors to the front desk of the jail where the two officers were waiting for him. They walked him out of the front door of the jail into a waiting police car and drove him to West Springfield.

They brought him upstairs to an interrogation room where Charlie Banister and the two New York Cops were waiting for him.

"Hello Joe, how are we doing today?" Banister asked.

"What do you want with me?" Parisi answered.

"There's a couple of boys from New York that want to ask you a few questions."

"Questions about what?"

"Maybe I'll just let them ask the questions."

The two officers from New York were sitting at the back of the room. They got up and took a seat across the table from Joe Parisi.

"Do you know Enzo Fatini?" one of the officers said.

"Enzo Fatini? Yeah I've heard of him."

"How about Tony Demarco?"

"No, I can't say that I do. Why do you want to know?"

"Listen Bud, we'll ask the questions here," one of the officers answered. "Wasn't Enzo Fatini on the bridge the day you shot Carlos Sinafaldi?"

"Hey, who says I shot Sinafaldi? I don't know what you're talking about," Joe Parisi snarled back at the cops.

"Come on Joe, we know you were there."

"Yeah, well I got witnesses that say I wasn't."

The cops just seem to ignore what Joe had to say about it and continued asking questions as if he already admitted to it. "What was Fatini doing on the bridge that day?"

"I told you, I wasn't there. How would I know what he was doing there?"

"Did you get Fatini to go to the bridge to set up Sinafaldi?"

"Are you guys deaf or something? I told you I don't know what you're talking about."

"Yeah, well there's a couple of boys in New York who are saying that Fatini got ten thousand dollars from you to set up a meeting with Sinafaldi on the bridge that day."

"Yeah, well those boys are full of shit."

The two officers asked Joe the same questions over and over for the next couple of hours but Joe always gave them the same answers and refrained from admitting he knew anything about Fatini and whether or not he was on the bridge that day.

It was about noon that Anthony Bono showed up at the York Street Jail to meet with Joe Parisi. When he got to the front desk the guard told him that Joe wasn't there and was at the West Springfield Police Station being questioned by two cops from New York.

Bono got in his car and drove to West Springfield. He ran up the steps of the station and pounded his fist on the front desk.

"I'm Anthony Bono and I was told at the York Street Jail that my client Joe Parisi is here being questioned," he shouted to the Sergent at the desk.

"I don't know. I'll have to check for you." He got on the phone and called upstairs.

"Do we have a Joe Parisi here? There's a lawyer here named Anthony Bono. He says that Parisi is his client." The Sergent nodded and hung up the phone and looked up at Bono. "Mister Bono, why don't you have a seat and somebody will be down to talk to you in a couple of minutes."

Bono was livid as he took a seat. It was a couple of minutes later that Charlie Banister showed up in the lobby.

"Hello Mister Bono, what can I do for you?"

Bono stood up as Banister approached him. "The boys at York Street told me you have my client here talking to the New York Police."

"Yeah I think we do have him here," Banister answered.

"Well if he's being questioned then I want to be present."

"Why don't you wait here for a minute while I try to locate him and see what's going on."

Bono sat back down and Banister left the lobby and went upstairs where Joe Parisi was being questioned. He summoned one of the New York cops outside the room.

"You guys got to work quick. Parisi's lawyer is downstairs and says he wants to be present for any questioning. I can hold him off for a few minutes but I'm going to have to let him in."

"Can you give us a few more minutes with him before bringing him up here?"

"Yeah, I'll hold him off for as long as I can," Banister answered.

The New York cops kept on hammering away at Joe Parisi while Banister looked on from the room which was equipped with a one way mirror. Joe stuck to his story and refused to admit anything about knowing Enzo Fatini.

Meanwhile Anthony Bono was waiting in the lobby and getting more upset by the minute. He finally got up and approached the desk again after waiting for another twenty minutes or so. "What the hell is going on?" he snapped at the desk Sergent. "I want to see my client," he pounded his fist on the desk.

"Just a minute," the Sergent answered and got on the phone again. One of the detectives on the floor picked up the phone upstairs. "Is the chief around there?"

"Yeah, just a minute," he said, and went to locate Banister. He found him in the room next to where they were questioning Joe Parisi.

"Chief, the desk is on the phone wanting to talk to you. Banister went to his office and picked up the phone. "Hello this is Banister." "Yeah chief, this lawyer is getting pretty hot under the collar."

"Okay, tell him that I'll be right down."

Banister stopped by the room where they were questioning Joe Parisi and told the cops that he was going to have to bring Parisi's lawyer upstairs. He took his time going down to the lobby and found Anthony Bono pacing back and forth when he got there.

"Mister Bono," Banister said. "It appears that your client is here. Apparently the New York Police got a tip that your client was somehow involved with another murder in New York and they are questioning him about it."

"Why wasn't I notified about this? I want to be present for any questioning."

"I'm sorry Mister Bono, I guess it was just overlooked."

"I would like to see Mister Parisi now."

"Alright, follow me," Banister said, and led Anthony Bono upstairs to the interrogation room.

"Hello Joe," Banister said as he walked into the room. He took a seat next to Joe as the two New York Cops looked on. One of the cops turned to Charlie Banister.

"I think we're done here Charlie."

"You're finished with him?"

"Yeah we're finished."

"Mister Bono, it looks like we're done talking to Mister Parisi. I guess we'll be taking him back to York Street."

"You're done talking to him now that I'm here. What kind of bullshit is this?"

"No bullshit, we're just finished with your client. Would you like a couple of minutes with him before we take him back to jail?"

Bono glared at Banister and after pausing for a few seconds answered, "No that's alright, I'll talk to him at the jail."

Banister summoned the two officers that brought Parisi over from York Street to take him back to jail. They took him down to the side entrance where the police cars were parked. Bono left the police station out the front door and walked to his car.

Meanwhile Benny Gallo and Danny Montoya were parked across the street on the commons side. From where they were parked they had a clear view of the side door of the police station. As Bono got in his car and started to drive away the two cops were coming out of the side door with Joe Parisi.

"There he is," Gallo said as they came out the door.

The cops led Parisi across the parking lot towards the car. Gallo started his car and drove across the street towards them. Parisi and the two cops were out in the open between the side entrance and the car when Danny Montoya opened up on them with a machine gun. As soon as the shooting started Joe Parisi dropped to the ground. The two cops both drew their guns and started to return fire. One of the two cops was hit in the shoulder and went down right away. Montoya sprayed bullets at them and then Gallo took off. He had missed Joe Parisi again, managing only to shoot one of the cops.

Within seconds the outside of the police station was crawling with cops. Montoya and Gallo were already gone by this time. Parisi and the two cops were hurried back into the police station.

About a half an hour later he was taken back to the York Street Jail. Anthony Bono had been waiting at the jail for him and was getting quite annoyed by the time he arrived back there. One of the guards came out to where Anthony Bono had been waiting and let him know that Joe Parisi was back at the jail and that he could see him now. Bono followed the guard through a series of locked doors to the visiting area where Joe Parisi was waiting.

"What the hell took you so long to get here? I thought the cops were bringing you back when I left the police station," Bono said, sounding quite irritated about having to wait so long.

"Hey somebody was trying to kill me. They started shooting at us when we came out of the station."

"When?"

"When the cops were walking me to their car."

"Who was it?"

"Hell I don't know. They shot one of the cops." Joe Parisi replied. "It was probably some of Sinafaldi's boys."

"What were you doing over there anyway?"

"There was a couple of New York cops wanted to talk to me about Enzo Fatini. I guess he got gunned down last week in New York."

"Listen Joe, you don't have to talk to any cops about anything without me being present. If I hadn't come here to see you, I wouldn't have even known about it."

"Okay, okay. What am I supposed to do when they come and get me?"

"You tell them you want to call your lawyer."

"Yeah okay, I'll do that next time. But why did you come to see me?"

"I came to see you because we have a court date for your trial."

"When is it?"

"They set the trial date for September twenty fifth. Do you think we can keep you and your witnesses alive until then?"

"The way these guys shoot? They can't seem to hit anybody though they seem to keep trying." Joe laughed.

"Yeah well I want you and your witnesses to stay alive until the trial. Be careful and if they want to take you anywhere again I want you to call me."

"Alright I'll call you."

They talked for a few more minutes before Bono left the jail.

Charlie Banister was really upset that Benny and Danny Montoya had shot one of his officers in their attempt to get Joe Parisi. He waited until he got home that evening before phoning Gallo in Worcester.

"Benny, what the hell are you doing? You shot one of my men," Banister sounded off at Gallo on the phone.

"Sorry about that Charlie. We didn't mean to shoot your guy. We wanted to get Parisi."

"Listen, I want you to take your gunfight somewhere else. You want to get Parisi or Marvici then you go to Connecticut and get them. Stay out of my town. Do you understand?"

Benny told Banister that he understood and agreed to take it somewhere else. But the gun battles among the two factions were increasing. Just a couple of days after Banister told Gallo to take it somewhere else, another gun battle on South Main Street in Springfield saw another man, John Moaca shot and killed.

It seemed like every week someone else was getting gunned down. Joe Marvici and the members of the 'Familia' were aware of the danger and never went anywhere unarmed or alone.

The following week Joe and Bambino were driving down Main Street in Springfield after visiting with Joe Parisi in York Street Jail when someone opened fire on them riddling their car with bullets. None of the bullets hit either of them but there were twenty three bullet holes in the side of the car.

Agatha always worried about Joe every time he left the house. It was getting scary for her as the newspapers ran stories of shootings every few days. She tried to talk to Joe about getting out of the business but he felt that there was nothing that he could do right now. He had to keep looking after the business while Joe Parisi was in jail. Though the 'Familia' still had a lot of control over the territory in Connecticut, the business in Massachusetts was starting to slip since Joe Parisi went to jail. Benny Gallo was heading Sinafaldi's organization now and had continued to put the pressure on businesses to switch over to him. Some customers in Springfield had been abandoned the 'Familia' in favor of Benny Gallo lately.

The cops in Springfield were making it increasingly harder for Joe and the 'Familia' to do business as well by targeting the businesses that were buying from them. Benny took over where Sinafaldi left off by keeping the police on the payroll so they would know which businesses to harass.

Chapter 16

Joe visited Joe Parisi every week in jail. According to Anthony Bono, as long as Joe and Vinnie stayed alive to testify, Joe Parisi would probably get off the murder rap. Parisi believed that he was going to get off and be out of jail soon to deal with the situation in Springfield himself.

The Springfield cops were still putting the pressure on The Catenzaro Restaurant. About every two weeks they were conducting a raid on the restaurant. John got in the habit of locking the front door and watching through a peephole before opening the door. This would buy them a little time to get the booze off the tables every time the cops showed up to raid the place. Business at the restaurant was falling off because of it though. Many of their customers were choosing to go somewhere else to avoid getting caught in a police raid.

Danny Montoya was getting impatient waiting around Springfield, trying to get another shot at Joe Parisi. It was unlikely they were going to get Charlie Banister to arrange another chance to get Parisi before his trail. Montoya felt like he had been around Springfield long enough and wanted to go back to Chicago. However Benny Gallo didn't want him to leave yet. He had already paid Torrio twenty five thousand and wanted to get something for his money before Montoya left.

Getting Joe Parisi was going to be more difficult since Banister was refusing to let any more killing go on in his town. Benny and brother Tony and a few other members of their organization met with Montoya in Worcester at the beginning of September. Montoya was anxious to get out of the area but Gallo wanted him to make another attempt at killing Parisi's witnesses before he left. Joe Parisi's trial was set to begin on the twenty- fifth of September and there was a good chance he was going to walk away from the murder charge if Joe and Vinnie showed up in court and testified that he was with them and nowhere near the North End Bridge.

"How long am I supposed to stay around here?" Montoya argued with Gallo.

"Danny, I paid Torrio twenty-five thousand for you to get rid of Joe Parisi," Gallo said, making his point. "So far you have managed to miss everybody. I want you to stay here and shoot somebody important before you go back to Chicago."

"Who am I going to shoot who's so important? I can't get to Parisi."

"Let me explain something to you Danny," Gallo leaned across the table towards him. "I want to take over Springfield. I want to be the man who's selling the booze there. I want my competition to be eliminated so that I control that town. Right now Parisi and his mob are my biggest obstacle to being able to take over. If he gets off this murder wrap he's going to fight me for it. If that happens there's going to be more killing and there's a chance that I will lose. Okay, so getting at Parisi is going to be hard, but he's in jail and if he stays in jail then he's going to have a hard time defending his business in Springfield. We got to go after his witnesses. Without them he's going to go to jail for a long time."

"Alright, I'll stay for a little while longer. But I want you to set these guys up so we can get them. And I'm getting out of here when we do."

"Don't worry you can go back to Chicago when you get these guys," Benny answered. "I want you to go to Connecticut with a few of the boys and start keeping watch on these two guys. Joe Marvici is living in Waterbury and Vinnie is looking after the Catenzaro Restaurant in New Haven. Follow them around and find out where they go and what they do every day. Then when an opportunity presents itself 'bang'," Benny made a motion with his hand like he was shooting a gun, "we get these guys."

Montoya smiled at Benny, "Okay Benny."

Gallo sent Montoya and a couple of other guys to New Haven to keep watch on Vinnie and another car with three more of Gallo's men went to Waterbury to keep watch on Joe.

Both Joe and Vinnie had already been shot at a couple of times and were trying to be careful when they went out in public. Joe was in the habit of never leaving his house by himself. Whenever Joe had to go anywhere a car with armed men would pick him up in front of his house and take him to where he wanted to go. He never went anywhere without some gunmen to protect him.

It was towards the end of August when a car with Gallo's men showed up down the street from Joe's house in Waterbury. At the same time Montoya and a couple more men started to keep watch on the Catenzaro Restaurant in New Haven.

Savako and Rocco came to pick Joe up the first morning that Gallo's hoods showed up down the street. Joe walked out of the house and got into the car. Savako drove away and drove right by the car with Gallo's hoods. Savako looked at the men in the car as he drove by. As soon as he passed them they started their car and turned around and followed Joe's car.

"Hey Joe. We got somebody following us." Savako said as he watched them through the rear view mirror.

"Oh yeah! Is it the car with the three guys in it we just passed?"

"Yeah they turned the car around and now they're behind us," Savako answered as he watched through the rear view mirror.

Gallo's hoods kept a fair distance behind as they followed them through Waterbury.

In the back seat Rocco cocked the bolt on a machine gun and was ready to shoot if he needed too.

"Let's take them for a tour," Joe directed Savako. "Drive around town and see if they stay behind us."

Savako drove all around Waterbury while going up and down the same streets more than once. The car stayed well back but continued to follow them. Savako then drove to the Catenzaro Restaurant in Waterbury, and pulled the car around to the rear entrance. Savako and Rocco stayed with the car as Joe went inside.

As Joe entered the restaurant from the back door Serafino met him at the door. "Hello Joe. How are you today?"

"I'm good Serafino. But... we got some hoods following us today."

"They followed you here?"

"Yeah, they're right down the street. Savako and Rocco are outside by the car keeping an eye on them."

"Do you know who it is?"

"Not yet but we're going to find out," Joe answered. "Get Vinnie on the phone. I want to talk to him."

Joe sat down at the table by the kitchen and waited for Serafino to bring the telephone to him. "Vinnie I got some hoods following me this morning."

"Oh yeah?" "Yeah, they were waiting outside my house this morning. Savako and Rocco picked me up and they followed us to the Restaurant."

"Do you know who they are?"

"No not yet but I want to find out."

"How many are they?"

"There's three of them in the car."

"Should I get a couple of boys and come over there?"

"Before you do that Vinnie, take a look outside the restaurant and see if there's any cars parked on the street with people in it, they might be watching you too." "Okay I'll be right back." Vinnie looked out of the front door of the restaurant onto the street. There were a couple of cars parked on the street in front and a couple in the parking lot. There didn't seem to be anyone in those cars, but then Vinnie turned his head and looked down the street and noticed a car with several guys inside parked about a half a block from the restaurant. He went back inside and picked up the phone.

"Yeah Joe, there is a car down the street with a few guys in it."

"Take a ride somewhere Vinnie. See if they follow you. And make sure that you take a couple of guys with you. Don't go alone. I'm here at the restaurant in Waterbury. I'll wait here for you to call me back."

Vinnie made a call to Antonio Rizzo and told him what was going on and asked him to come down to the restaurant and bring a couple of extra guys with him. Rizzo showed up about twenty minutes later with two other gunmen. They walked out of the restaurant by the front door in plain view of Montoya and Gallo's men. Vinnie got in Rizzo's car with the others and started down the street. As soon as they pulled away from the restaurant Montoya's car pulled out and followed them. Vinnie had Rizzo drive around New Haven the same way Joe had done in Waterbury, driving down some of the same streets more than once. Montoya's car stayed a safe distance behind but followed them wherever they went. After about half an hour they drove back to the Catenzaro and Vinnie phoned Joe back.

"It looks like they're watching me too. We drove all around town and they followed us everywhere," Vinnie told Joe.

"It's probably Sinafaldi's hoods. I want you to be careful Vinnie. Don't go anywhere without some guns for protection at least until we find out who they are and what they want."

"Okay Joe," Vinnie assured him.

Now that Joe knew that both he and Vinnie were being watched he got Serafino to drive him home. Gallo's hoods followed them to Joe's house and parked up the street again and continued to watch the house.

After returning to the house Joe got on the phone again and called Bambino in Hartford.

"Hey Romano, how are you doing?"

"I'm doing okay Joe. What's up?"

"I got a car with three guys parked down the street watching my house."

"Oh yeah, you know who it is?"

"No, but I suspect that it's Sinafaldi's guys."

"How long have they been there?"

"I just noticed them this morning and Vinnie's says there's a car with another three guys watching the restaurant in New Haven too."

"You better watch out Joe. You and Vinnie are both witnesses in Joe's trail."

"Yeah I know and the reason I'm calling you is I want you to put a few men together and let's confront them on the street where they're parked before they shoot somebody."

"Yea Joe, I can do that. When do you want to do it?"

"I'm going to call Masalino and tell him the same thing. Maybe we can do it tomorrow. I'll get the guys watching me first and then we'll go to New Haven."

Yeah, okay Joe, when do you want me to come down there?"

"Can you make it tomorrow morning?"

"Yeah, I'll be there," Bambino answered.

"Alright, I'll see you tomorrow. Give me a call before you leave Hartford."

Joe hung up the phone and called John Masalino in Springfield. He had the same conversation with Masalino, who agreed to follow Bambino to Waterbury and confront the guys watching Joe's house first and then go to New Haven and confront the guys watching the restaurant and Vinnie.

Joe spent the rest of the day inside the house looking out the upstairs window every once in a while at the car down the street. They remained down the street until well after dark. When Joe got up the next morning they were still there.

After seeing Joe looking out the window repeatedly Agatha figured out that something was going on. She looked out and noticed the car parked down the street with men in it. She tried to talk to Joe about it but he wouldn't tell her anything for fear that she would just get worried. He felt like this was a problem that he could take care of and saw no need to get her upset.

Vinnie had an apartment above the restaurant where he stayed that night. Antonio Rizzo and the two other gunmen stayed with

Vinnie. The next morning Vinnie looked out on the street and saw the car was still down the street with the three men in it.

Bambino made a call to Joe about nine in the morning telling him that he was ready to leave Hartford. John Masalino had just arrived and they were going to drive down together.

"When you get to Waterbury I want both of you to come to my house first," Joe said to Bambino. "We'll deal with these guys outside my house first and then we'll go to New Haven. I want you to come to my house and pick me up just like you're taking me somewhere. I'll come out and get in the car and I want John to approach the car from behind as soon as we start to drive away from my house. They will be paying attention to us as we leave the house and John can get the drop on them from behind. You tell John what I want him to do." Bambino arrived at Joe's in Waterbury just before eleven o'clock in the morning. Joe was keeping an eye out for him through the window. As soon as Bambino pulled up in front of the house Joe put on his overcoat and went out to the car. As he got in the car Gallo's men started their car expecting to follow them again. Agatha looked out the window as Joe left the house and watched as he drove towards the car parked on the street.

As Bambino started to drive down the street John Masalino approached in the other direction. Masalino and his gunmen pulled over behind Gallo's hoods as if he was pulling over to let the car with Bambino and Joe go by. Bambino slowed the car down as they got close to them. Gallo's men had focused their attention on the approaching car and before they knew it Masalino and his men had guns drawn on them. Masalino swung open the back door of their car and at gunpoint ordered them to get out of the car.

Joe, Bambino and the other gunmen got out of the car with guns drawn. Masalino had Gallo's men out on the sidewalk and ordered them to put their hands against the car. He frisked them and took a pistol from each one of them and a couple of machine guns from inside the car. Joe turned the driver around.

"What are you doing watching my house," Joe said angrily at the driver. "The driver just looked at Joe and wouldn't answer. Joe

cracked him across the face with the gun barrel. Blood streamed
from the drivers mouth.

"I'm asking you again. Why are you watching my house?"

Still the driver refused to say anything. Joe cracked him across
the face again this time loosening some teeth. The driver was spitting blood yet still said nothing.

"Let's just shoot them. Then they won't be watching nobody,"
Bambino said in an angry tone.

Joe put his gun to the driver's head and cocked it. "Maybe I
should listen to my friend," Joe said to the driver.

"Okay, okay, I will tell you. Just don't shoot."

"You better start talking," Joe pushed the gun against his head.
"Now, why are you watching my house?"

"My boss wants me to watch you and see where you go every
day."

"And who is your boss?" Joe shoved the gun against his head.

"Benny Gallo."

"Benny Gallo who worked for Sinafaldi?"

"Yeah that's right."

"It's Gallo's boys that are watching the Catenzaro Restaurant in
New Haven too?"

"Yea that's right."

"You know you could get yourself killed watching my house
like you're doing."

The driver just shook his head.

"Now you and your boys get the hell out of here and if I see you
watching my house again you're all going to be dead men. Do we
understand each other?"

The driver nodded.

Joe removed the gun from his head. "Now get out of here."

The driver and the other two men got in their car and drove off.
Joe had attracted some attention with the neighbors on his street.
Some of the neighbors were watching from their windows at the
happenings outside. Joe noticed that they were being watched.

"Let's get out of here. It looks like we have an audience." They
got in the cars and headed for New Haven.

The boys that they confronted in Waterbury had a few minute's head start on them and were driving to New Haven as well, trying to get there before Joe's and the guys and warn Montoya about them.

They got to the Catenzaro Restaurant a few minutes before Joe, pulling the car up beside Montoya's car.

"What are you guys doing here?" Montoya said as the car pulled up beside him.

"We got run out of Waterbury by Marvici and a mob of his men. I think he's headed this way."

"How many of them are there?" Montoya asked.

"Two cars, maybe about six or seven of them. They got the drop on us from behind. I'm just warning you because they're going to be here soon. We're getting out of here." The driver put the car in gear and drove off, going north back to Massachusetts.

Montoya started the car and started to pull away just as the two cars with Joe and Bambino pulled around the corner.

"There they are," Bambino said as Montoya's car passed them going the other way.

Bambino turned the car around and took off after them. John Masalino, after seeing Bambino turn around followed and the two went in pursuit of Montoya.

Montoya wasn't going to be caught easily. He sped through the streets of New Haven heading for the highway north to Massachusetts. Bambino and John Masalino followed in pursuit but were unable to catch Montoya's car as he raced through the streets and onto the Wallingford Trunk Road toward Hartford. Montoya had the faster car and was starting to pull away. After pursuing Montoya's car for a few miles outside of New Haven they realized that they were not going to catch him. By the time they got close to Wallingford Montoya had gotten so far ahead that they lost sight of his car. Realizing that they weren't going to catch him, Joe ordered Bambino to turn the car around and go back to New Haven. He felt that he could be sure that Gallo's boy's wouldn't be returning to watch his house or the Catenzaro Restaurant any time soon.

They all returned to the Catenzaro Restaurant to have lunch and talk about the situation.

"I think that we got to careful Joe," Vinnie spoke up. "If these guys are Gallo's boys then they probably don't want you or I to be able to testify at the Boss's trial."

"The trial is less than a month away. There's a good chance that they'll be trying to get us before the trial," Joe answered Vinnie. "We are going to have to be careful and not go anywhere by ourselves. Vinnie you and I got to have some of the boys with us each time we leave our house or any time we go anywhere."

Vinnie agreed and the others all concurred that they must be especially careful from now until the trial.

"I have to go to Springfield and see the Boss in a couple of days," Joe informed the others. "I'm going to need some of you boys to go with me."

"I'll go with you," John Masalino said. "I'll drive down from Springfield the night before and go with you.

"Rocco and I will go too Joe.," Bambino added. "Do you want to pick us up in Hartford or do you want us to drive to Waterbury?"

"I don't think those guys are going to come to Connecticut again. John, you come to Waterbury and pick me up and then we'll get Bambino and Rocco when we pass through Hartford," Joe said. "Vinnie, I want you to hang around the restaurant and keep a low profile. You keep Rizzo with you. We need you to stay alive to testify."

"Sure Joe. No one wants me to stay alive more than me," Vinnie laughed.

The meeting broke up right after lunch and Joe rode back to Waterbury with Bambino and Rocco and the two other gunmen. John Masalino followed them in his car. They dropped Joe off at his house in Waterbury. He got out of Bambino's car and walked back to John Masalino's car.

"I'll see you in a couple of days John. You can pick me up here in the morning. I'll give you a call."

"Okay Joe," Masalino answered. "Be careful."

Joe shook hands with Masalino and walked to the front door. The drivers of both cars waited until Joe opened the front door and went in his house before pulling away.

Agatha met Joe at the door and embraced him. "I'm so glad to see you Joe. I was worried about you."

He put his arms around her. "Don't worry my dear, I'm going to be fine." Agatha wanted to believe him and pressed him close to her. She said nothing and a tear slowly ran down her cheek as she held him.

They could hear the children playing in the next room from the entrance way where they were standing. Joe and Agatha gazed into each other's eyes and smiled at each other.

Joe stayed around home the rest of the day and the next day. Agatha couldn't seem to shake the feeling of uneasiness that had come over her. She was especially affectionate towards Joe as she had a feeling that something was going to happen to him. The morning that John Masalino was supposed to pick Joe up Agatha pleaded with Joe not to go to Springfield. She had a strange dream the night before in which she dreamed that someone was shot and killed. In the dream it was not clear who it was but it woke her up in the middle of the night.

She lay there in bed with Joe and looked at him sleeping peacefully beside her. It was an uneasy feeling that she couldn't explain except to say that she was worried that someone was going to try to kill him.

The next morning Agatha pleaded with Joe not to go to Springfield. Again Joe assured her that he would be alright as John Masalino pulled up in front of the house in the morning. Agatha cried as Joe left the house and got into Masalino's car. She watched from the window as they pulled away.

They drove north, stopping in Hartford and picking up Bambino and Rocco before driving the rest of the way to Springfield. Visiting hours at the York Street Jail were between one and four o'clock. They arrived there a few minutes before one. John and Rocco stayed with the car outside the jail as Bambino and Joe went in to visit Joe Parisi. They were led through a couple of locked doors into the visiting area where Joe Parisi was waiting for them sitting at a table. Joe and Bambino took seats across from Parisi.

"Hello Joe, how are you doing today?"

"I'm doing okay," Parisi answered reaching across the table and shaking hands with both of them. "How are you both doing?"

"Except for people trying to shoot us, we're doing pretty good." "Who's trying to shoot you?"

"A few of Gallo's boys been parked outside my house and parked outside the Catenzaro for a few days this last week."

"In New Haven?"

"Yeah, me and the boys ran them off yesterday."

"Who were they?"

"It was some of Gallo's boys. They were watching Vinnie and me."

"You sure?"

"Yeah we're sure. We got the drop on them watching my house and one of them talked."

"You boys got to be careful." "Oh we're being careful Boss. That's why we got the drop on them."

Joe Parisi leaned across the table towards Joe and Bambino, "Do you remember Dominic Perrotti?"

"The Italian fellow from Rhode Island?"

"Yeah, he's been waiting for trial for a couple of murders that took place last year in West Springfield. They charged him with killing a couple of guys from Connecticut."

"Yeah, I remember hearing about him."

"Well he just got out of jail this week. He beat the murder rap against him. They couldn't seem to find any witnesses to testify against him."

"Yeah, I remember hearing about him," Bambino spoke up.

"I've been talking to him while he was in jail with me. I think he may be able to help us out. I want you to go and see him in New Haven. I think that he may be able to help us get rid of our witnesses."

"You talked to him about it?"

"Yes, we talked about it. You need to bring twenty thousand dollars to give to him and he'll make the witnesses disappear."

"How do we find him?"

Joe Parisi had a telephone number written on his forearm. "Write down this number," he said showing his forearm to Joe.

Joe pulled a pen out of his jacket and copied the number onto the back of his hand.

"Find him and give him the twenty thousand. We got a little over two weeks before the trial. He'll take care of the witnesses before that."

"So he's expecting us to be in touch."

"That's right. You should go see him today. We don't have a lot of time to take care of this situation, so let's get together with him right away and make sure he has some time to take care of it."

"Okay Boss, we'll go to see him today."

"Good, now get out of here and go pick up the money and go see him."

The three men shook hands and Joe and Bambino left the jail. They walked out of the front doors of the jail to the car where John and Rocco were waiting for them.

As they were walking down the long steps at the front of the jail Danny Montoya and a couple of Gallo's hoods drove by.

"That's him," Montoya said in a low tone as they passed the jail. "That's Marvici coming down the steps." The car continued down the street past the jail and went around the block.

Joe and Bambino were just getting into the car across the street when Montoya's car was coming around the block towards the front entrance. Joe got into the driver's seat and started the car and pulled away down York Street onto Columbus Avenue. Montoya followed him, staying well behind them so as not to be noticed. Gallo had gotten a tip that Joe was going to visit Parisi in jail today and had sent Montoya to the jail to check it out. It was just luck that he happened to be passing the jail just when Joe and Bambino were leaving. "We got to go to New Haven to see a guy named Dominic Perrotti," Bambino said to John and Rocco. "The Boss made arrangements with him to get rid of the witnesses against him."

"Was that the same Dominic Perrotti who was in jail for killing a couple of guys from New Haven?" Masalino asked.

"Yeah that's the guy. I guess he just beat the rap against him. They couldn't find any witnesses to testify against him." Bambino continued to fill John and Rocco in on the details. "The Boss had a chance to talk to him before he got out and made a deal with him to take care of these guys for twenty thousand."

Joe stopped at a gas station and filled the car with gas before they left Springfield. Montoya pulled his car over to the side of the street when he saw Joe pull into the gas station. He waited there until Joe pulled back onto the road and then followed him, staying as far behind him as he could while still keeping him in sight.

Joe made a stop in Hartford at the Catenzaro Restaurant. All four of them went into the restaurant for a bite to eat. They sat at their usual table in the back of the restaurant close to the kitchen. While they waited for the food to be prepared, Joe used the phone at the front counter at the restaurant and called Dominic Perrotti.

He dialed the number he had written on the back of his hand. After several rings a man answered on the other end.

"Hello, I would like to speak to Dominic Perrotti."

"Who's calling?" the man answered on the other end.

"My name is Joe Marvici. I'm a friend of Joe Parisi." The phone was silent for a few seconds and then Perrotti answered. "Hello, Dominic here. What can I do for you?"

"Hello Dominic, this is Joe Marvici. I am an associate of Joe Parisi. I just talked to Joe Parisi this morning and he told me that I should get in touch with you."

"Yes, Joe Parisi told me that you would be getting in touch."

"I am on my way to New Haven to talk to you right now."

"Where are you now?"

"I'm in Hartford at the moment stopping for a bite to eat."

"And when will you get to New Haven?"

"I will probably be there by about three o'clock, maybe three thirty."

"Can we meet somewhere at four o'clock?"

"Do you know where the Catenzaro Restaurant is in New Haven?"

"Yeah, I know where it is."

"I will meet you there at four o'clock."

"Alright, four o'clock," Perrotti answered. "Do you have the money?"

"I will have it when we meet." Joe answered. Perrotti was satisfied that Joe would show up with the money and cut the call short, agreeing to be there at four o'clock.

Joe hung up the telephone and before he went back to the table telephoned Vinnie at the Catenzaro Restaurant in New Haven.

"Hello Vinnie."

"Yeah this is Vinnie."

"Vinnie it's Joe Marvici. I'm on my way to New Haven now. I'm meeting an Italian fellow at the Catenzaro at four o'clock. The Boss wanted me to meet with this guy and talk to him about doing some work for us. This is an important meeting Vinnie. It would be good if there were nobody else in the restaurant when we are having this meeting. Can you arrange it for us?"

"No problem Joe."

"Oh and one more thing Vinnie."

"What's that?"

"I need you to get some money together and have it there when I get there."

"Sure Joe, how much money?"

"Twenty thousand."

"Twenty thousand? Alright Joe. It'll be here when you get here."

"I'll see you about three thirty." Joe hung up the telephone and was going to join the others at the table when the phone rang. It was Rocco's brother calling, wanting to talk to Rocco. Joe joined the others at the table and told Rocco that he was wanted on the phone. Rocco got up and answered the call.

"Hello Rocco. Your wife's in the hospital, she's having the baby. Maybe you better get down there."

"Holy shit, I thought she wasn't having the baby until next week."

"Well she went to the hospital this morning."

"Alright, I'll get there right away."

Rocco went back to the table, "That was my brother. He said that my wife is in the hospital having a baby."

"Congratulations Rocco." Bambino said loudly, extending his hand to him.

"Yeah, congratulations," both Joe and John shook his hand.

"Are you going to need me to go with you or can I go to the hospital?"

"Hey Rocco, we're going to be okay. You go to the hospital and see your wife."

"Thanks Joe, I'll see you later." Rocco got up and left the restaurant.

In the meantime Danny Montoya and the other two gunmen were parked down the street on the next block from the restaurant watching for Joe and the others to come out. They were armed with 45 caliber handguns and machine guns, and spent the waiting time making sure the guns were loaded and ready to use at a moment's notice.

It was about two thirty in the afternoon when Joe and John Masalino got ready to leave Hartford for the drive to New Haven. Bambino walked with them to the street in front of the restaurant where the car was parked. Bambino checked the street in both directions as Joe and John got into the car. Montoya's car was parked far enough down the street that none of them noticed him.

As Joe started the car Bambino asked, "are you sure you don't want me to go with you?"

"Romano, we are going to be alright. Besides if we have any trouble we can take care of it," Joe answered and drew back his coat exposing the 45 caliber handgun. Both he and John were armed with 45's.

"Okay Joe, you be careful." Bambino reached in through the window and shook Joe's hand.

Joe pulled away and headed to the highway towards New Haven. Montoya noticed Joe's car pull away from the restaurant and waited until Bambino had gone back inside before pulling out and following them, keeping a safe distance behind so as not to be detected.

The two men were in a positive mood on the drive to New Haven. Joe had recently purchased a new Willys-Knight sedan and was enjoying driving it down the highway. It was a warm afternoon, the sun was shining and it still felt like a summer day even though it was the first week of September. The two men rode with the windows open as the wind blew through the car keeping the air cool. They were a few miles north of North Haven on the Wallingford-New Haven Trunk Road when Montoya decided to make his move. Until this point he had stayed far behind them, just far enough to keep them in sight. It was a long straight stretch of highway where Montoya picked up speed in order to overtake Joe's car. Montoya was driving a black late model Ford touring car. As Montoya was closing the distance between them, both the other men in the car crouched down in their seats with guns ready. Montoya had a pistol lying on the seat beside him as well.

As they started to overtake Joe's car, Joe could see the car approaching behind him through his rear view mirror but it looked to him like there was only one person in the car. He didn't think anything of it. He and John were talking when Montoya's car started to pull up beside them.

Montoya's car pulled abreast of Joe's car. At that moment John turned and glanced over at Joe. Montoya waited for the two cars were side by side before putting his hand on the 45 on the seat beside him. He was looking straight ahead and took his foot off the gas quickly slowing his car down to the same speed that Joe and John were traveling.

John was the first to notice the other car slowing down. He looked past Joe towards Montoya's car.

Montoya turned his head towards them and raised the gun from the seat pointing it right at Joe.

John looked past Joe and at Montoya a split second before he fired his gun.

"Look out!" John yelled out and reached for his gun. That very instant the two men who had been crouching down in their seats appeared with guns pointing at the two men. Montoya's gun was the first to discharge.

Joe reacted to John's warning by reaching for his gun but before he could pull it from his holster under his coat a shot rang out and a bullet hit him in the left forearm. Instantly the other two men started shooting at them with machine guns. A bullet hit Joe in the eye, killing him instantly. He slumped in the driver's seat and lost control of the vehicle, swerving off the road to the right. Montoya and his men continued to fire on the car even after the car went off the road and down the bank onto an empty lot.

John Masalino managed to shoot back at them twice before being hit himself. While firing back he was wounded on the side of the head. The bullet went through the lobe of his ear grazing the lower scalp, but it did not penetrate the skull.

After the car left the road Montoya and his men continued to fire at it until they got well past. Then he stepped on the gas and got out of there. Joe's car came to a stop in the vacant lot.

John, who was not seriously hurt, came to his senses when the car finally stopped. Joe lay slumped over the wheel. His eye was shot away and blood poured from the wound.

"Joe, Joe," John called out and then got out of the car and quickly went around to the driver's side and opened the door. He tried to get a response out of Joe but to no avail.

John stood over his friend and made the sign of the cross. He began to say a prayer over him. "Our Father, who art in heaven, hallowed be thy name......."

At that moment a car stopped on the highway. It was Reverend Lewis from New Haven. He had been driving down the highway some distance behind when he heard the shots being fired. He was not able to see who was doing the shooting but did notice that there were three men in the black touring car firing at Joe's car. By the time he arrived on the scene Montoya and taken off and was down the road out of sight.

Reverend Lewis stopped his car and jumped out and ran down the bank towards Joe's car. He ran up to where John was on the driver's side of the car. John cradled his friend in his arms, talking to him and listening for any sign of breathing, but there was none. Blood ran down Joe's face from the fatal wound in his eye. Masalino was bleeding profusely from the wound in his ear and the blood was running down his neck and soaking his coat on the shoulder.

"Is he alive?" Reverend Lewis said to John after getting close to him and seeing the eye shot away.

"I don't think so. I can't hear any breathing."

"Did you see who was shooting at you?" the Reverend asked.

"I did get a look at his face but I don't know who he was."

Another motorist who was driving by the two cars on the side of the road shortly after the shooting proceeded to North Haven. In New Haven Constable Herbert Carlson was having coffee with a fellow constable in a restaurant on the north side of town. His police car was parked in front of the restaurant. The motorist was going to drive to the North Haven Police station but noticing the police car parked in front of the restaurant, he pulled into the parking lot. Getting out of his car, he hurried inside. The constables were sitting at the counter when the motorist barged inside.

"There's been a shooting down the highway," he said in a frantic tone.

Constable Carlson got up from his seat asking, "Where and when?"

"Just north of town about four or five miles."

"Anybody hurt?"

"I don't know, I didn't stop but there was a car off the road and someone had already stopped to help. It looked like someone had been shot."

"Come on, let's go," the constable said to his partner and they hurried to the police car and took off north of town with the siren blaring. The police arrived on the scene and found John Masalino still holding Joe hoping that he would revive but to no avail.

Several cars had pulled over along the side of the highway and a small crowd had gathered around the car by the time the constable arrived. One fellow who had stopped investigated saw that someone had been shot. He went back to his car and drove north to Wallingford, notifying the police there about the shooting. Shortly afterwards an ambulance and the medical examiner from Wallingford were on the way to the scene. It was J.H. Duffum, a doctor from Wallingford and the medical examiner for the area who pronounced Joe dead at the scene. The doctor examined the wound in John Masalino's ear and bandaged it. The wound was not that serious yet it it needed to be bandaged to stop the bleeding. The bandage made the wound look much worse than it was.

While the ambulance attendants covered Joe's body and moved him to the ambulance Constable Carlson and the deputy took John Masalino back to the police car and into custody for questioning. They transported him to the North Haven Police Station for questioning. The ambulance followed the police to North Haven and continued on, taking Joe's body to the morgue in New Haven.

Aside from the obvious, the North Haven Police couldn't get any additional information out of John Masalino. The truth was he didn't know who the shooters were and was not willing to give up any information about the situation surrounding the shooting. After about half an hour of questioning, Masalino was allowed to make a phone call. He telephoned Vinnie at the Catenzaro Restaurant. It was already a little past four o'clock and Dominic Perrotti and a couple of his men had just arrived.

"Vinnie, this John Masalino. We had a little problem on the way to New Haven."

"What happened? Perrotti and his boys just showed up here."

"Joe and I were ambushed on the highway between Wallingford and North Haven."

"What? What do you mean?"

"They got Joe."

"What do you mean they got Joe?"

"They got him Vinnie, he's dead."

"Who got him?"

"We don't know who it was yet."

"Where are you now?"

"I'm in the North Haven Police Station. How about sending someone here to pick me up?"

"Yeah sure, I'll send someone to get you. But what do I do about Perrotti? He's here waiting."

"Give him something to eat. Just keep him there until I get there."

"Alright John, I'll think of something to tell him. I'm sending my nephew to pick you up right away."

"Okay Vinnie, you tell him I'll be waiting out in front."

Vinnie phoned his nephew Charlie, who lived in North Haven and asked him to go pick up John Masalino and bring him to the Catenzaro in New Haven.

Vinnie hung up the phone and paused for a minute. He thought I better call Bambino. He dialed Bambino's number in Hartford. After a couple of rings Bambino answered.

"Romano, John Masalino just called me from the North Haven Police station."

"What happened? Why is he calling you from the police station?"

"John and Joe were ambushed on the highway near North Haven."

"Oh shit, I knew we should have gone with them."

"Joe's dead."

"Joe's dead? What about John?"

"Well he's alive because he just called me. I sent my nephew Charlie to go pick him up. Maybe you better come down here. Perrotti is waiting in the restaurant right now."

"God damn it. I knew Rocco and I should have went with them. Okay Vinnie, I'm leaving right away." Bambino hung up the phone and called Rocco.

"Rocco, get ready we have to go to New Haven. I'm picking you up right away."

"What's going on Romano?"

"I'll tell you about it on the way. Just be ready, I'll be right over to get you."

"Hey Romano, it's a boy."

"Hey congratulations Rocco."

Bambino hung up the phone and drove to Rocco's picking him up and heading south to New Haven.

Bambino filled Rocco in on the details as he sped south on the highway, driving as fast as the car could go.

In the meantime Vinnie went over to the table where Dominic Perrotti and his boys were waiting. "My friends are going to be a little late. Can I get you something to eat?" he said giving a menu to each of them.

They each ordered from the menu while they waited.

John Masalino arrived with Vinnie's nephew Charlie about twenty minutes later. He walked in the front door and got Vinnie over to the side. "I know this is a very bad situation Vinnie but the boss is still in jail and we got to make a deal with Perrotti right now."

"Yeah, I know. Bambino is on his way too." "Do you have the money that Joe wanted you to get?"

"The twenty thousand?"

"Yeah, I got it here."

"That's good. They're waiting for us in the dining room."

" They are having something to eat."

"Okay, we'll try to keep them here until Bambino arrives but if they don't want to wait we are going to have to make the deal with him."

Vinnie and John went to the table where Perrotti and his boys were sitting. They were just finishing their meal. Vinnie introduced John to them and motioned for the waitress to clear off the table.

"Hello Dominic, this is my associate, John Masalino."

Dominic Perrotti stood up and extended his hand to John, "Pleasure to meet you," he answered. "What happened to you?" he asked, looking at the bandage on John's head.

"It's nothing. I just caught a bullet in the ear. It's not serious." John and Vinnie sat down at the table. "I was just talking to my Boss today in Springfield. He tells me that you will be willing to help us, shall I say, make some people lose their memory."

"Yeah, your boss and I had some discussions about the witnesses that might want to testify against him in court."

"You know who these witnesses are then?"

"Yeah, in cases like this I make it my business to know who they are."

"So we can expect you to see that they don't make it to court."

"That's right. I will make sure that they don't make it to court."
"The trial is in a little over two weeks so we will expect you to get right on it."

"There is a matter of the money." John turned to Vinnie and nodded. Vinnie got up from the table and went to the front of the restaurant, returning with a briefcase. He put the briefcase on the table in front of Perrotti. Perrotti opened it and looked inside briefly. After he was assured that the money was in it, he closed it and slid it over to one of his men.

"Don't worry my friend, those witnesses will never say a word at your boss's trial."

They shook hands on the deal and Perrotti and his men got up and left.

After they left the restaurant and the deal was done John and Vinnie went back to the table and sat down.

"What the hell happened out on the highway John?"

"It was a mistake to drive down here and leave Bambino and Rocco in Hartford. Joe might have survived it we had the extra guns with us."

"Why didn't they come with you?"

"I don't know. Joe didn't feel that it was necessary We were in Connecticut and somehow none of us felt like we were in danger. Besides Rocco's wife was having a baby and he wanted to go to the hospital."

"So what happened?"

"We were just driving down the highway and a car came up beside us. It looked like just one person driving. We thought he was just going to pass us and all of a sudden two other guys with guns came up and they all started shooting at us. Joe went for his gun when a bullet hit him in the arm. There wasn't much we could do, the next one got him in the eye and the car went off the road and they took off down the highway. When the car stopped Joe was already dead."

A little while after Perrotti left, Bambino and Rocco arrived. Bambino came through the front door in a rush and with Rocco right behind.

Vinnie and John were sitting at the table by the kitchen as usual and Bambino went right to the back of the room where they were sitting.

"John, are you alright?" Bambino asked right away, seeing the bandage around his head.

"Yeah, don't worry about me, I'm alright."

"I want to hear what happened." Bambino said. "Sit down and tell me."

John described the events after they left Bambino and Rocco in Hartford. After hearing the story of the shooting from John, Bambino and Rocco made the sign of the cross and said a quick prayer for Joe.

"Has anybody told Agatha yet?" Bambino asked.

"Not that we know of," John answered.

"Well we had better go and tell her. It's only right that she knows."

The four of them drove to Waterbury to tell Agatha of the shooting, knowing that she would not take it well.

Chapter 17

Agatha had been worried about Joe for some time now. The nature of the business he was in was reason for concern every day as it was. She stood at the front door and watched Joe get in the car with John Masalino that morning and as they drove away a strange feeling had overcome her. She remembered the dream she had where someone had gotten shot and killed. A feeling of fear and nervousness had passed through her as the car was pulling away. She made the sign of the cross and said a prayer that Joe would return safely. The uneasy feeling stayed with her all day long as she repeatedly looked out the window during the day, hoping that Joe would show up at the door.

While Bambino and the others were still on route to Waterbury Agatha was visited by Constable Carlson from the North Haven Police.

She was looking out the window hoping Joe would be returning soon when she saw the police car pull up to the front of the house.

"Oh, no," she said to herself as she watched two constables get out of the car and walk towards the house.

The children were playing in another room when the knock came on the door. Agatha answered the door and felt immediately distressed when she opened the door and the two police constables stood there in front of her. "Mrs. Marvici?"

"Yes," she answered.

"Are you by yourself?"

"Yes I am. Just me and the children," she answered. "But why are asking me that?"

"Mrs. Marvici, we have some bad news for you." "Oh no," she said and started to sob.

"Your husband is Joe Marvici?"

"Yes, yes," she sobbed.

"I'm sorry to tell you that your husband has been shot and killed this afternoon."

Agatha let out a loud wail and then collapsed in the doorway.

"No, no, he can't be dead," she wailed.

The two constables tried to get her up and into the house. She let herself be helped up and led back into the house and to the couch in the living room. The children heard their mother wailing and came into the room to find out what was going on.

"Is there someone you could call to come and stay with you?"

"Yes," she answered between sobs, "My neighbor Rosita." .

"Do you have a telephone number for Rosita?"Constable Carlson asked.

"Yes....it's in the book by the telephone," Agatha answered while pointing to the telephone.

The constable called Rosita who only lived on the next block.

Rosita answered the phone, "Hello".

"Hello, this is Constable Carlson from the North Haven Police. I would like to speak to Rosita."

"This is Rosita speaking."

"I am at the home of Agatha Marvici. There's been a tragedy in the family and Mrs Marvici has asked me to call you and ask you to come over to the house right away."

"What kind of tragedy?"

"Mister Marvici has been shot and killed."

"Oh my God," she answered and the line went silent for a minute.

"Rosita, are you still there?"

"Yes I'm still here." she paused, "Yes of course, I will be right there."

She hung up the telephone and held herself upright, leaning against the wall. Rosita was overcome with emotion. She covered her eyes with one hand and wiped away tears from her eyes.

"Savako," she called out. "Savako."

Savako was working at his desk when he heard Rosita yelling for him. Her voice had the sound of panic and Savako hurried to her.

"What's the matter Rosita?"

"I have to go to Agatha's. That was the police who just called." Tears were streaming down her cheeks as she talked. "Joe has been shot and killed."

"Oh my God," Savako replied. "When ?"

"It must .....have just .....happened," Rosita replied finding it hard to talk. "Let's just go."

The Marvici's house was only on the next block and Rosita and Savako hurried over to the house. The police met Rosita and Savako at the door and talked to them briefly before leaving the house.

They arrived to find Agatha crying hysterically. The children were still in the house and they could hear their mother crying. Rosita helped Agatha into the living room and sat down on the sofa with her. The children could hear all the commotion and came out to the living room and gathered around their mother. All of the children seeing their mother crying became quite upset and started to cry too although they did not understand why right away. All they knew was that something terrible had happened.

Savako heard a car pull up in front of the house. Bambino, Rocco, John and Vinnie had arrived.

Savako went outside to the car as Rosita stayed with Agatha and the children in the living room. By this time Agatha had been over taken by her grief. She cried hysterically as Rosita tried to comfort her and the children.

"What happened?" Savako asked Bambino as he was getting out of the car.

"John and Joe got ambushed on the highway in North Haven."

Savako looked over at John who was wearing the bandage on his head."Are you alright?" he asked John.

"Yeah, I'm alright but ......Joe didn't make it."

Constable Carlson recognized John Masalino as the four men got out of the car and approached the house. He raised his hand toward John trying to get his attention and John walked over to him.

"She's taken it pretty hard John." Carlson said. "I want to ask her if she wants to go to the morgue and see the body but this might not be the right time." The constable wrote down a telephone number and gave it to John. "Here is a telephone number for the morgue if she wants to go see the body later," he handed the paper with the number to John."There is nothing more that we can do now. We will see you later."

The two constables went to their car and drove away.

Some of the neighbors noticed the police car out in front of the Marvici's house and a few people came out of their houses and gathered on the street. Agatha's sobbing and wailing could be heard on the street as more people started to gather outside.

Maria and her teenage daughter Victoria, who lived next door to Agatha, saw the crowd of people gathering on the street and came to the house to see what was going on. They found Agatha and the children in the living room with Rosita. The children were gathered around their mother and were crying. Maria put her arm around Agatha and tried to comfort her while Victoria helped with the children.

The situation in the house was becoming a bit chaotic as the five men came inside. Agatha was wailing hysterically and the children were crying as well. Rosita and the two neighbor women were trying to help out.

Bambino motioned for the men to come into the kitchen, where they sat down around the kitchen table. It was an emotional time for everybody and even the men were feeling it.

They all sat down around the table. Everyone was quiet as the sound of Agatha and the children crying in the other room could be heard in the kitchen.

Savako looked at Bambino. "What are we going to do now Bambino?"

"The first thing we got to do is to bury our friend. And after that we got to find out who shot him and then we got to make sure that their friends are going to bury them.

Since Joe Parisi had been in jail Joe had been the number one man in the Familia organization and there was some indecision on who would take over now. It was either going to be Bambino or Vinnie that would have to be in charge now. They would have to be very careful now as Vinnie was the only witness left to testify for Joe Parisi. If something were to happen to Vinnie, Joe Parisi might be doing a long stretch in jail for Sinafaldi's murder.

The five sat around the kitchen table and discussed who would take the number one spot in the organization now. Because Vinnie was a witness in the case against Joe Parisi and already a target for those who wanted to see Joe Parisi go to jail they agreed that he should keep a low profile and Bambino should take over.

Bambino was a take charge guy and as soon as it was decided that he would take over he began directing the others right away.

"The first thing we must do is to arrange for Joe's funeral and then avenge his death." Bambino said. Vinnie and I will make the funeral arrangements. And Savako, I want you to stay around here and keep an eye on Agatha and the children. I want you to telephone all of the family, friends and associates that should know about the funeral right away." He turned his attention to Vinnie, "Vinnie these guys that shot Joe could very well be looking to kill you too. You got to be careful and always have a couple of guys going with you everywhere you go. If we lose you the Boss will not have a case. I want you to lay low, stay out of sight until Joe's trial."

"What about Joe's funeral?"

"Don't worry there will be a lot of people around you at the funeral, you'll be okay there."

Bambino got up from the table, "Alright let's go to the morgue and the undertaker and start to make the arrangements." The others got up and followed Bambino out to the car. Savako stayed behind as Bambino asked, first going out to check on Agatha and then making some phone calls.

They drove to the funeral home in Waterbury and made arrangements for the funeral before driving to New Haven.

They arrived at the morgue in New Haven and viewed Joe's body. His face was grotesque from the gunshot to his eye. Each man made the sign of the cross and said a short prayer while they stood in front of the body. Bambino arranged to have the body picked up and transported to the funeral home in Waterbury. From there they went to the Catenzaro Restaurant and Vinnie's apartment above the restaurant. They all stayed at Vinnie's for the night making sure that he had protection, just in case.

Danny Montoya and the other two gunmen arrived back in Worcester late that afternoon and met with Benny Gallo.

"Tell me that you got them both and now Parisi has no witnesses," Gallo said to him.

"There was two of them in the car. We followed them from the jail in Springfield. I think they are both dead but we didn't stick around to find out," Montoya answered.

"You didn't stick around to find out?"

"No the car went off the road and we just got the hell out of there."

"How do you know if they are dead or not?"

"It looked pretty bad for them. Like I said the car went off the road after the driver was hit. I don't know how anyone could have lived through that. We sprayed the car with bullets at point blank range. I think we got them both."

"But you don't know for sure?"

"No, we didn't get a chance to ask them if they were dead." Montoya was getting annoyed at Gallo's questions.

"Before you go anywhere I want to see proof that those guys are dead."

"Proof, what do want for proof?"

"I want to see the newspaper report, the obituary or something that says you got these guys."

"For Christ sake Benny. You want to wait until you read it in the paper?"

"Yeah that's right."

"What do you want? You want me to go back to Waterbury and get you a paper?"

"That's right Danny, I want to read it in the paper. And if you go to Waterbury and the paper says that they are not dead then I want you to finish the job."

Montoya glared at Gallo without saying a word.

"Now go back to Waterbury and find out if they are dead."

Montoya was none to happy about Gallo sending him back to Waterbury. But he and the two gunmen left early the next morning for Waterbury. They got into Waterbury the next day just after noon and right away bought a morning newspaper.

The headline in the newspaper read 'Local Man Slain, Another Wounded In Bootleg Battle.'

Montoya slammed the steering wheel in the car repeatedly after reading the headline. "Son of a bitch," he said each time he slammed the wheel. It turns out that one of the witnesses, Vinnie Parisi wasn't even in the car.

"Vinnie Parisi, that's the guy that runs the Catenzaro Restaurant in New Haven" Montoya thought to himself. "We got to go there and get this guy." Montoya started the car and pulled out onto Main Street in Waterbury. He had decided that they would go to New Haven and stake out the Catenzaro Restaurant again hoping to get a shot at Vinnie.

John Masalino, Bambino and Rocco had just come from the undertakers where they were making funeral arrangements. Joe's body had arrived from the morgue in North Haven that morning and the funeral was going to be held the next day. They had just gotten into the car and pulled out onto the street turning the corner onto main street. The two cars passed each other going in opposite directions. John Masalino was riding in the back seat and just happened to look up at a car passing them on the opposite side of the street. John looked over at the car as it passed them and he and the driver locked eyes, but only for a second. John was talking to Rocco who was in the front seat when the two cars passed each other. His reaction was a little delayed but it hit him a few seconds later that he recognized the driver. He was the guy that pulled up beside him and lifted up the gun off the seat and started firing the day before on the freeway in North Haven.

"Holy shit, there he is. That's him." John yelled out to the others and turned around and watched them go by.

"That's who?" Bambino said.

"The guys that shot Joe."

"What?" Bambino said quickly pulling a u-turn and going after them. He pulled a gun out of his jacket and laid it on the seat beside him. "Are you sure John?"

"Yes, I'm sure. I couldn't forget that face I seen just before the shooting started. That's the guy."

"Okay, we're going after them."

Montoya and the two others were unaware that John had recognized them and had turned around and was in pursuit. They drove casually through Waterbury and out of town on the highway to New Haven. Bambino followed them, staying a distance behind as they cruised down the highway. It was pointless to try to overtake them as they sped down the highway.

"We're going to wait until we get into Nantucket. We can overtake them in the city when they least expect it."

They followed them through Nantucket but they were unable to get close to them while driving through town. There always seemed to be a couple of cars between them.

Bambino was patient, keeping his distance as they followed them out of town.

Beacon Falls was a small town just a few miles south of Nantucket which probably wouldn't even exist except for the Rubber Regenerating Company that was there. It was close to noon when the two cars passed through Beacon Falls. Some of the plant employees lived right there in Beacon Falls and made a habit of going home for lunch.

As Montoya passed the plant there was a small amount of traffic coming from the plant, just enough to slow them down as they passed by. It was here that Bambino was able to close the distance between them, catching up to them and following right behind.

"Get you guns ready. This might be our chance."

The two cars slowed down for the local traffic as they drove by the rubber plant. Bambino waited until Montoya had a car in front of him before making his move.

Quickly and unexpectedly he pulled out around Montoya and passed.

Montoya and the other two men were completely taken by surprise when Bambino passed them and the three men started to shoot, spraying the car with bullets.

Some employees of the Rubber Regenerating Company were having lunch nearby and looked up when they heard the shooting start. The whole incident lasted for only about a half a minute and it was over. Montoya and the other two fired a few rounds back after Bambino had passed them and was speeding away. Montoya was hit in the shoulder but managed to keep the car on the road. One of the other men was grazed on the side of the head. Nobody in Bambino's car was hit at all.

It was just a matter of minutes before the police were on the scene but both cars had sped away by then.

The factory workers who were outside the plant having lunch were interviewed by the police, having watched the whole incident take place right in front of the plant. From where they were, as they watched guns blazing from the two cars, they were not able to tell whether anyone was hit or not. But in fact Danny Montoya continued to drive through the Borough until they were a fair distance from where the shooting took place before he pulled the car over to the side of the road. He was unable to drive any further and wanted one of the other men to take over. Montoya's arm was oozing blood from the bullet wound. His arm had started to go numb and the blood was dripping from his hand and running all over the seat. He took off his coat and ripped the arm of his shirt, wrapping it around the wound tightly to try to stop the bleeding.

"Take the wheel. Let's get the hell out of here," he ordered one of the other men as he tended to the wound.

It was too risky to just turn the car around and go back the way they came. They would have to drive right by the factory where the shooting took place again and the last thing Montoya wanted is to get pulled over by the police and have to answer any questions. They continued south towards Beacon Falls looking for the easiest way to cut over to the highway going north from New Haven.

Montoya grimaced from his wound as the car sped along, passing through Beacon Falls. The bullet was still lodged in his shoulder but stopping anywhere to have his shoulder taken care of was out of the question. The police would be looking for someone to show up at a Connecticut hospital with a gunshot wound. They had to get back to Worcester, Massachusetts before he could be looked at by a doctor.

It was just south of Beacon Falls that Bambino pulled the car off to the side of the road. He backed the car down a dirt trail facing the highway and waited. He had a hunch that if they were still alive Montoya's car was going to be passing them soon.

It was a short wait before Montoya's car roared past the spot where they were waiting.

"There they are," Bambino said and pulled the car out onto the road again.

Montoya was in a lot of pain from the bullet wound and was not expecting Bambino to get behind them again. It was about half-way between Beacon Falls and Seymour that Bambino caught up to Montoya's car. Montoya was unable to hold a gun in his right hand as his arm was not functioning from the bullet wound. Bambino drew close to Montoya's car before they even realized they were being followed. John Masalino and Rocco had guns ready and when they got close started shooting.

The driver was hit right away and as he slumped in the seat the car lost speed and crossed the road, went off the other side into the ditch, and plowed headlong into a tree. Bambino stepped on the brakes and stopped the car, backing up to where Montoya's car was wrecked in the ditch. Bambino, John and Rocco got out and cautiously approached the wreck with their guns drawn. Montoya was the only one in the car who was conscious and was trying to get his gun out of his coat with his left hand. He drew the gun and raised it up pointing it at Bambino as he approached the wreck. Bambino shot first hitting Montoya in the other shoulder and causing him to drop the gun. Keeping the gun drawn on him he slowly approached the car.

"Is this the guy John?" he asked Masalino.

"Yeah that's him."

"The guy that shot Joe?"

"That's the guy."

Bambino was standing right in front of Montoya and looking him right in the eyes, he said to him, "You killed my friend asshole and now I'm going to kill you," and then he pumped six shots into Montoya's head. Bambino reloaded his gun, then he turned to the other two men who were still unconscious and shot them in the head also. The road had been quiet while this was going on but suddenly they could hear a car approaching from the direction of Beacon Falls.

"Let's get out of here," Bambino said and they quickly got back into the car and took off.

Bambino felt a sense of relief and vindication as they drove on to New Haven, having avenged Joe's death this way.

They were already around the bend and out of sight by the time the approaching car passed the wreck. The two men in the car noticed it at the last minute and drove well past it before they finally got the car stopped. They backed up to where Montoya's car was and yelled out, asking if anyone was alive. After getting no response, the men got out and walked up to the car. At first they thought that the victims were injured from the crash but as they got closer to the car it was apparent that all three men had been shot and were all dead. It was a grotesque scene, with each man having multiple gunshot wounds to the head and faces covered with blood.

The two men got back in their car and turned it around, driving back to Beacon Falls and calling the police from there. The police arrived on the scene of the shooting about twenty minutes later. It was apparent that the three dead men in the car were somehow related to the shooting that happened a few minutes before, close to the Rubber Regenerating plant. The police suspected that the shooting was also related to the gunfight the day before near Wallingford, in which Joe Marvici was shot and killed. The police were not able to identify any of the three dead men as none of them were carrying any identification.

Bambino, Rocco and John Masalino continued on to New Haven and drove straight to the Catenzaro Restaurant. Vinnie was in the restaurant when they arrived. They all sat at their usual table by the kitchen and told Vinnie the news.

"We got the guys that shot Joe," Bambino said with a smile. "Shot the trigger man six times in the head. There was two others as well. Shot them in the head too."

"How did you find them? Vinnie asked.

"Lady luck gave us some help and John recognized them," Bambino said with a smile.

Vinnie went into the kitchen and came out with a bottle of wine and four glasses and they drank a toast to avenging Joe's murder.

Joe's funeral was held a couple of days later in Waterbury. The funeral service took place at Our Lady of Lourdes Church. Joe was very well loved and respected among his peers, and the funeral was attended by several hundred people, with over fifty cars in the funeral procession. There were friends, family and business associates present from Connecticut, Massachusetts, New York, New Jersey and Vermont. Even Louis and Julia Guyon had come from Chicago. Even Toni and Percy had come from Vermont to attend Joe's funeral. Two open cars filled with flowers followed the casket through the streets of Waterbury and to the Calvary Cemetery where Joe was laid to rest. The day before the funeral, Bambino went to Springfield to see Joe Parisi and filled him in about Joe's murder on the highway and the shooting of Joe's killers near Beacon Falls.

Joe Parisi, after hearing the news from Bambino, managed to present a strong face to Bambino but later when he was back in his cell was overcome with grief. He and Joe had become like brothers over years or since Joe married his sister. The day of Joe's funeral Joe Parisi refused to leave his cell the entire day out of respect for his comrade. It was his own way of paying his respects.

Most of the men attending the funeral were armed and ready just in case there were any incidents at the funeral. There had been a lot of people getting shot recently and no one wanted to take any chances that there would be a gun fight during the funeral. Vinnie was especially well protected during the funeral and procession.

Agatha and the children rode in the car following directly behind the car carrying the casket with Joe's body. John Masalino whose head was still wrapped with a bandage, and Agatha's brother John Parisi rode in the car with her and the children. Agatha's heart was heavy with grief and she cried and and wailed in the church and for the entire funeral procession. She was especially overcome with grief as they lowered Joe's body into the ground.

Bambino, John Masalino, Rocco, Savako, John and Vinnie Parisi and all stood in the front of the grave as they lowered Joe's body. Italian men were always very guarded about showing any emotion. But all of them had a hard time hiding their feelings that day as they approached Joe's casket, picking up a handful of dirt and tossing it into the hole on top of the casket as it lay at the bottom of the grave and saying a last good bye. The Catholic priest stood over the grave and prayed as each person in the group filed by the open grave and paid their last respects.

Agatha cried and wailed uncontrollably as the casket reached its final resting place. Many of the women gathered around, her trying to console her as she broke down in the last minutes beside the grave.

It was a sad and solemn scene that afternoon as the women grieved and men held back tears, trying to wipe them away without being noticed. Agatha's mother Columbina and sister Mary-Angela kept close to her and helped her to the car when it was time to leave the cemetery. Rosita and the neighbors Maria and Victoria looked after the four children as Agatha was too emotionally distraught to be able to.

The funeral procession then moved to the banquet hall in the basement of the church for the reception. The hall was full to overflowing as over two hundred people crowded into the hall. Agatha managed to get her grief under control by that time and sat at the front of the hall surrounded by the children, her mother Columbina and sister Mary-Angela and the neighbors Rosita, Maria and Victoria. Everyone there eventually filed by and paid their respects to Agatha. As with many funerals the reception was a testimonial to Joe with many of his friends and family sharing their love and respect for Joe with stories about him.

The reception went well into the afternoon, finally breaking up around dinner time. Agatha was accompanied home by her mother, sister and Rosita who continued to stay with Agatha for a couple of weeks after the funeral, helping out with the children and comforting Agatha when she was overcome with emotion.

While the women stayed with Agatha the men had a meeting at Savako's house. Bambino, Vinnie, Rocco, John Masalino, John Parisi, George DiMaria, Serafino Parisi all went to Savako's house after the funeral. The meeting was also attended by Joe Popsadoro and Pasquale Lucariello. There was a clear need to discuss where the Familia was going from this point on. Joe was dead and Joe Parisi was still in jail and the trial was coming up in just a couple of weeks.

In spite of the the problems that the Familia were having in the Springfield area the operation in Connecticut was flourishing. The demand for booze was continually growing and they were now being supplied on several different fronts. Over the last few years they were getting less whiskey coming from Quebec and Vermont and more coming from the south through the docks in New York and Connecticut ports.

The bootleggers and speakeasies that sold the booze to the public had been doing an increasingly larger volume of business all the time.

They were not having problems with the police in Connecticut like they were having in Springfield. Benny Gallo had taken over Sinafaldi's operation in Massachusetts and was keeping the police in Springfield on the take. The Catenzaro Restaurant had been raided by the police several times and so had many of the speakeasies and bootleggers that sold booze for the Familia. These raids by the police in Springfield had caused some businesses to move around the city and some to close altogether. A few businesses jumped ship and were now being supplied by Gallo's operation. Compared to the operation in Connecticut, business in Springfield created many more problems.

There was talk at the meeting of pulling out of and conceding the Springfield business to Gallo and just concentrating on business in Connecticut. The biggest problem with doing that was that many of the Familia families still lived in Springfield. Most of Agatha's family still resided in West Springfield and now that Joe was gone she wanted to move back there and be closer to her family. Both Columbina and Mary-Angela encouraged Agatha to bring the children and come back to West Springfield.

Chapter 18

Over the years Joe had always kept in touch with his family in Italy, writing to his mother Katherina every couple of months and continued to send her money. Agatha had almost forgotten about Katherina with all that had happened since Joe was shot and killed. One day about a week after the funeral a letter arrived for Joe from his mother in Italy. Agatha opened the letter. She was unable to hold back tears as she read the letter. Katherina truly loved her oldest son as was apparent from her warm words. She wrote about all the latest news about Joe's sisters and brother Francesco, who had just bought a truck with the help of money that Joe had sent to her. It was not a new truck, but an older one that he had gotten a deal on from a man in Rome who had shipped it from America years before. It seems the Italian man was moving back to America and did not want to ship the truck back there. Francesco had traveled to Rome to buy the truck and drive it back to Carrafa. He was very proud of his truck and was the only one with a truck in Carrafa. When Francesco bought the truck only one of the two headlights was working. Francesco drove the truck back from Rome with only the one headlight. Parts such as headlights were not easy to find in this part of the world. Francesco's truck was easy to identify in Caraffa, especially after dark and was given the nickname of 'the one eyed truck'.

Agatha cried as she read the letter. It was obvious that Katherina loved her son very much and looked forward to receiving letters from him. She knew that she would have to write to Katherina and tell her that Joe had been shot and killed.

Over the next few days Agatha composed the letter to Katherina in Italy. It was a very difficult letter to write and she broke down in tears many times while doing it, sometimes soaking the letter with her tears. Agatha finally finished it and sent it in the mail. It was one of the hardest things she had to do after Joe's death.

The mail was slow to be delivered and took over a month to reach Katherina in Italy. At first she was elated to receive the letter but noticed right away that it was not in Joe's handwriting. A feeling of fear came over her as she quickly tore open the envelope. Katherina was in the kitchen and sat down as she unfolded the letter and began to read it. She let out a loud cry from the shock of the terrible news and broke down crying at the table. Francesco was outside in the garden when he heard Katherina crying. He immediately dropped what he was doing and rushed inside to see what was the matter. Katherina was at the kitchen table and was crying profusely.

"Mama, what is the matter?" he asked.

"Guiseppe...." was all she could say.

"What?"

Katherina slowly reached for the letter and handed it to him.

"Oh my God," Francesco said as he read the words of his brother's death.

Francesco made the sign of the cross and said a short prayer as he held the letter in his hands. He then turned his attention to his mother and wrapped his arms around her. They both cried while holding on to each other.

"Francesco, you must tell your sisters," Katherina sobbed as she talked.

"Will you be alright Mama?" he asked.

"Yes," she said while still sobbing." You go and tell your sisters."

Francesco left his mother and went to each of his sisters who lived close by in Samo and told them the bad news. Each of them went immediately to their mother's house knowing that she would want them to be there to share her grief.

Katherina still sat at the kitchen table with the letter in her hand, just as Francesco left her, when the girls arrived. They surrounded their mother and held her as they all cried for their dear brother.

It was Italian tradition at that time for a brother to be concerned for his deceased brother's family in the event of his death. It was commonplace for an unmarried brother to step into the place of his deceased brother and take care of his brother's family. Not being married, Francesco felt it was his duty to go to America and take Joe's place with his family.

Katherina talked to Francesco about this and it was decided that Francesco would have to go to America and look after his brother's family.

The next day Katherina wrote a letter to Agatha back in America. It was a difficult letter for her to write. She offered her deepest condolences to Agatha and the children, also asking how they were going to be able to get along without Joe there to take care of his family.

Agatha was already aware of the tradition in Italy of unmarried brothers being obliged to look after their brother's family in the event of the brother's death. Katherina wrote that she was sending Francesco to America to take Joe's place in the family and look after her and the children.

Family traditions were very strong in Italian families at this time in history and Francesco did not questions his mother about this. He accepted that this was his fate and his duty and he was bound to carry it out in respect for his brother and the family. Francesco booked passage on a ship bound for New York within a couple of days of hearing the news about Joe. He first traveled by car to Naples where he caught an Italian ship, the Dante Aighieri, to America by way of Lisbon, Portugal.

Katherina sent the letter off to Agatha right away in the hope that it would get to her before Francesco arrived in New York. Francesco boarded the ship a little more than a week after receiving the letter from Agatha.

Francesco could be seen standing on the deck of the ship a lot of the time during the voyage to America. He spent many hours there with the wind in his face watching the waves and the ocean go by, contemplating his future. He was not the adventurer that his brother Joe was and would have been happy to spend his life in Italy, close to his mother and family, but he felt like it was his duty to make the trip to America and take care of his brother's family. The days went by slowly as the ship cut its way across the Atlantic waters to New York. The ship took more than two weeks to make the voyage to America.

In the meantime, back in America, Joe Parisi's trial for the shooting death of Sinafaldi was coming up. Vince Perrotti was not able to knock off the witnesses and other attempts by the Familia to kill Sinafaldi's driver and bodyguard failed and both of them made it to court alive and testified against him. The trial was attended by members of the Familia and Benny Gallo and a number of his hoods. Vinnie Parisi arrived at the courthouse surrounded by at least a half dozen armed members of the Familia. The police were stopping people at the door of the courthouse and searching them for weapons before letting anyone inside. Vinnie was accompanied inside the courtroom by John Parisi, John Masalino and Romano Bambino. Each of them was unwilling to turn their guns over to the police so they gave them to their comrades, who would be waiting outside the court house before going inside. Gallo and the two witnesses arrived just after Vinnie had gone into the courtroom. They were being very protective of the two witnesses and surrounded them with a mob as they walked up the steps and entered the court house.

Tensions were high even outside the courthouse where both factions had armed men hanging around. The police had a strong presence outside and inside the courthouse as well.

This was a high profile trial and there were newspaper reporters from Eastern Massachusetts and as far south as Connecticut and north as Vermont. Even a couple of reporters from New York were there to cover the trial.

Joe Parisi was led into the courtroom by two uniformed police officers. Anthony Bono had already taken a seat at the defense table when they came through the door into the courtroom. Bono got up from his chair as Joe Parisi approached and shook hands with him. He leaned toward him whispering something into his ear before the two took a seat. Joe Parisi was dressed in an expensive suit and had a white carnation in his lapel. Parisi turned and looked around the courtroom before taking his seat. Vinnie, Bambino and John Masalino were all sitting in the front row close to the defense table. Joe's glance around the room had located them. He gave them a slight nod before turning and taking a seat.

The judge called the trial to order and the prosecuting attorney began with opening remarks to the jury. He stated that he had evidence to prove that Joe Parisi had gunned down Carlos Sinafaldi in cold blood. His evidence would prove that Parisi had in fact set a trap for Sinafaldi on the north end bridge that day and closed in on him with a mob of gunmen and shot Sinafaldi at point blank range and then shot both his driver and bodyguard, leaving them both for dead. He went on to say that both the driver and bodyguard had survived the attack and were in court today, as he turned toward them, pointing at them and telling the jury that they were here to give evidence that it was Joe Parisi who had carried out the attack.

Though Joe Marvici was not there to testify, Vinnie Parisi was, and he was still able to offer an alibi for Joe Parisi. The trial was a trial by jury and though the driver and bodyguard gave evidence that they had seen Joe Parisi shoot Carlos Sinafaldi from his car on the bridge that day, the testimony of Vinnie Parisi was enough to cause some doubt as to what really happened.

This caused the jury to take a long time coming to a decision. Most of the members of the jury agreed that the evidence showed that Joe Parisi had in fact gunned down Carlos Sinafaldi on the bridge that fateful day. However there were two jurors in the group that had doubts about the shooting based on Vinnie's testimony that Joe Parisi was in Connecticut that afternoon. Testimony also came out in court that Joe Marvici had intended to give evidence to back up the claim that Joe Parisi was in Connecticut that day but he had been shot and killed before the trial. The two jurors believed that with Joe Marvici's testimony it was enough to cast doubt on the charge of murder in the first degree. Things got pretty hot among the jurors because of the two that would not vote guilty on the murder charge.

When the jurors had not come to a verdict by the second day Anthony Bono was encouraged. The longer it went on the better the chance they were going to acquit Joe Parisi or at the least find him guilty of a lesser charge. It was on the morning of the third day that the jury finally came to a verdict. Anthony Bono received a phone call that morning saying that the jury had reached a verdict and he should come to the courthouse as soon as he could. Bono called Romano Bambino who was staying in Springfield at John Parisi's house, and let him know that the jury had reached a verdict. Romano, Vinnie and John Parisi and John Masalino went to the courthouse right away. Gallo and his boys were already there when they arrived.

After everyone was seated in the courtroom the Jurors filed in and sat down. The Judge was the last to enter the courtroom.

"Foreman of the jury have you reached a verdict?" the Judge said addressing the jury.

"Yes we have," answered the foreman, standing up to address the Judge.

"And how do you find," the Judge asked.

"On the charge of murder in the first degree, we find the defendant not guilty." A murmur swept over the courtroom. "And on the charge of murder in the second degree we find the defendant not guilty." Again a murmur swept over the courtroom.

"And on the charge of manslaughter we find the defendant guilty." This time people started talking and the courtroom became quite noisy. The Judge pounded his gavel,

"Order in the court" he said several times before the crowd quieted down. At that point the Judge discharged the jury.

The Judge waited until the jury filed out of the courtroom before passing sentence on Joe Parisi.

"The court orders that Joe Parisi, on the charge of manslaughter, serve ten years in the state correctional facility with a possibility of parole only after seven years served." The judge paused for a few seconds before declaring the court adjourned. The murmur in the courtroom became quite loud as the judge exited the courtroom and the County Sheriff and two of the deputies surrounded Joe Parisi and led him out of the courtroom.

Anthony Bono had a few words with Parisi before the Sheriff led him away. "I'll be in to see you this afternoon Joe," he said to him as they were leaving.

Bono had a short conference with Bambino, John Masalino, Vinnie and John Parisi in the hallway outside the courtroom before leaving for the jail where Joe Parisi was being taken.

"So what do we do now?" Bambino asked Anthony Bono.

"Well we can appeal the decision but it's a good chance it's not going to do any good," Bono answered. "I'll go talk to Joe and see what he wants to do. Can I get in touch with you fellows after I talk to him?"

"John Parisi stepped forward,"You can call on us at my house. We'll go there and wait for you, Mister Bono." John wrote his telephone number on a piece of paper and gave it to Bono.

"Okay, I'll be in touch as soon as I talk to Joe," he said. They all shook hands before he left for the jail.

The four men left the courthouse, meeting up with the other Familia men outside, and retrieved their guns from them. Gallo's men had already left the courthouse by this time and the reporters had also left, wanting to be the first to get the story out in the newspaper.

The men talked among themselves for a few minutes before leaving for John Parisi's house to wait for Anthony Bono's call.

Bono arrived at the York Street jail a short time later and was let in to see Joe Parisi. Parisi's spirits were pretty low after having been convicted and sentenced to ten years. Somehow or other Joe Parisi believed that he was going to get off for killing Sinafaldi.

"If I got to do the time then I'm glad the son of a bitch is dead," was the first thing he said to Bono. "What's the chances of winning an appeal?" Joe questioned Bono.

"An appeal only is successful if we have an angle or new evidence. We can try it Joe but there's a good chance that the court will not give us an appeal."

Joe Parisi lowered his head and, taking a deep breath, he looked up at Bono. "So this is pretty well the end of it? I'm going to do ten years in here?"

"You could get paroled in seven. But you got a better chance if you keep your nose clean while you are in here," Bono answered. "I can file an appeal Joe, but there's no guarantee that we'll get one or that it will be successful."

Joe paused for a few seconds, "Alright Anthony, you file for an appeal and we will see what happens. In the meantime I'll just wait for you in here." Joe looked up at Bono and laughed.

The two men shook hands before Bono called for the guard. "I'll keep in touch with you Joe," Bono said as he was leaving.

Bono left the jail and phoned John Parisi. "Hello John, I just came from the jail. We discussed filing an appeal but I will tell you the same thing I told Joe. Without new evidence winning an appeal is probably unlikely."

"Are we going to try anyway?" John asked.

"Yeah, we can try and you never know unless we try but don't be surprised if it doesn't work."

"Okay Mister Bono, I'll tell the others."

John hung up the phone and passed on Bono's comments to Bambino and the others. The telephone rang a few minutes later. It was Agatha calling from Waterbury asking how the trial turned out for her brother.

"Not so good. Joe got ten years," John told her.

He could hear her break down crying over the phone. "Agatha, is there someone there with you?" John asked. "Yes. Mama and Mary-Angela are here and so is Rosita."

"That's good. I'm going to come to see you today." John said. We just talked to Anthony Bono a few minutes ago. He said that here's probably not a very good chance of winning an appeal."

Agatha sobbed over the phone. "Alright John, I will see you when you get here."

Agatha hung up the telephone and continued to cry. This had been a terrible time for her. First Joe being shot and killed and then her brother convicted and getting ten years in jail. She sat down next to the telephone and continued to cry. It was Mary-Angela that first noticed her and came over to try to comfort her. Agatha sat with her hands covering her face and cried, not being able to control herself. Mary-Angela stood over her, rubbing her back, but she too could not control her emotions after Agatha told her about Joe being sentenced to ten years in prison.

After the call from Agatha the mood at John's house was somber. It was going to be a challenge to keep the Familia's business going with the loss of both Joe Marvici and Joe Parisi. However John Parisi still did not want to get involved with the bootlegging business and preferred that Bambino, Vinnie, John Masalino and the others work it out for themselves without him.

John announced that he was going to drive to Waterbury to see his sisters and his mother and that the meeting was over. Bambino tried to talk John into taking over for his brother without success. The meeting broke up and John left for Waterbury right away.

It was later that afternoon that a letter from Katherina arrived at Agatha's house in Waterbury from Italy. Agatha had just talked to her brother John minutes before the postman delivered the letter to her house. Mary-Angela had noticed the postman walking up to the house and went to the door and received the mail. The postman was an Italian man named Vito that had been delivering mail to the Marvici house for several years. He had also attended Joe's funeral and showed his concern for Agatha by asking Mary-Angela, "How is Mrs. Marvici doing?"

"She's doing better," Mary-Angela answered as she took the mail from him. They made small talk on the porch for a minute or so before Vito continued on his route.

Mary-Angela went back into the house and passed the mail on to Agatha. There were two letters. One was from from Chicago from Louis and Julia Guyon and the other was from Katherina.

Agatha opened the letter from the Guyons first. It had been years since they had met Joe in Chicago and they often wrote to Joe to keep in touch over the years. This letter was written before Joe's death. Julia Guyon wrote about all the news from Chicago. Agatha cried as she read the letter.

She then opened the letter from Katherina. Katherina's letter started out by offering Agatha heartfelt condolences for the death of her husband. She went on to say how much Joe would be missed by everyone in the family. Agatha wept again as she read the letter. Her tears dripped upon the pages as she tried to keep reading Katherina's letter. Katherina then told her that she had sent Francesco to America to take Joe's place in his family. He would be arriving on the passenger ship the 'Dante Aighieri' that would arrive in New York the first week of October.

Agatha dropped the letter on her lap after reading it. Her hands covering her eyes, she began to cry some more. Mary-Angela went to Agatha and put her arms around her shoulders, comforting her.

Agatha looked up at Mary-Angela and sobbed as she told her that Joe's brother Francesco was on his way to America to take Joe's place in the family.

"When is he coming?' Mary-Angela asked.

"He is on his way as we speak," Agatha answered. "Joe's mother Katherina has already sent him on the boat to come here." Agatha passed the letter to Mary-Angela. Mary-Angela quietly read the letter. After reading it she looked up at Agatha.

"What are you going to do?" She asked.

"Mary-Angela," she answered. "I just lost my husband and now our brother has gone to jail. I cannot accept another man in my life right now. It is too early for me. I am still in mourning for my husband."

"But my dear sister, Francesco is already on his way. What will you do?" "I don't know what to do," she answered and then put her hands over her face and started to cry again. This was clearly not the time for Agatha to make this kind of a decision. Mary-Angela sat down beside her and put her arms around her sister to comfort her.

Both Columbina and Rosita entered the room after hearing Agatha's sobs and tried to comfort her. Mary-Angela told them of the news of Francesco's voyage to America to take his brother's place in his family. Agatha was still too distraught to talk though she cried harder as Mary-Angela told them what Katherina had written in the letter.

It was a couple hours later when John arrived in Waterbury. The mood was somber at the house when he came in the door. Agatha burst into tears when she saw her brother.

He put his arms around her and held her as she tried talking about the situation. Agatha could not talk while sobbing and it was Mary-Angela who told John what was going on while Agatha cried.

John held Agatha at arms length for a minute and looked in her eyes. "This upsets you my dear sister".

"Yes," she said.

"And why does this upset you? This is Joe's Brother. He wants to take care of you and the children."

"No, I cannot do this. I want him to go back to Italy."

"But why? This may be a good thing for you."

Agatha stopped her sobbing for a few seconds and looked John in the eyes.

"What if he gets involved with the business and he is killed too? I will not be able to live with that."

John looked lovingly at Agatha. "What do you want to do? He is already on his way."

"We must tell him to go back to Italy."

"You are sure about that?'

"Yes, yes, I am sure," Agatha answered.

"But he is already on the ship on his way."

Agatha paused for a minute and wiped the tears from her eyes. "John will you go with me to New York and meet the ship? Then I will tell him to go back."

"Of course I will." John answered. " When does the ship get to New York?"

"Katherina's letter said the first week of October."

"I will call New York and find out when the 'Dante Aighieri' will arrive. Then we will go together and meet Francesco and send him back to Italy."

It was already the end of September just a few days from the 1st of October, when John telephoned New York to inquire about when the ship was arriving. After several telephone calls he was finally able to track down the information. The 'Dante Aighieri' was scheduled to arrive in New York on Sunday, October 5th at Pier 1, Chelsea Piers at 9 o'clock in the morning.

After getting the information about the ship and with it Francesco's arrival in New York, John made a plan to take Agatha to New York to meet the ship. Columbina agreed to look after the children while they were gone and it was decided that Mary-Angela would go with them to New York too.

John stayed in Waterbury that night and left for Springfield early Monday morning in order to get back to Springfield to open the the Catenzaro Restaurant.

He telephoned Agatha several times during the week to check on her. He decided that they would drive to New York on Saturday, October 4th and stay in New York overnight and meet the ship the next morning.

John left for Waterbury late Friday afternoon and stayed at Agatha's once again. They left the next morning for the drive to New York.

Agatha had trouble sleeping that night. Her mind was racing about the meeting with Francesco the next morning. She knew a lot about Francesco from things that Joe had told her but had never met him. As she lay in bed trying to sleep she went over and over the meeting with Francesco in her mind. Agatha tossed and turned all night with visions of the meeting the next day and what she would say to Francesco to get him to go back to Italy on the next ship. Agatha finally fell asleep in the early morning hours and awoke a few hours later to the sounds of the children.

Columbina was feeding the children breakfast when Agatha woke up. John and Mary-Angela were both awake and sitting in the kitchen having a cup of coffee when Agatha came in.

There was no rush to set off for New York right away as Francesco's ship was not due to arrive until the next morning.

It was late in the morning, about eleven o'clock when they set out on the drive to New York. It had been years since John had been to New York.

It had been a long time since John spent any amount of time with his sisters without a lot of people around and they enjoyed their time together driving to New York. They got into New York Friday evening and checked into the Clarion Hotel on Canal Street located about six blocks from the the Chelsea Pier One.

The Chelsea Piers were spread out on the southwest side of Manhattan Island jutting out into the Hudson River. Agatha and Mary-Angela shared a room and John was in the next room on the twenty second floor. John anticipated that Francesco would have to stay in New York at least a day or two before the 'Dante Aighieri" would be going back to Lisbon. Having a separate room, John planned to have Francesco stay in the room with him.

After checking into the hotel the three of them went to dinner in the hotel restaurant. It was a busy place as New York was a bustling town especially that close to the Chelsea Piers. Though John had been to New York before both, Mary-Angela and Agatha had not been there since they came to America in 1913. Even then they were only there for a short time and didn't really remember much. The big city was very different from Waterbury and Springfield. There seemed to be thousands of people on the street at once, something you would never see in Waterbury.

Agatha was nervous about the meeting with Francesco. If he was just coming for a visit it would be different. But he was coming to be Agatha's husband and the father of her children. She was very conscious of hurting Francesco's feelings. Since he was Joe's broth-er, that was the last thing she wanted to do. She was restless during the night and got little sleep. The thought of meeting Francesco the next day kept her awake most of the night. Agatha finally fell sound asleep in the early morning hours. She awoke with Mary-Angela lightly shaking her.

"It is time to get up and go meet the ship," she heard Mary-Angela saying to her when she was waking up.

When Agatha opened her eyes she could see that Mary-Angela was already dressed and almost ready to leave.

"I waited as long as I could before waking you."

"What time is it?" she asked.

"We have about an hour before the Francesco's ship comes in." Mary-Angela then left the room, going next door to John's room.

Agatha was up and had gotten dressed by the time Mary-Angela returned.

They went next door and knocked on John's room. He came out and the three of them left the hotel and drove towards the piers. Even in 1924 it was hard to find a parking place in New York and they ended up parking several blocks from Pier One.

By the time they arrived the 'Dante Aighieri' was already tied up at the pier. Great big letters on the bow spelled out the ship's name. The gangplanks were just being lowered and it was a few minutes before the passengers started coming off the ship. The 'Dante Aighieri' carried about fifteen hundred passengers, most of whom were immigrants coming to America. Francesco was not aware that Agatha had come to New York to meet him. He had planned to take the train to Waterbury as soon as he could.

Since neither Agatha, Mary-Angela or John had ever met Francesco before, they did not know what he looked like. Both John and Mary-Angela called out his name, as the people filed by them coming from the ship. Another man named Francesco, upon hearing his name called approached John.

John asked him, "are you Francesco Marvici?"

The man answered that he was Francesco Cordova before going on his way.

They stood beside the ship as the mob of people coming from the ship filed by. The two sisters were dressed in black as they still were in mourning. John was also wearing a black suit. Suddenly a man approached them, having heard his name called out..

"You are looking for Francesco Marvici?" he said.

"Are you Francesco Marvici?" John asked.

"Yes, I am, "Francesco answered.

"And Joe Marvici was your brother?"

"That's right, he was my brother."

"I am glad to meet you, Francesco. My name is John Parisi and these are my sisters Mary-Angela and Agatha, Joe's wife."

Francesco reached out and shook John's hand. Francesco was a tall man, much taller and more slender than Joe. He was also dressed in a black suit and an Italian fedora hat.

"It is my pleasure to meet you," he said to John. Then turning to Mary-Angela he offered his hand. "My pleasure to meet you Mary-Angela." He then turned his attention to Agatha and smiled and offered his hand to her. "My dear Agatha, it is my pleasure to meet you." Francesco took off his hat and put it across his heart. "I offer my condolences to you for the loss of my brother and your husband, from myself and from my mother."

"Thank you Francesco," she replied.

The crowd of people still filed by them as they talked. "Let us go someplace and sit down and talk," John suggested. They started to walk back towards the John's car.

Before reaching the car they came across an Italian restaurant and decided to go in for something to eat. Francesco kept Agatha by his side. He was glad to be off the boat and to be walking with Agatha beside him. It was obvious to John and Mary-Angela that Francesco was quite interested in Agatha partly because of the sense of duty that he felt for his brother to take care of his family and partly because she was a very young attractive Italian woman. They entered the restaurant and sat in a booth in the back of the dining room. Mary-Angela and Agatha sat next to each other on one side and John and Francesco sat facing the two sisters.

Agatha and Mary-Angela made small talk, asking questions of Francesco about his family back in Italy.

At first they avoided talking about Francesco's reason for coming to America. The waiter came to the table and took their order. Francesco tried to order a bottle of wine but was informed that because of the prohibition laws in America the restaurant was not able to sell any alcoholic beverages as they could in Italy, where alcohol was still legal.

The waiter brought a pot of expresso to the table and four small expresso cups and poured a cup for each of them before taking their order. As they waited Mary-Angela asked Francesco question after question about his family and life in Italy. It had been years since she had been there and she was very interested in hearing any news. Francesco was polite as he answered Mary-Angela's questions though he was distracted by them. He was, in fact interested in Agatha and wanted to turn his attention towards her but did not want to be rude to Mary-Angela. But Mary-Angela would not stop talking, giving no one a chance to say anything until John finally spoke up, "Mary-Angelo, will you please shut up?"

It was then that Francesco asked Agatha to tell him about his brother and how he died.

"It is very hard for me to talk about," she answered.

"I understand," Francesco replied. "Maybe later," he said, thinking that he would stay as he had planned.

It was John who broke the news to Francesco.

"Francesco, we came to meet your ship because we want to talk to you."

"Yes?"

"We want you to go back home on the next boat."

"But why? I came here to take care of my brother's Family?" He looked over at Agatha. She looked straight ahead, careful not to look at him.

"That's just it Francesco. Agatha and the children have her family around to take care of them. And your brother was shot and killed by hoodlums. And if you come here they will kill you too."

"Why would they kill me? I have done nothing to them."

"These enemies of your brother will see you as a threat and they will try to kill you."

So I should run away from these people?"

"Yes, you should go back, and not get involved."

"Who are these men who killed my brother."

"Look Francesco, there is a war going on out there and a lot of people are getting hurt and even killed. That is the life your brother chose and he ended up dead. Don't come here. Go back to Italy."

Francesco leaned back in his seat and put his fingers to his chin and paused. He then turned towards Agatha and asked, "How do you feel about it Agatha?"

She slowly turned her head towards Francesco and said, "I want you to go back to Italy. It is too soon Francesco, I am still in mourning for my husband. And what my brother says is true. Somebody will kill you too. I do not want you to stay, please go back to Italy." This was a turn of events for Francesco. He hadn't contemplated being asked to go back. Again he sat back in his seat and paused a moment.

"You go back to Italy Francesco. My sister doesn't want you here and besides it's too dangerous, you'll be killed," Mary-Angela blurted out.

John held up his hand toward Mary-Angela as a signal to 'not get started'. He then looked at Francesco and said. "She's right, Francesco. This has nothing to do with you as a person, this has to do more with what is going on here and we want to protect you from it."

"I had not thought of this possibility before now," Francesco replied. "I understand what you are saying but it is a custom for a brother to take care of his brother's family in these cases."

"We are in America, Francesco, some of the customs from the old country are not being practiced here. Your brother's family will be taken care of even if you go back to Italy. You don't have to worry about that."

Francesco looked over at Agatha, "What do you think about this Agatha?"

She looked up at him and looked him right in the eyes. "I want you to go back, Francesco. The time is not right for you to stay here in America. Please believe me that it is not because of you that I say that. I have great respect for you, my husband's brother, and Joe would be proud of you making the effort to be sure his family would be taken care of but it is not the right time for me to have another man in my life." She looked at him with caring eyes. "Please tell me you will go back home?"

"I would not force myself on you my dear Agatha. If it is your wish for me not to stay here in America with you then I will not stay. But it is with deep regret that I would travel back to Italy." Francesco took Agatha's hand and kissed it.

"When will the ship leave for Italy, Francesco?" John asked.

"I will have to find out when it goes back. I did not concern myself with the ship's schedule because I did not know that I would be taking it back home again."

"We will stay here in New York with you until your ship leaves and keep you company."

Agatha looked at Francesco and was overcome by a wave of emotion. Tears started to well up in her eyes and trickle down her cheeks. She wiped her eyes while trying to hold back the tears. Mary-Angela took a tissue from her purse and passed it to Agatha.

"Please do not cry Agatha. Everything will be alright. I am grateful that I got to meet you and John and Mary-Angela. I feel good knowing that you are all right and that you will be taken care of. My mother and my sisters will be happy to hear about you.

It was close to noon when they finally left the restaurant and walked back towards pier one where the 'Dante Aighieri' was tied to the pier. They asked a uniformed policeman where they could find out when the ship would depart for Europe. The policeman directed them to the Pier One ticket office that was located at the south end of the pier. There was a line-up in front of the ticket office and the four of them got into the line. It took about twenty minutes for them to move up the line to the ticket window. John spoke to the man at the ticket window, asking when the ship was scheduled to depart back to Naples. The ticket agent was an Italian man who replied, "The 'Dante Aighieri' will be departing on October 7th at 8 o'clock in the morning. If you are going on the ship then you must be there by 7 am."

"I would like to pay passage for one to Naples," John responded.

"Name of passenger?" he asked.

"Francesco Marvici."

John paid for the ticket, "Here you are," he said to Francesco as he turned and handed him the ticket.

After buying the ticket they all went back to the car and drove to the Clarion Hotel. Francesco moved into the room with John next door to Agatha and Mary-Angela. They had the rest of the day and tomorrow to wait in New York before Francesco's ship left for Naples. Since Francesco had never been in New York before they decided to take in some of the sights while they waited.

Later that afternoon they left the Clarion Hotel and and drove around the city. Francesco had never been in a city like New York and was impressed by the tall buildings that surrounded them. John drove up and down the avenues that went north and south through Manhattan with rows of tall buildings that had them looking skyward out the windows at the tops of the buildings.

John picked up a map of the city in the hotel lobby that pointed out some of the city's landmarks.

It was late in the afternoon that they returned to the hotel. After resting in the room for an hour or so they went to dinner in the hotel restaurant.

Francesco was a complete gentlemen to the ladies but it was fairly obvious that he was attracted to Agatha, though it was Mary-Angela who was taken by Francesco and kept her attention focused on him.

The next day they spent the day taking in some of the sights in New York. After a boat ride to the Statue of Liberty they visited the Empire State Building. Francesco was impressed by the view from the observation deck. New York was truly a beautiful city and made more beautiful when looking at it from this high point. They were truly in the clouds at the top. Clouds would surround the top of the building for a while and then clear, leaving them with a spectacular view.

Again they had dinner in the hotel restaurant that evening. They stayed in the restaurant for hours after dinner. They mostly talked about Joe. Francesco told them stories about Joe when he was a young man in Italy. Francesco recounted Joe's presence in his mother's house after their father had gone to America. Francesco always looked up to his older brother, being much younger than him. Francesco was just a young boy when Joe made the decision to go to America. He could still remember the day when Joe left his mother's home. They were always excited to get letters from him and of course he always sent money to his mother.

Francesco remembered very little about his father, Pasquale. He was very young when Pasquale went to America. He did remember his brother though. Francesco was just eleven years old when Joe left Caraffa. He remembered the day that Joe left, with the whole family lined up to say goodbye. Francesco recounted the time to Agatha, Mary-Angela and John.

Agatha too had high praises for her late husband. She thought him to be a kind and loving man to her and the children. Albeit the dangerous business he was in he always provided very well for them. All the talk about Joe brought up emotions in Agatha as she wiped tears from her eyes.

Mary-Angela put her arm around Agatha, comforting her.

The time flew by and it was getting late when they left the restaurant to go back to their rooms. They all had to be up early for Francesco to board the 'Dante Aighieri', which was scheduled to leave at 8 am. They said goodnight and each went to their room.

John and Francesco got into their beds and turned out the lights. Francesco lay there in the dark thinking about everything that has happened.

"Too bad it worked out this way," he said out loud.

"Yeah, it's too bad Francesco. I would have liked you to stay around now that I know you," John replied.

"But you are not the one who it has to matter to."

"Yes I know."

"It also bothers me that my life could be in danger if I was to stay. That someone I don't know would want to kill me."

"There is a war on with this prohibition thing. Lot of people getting killed. You don't want to get mixed up in that."

"How did my brother get mixed up in it?"

"He was in the booze business before it was illegal. He just kept on, that's how."

In the other room Agatha and Mary-Angel were about to get into bed.

"He is a very nice man ," said Mary-Angela."

"Yeah, he is."

"But you still want him to go?"

"Right now I cannot have another man in my life. I still have to get over Joe."

"That's too bad," Mary-Angela said as she shut off the light.

They were all up early and had breakfast in the hotel restaurant before going to the pier where the 'Dante Aighieri' was waiting. They accompanied Francesco as far as they could, stopping at the gang plank where the passengers were loading and the officers were taking the tickets.

"Good luck Francesco. It has been a pleasure to meet you and I hope we will meet again," John said while shaking hands with him.

"It has been my pleasure to meet you John, and if you ever travel to Italy please do come and see me."

Francesco then turn to Agatha, "Agatha my dear, I feel fortunate to meet you and get to know you, my brother's wife. I am sad that I must leave you. I only hope that we will stay in touch and maybe meet again in better circumstances." Francesco embraced and her and kissed her on both cheeks. Tears trickled down her cheeks as they said goodbye.

He then turned to Mary-Angela. "Mary-Angela my dear, I hope you will look after Agatha and help her get through this hard time. I am happy to meet you and I hope you will look for me if you come to Italy."

"You are a very nice man Francesco and I am sad to see you go. I will look for you when I travel to Italy." They kissed and Francesco picked up his bag and gave his ticket to the officer and walked up the gang plank to the ship. They stayed on the pier for a few minutes and watched Francesco disappear into the belly of the 'Dante Aighieri'.

The drive back to Waterbury seemed longer than ever for Agatha. Her mind raced back and forth wondering if she did the right thing by sending Francesco back to Italy.

"He is such a nice man," Mary-Angela commented several times during the drive. The mood in the car was somber and quiet.

The "Dante Aighieri" sailed out of New York Harbor and was soon riding the swells on the open ocean. Francesco found some solitude on the deck and, leaning on the railing, thought about all that had happened. He thought about Agatha and his brother and his brother's children whom he had not met.

The wind whistled across the deck and the waves smashed into the side of the ship as she cut her way across the Atlantic back to Europe.

THE END

CPSIA information can be obtained
at www.ICGtesting.com
Printed in the USA
BVHW072001200921
617105BV00001B/2

9 781425 117368